PRAISE FOR *THE MEANING OF FEAR*

"What do we do with the wounds that won't heal? And what do those wounds do to us? *The Meaning of Fear* is a gripping novel that traces the hairline fractures of trauma through a small community in Michigan, defying the neat divisions we try to enforce between past and present, victims and violators, and the terrors and graces of intimacy. What drives Paul and Lea and everyone else in this suspenseful novel is a shared hope—and dread—of release."

—Bryan Furuness, author of *Do Not Go On*

"'The culling of bucks, while not prohibited, was discouraged,' Thomas writes in her beautifully rendered and deeply intelligent debut novel, while 'controlling the female segment of the population is critically necessary.' And so the suburban cull begins. When forests become farms and farms become housing developments, wildness and violence, we're reminded, remain. Thomas is a master of this landscape, and in her exploration of the place where fear drives her characters between the instinct for revenge and the longing for mercy and forgiveness. A great read."

—Susan Neville, award-winning author of *The Town of Whispering Dolls*

"What a bold, wise writer! I am in love with Laura Thomas' luminous, empathetic worldview. She is a connoisseur of interiority and nuance. I was utterly enthralled by *The Meaning of Fear*, a remarkable feat of characterization. The narrative delves into the lasting effects of trauma and abuse, masterfully detailing how perceptions based on personal experience and bias sometimes lead to misunderstandings and misjudgments. The story highlights the ripple effect of all our choices and offers the reader a powerful picture of what it means to be human: the messiness and beauty and the enduring capacity for hope."

—Kelly Fordon, award-winning author of *I Have the Answer*

"As its title suggests, *The Meaning of Fear* explores through precisely drawn and utterly believable characters the many ways fear shapes us: through brutality, abuse, neglect, and betrayal. As a result of their past traumas, Lea and Rilke are complicated people, both victims and aggressors straining to find balance and happiness even as their thoughts and behaviors are inspired by past wounds. We walk a tightrope beside these characters, deciphering actual reality from one filtered through their trauma in a masterfully delivered novel of suspense. Will they betray in a learned and potent response to fear? Will they exact revenge on their abusers? Will they forgive and move forward? Thomas's skill in drawing memorable parallels between past and present events, places, and conflicts results in an intricate and satisfying story that drives forward with clarity and ingenuity. This book is literally novel; you will never read another one like it."

—Dorene O'Brien, award-winning author of *What It Might Feel Like to Hope*

"This riveting, richly layered novel engages on multiple levels. It's a searing exploration of the long reach of trauma, and of how it can limit our ability to trust or love. It's an unsparing examination of how relationships can fall apart, or find promising ground. It's also a moving exploration of how we can persist—and perhaps find reasons for hope—even under the most trying circumstances. And, finally, it's a compelling mystery that will keep you guessing until the final pages. Both unflinching and compassionate, *The Meaning of Fear* is an unforgettable novel."

—Beth Castrodale, author of *The Inhabitants*

"With gorgeous and precise language, Thomas escorts us through a labyrinth of memories to arrive at a rural Michigan town where her characters find themselves revisiting their past lives. They relive their pain as they struggle to be understood, be seen, be loved through human interactions that could verify their existence or make them run from their past. Thomas's characters figure out some understanding of themselves in unsuspecting ways that could help us gain strength as we travel with them in their search for ways to overcome their fears through confronting them. All of this takes place in what on the surface could easily be mistaken for a quiet Michigan community. *The Meaning of Fear* challenges us but also provides a path to reflect and grow. And maybe find love."

—Lolita Hernandez, award-winning author of *Making Callaloo in Detroit*

"*The Meaning of Fear* pulls readers into a sharply drawn landscape. In it, just as the edges of suburban and rural life overlap, the central characters' past traumas intersect with the present, shaping it and threatening to unravel them. *The Meaning of Fear* trains an unflinching eye on the darkest aspects of suffering and survival. A tense, taut read."

—Megan Schikora, author of *A Woman in Pink*

"In *The Meaning of Fear*, behavioral researcher Lea Johnson grapples with the haunting interplay of trauma, revenge, and redemption as she confronts the shadows of her past. In an unflinching exploration of fear and resilience, the novel navigates Lea's struggle with her husband's obsession with guns and her evolving bond with a police officer investigating events swirling around her home. A gripping story that keeps readers on edge until the last page!"

—Maryka Biaggio, author of *Margery and Me*

Also by Laura Hulthen Thomas

States of Motion

THE MEANING OF FEAR

Laura Hulthen Thomas

Regal House Publishing

Published by
Regal House Publishing, LLC
Raleigh, NC 27605
All rights reserved

ISBN -13 (paperback): 9781646036783
ISBN -13 (epub): 9781646036790
Library of Congress Control Number: 2025937264

Cover images and design by ©studiochi.art

Printed in the United States of America

Regal House Publishing, LLC
https://regalhousepublishing.com

For Mom, whose love and courage gave me the way through

But it is utterly impossible I can ever be revenged,
and therefore I cannot forgive him.

—Emily Brontë, *Wuthering Heights*

Don't become a mere recorder of facts,
but try to penetrate the mystery of their origin.

—Ivan Pavlov

PART 1

FEAR CONDITIONING

1982

Lea

I

The day *he* came back, Lea was in the driveway, squatting in a gravel pen she'd built to capture ants. A black line streamed over her bare feet on its way to the nest in the corral's center. Sometimes she would squeeze a few in the calloused patches between her toes. Abundant ants, restless to reach home. Their single-mindedness made them easy to trap.

He saw her, of course. She was in plain sight and made no move to hide. Under his arm he carried an ugly gray rabbit like a football. She had to look twice to see whether it was live or stuffed. His special-for-her gaze rested on her as it always had. Lea was thirteen then, a late bloomer, her mother called her. Straight-line hips. Hard, shallow breast buds. The training bra snagged her nipples. Her mother had scolded her to wear it that day, grow up, dress *appropriately*, but the chafing stung, and anyway she already knew that what she wore would never ward him off.

He walked past her up the drive and strode up the cement steps to the concrete porch. What was he doing here? He'd promised not to come back if she didn't tell. Well, she hadn't; she'd kept her word. He scratched the rabbit between the eyes. He was still handsome. The pale skin like blank paper. The deep black hair curled at his neck. The mustache trimmed in a neat patch over his red lip like an inkblot. Shouldn't he be ugly after the ugly thing he did? *They did.* Maybe that was why he was still so good looking. Maybe he wouldn't appear ugly to the world if she'd sort of gone along.

His knock summoned her mother to the door. She opened the screen and parted her lips as if tasting every word he spoke. She always breathed through her mouth. *Chronic sinusitis* was what Lea had been told was the matter with her mother. Gunk made her breath stinky. Hard to be anywhere near her, yet there he stood, taking it. To hide her red, swollen eyes she was wearing her thick shades, the reflective Jackie O discs that were fashionable when her mom was Lea's age. She'd cried all that morning, seized by one of those sudden jags that made Lea talk long and frantic. Her mother had finally kicked her outside. Now he was staring into her pitch-black lenses at his own reflection, patiently explaining.

Lea couldn't hear them, but he had to be telling her mother the whole story. Well, good. She'd be released from her promise not to tell. Her parents would quit nagging her about her sulking. They'd quit squelching the talky bursts that followed her silence, those hour-long stories she'd weave, one thought rambling into another like mismatched beads Lea had to string into something pretty. If he always intended to tell, why hadn't she gone ahead and done it first? What had their pact been for? Why attach rules that only she was expected to obey, as if he were nothing to her but just another parent?

The strong line of his shoulders shifted as if he might hug her mother, comfort her over the bad news about her daughter. Lea wanted to run to the porch then and make him hug her instead before her mother fetched the gun and shot him for what they'd done. Hanging over their mantel was Grandpa's Mauser rifle, the one he'd taken from a German soldier's corpse on the field of battle. That's how her mother always described the trophy, *taken from a corpse on the field of battle*. Grandpa was a hero. He'd known how to fight a war and what to take from the battlefield after a triumph. Her mother was a hero's daughter. She would know these things too.

The sun whitewashed the gravel and frosted the cement porch with a glaring light. Through the sharp gleam the rabbit changed hands. The soft gray ears grazed her mother's chapped knuckles, red-rimmed knobs like her eyes under the shades.

Lea turned her attention to the ants. She chose a jagged-edged gravel fragment studded with mica. The chunk was big enough to cover the whole line of ants marching over her foot. Still, she was selective. She squished hard enough for the stone to cut her skin. Slow, thick blood trickled over the crushed ant. The line scattered and then fell quickly back into order, skirting the dead body like a stream's current around a boulder. She'd remember this moment in high school biology, and again as a researcher, as her first observation of instinct's unmerciful march.

The screen door clapped shut. Lea didn't understand why her mother would take the rabbit except maybe she didn't want to hurt it when she shot him. His shadow joined with Lea's. They were touching again down here at the gravel even though, now that he was close to her, she didn't want to hug him anymore. Oil and sweat, and some sweetness she couldn't place, spoiled the clean air. Lea didn't look up. With the bright sun behind his head, his face would be hidden. Nothing to see.

Lea shifted her bare feet in a sprinter's starting crouch. When her mother fired the Mauser, she would have to scoot out of the way fast. Lea had to keep him in the driveway while her mother got the gun. She let the embroidered neckline of her peasant blouse fall open a bit. Bait for the catch, but she wished now she were wearing that bra.

His shoe knocked over one of her gravel walls. The ants scuttled to the break.

"Hello, sweetheart." His voice special, as if they'd parted just the day before, although since they'd last seen each other, the winter had disintegrated into this warm sticky spring.

Did he want to hear her voice? His was the same. A dip in his tone like the even swoosh of a swing. She shrugged.

"How are you?" He sounded hurt at her silence.

It was good that she could hurt him. When would her mother get out here? She mumbled, *fine*. From the apple tree in the front yard a bird trilled two notes, hi-lo, probably a chickadee. She was memorizing bird calls that spring, something else to do besides play with the ants, when her mother sent her outside. Were the blossoms out by then? Could she also hear bees buzzing at the pink-tipped blooms, their faint kazoos piped through the air? Beyond the apple tree and a row of lilac bushes the lawn sloped to the dirt road. His rusty old truck was parked on the grass. He hadn't pulled into the drive, maybe afraid he'd hit her by accident even though she was right there in plain sight.

His shadow shifted. His arm melted into her head. "I brought you a bunny for a present. I remember you said your hamster died."

Oreo had died a long time ago. She was too old now to miss him anymore. Rodents were for kids who didn't know anything about what made a good pet. What Lea wanted now was a dog, the bigger the better. A cuddly gentle breed but with a huge chest and fangs. Terrifying on the outside, loving on the inside.

Maybe he was remembering only that she'd told him about the hamster, and the telling made the death seem recent. He cleared his throat.

"Bunnies are stronger. Not so susceptible to every little thing. They make good pets. I asked your mom if it was okay just now. Do you like bunnies?"

Lea hated bunnies. When she was a kid *The Velveteen Rabbit* had scared her to death. Instead of comforting the sick boy, burning up with scarlet fever, the parents took away his favorite stuffed toy and banished him to the seaside. Any normal kid would die outright from such cruelty, but the boy had gotten better, so maybe it was all right. But why burn all of his toys while he was gone? Why not just spray them with bleach like her mother used to?

"I guess I like them," she said.

"Lots of girls do."

Their shadows drew apart. The ants abandoned the opening he'd kicked, streamed back to the nest.

She glanced up at the porch. The door was still closed. Maybe her mother was having trouble loading Grandpa's rifle. Keep him here, hold him fast. Still, her hand crept to her blouse and scrunched it closed. Willed the door to open, the same door she'd opened to him when she was home alone and wasn't supposed to let anyone in, but he was there to fix the furnace, her dad had called him to come right away, so Lea wouldn't freeze to death, he'd said, and he had a toolbox. She'd flirted with him that day, and plenty of other times too. Whenever he hung around drinking beer with her father, she'd wander into the den or onto the deck, pull her bare legs up to her chin for him to run his gaze over. Met his eyes a couple of times without even blushing. Once they'd held hands when her father was in the kitchen fetching more beer. Wasn't she old enough to know exactly what she was doing?

"Do you want to know what's special about this bunny? Other than it's for a special girl?" The deep secret music of his voice used to thrill her.

She mumbled, "I guess."

He squatted down to her level. He wanted her to look at him. She searched instead for the ant stragglers. "It's not a tame one from the store. It's wild. I caught it."

How he'd managed *that* would be another string of terrifying imaginings she'd spend years trying to quash.

He touched her chin, tilted her gaze to his. Friendly eyes, black as sunglasses; and it wasn't hard to look at him after all. Maybe she was braver than she thought. "It's not easy to catch a bunny and not hurt it so it can't be a pet to anyone."

"Okay."

"So you can feed it anything. Because it's used to eating what it can find. You don't need to go to a special store to get special food." His long nail nicked her chin when he let her go. "It was hard to do. To catch her."

She was meant to be grateful. "Thank you." She tried to sound ungrateful.

"I'll come back sometime. Help you feed her."

He'd seen the gun displayed over the fireplace many times. He'd asked her dad to tell him the whole story once. Why wasn't he scared to show his face here? A bird's shadow, maybe a chickadee, flitted over the gravel. Lea selected the ant milling over his toe. The boot's leather crown wrinkled under his crouch like ripples of brown water. She rubbed the worn leather with the gravel as if she were polishing the shoe. He waited until the ant was crushed, then wet a finger and washed it away.

"That's cruel, sweetheart," he said. "Like tearing the wings off flies. I knew a kid who did that. He was bad news."

Lea knew a kid who had pulled the wings off a monarch butterfly, and a girl, too, but she didn't tell him that.

"This is how you get rid of them." He stood up, nudged the nest's mound with his boot. Fine grains cascaded into the hole. "See? Easier that way. But it won't keep them down for long. You need poison for that."

She looked up at the hollow of him, his silhouette cut out from the sunshine like a paper doll. He might have blown her a kiss goodbye, she couldn't see. He walked down the drive and disappeared into the day's glare. The motor sounded as rusty as the truck.

Lea went after her mother to find out why she'd let him get away. The house was still, as it often was because of her mother's condition. The day's glassy brightness made the familiar rooms caverns, or maybe her eyes refused to adjust to the gloom. On the dining room table, the bunny was dumped in the old hamster cage. The water dispenser was empty. The shavings smelled of mold. Lea went to the den. Above the mantel, huddled in the flagstones, the Mauser lay on its pegs. The grainy blond wooden stock and barrel gleamed as if her mother had chosen to polish the gun instead of use it. Her mother knew how to shoot this gun. Once she'd pointed it at Lea's dad during the loud fights they used to have before the sinusitis became *chronic*. The gun wasn't loaded. The trigger's hollow click made her dad laugh, as if her mother were playing a prank.

So by the looks of things her mother hadn't disappeared inside the house to prepare to defend her daughter. Doubly bad news, because this time he'd left with a rule change. He planned to come back.

He must mean for them to keep being lovers.

And since, after what he'd told her, her mother hadn't shot him and was even taking care of the bunny, sort of, she must approve.

Down the hallway a light burned. Her mother's bedroom door was closed. Lea rapped lightly, *Mom,* and cracked the door to see a mound of blankets burying her on that bright warm day. The sunglasses stood rickety on uneven earpieces as if she'd bent them on her way to her room. A bottle of pills to treat her sinuses lay empty on its side near the lamp. Her vodka bottle stood next to the pillbox, the cap screwed on neatly. Beer was all her father ever drank. He left *the hard stuff* to *my lovely wife*, he always said. Lea could never tell whether he was joking or not. Her mother kept her bottles in her nightstand, some in her sewing cabinet, never in the kitchen. Lea wondered if her dad knew how often her mother replaced those bottles.

Her mother must have gone to sleep to escape the news of her daughter's *defilement,* a word Lea had read in a tale. A heaviness in the air, the sour scent of resting up before facing the truth, but whom would she confront upon awakening, him or her daughter?

Anyway, her mother wasn't going to be a hero.

The first order of business was to fill the water dispenser and carry the rabbit to the garage. No animals in the house. After the hamster died that became the new rule. She slid the cage on a low shelf tucked in dust and gloom. When her father pulled into the garage, his fender would graze the bars, hide the animal from view.

Then back to the ants to await her mother's awakening.

II

Not only did her mother survive his visit that day—he'd never even confessed—but the blistering memory of her mother's deep sleep made hard and fast truth out of childish supposition. Such news would make any mother want to kill herself, Lea reasoned. Sometimes heroes did that, absolved the family dishonor by taking their own life. It was how Lea forgave her mother for not shooting him. The real truth was that her mother had already swallowed those pills when he came to the door. He'd interrupted her long slumber, not caused it.

For years Lea thought her father's desperate attempts to awaken her mother when he found her that evening, his frantic call for an ambulance, her mother's confinement to her bed for weeks after she came home, proved he'd told the whole story. When her father yelled at Lea, *why didn't you call for help?* she thought of how hard he'd gripped her shoulder and told her to take her clothes off. How she'd obeyed him, her fingers moving haltingly over buttons and elastic because she couldn't even feel them. *I couldn't,* she tried to explain, which made her father furious. She understood his rage, shared it, even. Couldn't she have gotten away somehow, or at least said *No* out loud? But her father was forgetting that no one had been home, so what difference would calling for help have made? At the time it didn't occur to her that her father meant, *help your mother.* Lea assumed that by then her mother had told her father about the defilement, that they were all dancing around the same unspeakable thing.

As the weeks dragged on and her parents never mentioned him, Lea never dreamed of bringing him up. It was about that time that she approached Officer Friendly in school when he was warning the class about drug danger. Officer Friendly called his talk D.A.R.E., which to Lea sounded more like an invitation than deterrence. After the talk was over and she'd had the guts to approach him, she didn't make herself at all clear. She mixed up the telling of what she'd done with him with how he'd then tried to kill her mother. When the officer looked concerned, Lea's teacher stepped forward. *Suicide attempt.* Everyone in the class could hear her stage whisper. Officer Friendly patted Lea's shoulder kindly. No reason to investigate any further.

One last faith, that if she fed the bunny exactly as he'd instructed, the rabbit's health would ward him off. During her mother's hospital stay, when Lea was often left alone in the house for him to come for her any time he pleased, she loaded the cage with all of the vegetables she hated. Limp salads pickled in vinegar, mushy cooked carrots, slippery canned green beans. She fed it sweets, too, bits of fudge and cookies. The rabbit's belly bulged. It developed guarded, knowing black eyes and a sly way of moving as if anxious for the day it would outgrow the cage and return to the wild. Lea never knew if it was male or female. Did she know how to check at her age? Of course she knew. She must have refused to learn the sex. She'd forgotten he had called it *her*.

Why didn't she release it in the yard before her mother came home, before her father discovered it? When Lea came out to feed it one evening, her father had set the cage on the station wagon's hood. By then the enormous belly pressed through the bars. The rabbit's eyes were narrow and short-sighted from the chronic gloom. The orange light from the dusty garage window startled it. It shied from the sun, pressed its flab tight into the cage's corner. "Where did this come from, Lea?"

Lea told. Waited for his reaction at being reminded of all the trouble. She still believed he'd told her mother all about what they'd done. Would Dad blame him or Lea for her mother's condition? Well, now the rabbit was the charm to find out.

"How thoughtful of him." Her dad smiled, the first pleasure she'd seen in weeks, months really. Not since her mother had pointed the Mauser at him and he'd laughed. "I didn't know he'd been by. Too bad we've been out of touch. A pet will be a nice plaything for you, won't it?"

How was a rabbit supposed to play? But she didn't say this out loud.

Her father gave her an uneasy look, as though he wished he didn't have to talk to her at all. "Your mother's illness is hard, isn't it, sweetheart." He said this like a fact, not a question she was expected to answer.

She did anyway. She allowed as how it wasn't all that hard because her mother slept so much.

Her father disapproved of her attitude. She could tell because he petted the bunny's floppy belly through the bars instead of giving her a hug. She wanted to scream, *don't give me away*, because what else could such pleasure mean at his gift?

"I hope you said thank you."

She curled her fists at her hips. At least she didn't have to lie about that.

"I'll build your bunny a cage out back, honey. Animals need light, a roomy place to live. You shouldn't have put it in the garage. They're like us, Lea, okay? Animals need what we need. The basics, anyway. Understand?" Her father rubbed a finger between the rabbit's dim crafty eyes. "After your mother is all better we'll give him a call, invite him over for dinner. Thank him properly for thinking of you."

The magical notion that keeping the bunny fat was her warding charm vanished with her father's pledge. Lea stopped feeding the rabbit. The animal's slimming took longer than she imagined. After a week it was still huge. It drank greedily when Lea filled the water dispenser. It butted its crown against her palm, licked at the sweat and dirt between her fingers. The longer the bunny kept its fat, the more affection Lea came to feel for it. Because it didn't change appearance, it couldn't be in pain, she reasoned. Its refusal to suffer was a show of loyalty.

Or a sign that her fear of him would never show.

III

Her father's pledge to invite him back meant her parents had decided to restore her honor by giving her away, like a village girl to the bandit who'd defiled her. Would they braid her hair with flowers, dress her in white, parade her through town as if the arrangement were a wedding, not a sacrifice? Her mother's suicide attempt was a necessary response to *the field of battle*. No one would blame Lea directly for her mother's enduring despair. But giving her to him was an atonement that made sense.

That these assumptions were fantastical and irrational, that such cruelty contradicted her parents' competent, if sadly distant, treatment of her, never crossed Lea's mind. The imagination she possessed. The fear she carried. The tale she spun of the village girl and the bandit, handsome to all the world, his villainy shown only to her, was a way to cope with impulses she didn't understand. Crushing the ants. Starving the bunny. Her own missing appetite for food, for friendships, for the normal passions other girls her age pursued with clumsy single-minded quests for affection. A hero was her last hope.

One sweltering day, it must have been late June, Lea climbed the attic stairs to rummage through some boxes. What had she been looking for? She couldn't recall anything being worth enough to her that summer to leak sweat, dizzy and disoriented, in the dismal heat. She must have gone after some long-forgotten obsession, a little-girl doll she suddenly wanted to play with again, a book she wanted to reread.

She found instead a box marked *Eagle's Nest*. Inside was a photograph of her grandfather sipping wine on a marble terrace, a lead-gray sky blending with the mountains behind a caramel-brick chalet. Grandpa had had bright blue eyes, but the black-and-white photo erased their color, made everything in the photo look like stone. He was squinting at the camera the way he used to squint at Lea before he died. Angry and scared, warding her off as if she'd caused his stroke. Her mother had explained that Grandpa didn't mean to look that way, he didn't even recognize Lea anymore. The wineglass in the photo was still full. She flipped it over. *Hitler's wine 1945* was scrawled on the back.

From a wad of yellowed tissue paper Lea pulled a red marble chunk, dull as old blood. Folded neatly underneath the marble were two satin dresses dimpled with stains. The hems rustled on the pine floor when Lea held them up to her shoulders. In the pale light of the bulb dangling from the ceiling, the crimson and lavender silk shone like wildflowers.

She set the dresses aside and pulled out a thick handkerchief. Wrapped inside she found five cigar-sized torpedoes capped with steel. Maybe they were toys, since real torpedoes were enormous. The close, dusty air was getting to her. Her sweat dripped onto the crimson dress draped over her bare toes. She wiped her neck with the bodice and took out another tissue-wrapped packet. More photos, but the paper was sturdier than photographic paper and the drawings on the cards were larger than Grandpa's snapshots. One showed Hitler with his head squished between a naked woman's fat round breasts. In another Hitler's stern salute collided with the mud-brown saucers ringing a woman's nipples. The women's arms were draped around Hitler's neck. Their wide-mouthed hungry grins leered down on his greasy, tousled hair. Why was Hitler dressed in uniform while the women were naked? But with Lea, he hadn't undressed either, except to open his belt and pull down his jeans and underwear.

More cards, decorated with foreign words. One cartoon was split into two panels. In the left panel a tired soldier hunched behind barbed wire. The bodies of fallen soldiers hung limply from the tented wire fence. In the right panel a naked woman in a fancy room brandished a champagne glass and snuggled on a man's lap. Outside the window behind her nude shoulder, the Eiffel Tower's black skeleton shone starkly on the white paper. On the table next to the armchair was a photo of the tired soldier in ordinary clothes kissing the woman. The man she was snuggling with now wore ordinary clothes. He'd wedged his hand between the woman's spread legs. The woman's lips curved around the champagne glass as if she was enjoying her drink but Lea thought she saw pain in the woman's flat inked eyes.

Lea thumbed through the drawings. Soldiers with naked women flung over their shoulders like sacks. Soldiers bumping into naked women from behind, the women bent double to the ground. Foreign words unfurled like triumphant banners over the scenes, showy script, fancy exclamation points. Warnings or boasting? Impossible to tell.

The last card showed a pretty village girl framed by plump blond braids. She was lying on her belly, hands cupping her chin, dainty slippers crossed at the ankles, a daisy stem tucked in her smiling lips. Behind her stretched a field thick with wildflowers and grass. Above her unfolded a white, empty sky. The girl's expression was peaceful, happy in that daydreamy way, maybe because she was the only girl in the bunch with her clothes still on. But what was she dreaming about? The empty sky offered no clue. Lea rubbed at a smudge above the girl's head. She held the card up to the bare light bulb to inspect the dirt. Smack dab in the blank sky the ferocious snarl of a soldier grinding on top of the girl jumped out at Lea. His hairy, muscle-roped hands choked the girl's white neck. Her pretty dress was torn to shreds. The plump braids flopped into her gaping mouth. Her legs wrenched like broken toothpicks under the soldier's thrusting. The daisy she'd been chewing on lay crushed beneath her arm.

Lea cried out and dropped the card. The soldier and the suffering girl winked out of sight. The village girl was alone again with her happy dreams and the empty sky. Her defilement lurked above her, hiding in wait for the next ray of light.

Lea fought back tears. Why did Grandpa have these wicked, dirty cartoons? Had he fought the Germans to rescue these poor women?

She laid the cards next to the toy torpedoes. The steel tips gleamed in the dim light. The rafters creaked in the heat. A moldy smell like her mother's breath seeped from the satin dresses. He'd done some of these things to her, things she thought had never been done to any girl. But if what they'd done could be drawn, they must be common things, nothing special, like that village girl with the daisy.

She picked up a torpedo. Why would Grandpa have toys in this box, toys he'd never given to her?

She glanced back at the cards, picked out one with a grinning soldier ramming into a woman's behind. His gun was slung over his shoulder. It looked like Grandpa's Mauser.

She pressed the torpedo's sharp tip, studied the deep impression it dimpled in her finger. Too small to be real torpedoes, but were they just the right size to be bullets for a big gun?

The field of battle stretched before her as if a magic carpet had flown straight to her feet to take her there. If she dragged a chair to the mantel, she could easily reach the Mauser. Her sleeping mother wouldn't hear a thing. The fat muumuued neighbor lady wasn't out today on the back deck sipping Tab, settling her hawk's eye on Lea, poor thing, playing all by herself while that sicko mother neglected her. Their overgrown lawn bounded a stand of oak trees, and the trails through the woods led to abandoned cornfields. She could easily spirit the gun away.

She knew right where he lived and could walk there.

Lea piled Grandpa's treasures back into *Eagle's Nest*. Except the dirty photos. Those she tucked into her sundress pocket.

Lugging the gun proved the real chore. Lea could barely lift it over the hooks. She hadn't expected it to be so heavy. A peg caught the trigger guard, almost sending her tumbling to the carpet. She was awkward back then, bony-weak. The gun was almost as long as she was. But Lea managed to get it out of the house and drag it across the yard to the protected path without being discovered. She didn't dare think about how she would heft the gun when it came time to aim.

She was tromping through the cornfield, the Mauser bumping along at her heels, when she burst upon a girl smoking in a clearing. That new girl, Dinah, the one who'd pulled the wings off the monarch butterfly. Dinah's bare toes were buried in the furrows. The cigarette dangled from her hand, ashing on a mound of dried husks.

She shared none of the surprise Lea felt stumbling onto her. Her gaze rested on the barrel poking from Lea's fist. "That's not the way you carry it."

The same calm assurance she'd shown over the butterfly's torture. At her feet, a filament of smoke unwound from the husks.

"It's heavy." Lea drew the gun to her chest.

"Are you shooting with the boys?"

Lea thought Dinah had said *at the boys* until a shot rang out, followed

by a metallic plinking on tin. Whoops drifted through the narrow rows
of corn. She shook her head.

"Can I watch you shoot?"

"There's nothing to watch."

Dinah studied her skinny arms, her flat, plain body. Sizing up
whether Lea was capable of doing anything interesting. She must have
liked what she discovered. She pulled on the cigarette, held the cloud
in her lungs. She dropped the butt and ground the husks with her bare
heel. The smoke curl winked out. "No reason I can't tag along, then."

She might need help loading the gun, was Lea's thinking. She allowed
Dinah to trail her, said nothing when Dinah lifted the Mauser's stock
as if they were village girls hauling the water bucket home. When Lea
wound her way toward the boys, toward the wrong way out, Dinah
nudged her east, the rifle her rudder.

His house was isolated on the outskirts of town, a cobblestone
plunked down in stark Southeast Michigan cornfields not yet thought
of as real estate. The girls crossed a dirt road to wade through a grassy
field scorched from the heat and lack of rain that summer. A flatbed
farm truck sped by. Gravelly dust skittered along the road in front of a
white concrete apron. A short road divided the opposite field, ending
for no good reason in the middle of the corn. She would learn later that
the unfinished street was the beginning of a new subdivision, but on
that day the nowhere road seemed like an abandoned mistake.

When the truck rattled past, Dinah lowered her end of the rifle to
bury the weapon from sight, but out there, back then, no one would
question the sight of a gun in a field filled with pheasant, not even
if girls were carrying it. Their rustling traipse through the long grass
should have raised a bird. By now a flash of green and gold, a glorious
pinwheel against the broad white sky, should be casting a shadow on
the girls. But the sky stretched empty and clean like a yawn. His house
and the clump of oak trees behind it were lonely bumps on the horizon.

He was unlikely to be home, Lea realized, too late. In her girlish
view of summer's unmoored routines she hadn't thought that, like her
father, he'd be at work. She'd hauled the Mauser all this way for nothing.
Sweat streaked her back and heels. Salt burned her eyes. She'd have
to face Dinah now. Admit to poor planning and the narrow vision of
imagination where deeds are descendants of foolish impulse.

But then there he was, behind the cobblestone house, walking across his clipped grass into a wildflower carpet partly shaded by the oaks. Sunny buttercups, royal purple dragon catchers, white aster parted under his boots. Daisies popped their golden eyes as he passed. Crimson clover tongues brushed his legs. He waded carelessly through the color as if sloshing upstream. He looked ridiculous, padded in a full bodysuit of whitewashed armor. With a helmet hat, black mesh lumped at his neck. Why was he so protected? Had he sensed she was coming for him like those crafty bandits in the tales?

Dinah touched her bare shoulder. "That him?"

Lea nodded. That Dinah would know he was the one Lea was after did not strike her as strange. Already she took for granted Dinah's guessing things about her that Lea would swear she'd never revealed. But maybe she just couldn't remember telling Dinah all about him as they lugged the gun through the corn rows.

"Don't hurt the bees."

"What?" Lea brushed the sweat from her eyes. The sun glanced off the flowers' bright colors. Thick perfume rolled to her on the humid air.

Dinah pointed. A tall column of stacked boxes rested on pallets in the oak glade. That's why he was dressed the way he was, it was stupid of her not to realize. That he would be a keeper of bees jarred her, that he coaxed honey from them! He'd been as ruthless with the ants as she had. He'd filled their mound with a casual swipe of his boot. How could he tend bees?

"Do you know how to load this thing?" Dinah's voice floated to her from a distance.

Lea took the handkerchief from her pocket, unwrapped the bullets. The sharp torpedo tips would rip through that suit, they'd rip through anything. She handed the rounds to Dinah.

Together they figured out how to work the bolt action by removing the pin. The rounds chambered perfectly. Five shots. But after the first he'd run away, or run toward her, snatch the weapon, turn it on her. She had one shot.

"You're too far away," Dinah warned.

Lea couldn't move closer to him. She couldn't move at all. She hefted the gun, settled the silver guard into her shoulder's bony cave. The stock lodged smoothly under her arm. Harder to lug the gun than to raise and aim. She felt light, steady. A cold band tightened around her belly like a strap of ice.

Dinah placed a hand on the barrel as he lifted the beehive's lid and pulled out a frame. "You won't hit anything from here anyway. Wait until he's away from the bees."

Lea pressed the trigger.

Dinah's hand flew from the barrel. The kick knocked Lea backward into the grass. The gun landed above her head. The pure silence baffled her, as if the gun's report had sucked in all the air. Instead of him she faced a white, empty sky.

PAUL

I

Those two girls made Paul late to afternoon chores that day, and that's how the whole trouble began. He'd been plinking cans, that summer's entertainment, with a couple of farm boys in the next county. Which wasn't as far as it sounded. The county line bordered the Rilke farm's southernmost field. An easy hike to hang with Rick and Ed, shoot the shit as well as cans, spend a few hours away from Papa's short fuse over Paul's minor deviations from the way Papa liked things done.

Rick, who could turn both thick and mean for no good reason, had decided to ditch the log they were using and shoot a can off the back of his old man's dog. Ed's boombox was blaring John Cougar's "Jack & Diane" until the dog's shaking and laid-back ears made Paul feel sick and he cut the effing music. The pooch was a tall, skinny black mutt who minded well and was sweet too. Paul could understand the urge to disrespect a father's possession but why hurt a poor old scraggly thing? With Rick's crappy aim, the dog was bound to be wounded, or worse. Shoot up your old man's Prince Albert in a Can, or the *Playboys* stashed in the closet, but lay off the dog. Which is exactly what Paul told Rick. Which earned a shove from Rick, along with some lame insults as tame as his old man's *Playboys*. Ed snickered. Ed always went along with whomever was in charge, and Paul—sprawled at the base of a maple tree, where Rick had knocked him—had been taken out of the leadership pool. Rick loaded his rifle and walked over to the dog standing still and hollow-eyed in a patch of dried-out leaves and stalks; he hollered *stay!* even though the dog hadn't so much as flinched. Rick steadied the can on the pooch's bumpy spine. Paul's gut flip-flopped.

He was back on his feet and going for Rick's gun when those two girls crashed out of the corn into the clearing, gasping as if they'd been running for miles. The pretty girl with the curly black hair magnetized the air. The sun blazed hotter the moment a girl like that popped into things. At fourteen, shy Paul Rilke wasn't in the habit of staring at girls so long and hard it was like copping a feel, and he never would be that man as an adult either. But the bust-to-butt ratio in the tight tank and shorts couldn't be ignored. Her dark eyes laughed at the boys even before they regained sense enough to play fool.

Like the other boys, Paul didn't notice the mousy girl right away. With her stringy brown hair and rumpled, saggy dress, it seemed her only goal in life was to avoid attracting attention. The boys sure noticed the German Mauser she was dragging, though. While the guys ogled her friend and that amazing gun, the girl stared at the poor dog. The dog gazed at her right back, as if they were old friends. Usually that dog avoided looking at anybody. Probably Rick's dad cuffed him hard to get him to mind, and that was why he always slithered around with his eyes pasted to the earth.

The girl took in the can, and the dog's trembling, and then looked at Paul as though it was all his fault. Well, it wasn't and it was, and he wanted to explain himself, but he didn't need to say a word for her to put the boys and their stupid cruelty in their place, all right.

After the gutsy stunt she pulled, Paul swore to remember that mousy girl. Find out where she lived, what school she attended. But after the girls took off back into the cornfield, and Rick started griping about what lie he could tell his dad about what had happened to the poor old dog, Paul hustled home, late again for the milking. By the time he reached the dairy shed he was jazzed up, ashamed of the guys and especially himself. While he settled in to milk the first cow, he vowed to search for that girl starting tomorrow. Then he saw the bright-red swelling that had already spread to half the cow's udder. Mastitis—which wasn't the end of the world, but could be Paul's fault and that *could* be the end of Paul's world if Papa was in the mood to end it. Paul hated milking. He hated cows. He hated the dairy shed, a dank and rickety barn, muddy and smelling of hot hides and shit. The shed was huge, big enough for a whole production herd, but the Rilkes kept only a handful now. Because Paul had told Papa he hated milking, Papa had made it his job.

That was Papa's way, to force Paul to do exactly what he most disliked, all because Mutti defended Paul as sensitive. What Paul was most sensitive to was hurting animals. Clearing the traps. Air-gunning groundhogs and chipmunks and rabbits. Papa meant to teach him that dealing with pests was just another routine chore around any farm, but harming anything really bothered Paul. Once Papa ordered him to drown a barn cat's useless litter. Paul smuggled the kits to his teacher, who promised to give them to the Humane Society. When the next litter emerged, Paul outright refused to dispose of the kits, the only time he could remember standing up to his father.

Milking wasn't harming cows, but Paul still had nightmares about what had happened to bring their herd to the size where Paul was the only one needed to milk. He hated working the teats, sweating bullets while cheek to flank with a cow whose patience for this whole operation had been bred into it. Papa wouldn't let him use the old milking equipment either, since there were so few cows. So Paul was half-assed about milking on time, which meant he could have caused the bright scarlet mass glowering at him now.

Paul sighed, patted the cow's haunch, and went to find Papa, more to get that unpleasantness over with than out of any emergency about the animal.

❧

Paul's earliest memories of cows were sickening flashes of glazed, suffering eyes sunk deep into gaunt heads. Bodies wasting to spindles that looked like Papa's sawhorses. Hides eaten bare by runny, smelly sores. Hooves swelling and twisting into gruesome shapes that would crowd his nightmares. Back when Paul was five, the Rilkes, like almost every other Michigan dairy farmer, didn't know they were giving feed contaminated by flame retardant to their animals. By the time the error was discovered, the Rilkes' stock was beyond saving.

There was nothing to do but corral the herd into a pen. Paul's first experience of the catastrophes that caring for animals could come to was of the ghoulish cows stumbling about like Papa late at night, when Mutti had to lay hands on him and lead him gently to bed. Only instead of soothing the animals to sleep like Mutti did for Papa, Papa shouldered a long rifle with a fat scope. Paul had crouched behind a bush on the slope overlooking the pen to watch, although Papa had told him to stay inside. He was too young to know that the cows had been poisoned. To him, their illness appeared sudden, mysterious, illogical, and unfair like the flu that had taken his opa last year. As Papa fired his rifle, the cows fell one by one. The live ones didn't seem to know why the cow next to them had fallen, or that they were next. Maybe they were too sick to care. Later, his mutti would call this *mercy killing*. Paul wanted nothing to do with whatever mercy was if it led to what Papa did to those cows.

Long after he should have outgrown such babyish terrors, Paul still suffered vivid dreams where sometimes he had to take up the rifle to take care of the problem. Now, as he poked around looking for Papa, thinking of the mastitis's angry red swelling and the heat it gave off was making him sick. Papa wasn't in the fields, or in any of the outbuildings. This close to dinner he could be in the kitchen with Mutti, so Paul hiked up Scipio, the two-lane county road that bisected their land, toward the house. The sun's glare on the pavement made him woozy. He blamed his dizziness on the sick cow, not the still, humid air. From the road the house looked empty. He couldn't see Mutti through the kitchen's front window, her usual spot this late in the day. If she was standing there, she would wave to him, and he would wave back, and his upset over the cow would be soothed.

He took the porch steps two at a time and pushed open the screen door. Thinking back on it, although his memory would amplify the strange noises rasping down the hallway, the sounds couldn't have been too dramatic; Caroline was napping in her room just up the stairs from the library, and she didn't come down right away. Paul couldn't remember when he'd begun tiptoeing down the hall, his breath locked tight in his chest. He couldn't tell whether the grunts and moans were human or animal, whether the cries and thumps meant someone was beating something. He stopped at the staircase to listen. The commotion lay behind the library's heavy sliding doors at the end of the hallway. He would remember telling himself to breathe, to move quickly but quietly to help. It didn't occur to him to call out for his mutti, or for Papa. Maybe he'd been too scared.

The library's oak doors were so heavy he usually couldn't open them without rattling, but that afternoon the sliders tucked quietly into the wall. The noises floated past, still muffled. This could only mean whatever the trouble was wasn't near the door but lay deep inside, maybe by the built-in bookcases flanking the stained-glass picture window. He stepped into the room.

Papa was leaning against Mutti, who was pressed against a bookcase. Papa's big, clumsy hand was on her shoulder. His other hand was clamped just below her throat. They were nude, which should have sent Paul running, but instead set the muscles in his legs and arms tingling and thrumming so he couldn't move at all. A row of books behind Mutti's head had toppled like a spent accordion. Mutti used the library as a sewing room. There stood her Singer, over near the closet door, the sunny fabric of her next project, curtains, or maybe a new dress for Caroline, bunched up under the needle. The cutting table stood next to the bookcase. The family thought of this as her room, so Papa being in there at all was all but forbidden, in Paul's eyes.

He wondered why his mother didn't shout for help, or push Papa away. He shifted to look at her face. Her eyes were closed. Her hair flowed loose around her shoulders, draped down her back. Paul stood there, throttled into silence. The air, sticky and sour, wasn't fit to breathe. The thumps and moans and groans crashed into him, melted through his skin, tingled down his arms and legs, *move move*, but instead of rushing to save his mother Paul was back over the threshold, sweat streaming; he was going to chicken out, he was. A creak fluttered down the stairwell behind him. A hiss clouded the suffocating air. His mother's mouth had fallen open. She was whispering, *yes*, as if what Papa was doing was okay, just fine, which didn't make any sense.

And then it did, the way that mousy girl's dirty German postcards had made sense.

Paul backed up into the hallway, but before he could slide the doors shut, a book at Mutti's shoulder tumbled to the oak floorboards. Papa, grunting, tossed a look over his shoulder. Paul shut the doors. Waited for Papa to rush out and thrash him good. When he didn't, Paul relaxed a bit. Maybe he hadn't been seen.

A soft pulsing reached him then. Socks shuffled on the hallway oak.

Caroline was heading toward the library, yawning, cradling the house cat. "Where's Mama?"

"Sewing." Paul led his sister to the kitchen to fix her a snack. Moving slow and clumsy, he dug from the fridge a big bowl of chocolate pudding, her favorite. She was eight, too old to nap at all, let alone sleep so late, but that's the way that summer went, stumbles and setbacks and downright horrors on the way to growing up, and it had been so damn hot that day, who wouldn't want to sleep through it? Paul felt like he was sleepwalking now. He watched the house cat, a pretty kitty with lacy tiger stripes on her head, lick pudding from Caroline's fingers. That cat had gotten so fat lately he should make Caroline quit feeding her so much. He recognized, now, the sour odor in the library. His father was drunk. Maybe his mother was too. He hoped so. Even later he would come to believe they were too smashed to know what they were doing. Better that than to think her *yes* meant *yes*, that this wasn't the first time she and Papa had done this while Paul was out milking and clearing traps and mercy-killing little critters.

The dainty, gentle way the cat's pink little tongue lapped at his sister's finger raised babyish tears Paul was careful to wipe away. When Papa and Mutti finally emerged from the library, fully clothed, he'd already cleaned the chocolate from the cat's whiskers and locked her back in his room where Papa wouldn't see her. The cat was a secret between Mutti, Caroline, and Paul.

Papa grabbed a beer from the fridge and slammed the screen door on the way outside without looking at Paul sitting quietly at the table. Caroline fetched potatoes from the pantry. Mutti moved to her usual spot at the sink. Paul dared to join her and took up a rag to dry the dishes she was scrubbing. Her black hair curled at her shoulders. The bun she always wore was usually neat and tidy, no stray hairs at all. She must have been in a hurry to make herself decent.

The longer she was quiet, washing dishes as she always did, the more Paul flushed until she couldn't help but notice the red blotches staining his cheeks. If she guessed then that he'd seen, he couldn't blame her for keeping silent; what would she have said to her teenage son about catching his parents doing what they'd done? Especially since the Rilkes never hashed out any damn thing. The real trouble was, Paul would come to understand, that there was no use blaming his papa, either. Not as long as Paul's mother insisted on loving the man through all troubles, till death did them part.

II

Paul never did tell Papa the cow was sick. Maybe he just forgot, or maybe some deep and lonely part of him hoped that discovering the cow's suffering for himself would shock his papa into remorse for other sufferings he'd inflicted. On Mutti. On Paul. On those other cows, the ones he'd culled so expertly, barely missing a shot. But when Papa discovered the mastitis, he gave Paul a light strapping, treated the animal with antibiotics, and never mentioned Paul's irresponsibility again. He never mentioned the library, either, which convinced Paul that he'd slid those doors shut in time.

That July, Paul turned fifteen. He'd quit plinking with the guys, or doing much of anything except hard labor. For weeks he'd power-washed, scraped, and painted a run-down old shed Omi had used for shearing and carding back in the days when the farm had kept sheep. Omi, who was Papa's mama and sweet as Papa was sour as Mutti used to say, spent evenings spinning yarn and telling Paul stories he couldn't remember a lick of now. As he worked, he wondered if his papa had been a different man when his mother was still alive, and whether that difference had been better or worse than the man he was now.

Papa happened by one humid afternoon when Paul was stretched on a ladder, cutting in the paint under the eaves. He lurked at the ladder's base, head tipped up to stare at Paul's efforts. Sweat piddled down his neck, from the heat, or the nerves Papa raised.

Cosmetics is the last part of the job, son.

Which Paul took as criticism until Papa packed him over to the old cannery across Scipio Road from the farmhouse and informed him that they, together, were going to fix the place up.

Build me some comfort for my dotage, he joked. Paul took *dotage* to mean *drink.* Papa drank alone in the cannery most evenings, and maybe some during the day too. At least, there were long stretches when Papa went missing from the fields or the house, so Paul drew his own conclusions.

They set to work, together, that very afternoon. Because his father never maintained anything, Paul had assumed he lacked the skill of the trades, but Papa set to ripping out the rotted wall studs and replacing them with his own expert carpentry as if craftsmanship were a second skin. He buttressed every rotted stud with dimensional lumber and plywood and then finished the walls with polished pine. He replaced Omi's rickety shelving with fine built-in pine cabinets. He taught Paul to fashion doors for the cabinetry and hang them on oiled hinges. He showed Paul how to wire the place for lights and how to run a gas line for the kitchenette. He had Paul plumb in the bathroom fixtures. When the interior was finished, the whole job taking them, together, just six weeks to accomplish, Papa returned to the fields full time, leaving Paul to paint the exterior any color he wanted. Paul wanted something eye catching, so he'd picked a deep burgundy, a shade related to, but richer than, a traditional barn's hue. Papa never said anything about the color but made some approving remarks about the quality of the work. The guest cottage, he labeled it from then on, and swapped the rusted old cot that used to crouch under the far window for a roomy double bed.

Then Papa overnighted in the cottage some. On those nights Mutti stayed at the farmhouse, or at least Paul never caught her slipping out in the moonlight, crossing the road, loose hair flowing in the breeze. His parents' separation must mean some family good had sprung from the trouble in the library. Paul decided to feel honored that Papa had used his labor on the guest cottage to create civility, safety, even maybe harmony. Together Papa and Paul had built a fine place of exile for those times when the man of the house couldn't control himself. Papa quit strapping him for minor infractions, quit shoving the air rifle into his hands. Quit speaking to him, really, Paul realized later when he looked back on that summer.

Paul also learned everything he knew about building and maintaining a home from Papa that summer. Despite everything that happened between them later, he carried appreciation for that much, at least.

III

Once Paul made Mutti laugh when she'd sent him to fetch the milk bottle from the pantry table, *kitty corner*, she said, to the tall shelf, and he'd returned with a kitty instead of the bottle. That laugh left sparkles on his memory, because his mother worked so hard she didn't often pause long enough to see anything as funny.

"How on earth did that get in?" Her smile wrinkled her nose, just like Caroline when she giggled.

It's a house kitty, he told her.

Mutti had eyed the matted white fur, the brown socks that might be natural color or might be mud, the lady's fan of tiger striping radiating from between the eyes to the ears. "Take her back to the barn, Paul."

This was a few days after he'd refused to drown another litter, so a part of him hoped this little kit had escaped his papa's doing of the foul deed. Still, it was babyish to want to keep a kitten. So he told her Caroline had always wanted one.

Mutti laughed again. "She'll never stay in the house, son. When she's older, her heat will drive her outdoors. You understand?"

He did understand. He thought there were ways around that. He could tame her to the indoors. Caroline needed a pet, he argued again. His sister was lonely, teased at school by the town kids for her farm clothes and home haircuts. This being back before the subdivision boom dragged those town kids' behinds out to *the country*, as they called the township even though town was only five miles away down Scipio Road. Since Paul's quiet ways pegged him as dumb and he was also big for his age, bullies mostly steered clear, except for that jerk Jim Wagner, who wouldn't lay off the fat jokes. But Caroline, being a girl, endured torturous nonsense about her rural appearance and shy ways. Mutti brooded on Caroline but Caroline rejected her worry. They'd never been close the way Paul and Mutti were. He guessed that Mutti's concern for Caroline would soften her, although she'd simply said, "Your papa doesn't like cats in the house," and left it at that.

The pet cheered Caroline up, all right. Paul kept charge of feeding and cleaning the litter box, and he fetched the cat whenever she did manage to slip outdoors. Caroline kept charge of the affection. She was always combing the cat's fur with her own brush, which Mutti scolded her for but Caroline still did on the sly. The cat slept draped over Caroline's neck all night. Paul thought this had to be a bit dangerous, but Caroline insisted it comforted her. Looking back on it, Paul would see what scared kids they had been about the entire enterprise. They just called her the cat instead of bestowing a normal name. Entertainment and gratification centered on making certain the cat didn't get out of the house, not the cute tricks she performed while she was safely inside. The real excitement was keeping the cat secret from Papa. They managed this task pretty well. They shut her up in Paul's room because she'd already clawed to shreds so many of his possessions they might as well keep the damage contained. The litter box they stashed deep in his closet. When Papa was out of the house, the cat was released to tear around before she'd curl up in Caroline's lap and motor a purr, uneven as a busted engine's sputter.

Mutti put up with it for a while, but she had her limits. A couple of weeks after the library trouble, the cat destroyed Paul's Sunday shirt and he'd worn plaid flannel to church. After Papa scolded him for dressing like a field hand and disrespecting God, Mutti told Paul on the q.t. that the cat was getting to be too much. But she laid down the law nervously, which wasn't like her. Paul decided she must be terrified of Papa discovering their pet. She'd helped conceal the cat from Papa, which proved she was scared, didn't it? Maybe Papa had hurt her in the library after all, and Mutti's *yes* had really been a promise to do what he said from now on.

Before Paul had to make a decision one way or another on their pet's fate, one August evening, just after Paul and Papa had finished work on the guest cottage, the cat bolted outside when Papa opened the screen door on his way in. He'd cuffed her with his boot, raising a yowl. No amount of combing the barns had fetched her back. Caroline had cried a little when Mutti confirmed, "You can't keep a barn cat indoors forever," as if they'd learned a valuable lesson, and left it at that.

Late that summer, Paul and Caroline were curled up on the den sofa watching television. *Creature Feature* had just ended, *Mothra vs. Godzilla*, the Godzilla movie Paul loved best for the cool final showdown but Caroline hated because the mama Mothra ended up incinerated during the cool final showdown. The news blared while Paul and Caroline argued over whether Godzilla's atomic rays would be strong enough underwater to melt the cocoon the baby Mothras had trapped him in before he plunged into the sea. Paul had just about convinced Caroline that water, being naturally radioactive, would for sure make Godzilla even more powerful, when a jumpy black-and-white newsreel of a farmer shooting penned-up cows popped up on the screen. The footage so resembled his memory of Papa mercy killing the sick cows that he wondered at first if Mutti had somehow filmed it. But his papa didn't own a cap like the man was wearing in the news story, and Paul couldn't see the bush he'd hidden behind, or the Rilke farm's cornfields striping the horizon beyond the corral. Caroline watched with her thumb shoved in her mouth, a babyish habit she'd given up when she was four. The farmer shot another cow in the head. The footage cut to a newscaster, who informed them that from '73 to '74, nearly every resident in Michigan had eaten beef or drunk milk contaminated with PBB. A feed company had packed their FireMaster product into sacks similar to their NutriMaster feed supplement and shipped them to the Michigan Farm Bureau Services. While some Michiganders had developed cancer or thyroid diseases right away, for most the health effects wouldn't be known for years.

Caroline popped her thumb out of her mouth. "What's PBB?"

"Some chemical." Paul shrugged like it was no big deal, but in truth, he felt sick. "They just said what it was, dummy."

"I don't want that in me," Caroline told him.

Like Paul could do anything about what was in whom. But anyway, the math was clear. "It isn't in you. You weren't born then."

"Oh." Caroline brightened up, and then frowned. "You were, though. So were Papa and Mutti. So it's in you."

Paul shrugged again, *so what?* But his stomach was flip-flopping. The effects wouldn't be known for years. Would he feel these effects, when they came? Was he supposed to feel different now? Maybe he'd just grown used to the poison, since he was so young when it happened. Maybe he'd once been different himself.

Had the poison changed Papa and Mutti too? He couldn't remember how they'd been before. The memory of Papa felling those cows hit his gut hard; and then he saw, again, his father's hand at his mother's throat. A sour taste bubbled in his throat. Nerves, or the poison coming up his tube. How would he know the difference from now on?

Anyway, the three of them always treated Caroline a bit differently. Gentler, shielding her from the hardest work, the worst troubles. Paul always thought it was because she was a girl, and the baby of the family. Now he wondered if the chemical lurking in their bodies bound Mutti, Papa, and Paul together with grave effects that they would someday have to face together.

Mutti came in then, on her way out to the store, to tell Paul to fetch Papa because the slop sink near the furnace had backed up and if he didn't unclog it a fire might spark, so it couldn't wait. She didn't hear the news story. Didn't notice Paul and Caroline's somber quiet.

Well, the last chore Paul wanted while he was mulling over the poison inside was to deal with Papa. When Mutti left the house, he trudged down to the basement and tried to snake the drain himself. But the blockage wouldn't budge. Soon Paul was soaked in gray water. The old furnace spit like it was already drowned. He shop-vac'ed the water that had spilled on the concrete floor and sprinkled kitty litter to wick moisture. The cat had gone missing weeks ago, but Paul couldn't bring himself to get rid of her things just yet. He felt the hiss of the furnace like breath on his neck. He was worried to leave Caroline for the hazard the water posed, but he'd only be away a moment.

He told his sister to sit tight, locked the door behind him, and looked around. Since the farmhouse perched on a hill, Paul could see much of the farm from the backyard. Papa wasn't in any field, which meant Paul would have to check the guest cottage. With his gut still turning flips, he crossed Scipio Road at a run. Hiked through the line of pines and the fallow field toward the cottage. The papery bones of old husks crackled under his work boots. The guest cottage shimmered a gentle maroon under the blazing sun. He'd chosen a pretty color that stood up to the wear of glare and wind just fine.

Paul was sweating when he arrived breathless at Papa's door.

When Papa didn't answer, Paul rapped again. Listened carefully, heard only uninformative murmurs and rustlings, and then a come-in grunt. Was Mutti inside? Would he open the door to the sight of her against the wall, hair loose, whispering *yes*? But he entered to find Papa alone, sprawled spread-legged on the new double bed with a faded quilt bunched over his head. The raw flame from an unshaded lamp bulb lit Papa's bare arms. Paul hadn't been in the cottage since they'd finished the work. He was impressed with how the tidy room gleamed cleanly in the bare light. Buffed brown shelves glowed like shoe polish. The urethane streaks on the oak floor were burnished to a slick icy film. Even in his rubber-soled boots, Paul could skate to Papa if he wished.

Papa peeked at him. Flapped the quilt's bright edging with a peek-a-boo gesture that might have been playful coming from another man. "What is it, son?"

Paul cleared his throat. "The utility sink's clogged, sir."

"Snake it, then."

"I tried." From his slurry of vowels, Paul determined Papa was far gone already. A whiskey bottle stood on the kitchenette counter, half empty, the screw cap tossed aside. Paul pressed against the doorjamb. Papa rolled from the bed, stood up, shook the shivers from his legs one at a time. The crisp snap of denim rattled the room. "Mutti told me to fetch you." Paul hoped Papa would achieve the sense of his mother having sent him on this errand rather than Paul relying on him for help. "Water's leaking to the furnace."

"Shouldn't be leaks from a clogged drain. You check the pipes for bad seams?"

"No, sir."

"There's your leak." He glided to the counter, lifted the bottle, poured a shot glass full. Papa's size could still take Paul's breath away. Tireless labor had built up a rigid grid of muscle in his arms and chest. His height was nerve-racking, too, his girth outgunned by the limber stretch of his limbs. Papa looked like no one else, his mother had said once. As if rubber-band balls had been pinched together to form him. His eyes flashed at Paul over the shot glass. He swallowed the whole deal without a single bobble of the throat. Blame was about to be laid, for the faulty seam, for overlooking the real cause of the trouble. Paul braced for it.

Papa refilled the shot. "Shut the damn door. You're letting the heat in."

It couldn't be any steamier outside the cottage than in. Humidity poured from Paul's skin, now that he'd sweated out his run. His T-shirt reeked of sour gray water and the pus of his own perspiration. Maybe that strange odor had chemicals mixed in too. And Papa was holding out the shot to him. Dryness tatted Paul's tongue. He fought the impulse to run as hard as he could home.

Instead he shut the door.

Took the shot. Tipped back his head and tossed the whiskey down the way Papa had done. Choked like a baby on the sting of it. The losers at school drank themselves sick every weekend, but Paul had never touched a drop of alcohol in his life. He never would understand why he drank up then. He didn't remember being afraid of what his papa might do if he refused, but maybe fear felt like sleepwalking in moments like these, or maybe one of the effects of the poisons inside was to mess up what he was supposed to feel. Maybe Papa's feelings were messed up too.

Papa laughed at his babyish gagging and clapped him on the shoulder. "Better chase that cough." He poured him another shot full.

Paul drank in the manner of the first, all at once with a rigid swallow. He found Papa was right about the sting melting to a pleasant burn against his throat's leather. His vision cleared in the light's incandescent crown. A motor sputtered, a rumble that clotted his hearing and confused him for a moment. Once he'd located the sound, it would be the wonder of the rest of his days how he hadn't spotted her the moment he'd opened the door.

The lost cat lay purring on the oak floor behind a stainless garbage pail.

Her tail was wrapped around two tiny kittens, pretty little things frosted with soft, fine hair. They blinked at him with nearsighted, crystal-blue eyes. The bigger of the two was decorated with his mother's tiger striping between the pink, translucent ears.

For the very first time in his life, Paul believed Papa must love him after all, if he'd found the lost cat, spared her and her kits' lives, had even taken good care of them. Awash in gratitude, he was forgetting that Papa never knew about Paul's pet.

And Paul should have noticed, too, that the cat was protecting so few kittens.

He resisted the impulse to slide on his knees across the icy polish and take the cat in his arms. Instead he faced Papa, wedged a silly grin, and almost released the tears filling his eyes. "You found her."

Papa was drinking as Paul spoke. Once he'd drained the shot, he eyed the cat. She flicked her tail and roped it around her kittens. "Like hell. Snuck in here dragging her litter. Took up residence, didn't she. Got 'em down to two."

Down to two.

Paul felt a bit stupid, a bit confused. The room tipped. Surfaces gleamed under the streaming sunshine, the bare bulb. The cat warbled an off-key purr and then a hiss.

"You won't drown 'em, so—" Papa set down his shot glass. The eyes were glazed over again, waxy, shallow. Must be the effects of the poison. Those same effects, someday, would appear in Paul, he knew it. "You're a soft kid all right. Know how my papa taught me to get rid of pests?"

Paul didn't know, so he took care not to speak, or even move.

Papa strode to the pantry closet. He pulled from it a heavy-handled metal broom. "I was soft too."

Paul shook his head. Maybe if he'd managed to say something that bound the two of them together, *yes, sir, just like me, we're both soft,* Papa would have clapped him on the shoulder and poured them both another shot. *One for the road,* he might have said. *Let's go tackle that sink together, son,* he might have said.

Instead Paul kept silent, or more accurate to say, his throat was clogged as if Papa's fingers were clamped smack dab on his windpipe. "My papa knew how to toughen up a kid like me. Doing me a favor, he used to say. It was a favor too." Papa hefted the broom, as if Paul was supposed to know what to do with it. "Took me a long time to appreciate what your granddad was trying to teach me, though."

Before Paul could say anything, Papa moved swiftly on the cat.

His muscular back blocked Paul's view. The cat kept up her broken-motor purr under the broom head's wet, steady slap. The kittens fled sightlessly to the corner by the bedside table and cowered, their glassy sight too immature to see the obvious shelter of the dark space under Papa's bed. A wail, thin as gruel, sounded between the slaps. Paul became aware of blood pooling between Papa's heels. He hadn't noticed until then Papa's bare feet, the thin yellowing toes, the rough, chipped nails.

When it was over, Papa swiveled on the balls of his yellowed feet. His body was too bright, as if his skin were another of the room's gleaming finishes, and he was advancing on his son. Paul awaited his own beating with eyes closed against the crumple and the blood and the kits in the corner, crystal-gazed and shuddering. Breath wadded with whiskey dabbed his neck. Laughter sounded somewhere close by. Paul opened his eyes. Papa slung a taut arm around his shoulder, not as a fatherly gesture but to keep from falling down under laughter's gale. His droopy eyes ran with cloudy tears. His belly and chest flexed against Paul's arm and hip. The narrow space between them reeked of grain and gray water as if Paul's own odors were leaking from Papa now. A sound rose from Paul's throat, something painful that he recognized as his own laughter only because it hurt so much. Papa watched the fit take him with a drunkard's crafty glance. Just like that he quenched his own laughter the way he tossed down a shot full of drink.

"Got a choice here, Mr. Sensitive. Drown the rest. Or this."

And he'd handed Paul the metal broom, the head dented and dinged, the bristles speckled with blood.

No, Paul said. He'd said it out loud. The broom was in his hand, not because he'd taken it, but because Papa had shoved it there. He kept saying *no,* plain as anything. This he remembered.

"Pick your method. Or I'll tan your hide." Papa's tone was more explanation than threat. Paul's hide had been tanned good more than once. Which couldn't be the whole reason he didn't drop the broom and run straight out the door. To do what he'd done, he must have wanted to, else he couldn't have. He'd have to spend the rest of his life knowing this, being afraid of himself.

What happened next was very confusing.

He knew he'd picked up a dish towel from the kitchenette counter.

He knew he'd lifted the kits to the towel, but any recollection of what happened next collided with *no, no, no*, which he might have screamed out loud, might not have, a murkiness he'd come to appreciate as a mercy killing of his own memory.

PART 2

FEAR RESPONSE

2008

1

Although fear had chiseled the rules of her life, Lea would always be an adjunct to its cure. Neither scientist nor trainee, she managed others' inspiration. During the turn-of-the-millennium boom in Alzheimer's research, the Abel lab's steady gains in the understanding of the hippocampus, the ruler of memory, had nurtured new Alzheimer's therapies. Now that the war on terror showed no signs of ending, the grant money lay in conquering fear, not preserving memory. Abel's latest grant supported post-traumatic stress research for veterans. Lea instilled, and then extinguished, fear in mice. In the lab such feats were systematic products of biological prompts, not the intimate horrors Lea had known and still struggled to understand. But the *why* of the fear response was the concern of the neuroscientist, Abel, and the postdocs studying under him. Lea's job was to transform terror into neutral data.

In a spartan room adjacent to the conditioning lab, she used a computer monitor to observe her subject. Her presence in the lab, even out of sight, would disrupt the mouse's instinct, so Lea positioned a camera above the test cage and watched the isolated mouse scamper in a black-and-white video frame. She programmed a tone to coincide with a wave of electrical shocks conducted through the cage floor's metal grid. One or two rounds of shock were all it took to imprint fear. When she played the tone without the shock, the freeze response ossified the body in its last pose. A tail curled in curiosity, a neck craned in casual investigation, were captive to an exquisite stillness until the tone ceased, the threat passed.

After the fear response was ingrained, it was time to de-condition. For two days she would chime the single note without the shock and record how long it took for the mouse to become unafraid. With time, learned fear could be unlearned. But the mouse retained a shadow terror that could be measured neurologically. Original fear never leaves the subconscious. If fear of a musical note couldn't be erased, Lea didn't share Abel's hope for erasing the psychological pain of war or trauma.

Anyway, she didn't want to think about what might be left exposed in her memory if her own terror's linchpin was removed.

The animal husbandry staff fed the mice, filled water dispensers, cleaned cages. But the cage room across from the conditioning lab was reserved for Lab Will Care. Only the researchers cared for these mice, who matured without ever being touched. Successful conditioning required them to be handled for the first time as adults. Once acclimated, mice behaved like cats. Rubbed their bodies to her skin, eyes glittery, drunk on her touch. Ten days was enough to train the mice to come to her open palm, rely on her by sight, by smell, by sensation, hungry for the affection they'd never needed until Lea groomed them to crave it.

Today Lea was halfway to acclimation with her current subject. After five days, the mouse still skittered restlessly under her methodical stroking of his back and belly. Like the observation room, the acclimation lab was designed to be neutral. White walls, white tile, white plastic shelves overflowing with equipment. From the far wall a clock's second hand slid quietly from moment to moment, the hushed tick the only sound besides Lea's breathing and the click of the mouse's claws on the steel tabletop when she set him down. Lea scooped him up again, a soft bundle of brown with a white belly. She was practicing the motion of delivering him to the conditioning cage and removing him again, training him to accept without fear the sweeps of changing altitude. In a few more days, the mouse would trust her hand as he would trust a flying carpet's spell. She carried the mouse back to Lab Will Care, set him gently in his cage. Soon her essence would bedrock his sense of security, and then the fear conditioning could begin.

Lea peeled off her scrubs, threw them in the hamper by the security door, and made her way through the basement hallway. She rode the elevator to the Life Sciences Institute's top floor and entered the walkway crossing the lobby's lofty glass atrium. Through the curtain wall at the building's entrance, traffic wound down the street, glittering metallic under a high sun whitewashed by the cold. Smokers huddled around the building plaza's concrete planters as if the frostbitten remains of azaleas were warming fires. Below, a crew wheeled banquet tables on squealing dollies to the atrium's center. The screech echoed in the soaring glassy space like a touchy microphone. A fundraiser for Alzheimer's research was scheduled for tomorrow afternoon. Abel was giving the postdocs time off to attend. He'd offered her the time, too, but for Lea, seeking out trauma began and ended with research.

She crossed the walkway to the lab, washed up at the sink stationed inside the door, and went to her desk in the last bay cut into the countertop. Out the window, the university's unglamorous power plant roof, a dense thicket of pipes and valves clustered around a chimney, blocked the view of the ivied graduate library and the brick dorms rimming the campus. The Life Sciences Institute was a model of green efficiency, but when the power blinked off, the power plant kept the lights on as reliably as it had for half a century. There had been talk recently of closing off parts of Life Sciences, mothballing whole corridors, abandoning the south wing. Fifteen years ago the university had driven deep stakes into biomedical research. Life Sciences had coaxed top researchers to modern labs, encouraged risk, all but guaranteed reward. Now the Abel lab was a holdout in independent science's losing war. Many labs had already folded, the researchers absorbed into corporate research. In hindsight Life Sciences could be considered a reckless gamble, but who could have foreseen that the war on terror would so curtail public funding for the war on disease?

Two bays down, Abel was speaking quietly into his phone. His daughter, Michelle, perched on a stool, coloring. Michelle, an epileptic, must have a medical appointment. Tom, one of the postdoc trainees, stood waiting for Abel to end his phone conversation. Tom's study of mesial temporal lobe epilepsy was personal to Abel, one he still insisted on funding out of the dwindling PTSD grant.

Temporal lobe seizures were hard to detect. Until Michelle was three, Abel himself hadn't spotted his daughter's quiet recessions from motion and sensation, like being suspended in a wave's backswing. Lea witnessed a seizure only once, when she picked Michelle up from daycare to help Abel out of a scheduling jam. She'd had Kurt and Bunny with her, so she decided to treat the kids to ice cream. She'd gone for more napkins to clean up the creamy rainbow streams the waffle cones wept in the heat. When she returned to the bench, her kids were ringing Michelle like a protective fence. Michelle was sitting stiff, expressionless. Ice cream bubbled mildly from her lips. A lavender and pink slurry had pooled in her lap, soaking her sky-blue shorts.

Did she turn into a doll, Mommy?

Bunny had described Michelle's waxy skin, stiff limbs, and lifeless eyes perfectly. When she came out of it, Michelle blinked and resumed lapping at the cone as if the moments had never been lost.

Michelle tugged on Tom's shirt and held out a blue crayon. Tom glanced impatiently at Abel. Back when Lea started her career at Worcester Polytech, before she had kids of her own and understood how impossible it was to staunch the bleed between work and family, she'd resented Cameron Jeffers's domestic life spilling into the lab. A spat with his busy scientist wife over missed child responsibilities. The call from the kid himself, sick or stranded or otherwise marooned. Lea's own family had bottled their emotions. She would never have dreamed of calling her father at work. She'd never have approached him with a problem at all, and her mother suffered from chronic sinusitis, the diagnosis her father preferred over suicidal drunk. But at her stage of life now, mid-thirties, two kids, a marriage she and Jay were shredding to bits, helping Michelle to draw while she waited for the boss would be a welcome distraction.

Tom finally took the crayon and bent reluctantly over Michelle's drawing.

Abel snapped his phone shut and answered Tom's question. Tom moved to the scope in the next bay. Abel looked over Michelle's wave, *look, Daddy*, to rest a gaze on Lea. His long reliance on her to carry out his imagination's practical applications had cultivated a shorthand sympathy between them. Lea had shared a version of this sympathy with Jeffers, but back then she'd been a promising researcher, still untested. Jeffers's job was to train her to move past her natural aptitude for discipline to invention's messy play. She'd failed Jeffers's test, all right. Abel had hired her not as a researcher with promise, but as a sidetracked career scientist who had chosen lab management for family reasons, or temperament. Not everyone was suited to the tedium of discovery or the funding chase. Abel respected what he assumed was her choice.

When she proved her ability to anticipate the lab's needs, their connection matured to signals. A glance caught her attention. A slight dip in her expression caught his. *We're better than married*, he'd said a few months ago, after they'd managed a grant cancellation efficiently, as if bad news was merely another project launch. No layoffs, no interruption of the work, accomplished with no collateral tensions springing up between them, the managers of catastrophe. Abel knew by then that she and Jay were on the outs. Lea knew that Abel and his wife, Pat, were struggling with Michelle's chronic care. That neither took Abel's remark as a come-on proved how right he was.

By the expression in Abel's eyes now, Lea knew that the phone call had not concerned Michelle.

Kate, another postdoc, swiped into the lab. The harsh buzz that filled the room was purposefully grating, another security measure. While the others could ignore it, Lea always checked to see who was coming in. Not that the Abel lab drew the attention of activists. Research on neuronal function and behavioral output was, for the mice's welfare, uncontroversial compared to the oncology research she used to perform. The oncomice she'd made for the Jeffers lab were bred for tumor growth, gruesome engineering that was an easy target for animal rights protestors. The Abel lab's transgenic mice were designed to lack behavioral genes, the animals more tool than subject. But although the stunt Dinah had pulled was now years in the past, Lea couldn't ever again risk a breach. Checking the door in response to the buzz was so automatic, she barely noticed when her guard was up.

Kate joined Tom at the scope and took up a computer keyboard to record results. Abel stroked Michelle's hair, *great job honey, sit tight*, and moved to pull a stool to Lea's side.

"The DOD canceled." The next modest grant in their slim pipeline, the only grant in that pipeline after the current funding ran its course.

"Okay." News she'd received so many times over that past year it was pointless to react.

"How long?"

He meant the budget, operations, staffing. She'd made all the cuts she could, and he knew it. "Operating as we are, a few weeks."

"We won't hear from the CDC until January."

"I can't tell you what you want to hear, Mike."

Abel tucked a finger into the palm of his other hand and made a fist around it, his nervous habit. She referred to it as holding his own hand. His black hair, speckled now with gray, curled at the temples. Narrowed blue eyes stared past her to the window, the billowing smokestack, the glittering cars on the road below, but at the moment he wasn't seeing a thing. Lea waited. Behind Abel, Michelle crouched over her drawing. Six medication adjustments in two years. None had controlled Michelle's seizures without also leaving her nearly catatonic.

Abel was going to have to give up the temporal lobe research. Lea thought through how much operational time this might buy. She was startled to see that Abel was again gazing at her as if he were the one waiting for Lea to finish brooding.

Abel spoke before she could. "We'll have to cut husbandry."

She'd faced last resorts before. The drastic never resulted in a long-term solution. "I'm not going to do that."

"We'll have to trim anyway to make it through this round of results."

Cut. Trim. Euphemisms she couldn't stomach even after years in the profession. "I'd rather explore alternatives."

"Like closing down?"

"Like prioritizing what we get paid to do. Which at the moment is not epilepsy research." Lea glanced at Michelle. She was meticulously filling in her drawing's blank spaces with a fiery amber crayon. The picture could be a sunrise. Or a ring of fire.

Abel followed her gaze, opened his fist, clamped it closed again. "If we euthanize half, how long can we hang on?"

Managing death was her job, but for what ends mattered to Lea. Of course she'd made cuts before. For the Abel lab, when the downturn started, but that operation was small scale, one she could fulfill with the older mice who would die anyway within a week or two. For the Jeffers lab she'd had to perform large-scale euthanizing on rats, dogs, chimps that were too sick to offer for adoption. It was the one task she couldn't view with the scientist's detachment. She felt beholden to the bodies the animals had given to her, the trust in their eyes she herself had conditioned them to feel. What Abel was suggesting, and it would only be a suggestion for a few moments more, involved euthanizing the young. The choices of which subjects would live and which would die would have nothing to do with age or physical condition, everything to do with their queue in the research process.

"Lea." Abel met her gaze. She saw the determination she expected to see. She wished she could also see regret. Or grief.

She also saw the results of the reduction as if the accounts were before her. "We could operate until January, yes."

Abel rose, walked back to his desk to help Michelle put on her coat. Michelle left her drawing to hug Lea. She returned the hug, and Michelle skipped away. Abel didn't look at Lea as he swept Michelle up toward the door over her squeals that she was *too big, Daddy.*

The security latch on the lab door buzzed Abel into the hall. Lea watched Michelle squirm in her dad's arms. After her seizure outside the ice cream shop, Michelle had watched Lea mop the mess from her lap with a distant curiosity, as if the ice cream had melted onto someone else. After Lea's shock wore off, she'd felt a jealousy at the easy erasure of time Michelle would never miss. Anything could be done to her and she'd have no memory of the damage, nothing at all to fear.

Or regret.

Lea thought about going home early, except that facing Jay was more troubling than carrying on with her job. She'd made plans to go out that night. Arriving home late would help them avoid each other, a break she thought they both could use. Since Kate and Tom needed another subject to record before the day ended, Lea trekked back to animal husbandry. Once downstairs, she went to the cage room that housed the mice who had completed their de-conditioning. Imprinting fear had altered their neurological patterns. These patterns could now be recorded. Fear would have substance as waves on a monitor, the effects on the hippocampus as visible as a web of veins under the skin. Looking at the rows of subjects now, Lea felt sick. If the mice waiting for conditioning were euthanized, if the data slowed to a trickle and then stopped, would she have forced these animals to suffer terror for no good reason?

Through tears she pulled on a pair of gloves, scooped up a subject, and carried him to the euthanizing table.

2

After she packed the brain in dry ice, a grayish ball no bigger than her thumb, and stored the sample in the lab refrigerator, Lea left for home. When she reached the freeway ramp, westbound I-94, the most direct route home to Scipio Township a few miles out of Ann Arbor, had closed. She took the route along the Huron River, sparkling under a platinum late-autumn sun, and crossed the bridge back over the freeway. Below her, cars idled at a standstill. Clouds of exhaust streamed from tailpipes. The long line marched into the sun's low sulk on the horizon. The wreck causing the backup was out of sight, hidden by the sun's blinding glare.

By the time she pulled into her driveway in the Centennial Farms subdivision, dusk had fallen. She'd be able to duck out to Karla's soon then. Jay's Expedition was parked close to the front door, as usual, as if he needed, even now, to dart to safety. The house had two front entrances, one jutting into the driveway, shaded by a columned porch, the other around the south side of the house facing Scipio Road. The reassurance of another way out had sold Jay. Last year a gang of teens had lured him out of their house in town and beaten him into a coma. A random attack, no apparent motive. Nothing was taken from his wallet, or the house. Lea had always wondered if the kids had targeted Jay as a dare, nothing more. Although the attack happened in the middle of the day, the neighborhood of working professionals had been deserted. Lea, home by chance for a quick lunch after errands, had found him curled up in their driveway, soaked in blood. Since Jay had taken the week off to work on the house, at first she'd thought, stupidly, he'd merely fallen and spilled a can of paint.

Shortly after he'd recovered enough to come home, Jay insisted they move out of town. To Jay, the Centennial Farms house felt secure, but preparing for the next attack wasn't exactly Lea's idea of a fresh start. Jay had said her reluctance to move, to force the kids to change schools, to buy a house they couldn't really afford, was the start of her heartless lack of sympathy. Well, maybe he was right, but they were way past accusations now. For months they'd been living as roommates. They cared for the kids, maintained the house, spoke to each other as little as they could. Lea couldn't bring herself to ask Jay whether he didn't want to give up on their relationship, or simply wasn't yet strong enough to leave. She couldn't ask herself the same question.

As she slammed her car door, she spied Kurt across the yard, breaking the rule never to venture beyond the row of pines along the road's shoulder. Scipio was one of those county roads without a speed limit, or so every lead foot around here assumed. He stood with his back to her, legs apart and arms crossed, mimicking his father's favorite bull-headed pose. A man Lea didn't recognize was bent over her son. A John Deere cap shielded the man's eyes and face. He was holding a cable looped around one arm. A utility belt draped with heavy tools sagged to his hips. A muddy F150 had backed up a dilapidated wood trailer across her lawn. This early in November, the weather hadn't been cold enough for long enough to freeze the earth solid. Tire marks furrowed the brown grass like hastily plowed rows.

"Honey!" she called. The cold air shrank her voice to an echo. She waved, *get away from there*. Kurt didn't move. The man waved back, as if her *honey* was meant for him.

Jay was nowhere in sight, failing, as usual, to keep a close eye on the kids. He'd been an attentive parent before the attack. She'd assumed that the incident would make him overly cautious. Jay's healing had the exact opposite effect, although lately his neglect seemed less like something he couldn't control and more like an open revolt against what he'd decided was her hovering over Kurt and Bunny's every move. Maybe he'd just been humoring her fears, back when he'd been so careful.

She jogged across the lawn. The man motioned her over as if she'd kept him waiting. When she reached Kurt, she stroked his head. Her fingers snagged prickers tangled in his hair. Fiery red and gold leaves clung to his back. He'd been traipsing in the ravine at the east side of the house again, no coat, no mittens, no hat. "You okay?" She almost added, *did he hurt you?*

"He's getting ready to shoot the fawn," Kurt told her.

"It's the wrong season for fawns." The man answered Kurt by addressing Lea.

Lea removed her coat and draped it over Kurt's shoulders. "Excuse me. Who are you?"

The man touched his cap. "Wildlife Service." The thumb and the forefinger of his hand were lopped to the knuckles. Scars from old burns striped his wrist, glistening in the fading sunlight like strips of cellophane.

"What's going on here?" Behind the man, the trailer's metal tailgate yawned open. The bed was loaded with gear, platforms and railings, black canvas straps, yellow winch hooks, yards of loose tweedy rope. A Bowie knife tucked in a leather sheath lay next to a pair of antlers tangled up in rope. A shotgun with a rusting barrel lay slung on the rope's coils, looking as if it hadn't been fired in years.

"I saw her." Kurt pointed to the ravine. "Right down there." The home's former owners, both in real estate, had maintained the landscaping as meticulously as if the yard were another room to clean, but they'd let the eastern boundary grow wild. Weed grass and scrub brush scalloped the lawn's edge like torn lace. Beyond the ravine stretched an abandoned cornfield. Old papery stalks bowed at half-mast, frozen in neat rows. In the middle of a field a lone cottage hunkered like an aid container dropped far from the need. "At the corn."

"The corn?" She thought he meant the field. "I don't see a fawn, honey."

"Down there, Mom." Kurt jabbed his finger. "At the bait site."

"The *what?*"

"The bait site, ma'am." The man's clean, straight teeth, creamy clear skin, his freshly washed and pressed jeans, suggested a sound mind and body. But his squinting eyes under the cap's brim were rimmed red, and a sour, musty odor, like a root cellar gone to rot, drifted from his mouth when he spoke.

"Who are you, again?" Lea demanded.

From the depths of his jacket pocket the man produced a badge ID. *Wolverine Wildlife Control Service. Gary Starkey, Certified.* What he was certified in exactly was left blank.

Kurt tugged her hand. "Wildlife means *fawns*, Mom."

"Grown-up deer, son. We don't shoot the little ones."

"We don't shoot *anything*. What in the hell is going on here?" When Lea swore, Kurt dropped her hand. A stiff breeze rifled the tall grass, shuddered through the bare tangles of branches, and cut through Lea's blouse.

"Setting up for the deer cull." The more agitated she grew, the calmer the man seemed.

"I don't know anything about this." A fib. She *knew*, all right. She'd just forgotten the cull began tonight.

When she'd learned from the neighborhood association that, come late fall, sharpshooters would fill her subdivision's trees, Lea had driven straight to the county office to complain. The information sheet the brisk young woman behind the desk handed her *in response to your inquiry* explained the cull as a painless euthanasia. The herd reduction was divided into phases. During the first phase, sharpshooters would target does from safe and supervised bait sites. The maintenance phase that followed lasted a week. Incentives were set for qualified volunteers to harvest at least one doe. More substantial cash rewards were given for the most does culled at the close of the hunt. The culling of bucks, while not prohibited, was discouraged. *Controlling the female segment of the population is critically necessary*, the sheet noted. A forlorn graphic of a hand-rendered ink outline of a deer, head cocked in caution, a front hoof raised tentatively as if to flee, was printed in the handout's bottom margin.

Behind the brisk young county clerk, two cops hunched over worn laminate desks strewn with carbon paper, as if the computer sitting blank and idle at another empty desk was a last-ditch resource for true emergencies. The good-looking one with a sculpted build and silky dark hair had glanced up at her briefly when she'd first entered. He'd checked her out, dismissed her unimpressive figure cocooned in a loose cable sweater and old jeans, her plain brown hair, her anxious expression. The overweight one, inexplicably wearing tear-drop reflective shades indoors, hadn't looked at her at all. As she'd stood staring, first at the handout, and then at the clerk's smiling firewall of Midwestern distance, the overweight cop dropped his pen tiredly as if he'd encountered a question he couldn't answer, leaned back in his chair, and tilted his lenses at her. Not overweight, the shift of his body revealed, just big, all muscle. The shades beamed at her in the room's harsh fluorescence. He might have been looking straight at her, or past her dismissively as the good-looking officer had done.

The shades were a masculine parody of her mother's favorite costume, the gigantic sixties-era sunglasses she had used to accessorize her suffering.

The lenses reoriented back to the paperwork. For a heavy man the cop's features, at least what she could detect behind the glasses, were delicate; rosebud lips, a soft rounded chin, uncombed hair the color of a beer bottle. He set upon the form as if something in their glancing exchange had answered the question that had stymied him. How he could see anything at all through the dark mirrors shading his eyes stymied her. Her aversion to cops rose in her then. The promise of security that was only for show. She balled her fist. The handout crinkled.

This same big cop would show up on her stoop a few weeks later to write up the report after their house was robbed. He would meet her questions about recovering their stuff with condescension, as if she were stupid to wonder if stolen goods might reasonably be sought, even found.

The clerk asked whether, after studying the information sheet, she had any more questions.

"Yes, I have a question," Lea said. "This all seems very dangerous."

The clerk waited patiently for Lea to realize she'd made a statement, not a question.

Lea crossed her arms. "I have young children."

Which was another statement. The shades tilted her way again.

The cull took place with close cooperation from the sheriff's office, she was told, and she was also told there had never been an *adverse event*, and there were community forums where she could provide feedback on the impact on her neighborhood and if she had any other questions, which she didn't, then *all right have a great day*.

Lea had left wondering about the young woman's definition of adverse events.

"Your husband gave us the all clear," Starkey informed her now.

"He did?" She and Jay had agreed not to allow a shooter to stage so near the house. Hadn't they? "I didn't give *my* permission."

"Well, technically the county owns the old creek bed here."

"Look, I'm not about to have some guy shoot deer from my tree."

"Trained service sharpshooter," Starkey corrected. "Which *is* your husband, ma'am."

"Excuse me?" Now she knew the man was drunk. Jay had attended all the association meetings about the cull to protest it, not participate in it.

"My fawn ran away," Kurt said. "Daddy scared her."

"Daddy scared her?" Lea said.

"When he went up the tree." Kurt pointed to a cottonwood.

Lea stared up at the gray fan of bare branches. Where Kurt was pointing, a single dead branch stretched from a nearby oak, forked like a divining rod. "Daddy's in the tree?"

"Your husband is making some adjustments to the stand there." Starkey bent down over Kurt again. "You wanna hike down to the creek bed, son? I can show you there's no fawn for sure."

"She won't come back until later," Kurt said scornfully.

When she feels safe, Lea almost added. Between the prongs of the branches Jay's leg swung into view. Now that she'd seen one part of him, she easily saw the rest. A puffy tan jacket bulking up his thin shoulders. Cropped silver hair catching the sun's last wisp of white light. He dropped to the ground from the lowest branch into a pile of leaves. A rustling radiated from his boots like waves from a skipping stone. She never would get used to his hair so short, the way the nubs dusted his head like frost shavings. His round face had thinned alarmingly this past year, accenting the scars on his pale cheek like the nicks of a skater's blade on ice.

"Did you tell this guy he could kill deer on our property?" Lea said when Jay was close enough to hear her.

"Kurt, buddy, where's your coat? Your mom's freezing." Jay slipped off his jacket and draped it around Lea's shoulders. What had he been up to at those association meetings? She'd been certain he felt as strongly as she did about how dangerous it was to stage sharpshooters so close to family homes.

"Herd reduction, ma'am," Starkey corrected. "And I'm not the shooter."

"This guy tells me you are," Lea said. "I mean, that's ridiculous, right?"

"Don't overreact, Lea," Jay said quietly.

"You could make a mistake, Daddy." Kurt crossed his arms. "It's dark when you shoot the mamas."

"I know how to tell them apart." Jay ruffled Kurt's hair.

"Well, I'll be clearing out now. You're all set to start rolling tonight, Mr. Johnson." Starkey jangled the cable looped on his arm.

"Rolling?" Lea glared at Jay.

Jay's jaw knotted. "I'll be in touch in the morning, Gary."

A sharp breeze swept the brush and wild grass at the ravine's edge. Kurt gasped. "Mom!" He wrenched away from her hand and shot toward the rustling.

Jay grabbed his shoulder. "Whoa, son. Too late to go exploring."

He'd checked Kurt just in time. A deer the size of a pony burst from the swaying grass and galloped wildly past Starkey. The spots on the animal's back gleamed like a band of fallen stars.

"I'll be damned," Starkey said.

"Run, fawn, run!" Kurt twisted away from Jay's grip, cupped his hands to his mouth. "Don't come back tonight!"

The fawn streaked away as if obeying orders, galloping straight for Bunny, who was traipsing across the yard. Her sheer gossamer nightie billowed in the cold breeze. No coat, barefoot, looking for her family. Jay had left Bunny in the house while he was out here climbing trees and scaring their son. At six, their daughter was old enough to be okay for a few minutes parked in front of the TV, but Bunny hated being left alone and Jay knew it. She shot Jay a furious glance and bolted for her little girl, shouting at the fawn until it veered away from Bunny and disappeared into the pines.

3

Inside the house Lea carried Bunny to the den. The television was blaring. *My Little Pony* was on, which Jay knew scared the crap out of Bunny, although Lea could never figure out what about the hippy-trip pastels and soft-core conflicts made her so afraid. Bunny had arranged her stuffed animals in a semi-circle on the oak floor: a possum mother and babies, a plump white mouse with gingham checked ears, her beloved moose with the missing antler Kurt had ripped off last year during a spiteful tug of war. Their flat beady eyes took aim at the screen over Bunny's miniature Staffordshire tea set laid out primly on a scrap of cloth. One of the baby possums was plunked headfirst into a teacup full of chocolate milk. The room reeked of cleaning fluid. The Mauser lay on a sheet with a bottle of Tru-oil and some rags. Her grandad's trophy had been locked up in her various homes' attics since her mother passed away. What was it doing here where the kids could mess with it?

Lea set Bunny down among her animals and draped a tattered crocheted throw over her shivering legs. Behind her, Kurt was chattering on to Jay about the fawn—*she got away didn't she, Dad?* Lea turned to confront him, but Jay was holding the line on ignoring her. He took Lea's coat from Kurt's thin shoulders, reassured him *yes, she'll be fine.* Kurt sat down next to his sister and switched the television to a nature show, a fast glide through the deep woods up north somewhere. A low, pulsing drumroll beat time as if the camera were closing in on the target. Under the throw, Bunny fiddled with something hidden in her lap.

"Why is this out?" Lea pointed to the gun.

"That's mine!" Kurt snatched Bunny's toy.

Bunny wailed. "Daddy said I could play with it."

"Guys, be careful with that," Jay warned.

Lea looked at the toy. Which wasn't a toy, but a *gun*. Jay's old Ruger, the pistol he'd used for target shooting when he was a kid. Lea took it from Kurt. "Honey, I don't ever want you to touch a gun again, do you understand?"

"Daddy said we could." Bunny fingers were lodged in her mouth. Lea thought she'd outgrown sucking her thumb last year.

"I say you can't." She hadn't seen Jay's boyhood pistol in years. Hadn't *ever* seen it out of the dented steel case he stored it in. "Jay, what is going on?"

Jay shrugged. "I wanted to polish the antiques."

"The antiques?"

Kurt said, "Daddy said it wasn't dangerous."

Lea glared at Jay, and then smiled at Kurt. "Mommy and Daddy need to talk. Watch your show, sweetie."

Lea walked to the kitchen and slammed the gun down on the island. As usual, the sink brimmed with dirty dishes. The countertops were streaked with grease and crumbs. The more Lea worked, the less Jay cleaned up from the day. Yet when she'd asked if she should cut back, take some pressure off his time at home, perhaps free him up to go back to work, he'd asked her what job she had in mind for him. His career as a software programmer was over, but with his military background he could take on security work, couldn't he, even in this terrible economy? She hadn't told him how precarious the Abel lab's finances had become. Funding downturns had always been cyclical. That this contraction might not end did not chip at her resolve to keep her worry to herself.

Jay took up a post on the other side of the island, as far away from her as it was possible to be in this room. His eyes focused on their usual point in the empty space just above her right shoulder. They weren't exactly out of the kids' earshot, but Lea couldn't keep her voice down. "What do you think you're doing?"

"I asked you not to overreact." His tone was mild, careful, managing her. He'd turned at an angle to her, unconsciously—or consciously— hiding his scars. Lea was facing what he jokingly referred to as his *good side*, the left cheek that had healed up properly. This side of his mouth smiled as easily as it used to, the muscles supple, free, healed. When he smiled at her anymore.

"Why are the guns out?"

Jay peered at the space above her arm. "I told you. I'm cleaning them."

"In front of the kids?" She refused to believe he was being obtuse on purpose. His injuries had knocked his wiring loose. He wasn't himself, newly careless with dangerous things, avoiding eye contact, acting like she was the one who'd assaulted him. They were prone to dustups now that just barely skirted rage. She'd catch him crying sometimes in secret places, an upstairs closet, or the attic landing. Through his tears he'd deny he was weeping. She more than anyone ought to understand what he was going through, the way the brain reorients perception, bewitches the body to adapt to fear.

"I used to love looking at my dad's collection."

She'd never once thought of the guns, relics from their past lives, as a collection. "How could you leave the kids alone with those guns lying around?"

Jay's jaw tightened, one of his subtle tics. She had to watch him carefully to know how he was feeling, but her interpretation was only ever a guess. "Gary knocked before I was finished." *Gary*. She had to think a moment before she remembered who that was. When had the wildlife service guy become her husband's familiar? "Anyway, your mother hung that gun above your fireplace when you were a kid."

"It was up high." Cradled on hand-crafted oak pegs screwed right into the flagstone, one of her earliest memories. Jay didn't know that what he thought of as an antique was a weapon she'd actually used. She hadn't told him about that. Only Dinah knew about Lea's clumsy attempt at revenge. "I don't want my kids anywhere near a gun."

Jay brushed his hand along his head. He used to run his fingers through his hair when it was long enough to flop in his eyes, smooth it back along the line of his part. His fingers rubbed his scalp now as if startled by the bristles. *All that's left.* She'd asked him to grow his hair out again, like it used to be. He'd told her he preferred it shorn. "It's a target pistol, Lea." He took up the Ruger to rub at a dimple of rust on the barrel's dulled steel snout. "And I disagree about the kids. I think they should learn about guns, and how to handle them safely."

"How is it teaching safety to leave weapons lying around?"

"They aren't lying around. We were cleaning them. Anyway, teaching them what to do if a gun is unattended is part of safety training."

"They're little kids, Jay."

"I was Kurt's age when my dad taught me to shoot. Guns are always going to be a part of their lives. I want them to know how to handle them and not be afraid."

The refrigerator clicked, settled into its orderly hum. The tumble of fresh ice from the maker rattled the freezer door. She was still wearing his coat. The leather held the scents of late autumn: wet leaves, browning grass, the faint clingy sweetness of pine. How had they moved so far apart on their parenting? She couldn't ever recall Jay saying anything about teaching the kids about guns. "So what's this about you shooting deer?"

"I signed on, yeah." Jay set the pistol down on the counter between them and faced her. The light over the kitchen sink glazed the harsh red stubble the evening's cold had flared on his skin. Seeing him head-on was still disorienting. His features were asymmetrical, the right side of his cheekbone and jaw waxy and drooped as if he'd melted. His nose crooked sharply where blunt, vicious blows had dismantled the straight ridge between his eyes. The surgeon had reconstructed it with the remaining bone fragments. A sharp jag had been the best of the hoped-for outcomes. The long scar along his cheekbone, the one Bunny liked to trace with her fingertip, was beyond cosmetic repair, but the cut had been *straightforward*, the surgeon's term, destined to heal cleanly.

Everything had healed up, without apparent complication, or so she'd been told. The grave damage to the skull. The dislocated kneecap that had hobbled Jay from crawling back into the house to call for help. The shattered index finger caused not by the attack but by clutching his car key so tightly. Of all his injuries, this last had disturbed her the most. The kid's ploy had been to ask for help with his car. Jay would have grabbed the key just before stepping outside to be jumped by the kid's comrades hiding in the bushes. Had he used this single key to fight back, or had he held on to it with all his might to make it through the beating? His memory of the attack was so hazy, he couldn't tell her much about what had happened.

"Okay." She drew a breath and decided to let that hostility slide for the moment. "I thought we both agreed that the cull was dangerous. And inhumane."

"I volunteered."

"Without telling me?"

"I knew what you'd say. Which is, in fact, exactly what you're saying."

Lea's gut turned over. More than once she'd cried to him over euthanizing animals for any reason other than research. Dinah used to demand that Lea explain why killing for scientific purposes didn't also feel cruel. Dinah had been deep into her animal rights crusade by then.

Her organization's tactics favored spectacle over animal welfare, so Lea dismissed Dinah's accusations as motivated by politics, not by any real concern for the animals.

Jay had always offered the right comfort, with words like *painless,* and *mercy.* And *duty.* Did he really view a deer cull the same way? He had seemed to agree with her that there were more humane ways to address overpopulation than killing does. "Why did you volunteer?"

"I took the training and realized it felt good to shoot again. I loved it." Jay met her gaze then. Steady gray eyes, once so kind. Hardened, now. She preferred it when he stared at the dead space above her shoulder. "What do you love to do these days, Lea?"

Answering with the truth, *nothing,* would put him in the right. She was almost used to the hostility in his voice. *Forget love. Do you even like me anymore?* he'd asked recently when, nearly a year after the attack, she still couldn't make love.

Jay used to urge her to talk to someone about her distance from him and even the kids, about what he called her inability to feel. Well, she could feel, all right, just not what he wanted her to feel. Anger, for one. Not at Jay—how could she be? Not at the attackers, either, the three teens who'd never been caught. They were an anonymous cluster to her, like the prickers in Kurt's hair. Right after the move to Centennial Farms, Jay had seemed less erratic, almost at peace. For a short while their rift felt reversible. Then, just a week after they'd unpacked the last box, the house was burglarized. Jay insisted his attackers had found them and broken in as a warning. Lea refused to believe that the theft of a big-screen TV and a few gadgets meant they were being targeted. Still, they were—again—terrified, and pretending not to be.

And now he was telling her he'd trained to euthanize deer, knowing this would upset her, and kept it a secret too. How was she supposed to feel? "Can't you see how terrified Kurt is?"

"Don't use the kids against me."

A rifle shot blasted from the television. Bunny ran into the kitchen, clutching the possum. The babies bounced from the jiggling tail. "The show is *too loud.*" Bunny buried her face in Jay's coat.

Lea stroked her hair. "It's not real."

Jay turned away to open the fridge. Lea hurried to the den. Kurt was crouched too close to the screen. Bulky men in hunter's orange and army fatigues stooped over a ten-point buck bleeding from the chest.

One of the hunters produced a field dressing knife from the pocket of his vest. Lea stepped over Kurt to switch off the television.

"Don't turn off our nature show." Kurt tugged at her pant leg.

"That's not a nature show, sweetheart."

"Daddy says it is." Kurt scooched back from the screen. "Is Daddy going to dress the deer after he shoots them?"

"Daddy isn't going to shoot anything. Anyway, I don't know who dresses the deer, honey."

"Deer get dressed with knives?" Bunny had stepped back into the den and was staring at Lea with round eyes.

Lea cleared her throat. "Not *get dressed* dress. Dress like prepare."

"Prepare for what?" Kurt asked.

Lea hesitated. "Prepare to take the deer out of the woods. To make into venison."

Jay stepped into the den.

"What's venison?" Kurt asked.

Jay ran his fingers through Kurt's hair, snagged another pricker. "Deer steak."

Lea felt the weight of Jay's hand on her son's head like a headache. The odor of gun oil would take days to air out. She looked around for her purse, wishing she'd found a reason to go straight to Karla's after work. She remembered that Kurt confronting Gary Starkey had distracted her. The purse was still in her car. Lea headed to the foyer.

"Where are you going, Momma?" Bunny asked.

Lea had breezed by the kids without a kiss goodbye. She waded back through the tea party menagerie to kiss Kurt's tangled hair, and then Bunny's crown. "Book club, sweetie. Momma will be back soon."

Jay turned the television back on and switched the channel to a merciless Tom and Jerry chase. Bunny lodged her thumb in her mouth. Kurt was all dirt smears and prickers. Leaves and sodden threads of muddy grass wound across the polished oak to the kitchen like a groomed trail. How could she leave this mess?

Then again, how could she come back to it?

The Mauser stood gleaming on the hearth, the only clean thing in the room. She didn't think the gun would ever look the way it used to when her mother was taking care of it. Bright, massive, Lea's only protector and her best hope. Jay had polished it up beautifully, she had to admit. Lea still had those huge bullets stored away too. She'd never considered getting rid of them, or the gun, but how could she continue to keep them the way Jay was behaving?

Jay squatted with the stuffed animals. Bunny poured chocolate milk from her teapot and passed the cup to her dad without spilling a drop. From petrified to posh, just like that. A clownish chocolate smear perched on Jay's top lip. "Go have fun. We'll order pizza."

He set down the cup, drew Bunny into his lap with a ticklish hug that raised happy giggles. Bunny rubbed her nose with his, their favorite game, their secret code, their way of kissing. The kids didn't know anything was off with their dad. The scars, the crooked nose, they'd accepted as *Daddy getting all better*. She'd reassured the kids that Daddy would be fine long before she believed it herself. Watching Bunny cuddle with Jay now, Kurt resting his head on his dad's arm, it was clear they'd both succeeded in moving the kids past any lasting fears. In fact, to the kids Jay might seem better than ever. Before the attack, he'd always worked long hours. Now that they were home with him, the kids treated him more like a pal than a father. At times their happiness left Lea feeling like they had closed ranks. Or maybe Jay was right and she was the one who had closed off—working more, scolding more, worrying more. Maybe she was making too big a deal out of Jay's lax, messy parenting. Maybe he even had a point about the guns. Hadn't her grandpa's trophy been there for her when she needed it?

"Just be home by midnight," Jay called after her as she headed out the door.

She didn't answer him. No way was he going to be a sharpshooter tonight, but she'd deal with that later. She slammed the door on his cheerful voice and the plume of her kids' giggles.

4

Paul Rilke was back patrolling nights after a two-week hiatus, and a couple of hours into a grueling shift, exhaustion was messing with him. A lurid struggle with a wife-beating thug had kicked off the evening. The man had a history of run-ins with the county sheriff's office; he should have been put away a long time ago and saved everyone a lot of hassle, the poor wife most of all. The woman involved was tough, someone he remembered vaguely from high school as one of the fringe gals who hung out in the shop wing with the automotive tech guys. She was giving it back so good that when Rilke first arrived on the scene he was confused as to who was beating on whom until he saw a bloody smear above her lip. Even so, Rilke had to threaten to cuff her to the oven range to make the arrest on her husband.

Just after Rilke processed that individual, he was called to a gruesome pileup on I-94, yet another tragedy on the dangerously clogged artery that connected Chicago and Detroit. Wrapped in a veil of fog, the bodies of a young woman and her two little kids clung together in a minivan's mangled remains as if the mother had managed to hold her daughters close in their last moments. The semitruck driver had walked away unhurt. The worst part of Rilke's job was cleaning up such horrifying proof of fate's lopsided rules.

After he'd reopened the freeway's westbound lanes, Rilke headed to the off-ramp nearest the Costco lot to blow off steam by catching the light dodgers at the Dix Road intersection. The vision of the tykes' sad little bodies wasn't going to fade anytime soon. Budget and personnel cuts meant the sheriff's office couldn't respond to every fender bender that came along, so the traffic calls these days always involved grievous injuries and sudden, heartbreaking tragedies no one had seen coming.

Rilke pulled into the Costco. The Burger King lot was located kitty corner across the intersection. When Rilke was a kid, Costco was a different grocery, Schmidt's IGA. The Burger King had always been the Burger King except for the minimalist logo change on the sign from a picture of a plain old burger to a beige swoosh that didn't look anything like food. In between the stores, boulevards bisected by Michigan turns had replaced the old country lanes Rilke had grown up driving. The change obliterated the simple junction of Dix and Maple that marked the township's eastern border. Confounding signage illustrated the hook maneuver required to overshoot the light, execute a U-turn across the median a ways down, all just to end up back at the light to make the right. The sign's graphic looked like a snake's head craning to look back at the place where it used to belong.

Some motorists still squatted in the intersection flashing their left signal in defiance or ignorance. More often drivers used the Burger King parking lot to make the hassle-free turns allowed since the horse-and-buggy days. Rilke's watch at the Costco made it possible to jet down the boulevard to catch just about any illegal maneuver. Mostly he caught old locals, whom he let go with a warning and a shared eye-roll over stupid township planning. Girls, too, he let off with the stern act that caused some to make remorseful promises of good future behavior.

But the young guys, if they gave him any attitude at all, he messed with. Made them step out of the vehicle, frowned at the documentation, poked around for minor violations. Sometimes he called in the license just for how it looked. He ticketed any failure to make the proper adjustment to said attitude. That way, if the kid had come out to the township to vandalize property or drag race on the rural roads, well, corralled in the Burger King they stayed out of trouble, and wasn't everyone better off for it, too, the young man in question most of all. Minor but useful policing with tidy resolutions. Diligence concerning the minor violations was the cornerstone of overall civic order, a trendy philosophy, sure, but one Rilke believed in. Anyway, the routine would help nudge those little girls killed in the crash from his thoughts.

Rilke drove to a burned-out lot light and oriented the vehicle perpendicular to the parking space to align with his sight line. A stupid habit—although it made his observation effortless, it also made the county sheriff's logo on the door conspicuous. But he always parked kitty corner to the kitty corner because as a kid his mother was always saying to him that something was kitty corner to something else, and then he would poke around for the kitty. Mutti would laugh when Rilke would report, *There's no kitty in the corner.* Her laugh was something he didn't hear much. Long after he knew that she was describing an orientation, not an animal, he still pretended to look for the kitty until the funny day he actually found one in the pantry. Not too long after that, kitties stopped being anything he ever wanted to joke about again.

Thinking of his mother's laugh made him long for her voice. Although he was living in the guest cottage across Scipio Road from the farmhouse, a temporary deal until he sorted things with Jules, he'd kept his habit of calling her every night to tuck her in even though he could walk across the road and wish her goodnight in person. He cut the engine and the headlights. Bright lights from the store and the lot lamps shined up the parking spaces' toothcomb borders. The asphalt glimmered ice-black, glossy in the unusually brutal November cold. Rilke's vehicle crouched in the only patch of darkness. Across the street the Burger King sign flickered. The spooky fog that had caused the I-94 pileup west of Ann Arbor had popped up out of the frigid air, isolated to that stretch of the freeway as if springing a trap meant just for those little ones.

Rilke glanced at his watch and punched in Mutti's number. "Calling goodnight," he said briefly to her yawn.

"You're out tonight, then."

"Back at 'em." For a Tuesday, Dix Road was busy, holdover congestion from the freeway closure. Headlight glare splashed his windshield like it was raining flashbulbs.

"The news is talking about the crash on 94."

"Just finished up there."

"I'm sorry. Glad it wasn't worse." He knew what she meant, and it could have been too. Ten cars smashed up and only three fatalities, but things not being as bad as they could be didn't help those little tykes much, nor their mother. Nor the poor man who showed up at the scene to see with his own eyes that tonight was the night he'd lost his entire family.

"It was bad enough." He reached for a tissue in the glove box and blew his nose. He wasn't crying, he never cried, but she seized on the mournful noise as an invitation to offer up the usual tiresome career advice.

"I wish you'd give up nights for good. It's a bad idea to go back to the way things were."

"Nights are a great idea." He wadded up the tissue and tossed it into the door storage. He'd given up the night shift for those couple of weeks in a last-ditch attempt to please Jules. And what did he have to show for messing up his work life? Still living in his mother's cottage, that's what, no closer to moving back home. "Always have been."

"I'm worried about you out alone." A dodge, because she wasn't a worrier about what he did on or off the job. She'd raised him the way she'd managed the farm and Papa and Caroline, as if all trouble required of a soul was the good sense to rein it in.

"I'm not alone."

"You seemed better, working days."

Not really. He'd been assigned to liaise with the deer-cull contractor in addition to his regular patrol. The whole department knew of Rilke's squeamishness regarding animal control measures since the time he'd refused to empty the rat traps in the office basement to save the receptionist, Cheryl, the chore. Cheryl had chalked his refusal up to an unchivalrous attitude and hadn't let the incident go. Soon enough Rilke was the butt of office jokes, which no doubt inspired the leadership's serves-you-right order to traipse around Centennial Farms inspecting sharpshooter stands.

The most unsavory facet of that task by far was dealing with Gary Starkey, Rilke's and Julia's longtime neighbor, who owned the wildlife control service the county had contracted for the herd reduction. For days Rilke endured the man's gruesome stories about a groundhog who stubbornly survived several poisoning attempts and smoke bombs before succumbing to a few whacks with an axe, or the near miss of a kid's lost schnauzer that Starkey's sharpshooter had mistaken for a raccoon. Stories wholly lacking in overall entertainment value. The guy drank too much, which automatically put any individual in the category of a problem Rilke couldn't stomach.

"Define *better*," he said to Mutti.

"Paul, you'll brood out there." She didn't have to tack on Jules as the object of said brooding for Rilke to hear her name loud and clear.

"I won't brood."

"You *know* you will." She did sound worried. "Come up to the house for dinner tomorrow before you start work."

A Buick LeSabre turned into the Burger King and performed the predictable looping turn inconsistent with ordering up a burger at the drive-thru. "We'll see. Good night, Mutti. Lock your doors."

"Good night, Paul. Watch yourself."

"Check them. Windows too."

She hung up before he did. Rilke snapped shut his phone, shaking his head at his dumb self. Reminding his mother every night to lock her doors, when he more than anyone knew that the real danger, statistically speaking, lay inside the home.

Rilke waited until the driver executed the illegal maneuver before accelerating down Dix with his light flashing. The LeSabre, a burgundy nineties-model boat, pulled over to the curb promptly. He approached the driver's side window, obediently rolled down, awaiting him.

A full posse of young men stared out at him through fogged windows. The driver eyed him neutrally, projecting just enough clean-cut docility that Rilke didn't recognize the kid, not at first. The getup didn't help, either. The young man's spiffy attire included a white-and-navy striped tie, crisp white shirt—starched collar, even—and a navy blazer. An indistinct gold logo decorated the blazer's left pocket. Rilke couldn't make out the words stitched in navy thread. Some prep school for upper-class snobs from the 'burbs. All the kids sported the blazer deal. Joyriders, he assessed, probably out to ditch one of their own in unfamiliar back country to haze the poor bastard. The latest fad in stupid kid pranks from the upper-crust set, out to sneer at the rural rubes. Well, a run-in with the local sheriff out here in the sticks would add to their night's entertainment.

Rilke met the driver's *who-me?* gaze levelly. "License and registration, please."

"Did I break a law, Officer?" The kid's voice cracked. Familiar, the voice and the crackle. Rilke's last experience with this voice involved screeching obnoxious obscenities. Under the polished haircut lay the Nixon kid, looking snazzier than when he was setting fire to a metal pole.

A few months back, Rilke had spied Mr. Nixon crouched in the Costco parking lot at midnight, flicking his Bic intently at the base of a lamp as though he'd just discovered fire, not tried to start one. A simple warning situation, but when Rilke approached, the kid freaked out and pulled an eight-inch boning knife out of nowhere like he was working the deli counter. Nicked Rilke's arm right through his jacket. Lunged again after Rilke sidestepped, so he'd had no choice but to disable him. Banged up the kid's knee pretty badly, but the whole thing could have been worse for the both of them. The boy was out of his mind by the time the ambulance arrived, writhing and hollering despite Rilke's efforts to calm him down, punting outdated insults like *pig* and *fuzz*. The EMT had to strap him to the stretcher while the kid thrashed and cursed as if Rilke, not whatever junk he'd put in his young and able body, was his whole problem.

What the hell was the Prince of Pyro doing back here?

"Yes, you did. Know who I am, son?"

Nixon glanced at Rilke's arm. Did he think Rilke wouldn't recognize him? His nervous swallow popped his throat out like he'd inhaled a sucker. "Yes, sir. I mean, I don't really remember. Much. But I'm sorry, sir. Again."

Rilke maintained the impassive act. Nixon's apology and past clean record had drawn community service. Well, a citation that might invalidate his cushy plea agreement was just what Mr. Remorse had coming, wasn't it.

Nixon told Rilke he was going for the glove box and leaned to spring it open. The door hit the lanky knees of the tall kid in the passenger seat. Navy blazer, pressed khakis, eyes forward. Rilke studied the LeSabre's interior for evidence of a ditched comrade. An ownerless cell phone or blazer. An orphaned pair of pants. Sometimes these kids left their buddy stranded in nothing but underwear. Would be a long night tonight for the kid if that were the case. The temperature was forecast to plunge dangerously overnight.

No sign of a missing occupant. Every seat taken, every suited boy buckled as the law demanded. No open bottles or cans, except for a Pepsi nested in the driver's holder. No booze, no sign of drugs. The Buick's interior reeked of perfume. Some fruity womanish scent, although the rearview mirror wasn't sporting one of those dangling air fresheners kids used to mask the odor of weed. When Nixon took a plastic sleeve from the glove box, a fleshy rubber rod dropped to the passenger's lanky knees and rolled into the angular valley of the young man's lap. Felted deer antlers rolled around globes of plastic testicles.

Nixon snatched the accessory and stuffed it back into the glove box before the lanky kid could muster a reaction more efficient than a whispered curse. The men of the back seat stiffened, eyes bright and wide and fixed on the windshield.

Nixon fixed the innocent look in the vicinity of Rilke's forehead and handed over his papers. Rilke glanced down at the license. *Homer.* He'd forgotten the kid's first name. "Step out of the vehicle."

Nixon looked over at his buddy, who clicked the glove box closed after one last poke at the obscenity. "Be cool, man."

Wise advice from the sidekick. Nixon squared his skinny shoulders and exited the car. "What did I do, Officer?"

Rilke gave young Nixon the stare that signaled he was about to determine the young man's fate for the balance of his evening. "What are you doing way out here on a school night, son?"

"Nothing, sir."

"Why should I believe that?"

"I mean, not nothing." The kid glanced at his hands, which were shaking a bit now. Nerves, or the kid was freezing in just his blazer. "I mean, we're on our way home from a…sporting event and wanted some burgers and stuff."

"I don't see any food in the vehicle."

The kid swallowed hard again. "We decided…we weren't hungry. Once we got here."

Rilke glanced at the registration and then returned the documents. Nixon fumbled the hand-off. The license fluttered to the pavement, landed on Rilke's boot. Rilke made no move to pick it up. "Mr. Nixon, are you aware that you illegally avoided a red light?"

Nixon swiped the license from the road. His fingers brushed Rilke's boot. "No, sir. I mean, yes, sir. But we were just changing our minds. About the food. Just turning around."

"Is the distraction in your glove box affecting your driving judgment?"

"That's no distraction, sir." He glanced back at his companions. "It's a joke."

"Uh-huh." Rilke scanned the posse. The young men sat uniformly still, eyes forward like a synchronized team. "Any further distractions in the vehicle you'd like to bring to my attention?"

Nixon shook his head. Rilke flashed one more inspection at the LeSabre's interior then decided to let the thing go. The stoop of the kid's shoulders when Rilke told him to move along might actually have been a grateful bow. He was staring at Rilke's arm again. "I'm keeping clean, just so you know. Haven't missed any school or anything. And, *um*, I don't remember hurting you. I mean, I know I did it. I take responsibility. But I don't remember, you know?"

The Eddie Haskell routine was as transparent as a window. Clean and scholarly were the terms of his plea, so no points there. Still, the kid hadn't begged off the ticket. His eyes were clear. The demeanor was in line. Rilke had been such a straight arrow at this kid's age, he never could muster up any sympathy for poor choices totally within an individual's control. It had been easy for him to stay off drink and drugs, no problem at all. It still was easy. Then again, being a farm kid could drive one to stupidity, didn't Rilke know it. Farm work was thankless, lonely labor, and all a kid had to show for it was being teased by the suburbanite snobs at school. The Costco caper was just the sort of dumb stunt any bored teen might do to blow off steam. Add in the drugs and watch how a stupid prank turned into an assault on anything you cared to blame for your own screwups. Rilke knew all about that dynamic too.

Anyway, the kid had landed his cushy plea deal because Rilke himself had made out like the nick on his arm was no big deal, nowhere close to assault on an officer. In truth, the wound came about due to Rilke's half-assed response. When he'd pulled up to see what Nixon was doing, squatting so unnaturally at the base of a Costco light pole, he could have sworn the kid was messing with some small animal. Between the kid's fingers Rilke thought he saw fur, wriggling feet, a little mouth yawning open in distress. Hell, okay. He thought Nixon was smothering a kitten there. Made him sick. When the lighter blazed, Rilke thought he heard a yowl. Messed up his reflexes when Nixon stood up hollering, wielding the boning knife. Rilke was too distracted to talk the kid down. He never did see a cat book it out of there. Maybe he'd imagined the yowl too.

But if the kid was looking for a pat on the head, forget it. "How's the knee, Mr. Nixon?"

"Oh, that, that was no problem. Barely hurt."

"Drive straight home," was all Rilke said. "No more stops."

"Yes, sir." Nixon ducked back into the car and turned his engine over. Rilke walked back to his own vehicle. The LeSabre swung dutifully around the Michigan turn that would land the boys at the highway ramp. Legally.

Rilke parked back at the Costco and stared out the windshield. Those little girls in the minivan, all cuddled up in their mother's arms, seeped back to him. The mother must have moved quickly to clasp them in time. Both of the tykes had been sitting in the front seat, maybe one nestled in the other's lap. None of them had been belted in, a negligence that would have been charged as criminal had the mother survived. The stricken dad had related how the girls had worked out how to unbuckle their straps and crawl into the front seat, how he and his wife had to pull over to re-buckle them. He was sure his wife would have been trying to pull over when the accident occurred. Rilke recalled how Papa used to swing his arm in front of Rilke and his sister at sudden stops. Typical of Papa that a rare show of protection would also be an ineffective one. The mother must have obeyed the same useless instinct. He wondered if she'd known before she died that she'd succeeded in reaching her girls.

Just as he was pulling out of the Costco, a call came in. Disturbance at 118 Old Peach Tree Court. Another call from Gary Starkey about Julia's latest house party. Clearly Gary wasn't absorbing Rilke's lectures on minding his own damn business rather than Jules's. Every time Jules had house guests, rowdy or no, the man complained to the cops. Rilke headed for the same crazy turn to orient west into the township's heart, feeling, as the old-time locals did, every tick of that forced extra half-mile in the wrong direction.

5

Lea drove slowly past the half-built foundations lining the back of the Centennial Farms development. Work on the subdivision's next phase had halted abruptly last year. A row of topless concrete block rectangles stood like empty boxes missing their lids. A bucket loader was parked in the half-finished road, the scoop at half mast, as if the developer couldn't afford the gas to drive it away. Past a barbed-wire fence, an old cornfield unrolled into the darkness. The sub was named for the farm that had tilled the surrounding land for several generations. The original cobblestone farmhouse still stood across Scipio Road from Lea's house. She thought the farm family still lived in the house, although they'd quit farming. Maybe the recession had put them out of business; or maybe they'd sold enough land to the developer before the crash to give the labor up altogether.

Maybe the farm family had made out on the sale, but Lea and Jay had bought their Centennial Farms house at the worst possible time, at the height of the real estate market. A month after they moved in, around the time the Abel lab's grants were evaporating, home prices plummeted. Then Jay's software tech firm had officially let him go, after promising to keep him on at a reduced salary until he could return to work. That salary had been enough to afford the new place. Now, Lea's salary just barely covered the mortgage. With the house underwater, selling seemed like a worse choice than hanging on for a while until the market recovered. If it recovered.

Sinking so much into the move had been a bad idea from the start, but when she'd tried to persuade Jay to stay in town, pointing out that the stability might be better for the kids, he'd accused her of heartlessness, again. He'd asked how she could stand to live in a house that reminded them of the violence that changed their lives forever. How could she explain that she not only didn't mind but preferred it? Jay knew about what had happened to her as a kid, of course, although some of the details she'd kept to herself. She would never have wanted to move away from her childhood home just because of what that creep had done to her there. Why should she be the one to turn tail, run away and hide? Anyway, her parents never did find out what happened, so she was never given the choice. But she would have refused to leave, even so.

She couldn't refuse Jay, however, so here they were, in a worse than worthless house. If the lab ended up folding, they'd lose their home outright.

On Corn Row Drive, Lea's headlights lit up a line of cars parked along the shoulder in front of Karla's house. She pulled up behind a sleek blue sedan. Rust patches clustered on the fender. She cut the engine and snapped off her lights. The sedan's taillights continued to shine, livid white knots in the darkness. She'd need to tell the owner. As she walked up the road to Karla's, she curled her hands inside her pockets and brushed a set of keys. For a moment she was puzzled. She'd put her keys in her purse. Then she realized she was still wearing Jay's jacket.

Lea knocked lightly on Karla's door and stepped into an impeccably decorated replica of her own home. The flagstone foyer opened into a recessed den. An ash-gray sectional wrapped around a glass coffee table. Beyond the den the kitchen gleamed, all speckled granite and brushed steel. Bottles of wine and plates of finger foods crowded expensive Moebius end tables. A glossy chocolate cake heaped on a crystal stand ruled the coffee table. Smooth razor lines of jazz lapped at the muted buzz of conversation. No one was eating. Everyone was drinking. If these women were her neighbors, Lea wouldn't know. She had only met Karla because Karla had gifted her and Jay a bottle of wine when they moved in. Or was it vodka?

After hanging her coat on the rack, Lea scanned for a copy of the book to thumb. She hadn't read *Wuthering Heights*, that night's book, since high school. Although Karla had invited her to join her club every month since she'd moved to Centennial Farms, Lea had always sidestepped. She didn't like clubs. She didn't like to hang out with other people much, particularly women, if she was being honest. She'd always been a shy, private kid. Dinah had been her only real friend. They'd been so close for so long that after what Dinah did to her, Lea found it difficult even to want female friends, much less maintain them.

Karla, dressed in a fitted leather zippered vest, swept into the foyer to squeeze Lea's hand. A butterfly tattoo decorated the rise of her left breast. Karla's pale tipsy eyes glittered into Lea's. With her fitted jeans and busy black curls gathered in a bandana, she appeared prepped to roar off on her Harley rather than host a literary chat. "Lea. Glad you decided to join."

"Thanks for the invite, Karla. Someone left their car lights on." Lea wriggled her hand free.

"What's the make?"

"I don't know cars. It's a sedan. Dark blue."

"Ladies!" Karla cupped her hands. A saxophone's busy riff filled the sudden silence. "Anyone own a blue sedan?"

Two women stepped forward from a conversation cluster near the sofa. The younger, still dressed for a workday that required hose, pumps, and a navy blazer, tucked her straight hair behind an ear. "Am I parked illegally? There's a hydrant. I thought I'd pulled up far enough."

"Your lights are on." Karla turned to Lea. "Don't you know the make?"

"Maybe a Ford?"

The older woman said, "It's mine," and set her wineglass down on the coffee table. Her hands, crimped and swollen, shook slightly. She was older than Lea had guessed by her straight posture and loose bun of soft hair. An ivory-dusted widow's peak framed her narrow face. Shallow wrinkles edged her gray eyes. When she climbed the stair, she stumbled on the tread's oak lip. Her hip bobbled, popped lightly.

Lea stepped to her side, cupped the woman's elbow until she steadied. "Are you okay? I'm happy to take care of your lights for you."

She must have startled the woman by grabbing her too quickly, or perhaps her grip on the woman had pinched. She drew away, rubbed her arm. The loose skin between her eyes puckered. But she spoke pleasantly. "Thank you. But no. I'm quite capable."

"I didn't mean—" Lea began.

The woman gave her a crisp smile. "No, you didn't." Lea watched the woman sway to the foyer, favoring her hip. She tensed to sprint to the woman's elbow again when the shuffling feet reached an area rug's fringe.

Karla said, "That's Vivian. Her husband died recently, so she's, well, grieving. She doesn't belong to book club. She's just a neighbor. Most of these girls I know from work. But Viv thought it would do her good to get out of the house, have some naughty fun. You wouldn't think she'd be into it, would you? Your house faces Scipio, if I remember correctly. Aren't you a bait site?"

Vivian had navigated the treacherous rug safely to the flagstone's serene surface and pulled on her coat. Lea relaxed. "Excuse me?"

"Jay gave a terrific presentation on the deer problem at the association meeting." Karla led Lea to a side table and poured her a glass of red wine. "I didn't know what to think of the whole thing until he explained it. I moved in last winter after the cull was over for the season, so I didn't know anything about it."

So much for his promise to voice their shared objections to the cull. He'd planned to participate from the get-go. Lea took a generous gulp of the wine. Drops splashed her hand. She resisted the urge to lick them off. "Did he?"

Karla handed her a cocktail napkin. "You have a sharpshooter, right? How close to your house do they set up?"

Lea decided not to reveal that Jay planned to be her sharpshooter. "At the boundary of our yard. Overlooking the edge habitat. It's not close to the house at all." Now *she* was sounding like a handout.

"That's what Jay said." Karla settled on the sectional sofa two cushions in from the end.

Lea took another long drink, a doorstop Cabernet that buzzed right to her head. She perched on the sofa next to Karla. The sofa cushions were plush hip-swallowers that would thrust her knees up if she settled in and make it impossible to navigate her drink without spilling. Balanced on the edge, her knees knocked against the coffee table, but at least she'd be able to rest her glass among the clustered bottles of wine and vodka. Had the women memorized the book? She couldn't find a copy anywhere.

The others refilled their wine and settled on the sectional. Fewer book clubbers than Lea had perceived when she'd arrived. Women her own age, affluent, chatty, lightly tipsy.

"I'd worry about my kids if one were in my yard," Karla said.

"The sharpshooters only work at night." Defensiveness overpowered her irritation at Jay, although she didn't know why. Karla was hardly accusing her of negligence. "Anyway, it's only for a few nights."

"That's what Jay said. But I still think it's dangerous."

The owner of the other blue sedan said, "This from the woman who motors her kids around on a Harley."

"Only up and down my street," Karla said. "They wear helmets. It's perfectly safe." She leaned to refill her glass with vodka. Straight. No mixers in sight; not even lemon or lime wedges.

The front door slammed. Vivian emerged from the foyer. Steadier on her feet, her hip swaying only slightly now, as if the trudge to the car had lubricated her socket. Her gaze rested on the empty spot next to Lea, the only place left to sit. The pucker between her eyes trembled. The woman clearly didn't want to be stationed next to her. Lea slid closer to Karla and sat back. An invitation, or a truce for whatever skirmish her offer of help had unintentionally ignited.

Vivian shuffled reluctantly over. "May I sit here?"

"Jay did mention you had safety concerns," Karla said to Lea.

"Please." Lea smiled at Vivian, patted the cushion next to her.

Vivian sank in. Her thigh plopped over the soft cushion to press against Lea. The only graceful way to detach would be to scoot awkwardly back to her perch on the sofa edge. But Vivian would then tip over into Karla. Already she was using Lea's shoulder to keep upright, perhaps to relieve the weight on her sore hip. Lea gulped her wine down to a spill-proof level and felt suddenly ravenous. But no one else was loading the plastic plates stacked next to the appetizers.

"I'm very concerned, Karla." Lea struggled to ignore Vivian's breath on her neck. At least Jay hadn't completely shut her out.

"That's what Jay said. But he also said your kids were almost hit by a car that had hit a deer, so the lesser of the evils, I guess, right?"

Bunny and Kurt had witnessed a fender bender on Scipio. Hardly a close call. Lea had been outside mulching the flower beds when it happened. She didn't remember seeing a deer.

"Would you hand me my wine, please?" Vivian said.

"I'll get it." Karla sprang forward. Lea bobbed. Wine sloshed in the glass's belly. To prevent the drink from ending up in Vivian's lap, Lea grabbed the glass with her free hand. Her elbow dug into Vivian's side. The woman moaned.

"Did Jay say that, the lesser of the evils?" she asked Karla.

"No. I did. And then Vivian said evil had no place in the conversation." Karla passed Vivian's wine over Lea's lap to the wizened hand, bypassing Lea's attempt to relay the glass. "We're just doing what's necessary. But I don't think she heard me correctly. I was using evil as an expression, not an actual, *um*, thing. Right, Vivian?"

"I heard you correctly, Karla." Vivian took the glass.

"No, remember, at the neighborhood meeting. I think you confused what I said."

"I was not confused."

"Yeah, I *knew* you hadn't heard me right. Vivian lives on Harvest Way. There's a bait site somewhere there too. Lea has a sharpshooter," Karla told Vivian.

Vivian shifted. Her thigh rubbed Lea's leg. "You must be Jay's wife."

Lea drained her wine.

"Jay said you had safety concerns," Vivian continued. "Are there any questions I can answer for you?"

The owner of the other blue sedan was leaning over the table to fill her glass with vodka. "Safety concerns? How dangerous is this party?"

"Deadly, Bettina," Karla said. "But we're talking about the cull."

"What's a cull?"

Vivian said, "Managing the deer population."

"By shooting them," Karla said.

The woman sitting next to Bettina stared at Vivian. "Isn't that a bit extreme?"

"My husband died of Lyme disease, Jill." Vivian's tone was patient, as if she'd had to explain the threat of the deer many times before. "So, no. I don't find doing all we can to protect our health extreme."

"You don't die of Lyme disease."

Lea had determined to keep quiet, but the words had popped out. Vivian removed her weight from Lea's shoulder. The movement forced Lea to turn. No avoiding, now, the grief-hardened eyes, the tight disapproving pucker. "Are you a doctor?"

Lea took advantage of her brief freedom to reach for a refill. Vodka this time. The drink mixed with the wine pooled in her glass, tinted the vodka rose. The bedrock of jazz fell silent, stranding her voice. "I'm in medical research."

"I see." Vivian sipped her wine. Stared at Lea's glass. She must have poured a half-dozen shots by mistake. And she had no idea how to settle back between Vivian and Karla to avoid that angry stare.

Jill was saying to Vivian, "But still. There must be alternatives to hired guns."

"Trained sharpshooters," Lea said.

Bettina and Jill stared at Lea. "How many sharpshooters *are* there in this neighborhood?" Jill asked.

"Jay said there were three," Karla said. "They only work at night." Bettina glanced out the window behind the sofa into the darkness. "Late at night," Karla added.

Jill shook her head. "Glad I live on the golf course."

Music cloaked the den again, a dense arena rock anthem Lea hadn't heard in years. Karla poured another vodka shot. "Hate to break it to you, Jill, but this service also exterminates the critters on your course."

"Hardly the same thing." Jill glanced at Lea, as if wondering if Jay had anything to say on that score.

Bettina said, "Isn't it exactly the same thing?"

"Well, no, it's not," Jill said. "Groundhogs are rodents. Deer are— well, deer. At least they don't use sharpshooters on the ninth hole."

"They do, though," Karla said. "Jay said Falconry Fields have been using this service for years without a single adverse event."

"I think I would have noticed gunmen on my course," Jill said.

"They're discreet." Vivian hadn't spoken since Lea's comment on her husband's death.

Lea looked at Karla. "When do we discuss the book?"

Over the rock anthem's overwrought climax, the doorbell chimed. Karla leaped up from the sofa to answer the door. "That must be Heathcliff now."

After a flurry of rustling from the foyer, coats hung, greetings exchanged, Karla ushered in two young women dressed like teenagers in pastel halters and low-cut tight jeans, lugging cardboard boxes. In fact, Lea saw as they piled the boxes in front of the coffee table, they were teenagers. The older-looking one in the baby-blue halter couldn't be more than eighteen.

"You remember Jaclyn, ladies," Karla said. "My assistant by day, party consultant by night. Right, Jacky?"

The woman ripping the tape from a box seam looked up with a blistering smile. "Hi, I'm the Jacky in 'Party Girls with Jacky.' This here's my cousin. Sara, say hello to these ladies." Sara raised a busy hand loaded down with ruby nails and rhinestone rings. Like Jacky, Sara's tacky blue eyeshadow didn't quite distract from the thick charcoal ring around her eyes. Her lashes drooped under clumps of mascara. Both girls' lipstick gleamed like fresh blood. Glitter flaked from their eyeshadow as they moved, dotting the rosy blush on their cheeks. Why were these girls made up like that, and was that a dildo Sara was pulling from the box?

"Now, ladies, for the new faces, here's what you got to know." Jacky stood up straight. "I've been doing Party Girls for a year now. I started with Party Girls in order to own my own business like my role model Karla here does and to save for college, and a big thank-you to my role model Karla for hosting me and Sara this evening. Karla will receive fifteen Naughty IOUs and the Passion Mini-Wand for hosting us tonight and you ladies can also win big if you book a Jacky party tonight before you leave. Party Girls is an amazing company and I'm proud to be giving women all around the southeast Michigan region permission to enjoy their sensuality. Party Girls does not sell sex. Our products bring the romance to your relationship, not replace it. Nothing beats the real thing, the real thing being your spouses or partners. Now I can tell by looking that you all are not hung up by your sensuality, but remember, this is all just for fun."

Sara waved the dildo and grinned. Lea felt queasy. Probably just her empty stomach rebelling, not anxiety over these girls' fuck-me clothes and makeup and an enormous plastic penis that couldn't be any woman's idea of pleasure, could it? Lea hoped Karla and the others would think her sudden flush was the alcohol.

But Karla didn't blame Lea's distress on the booze. "Hey, Lea. Didn't I mention this was our annual naughty night? Sorry about that. *Wuthering Heights* is our code. I thought you knew."

The other women stared at her. Jacky said, "No worries, if you do feel some hang-ups. Perfectly normal. Party Girls puts you in a luscious relaxed and romantic zone so you can fully enjoy your partner and your body."

Lea buried her nose in her glass. The other women stopped staring at her to watch Jacky and Sara unpack the merchandise. Lotions, fur-lined handcuffs, pleasure beads, and vibrators joined the dildo and the glossy chocolate cake on the coffee table.

Sara handed a fleshy rubber vibrator to Vivian. To Lea's astonishment, Vivian took it eagerly. "You can pass this along, Mrs…"

"Vivian." Vivian held the vibrator up to the light as if inspecting it for quality.

"It's got a motor, Mrs. Vivian."

"Just Vivian."

Karla said, "Oh, shoot. I forgot to introduce all of you." Karla ticked off names. Vivian pushed a button. The rubber sheath wrinkled like a fleshy wink.

"Mrs. Vivian knows how to switch on the fun," Jacky said.

Vivian turned off the motor and handed the vibrator to Lea. "Would you like to pass that down?"

As if Lea wouldn't like to rev the motor, press the vibration to her palm, imagine what it would feel like to jazz a spot. Well, Vivian had misinterpreted everything about her except the truth of *that*. Lea handed the vibrator to Jill. Bettina was inspecting a fat purple vibrator. Karla was dabbing peppermint lubricant on the butterfly tattoo. Jill set aside the rubber vibrator to work the motor on some sort of plug with corkscrew grooves.

Sara handed Vivian a vibrator with buck antlers and patches of fur on plastic testicles. "You gals out in the sticks here always get a real charge out of Bucky," she said. Vivian didn't smile. Sara handed Lea an open box with three golden balls nestled in velvet.

"You apply that Revelation Lubricant to your button, not your butterfly," Jacky told Karla.

Karla kept dotting her tattoo as if the gel were cologne. "Just getting the feel."

Beside Lea, Vivian was waiting patiently to pass along the buck vibrator. Lea feigned fascination with the shiny balls.

"That's a demo tube," Jacky told Karla. "Go on and try it where it belongs."

Karla shrugged and disappeared into the kitchen. The ball Lea was inspecting slipped through her fingers and disappeared into the gap in the cushions Vivian's lopsided weight had opened.

Lea groped between the cushions while Vivian watched her calmly. "Can I help you find that?" Vivian asked.

"It's right here." Lea felt a foolish dread at the anticipation of her hand closing around the ball.

Bettina and Jill were engrossed in discussing the advantages of vibrating pleasure beads over the non-motorized variety, assessing noise, comfort, and ease of use as if comparing microwave ovens. Forgotten for the moment, the two consultants were drinking vodka and talking quietly. Sara twirled a rubber plug absently between her fingers like a shrunken baton. The alienation Lea always felt at girls' gatherings swept her, when the frank talk turned from who was cute and who had slept with whom to clinical observations and crude jokes while she fumbled for something to say, hoping no one would notice her silence and label her uptight.

Lea's squirming finally summoned Sara. "Something gone missing, Mrs.—?"

"Lea. I just dropped a *um* ball."

"It's not lost," Vivian said. "It's down there somewhere."

"Those are slippery," Sara said. "You don't need much lubricant. A top seller." She dug her hand between the cushions. Her sharp rhinestones grazed Lea's fingers. Sara straightened, clasping the ball. "You can try these, if you want. They've been sanitized with Clean and Simple Adult Toy Cleanser. It's a top seller. Jacky highlighted the Cleanser on your order form for your convenience along with the top ten products we are demonstrating for you tonight."

Karla returned, tossed the tube to Bettina. "This you need to try."

Bettina laughed. "I've got plenty of tingle of my own, I'll have you know. How about you, Lea?"

Bettina might have been trying to put her at her ease, but Lea couldn't help but feel that the whole room could sense she hadn't had sex in over a year. "I have sensitive skin."

Vivian placed the buck on the sofa table, tottered to her feet, and headed toward the kitchen.

"There's a formulation for that." Sara handed Lea a lavender tube swirled with hearts. GentleGel. "It's not harsh."

"It's a top seller," Jacky said.

There was no graceful way to pass along the product. Well, it wouldn't kill her to have fun. Lea rose, embarrassed, and wobbled, almost careening into the coffee table. She was more drunk than she'd realized.

Jacky took the box of balls from Lea and handed her another. "In case the gel makes you adventuresome. You know what to do with them, right? Instructions are in the box." Jacky studied her doubtfully. "These ones got a string attached. Best to be precautious."

Karla's cramped half-bath was down a tiled hallway off the kitchen. A scented candle flickered on a glass shelf over the towel rack. The flame shone weakly, a blue filigree caressing a blackened wick. A cloying vanilla scent clogged the room.

Lea switched on the lights and shut the door. She should be angry at Karla for dumping this surprise on her, but being angry at anyone, including herself, was beside the point. She'd linger in the bathroom for a decent interval and work on projecting a fun attitude.

A photograph graced the wall above the toilet seat. Strange misshapen gazelles streaked across a washed-out desert, their heads pale domes with great curved horns. She moved closer and realized the gazelles were motorcycles, racing in slow exposure. The great curved horns were handlebars, the domes helmets. The wheels were blurs, erased by speed, blending with the sand. The racers' legs popped from the images, lean, banded with muscle under skin-hugging leather. Bent at the knee as if the wheels' evaporation had forced the bikers to run. The print was signed. Karla's signature was a slanted scrawl.

It's perfectly safe, Karla had said about her children's neighborhood rides.

In her photography, too, she'd removed any peril. The play of light and the wheels' disappearance suspended the racers above the desert floor. The bikers were speeding so fast they'd achieved a perfect stillness danger couldn't touch, or fear.

Laughter filled the hallway. Women she didn't know, whose opinions shouldn't matter to her, were enjoying some harmless dirty fun. And here Lea was, hiding out in a stranger's bathroom. What was wrong with her, anyway?

The past year wasn't the first time her body had let her down. After the assault, she'd avoided men for years, until she met Jay in graduate school. Then a switch was thrown. They made love effortlessly, passionately. She'd been so excited to tell Dinah she'd finally met the right guy, that all along nothing had been wrong with her.

Lea stared at Karla's serene race. Back then, Jay was the beginning of the possibility of healing. Maybe, if she could just relax, she could be this possibility for him. Didn't she owe it to him to try?

Lea switched off the bathroom light. The candle flame flared in the abrupt return to darkness. She set the box and the lotion on the toilet tank, slipped her jeans down to her ankles, sat down on the seat. She lifted the box's lid. The candlelight buffed the three golden balls

tethered by a thin string. The flame's reflection flickered on the balls'
amber surface.

She squeezed a bit of GentleGel onto her fingertip. Peppermint
mingled with the cloying odor of vanilla. She felt a quivering, the promise of sensation. She parted her legs, dabbed the gel timidly, everywhere
but. *You apply that to your button, not your butterfly.* Lea squeezed another
dollop from the tube, inserted her finger between her legs. Realized she
was gritting her teeth, for heaven's sake.

The sensation wasn't so bad. Gentle, as promised.

She removed the balls from the box.

She fumbled between her legs, gasped at the pressure, and then at
the sensation of discomfort she should have learned, by now, to expect.

A slurping sound when her body swallowed the balls.

His sound.

Before she'd seen what he was doing near the furnace, she'd thought
the slurping was like the steady beat of waves against a hollow hull.
After she'd decided it couldn't be waves, of course—they lived miles
and miles from any body of water—she'd imagined a dog's lapping
tongue buried greedily in a water bowl.

The balls shifted sharply. A hard, swollen ridge raised in her like
erupting teeth.

Another shift, a rocking sensation. Pleasant, now that the beads had
slipped past the crest of discomfort. Lea pressed her knees together.
Unclenched her jaw and rocked with the beads. Her first sight of him.
What he was doing. She remembered still wondering about the noise.
So steady, at odds with his jerky hand and twitchy expression, his bright
lost eyes. Maybe it was wonder that had drawn her to move toward him,
not run away.

A knife-cut of passion nearly doubled her over on the toilet lid.

Jesus. How could she be thinking of *him* that way?

Horrified, hating herself, Lea groped between her legs to yank the
string. Where was it?

The light flashed on. Lea jumped. Vivian stood stock still with her
hand stalled on the switch as if to turn the lights right back off. She
stared at Lea's lap, and then at the velvet dimples in the empty box. "Oh.
I *am* sorry."

Lea flushed. "Excuse me. Can I have a moment, please?"

But Vivian made no move to leave. A stupid sense of panic welled up in Lea. She hadn't removed her sweater when she'd arrived at Karla's. Now the wool was pooling heat. Sweat trickled down her back. "It is fun, isn't it?" Vivian nodded at Lea's lap. "A little crass. But don't you find it liberating? You'd think that at my age, widowed, I wouldn't ever think about sex again. But I think about it all the time."

Lea fought back tears. "If I could just have a moment. *Please*."

"Too, you don't realize until it's too late that every little pleasure might be the last," Vivian said calmly. "You know, I can recall perfectly the last time my husband and I made love. Never would I have imagined that it would be the last time *ever*. Don't you find that odd? That I wouldn't somehow know? Wouldn't a thing like that be obvious? But you look distressed, dear." The woman's gaze lighted on her hand. "Can I help?"

"Well, there's a string, so it shouldn't be—"

Vivian interrupted. "They can be hard to remove, you know, if you don't use enough lubricant. But there's no need to get upset. I'm a nurse. Retired since my husband's illness. You don't know how many times I've seen women in the ER panicking because they think a ball is lost up there."

"I'm not upset."

"Most women don't think to just relax." Vivian pressed her index fingers together. "Remember those Chinese finger traps? You had to fight your instinct to pull your fingers apart. Giving in to the pressure was the only way to get free." Vivian surveyed Lea as if she were laid out on a gurney waiting for help. "My husband did die of Lyme. People do."

Why wouldn't this woman leave her alone? And she couldn't very well get off the toilet and push her out, could she? "I only meant to say that it's, *um*, a chronic condition."

"He suffered from psychosis. A rare complication. Rare until it happens to you. There were other losses. Nerve function. He needed a catheter. Then he couldn't control his bowels. It was very slow. But I can see you need help, dear." Vivian stepped toward her. "Just *relax*."

Lea closed her eyes. What else could she do except go along, wait for it to be over?

6

Gary Starkey did have a point regarding the constant complaints. Since Rilke moved out, Julia had been riding a circus wheel of wild parties seemingly designed to trash the home they'd agreed he'd return to after certain changes to behaviors were accomplished, certain demands of the heart fulfilled. Conditions he was working hard to meet, and would meet, and had in fact already met, like the day-shift deal. Her new freedom, as she labeled the parties, was all about rubbing his nose in, as was her way; more habit than malice, one of her many habits he understood, and forgave, always had, always would.

But when he pulled onto Peach, a quiet street in one of the older township neighborhoods along the city limit border, the cul-de-sac's crescent wasn't choked with the usual assortment of Volvos and F150s. A few months back, when The Marriage frayed to the point that he'd had to move out—she always referred to their relationship that way, with the capital letters digging trenches in her tone, and she'd even written it *capital t capital m* once in a note telling him not to drop by without calling first—right about that time, she'd landed a new job working for a tech start-up. The firm was only a start-up. She was only the receptionist. But just like that, Volvos started showing up at her parties, and pricier booze, and probably drugs, although Jules had been a health freak since their high school days.

Still, he had no doubt that Julia was enjoying trouble with him temporarily out of the picture. He'd expected her to cut loose after living with him for so long, and hell, a part of him encouraged some reckless behavior as a necessary purging of resentment on the path to forgiving him. Best to get it all out of her system before they got back together. They'd married young. Rilke's affinity for the night shift had raised some complaints over time. His predisposition to keep to himself raised others. Over their many years together he'd noted a pattern of restlessness which he thought constituted basic features of any long-term marriage, seeing as he'd had plenty of fed-up moments of his own. But Rilke knew this much about Julia. She projected the party-girl demeanor but she was his girl now and forever, that being a girl who relied upon stability and faithfulness and protection far more than she ever let on to anyone but Rilke.

Gary liked to present Julia's behaviors in the worst possible light whenever Rilke came around to check on the place. Rilke's moving out had downgraded Gary's snooping to outright spying despite Rilke's advising him in no uncertain terms to lay off. What the old man hoped to gain, Rilke didn't like to think about. Such thoughts led to unsavory suspicions that Gary had crossed a line in their relationship to an un-called-for father-son dynamic and was hoping Rilke would move back home less for Julia's sake than his own.

During a lunch break the previous week, Rilke had decided to poke around the Peach house to make sure Julia was keeping up the basic maintenance. He'd put his all into making their house stand out from the identical ranch homes that ringed the street, crammed window to window, the space between as dim and crowded as city alleys. The homes had been sided all alike in the cheap board and batten popular back when the township's first subdivisions sprang up. Rilke had replaced the ugly siding with Hardiplank. He'd painted it a bright jay blue, trimmed the windows cotton white, made the place really pop. The Culvers and that young couple, Grace and Tom, brightened their houses with bulb gardens and burning bushes when a bold paint job would do the trick much better, but at least the properties were maintained, everything kept up so nicely.

He owed it to the neighborhood, not to mention himself, to make certain their property was shipshape. When he checked the furnace, just a thin web of dust clung to the filter, so she'd remembered to change that, and salt brimmed the softener, and the solder repair he'd made to the bathtub plumbing was holding okay if the clean drywall was any indicator. Gary had waved him over as Rilke exited the side door to salt the driveway. Jules was always slipping on wet pavement, which had filmed over during the cold snap to a black wafer of ice. She'd never had the foresight to take care of any problem before it caused her some harm.

"Been noisy around here, Paul, with you gone." Always the same tiresome greeting. Gary's boiled-milk odor didn't exactly suffocate the brandy's ginger aroma. The man's toddy doubtless capped a night of indulgences, as the bloodshot eyes and tremors would attest.

"That right?" Rilke kept the tone neutral.

"Seems like something boisterous every night. Though I know it can't be so often." Gary had touched Rilke's sleeve. The right thumb and index finger ended in stumps at the knuckles. Scar tissue wadded at the joint like old, cracked rubber. Scars from an electrical accident at one of his rental properties some years back. The damage curtailed the old man's shooting accuracy, so he'd always hired out that end of the wildlife control business. Had periodically offered Rilke some cash under the table to do the work, an offer Rilke always refused.

"Thought we agreed you would knock off the calls, Gary." Rilke sowed salt pellets on the drive. Sprinkled some grains near Starkey's boot so the old man didn't lose a footing on Rilke's property. "Thought that was the deal we struck to avoid a fine for excessive complaints."

From across the court the neighbor kids slammed a door, tumbled down the porch steps, and waddled down the sidewalk in their puffy jackets like cute little boll weevils. Rilke and Julia had decided not to have kids, given that they'd both been knocked around as kids them-selves. Throttle both of their family lines together was how they saw the childless life, plus no danger of falling into unhealthy patterns despite good intentions and so on. But these cute little tykes always did make Rilke nurse some longings and regrets.

"Just trying to do the right thing here. You're like my own son, you know that." The man's voice projected, all right. The kids stared at Gary as they passed, all round eyes and fierce whispers, as if he were the neighborhood bogeyman. Not far off the mark. Rilke moved to salt the driveway's apron. The grains skated on the ice and rolled to the street. The problem of the ice was a problem with the driveway's drainage. Another item he'd deal with when he moved back home. "Plus, things do get rambunctious in there. Hell, half the time I'm making the call out of regard for her damn *safety*."

"Okay, let's dial it down." The man's odor overwhelmed the air Rilke was trying to keep between them, and he could do without the son crap. Anyone who knew anything about Rilke knew he needed a second pa like he needed a hole in the head. But his disgust was misdirected, he had to admit. Gary had always been a bit loony and the drinking had crossed certain acceptable boundaries but he was, deep down, although almost by now goddamn *buried*, an all right guy. Just lonely, which did mess with a guy's overall outlook over the long term. "I'll talk to her. But, Gary. Stop the calls. I'm not going to warn you again."

And talked to her he had, that same evening, on the cedar porch he'd built. Rilke would be well within his rights to force *her* to live in Mutti's guest cottage while they worked through the problems. But he'd kept the conversation low-key and reasonable. He touched upon the behaviors that posed challenges to her own health and safety, not to mention The Marriage getting back on track where it belonged. He outlined the compromises he was willing to make to roll things along in the right direction. Jules took it all in, he thought. He'd fallen silent, marooned by her beautiful green eyes and her stubborn, full-lipped pout that tonight looked just a crinkle short of a smile.

"Did you come in the house today while I was gone?" she asked.

Rilke was taken aback. Although she was always diverting from the subject at hand, for once she'd looked like she was concentrating on what he was saying. "Just came by to check on things."

"I told you not to do that anymore." She'd actually looked uncomfortable. A dusting of fear inhabited the way she was avoiding his eyes. "I made it clear where things stood."

"I salted the driveway for you."

"I saw that. Look, Paul, you have to stop snooping around here."

"It's called checking on my property, Jules," he had told her.

"Meaning me?"

"Meaning the water softener."

"The water softener does not need checking."

"Okay."

"But maybe I do, right?"

"This is my house too."

"That why you show up to my parties?"

"I don't show up to your parties, Jules."

"You've ticketed my guests, Paul. Maybe the hydrant was blocked *once.*"

"I gave out a few for disorderly conduct, too, that one time," Rilke had pointed out mildly.

"You have a pretty low threshold on what constitutes disorderly. Look, you people have to quit accepting Gary's calls."

"I've told him to knock it off a bunch of times. Maybe he finally would if you knocked it off too." A response he would change now if he could.

Julia had pushed him, a hard thump against his chest he'd felt as a painful echo of his racing heart. Maybe he'd drawn too close—she hated his crowding her, another of his *stiflements*, her term for his care. "Look, Paul, my therapist says I need to enforce boundaries with you. So give me your key. Or are you going to make me pay to change the locks?"

"Your therapist?" She'd never had any trouble whatsoever enforcing boundaries in The Marriage. Her temper had obliterated any attempt he'd ever made to cross her threshold uninvited, not that he'd ever been anything but respectful. Julia needed, *thrived on*, one-sided rage, that side being her side of the encounter. Her dad had hit her growing up, badly enough to put her in the ER once. For all that she met anything she took as hassle with her own quick sunbursts of anger, she had a trigger about men. Rilke had always been careful in his dealings with her. Let her yell and push and feel safe and strong. He'd always backed off, as he was doing now.

To project his willingness to give her what she wanted, he'd handed over his key right there on the spot. Though of course he had a spare in case of an emergency. Which of course she *knew*. The key ritual had to be some kind of symbolic thing she needed at that moment, and the moment and the need would pass like every other moment and need, and they'd be one step closer to resuming The Marriage.

Whatever it took was fine by him.

He loved her and was true to her. She was, although she hadn't believed him when he'd admitted it to her, his first and only lover. He'd never looked at anyone before or since, as if every drop of desire he possessed was hers alone and it was just natural to love her as deeply and all at once as he had. Which was just the kind of sappy crap a man couldn't say out loud. Not to a woman like Jules, who had learned the hard way to trust only what that man did, not what he said.

As he idled outside the house now, the absence of the Volvos—in fact, any car at all—surprised Rilke. Julia's porch lights were darkened. A single light from the side bedroom illuminated the garage walkway. The scene was quiet when he cut his engine and stepped out of the car. A nice street of nice families. Most days kids were out playing while he was sleeping off the night shift. He missed dozing to the high chatter of happy voices worried about nothing at all, just the way it should be for kids. Centennial Farms, that development, built on what used to be the north fields of the Rilke farm, was a graveyard. Acre lots, sloppily constructed, overpriced mini-mansions and ghosts living in them, as far as Rilke could tell. He'd driven through that desert as part of his follow-up on Gary's work. The stand he'd repaired was near a populated road. He'd knocked on the door before spending all morning in the homeowner's tree and in all those hours had raised only the whistle of a whining dog locked in the home.

A while back he'd taken a call for a burglary in that subdivision, a minor theft on a nice family. Two young kids, good-looking mother. She let her husband do the talking while she took in Rilke's holster and nightstick like the minor theft was anything but routine just because the crime was against them. Rilke had to wonder sometimes at the sheltered outlook of some suburban types. So the residents existed, but it was quiet in that abandoned sense, not in the peaceful sense of the Peach Tree neighborhood.

Peaceful except for his own wife.

And except for Gary, who had flipped on his porch light and was standing in his driveway in robe and slippers, his knobby legs bared to the cold. "She's screaming in there."

Rilke approached him and immediately suppressed a gag. The man's breath poured spoiled milk and vinegar. "I don't hear anything, Gary. You drinking tonight?"

"I'm not drunk." The thick flow of his breath clouded in the cold air, drifting to Rilke in hard, sour beads. "Get in there, man."

"All quiet out here." Rilke made a motion at the man's shoulder. He would never lay a hand on an agitated individual unless he had to, even a guy he'd known as long as he'd known Gary.

"I swear there's trouble for real this time." Gary's voice dropped to a rasp. His odor recalled the sour tang of Papa's decay, etched on Rilke like a permanent stain. The slow erosion of the teeth and the linings of the stomach and the throat. Papa's appearance had never much changed through the years of decline, but the odor worsened until it became a presence, announced on the air before Papa entered a room.

Rilke rode out another bubble of disgust at the wreckage of this man, withering in the borders of his lonely person. "Okay, Gary. Let's call it a night."

Gary grabbed him. Since first contact hadn't come on Rilke's initiative, he could now cradle Starkey's elbow gently, propel him to the porch, dial down the agitation. Gary leaned into him and wrapped his arms around Rilke's waist, as if effective management of an old drunk were a show of affection. "You're a good sport, Paul."

Rilke didn't spook easily, but he had to admit the muffled scream that tore through drawn blinds and Hardiplank and the frigid air and Gary's soup of odors cut him in two. It was all the more startling because although he couldn't recall ever hearing Julia scream like that, the thin pitch of her cry was as familiar to him as her speaking voice.

"You hear that?" Gary cried with the smug pleasure of events working out as anticipated.

"Get inside." Rilke pushed the man toward his front door. "Stay there. Understand?" He barreled up the walk and scaled the cedar porch. Checked himself at the door, listened a bit, rapped sharply. A muffled thump that wasn't her soft tread coming for him leaked through the jamb's seams, and then a bang, and another scream, this one throttled mid-stream, and Julia's voice full on shouted words he couldn't quite make out but sounded like *stop no yes there* that raised a pounding in his throat and at the hard knobs of his temples. He fitted the spare key carefully, slid the bolt, and stepped into the darkened foyer.

A high keening blasted from the kitchen. He darted down the hall and made to pivot around the double ovens when a riot of light splashed his boots and he stopped short of seeing into the kitchen. Julia's pitch was hysterical and specific, like fear and love being mixed up and confused one for the other, *hit it right there no stop yes there yes yes* and Rilke stopped cold. *Jesus Christ.* Was she doing some party guy right there on his kitchen floor? The thumping now a full-on ramming and Julia screamed again like she'd bit off more than she could chew, or maybe the guy was hurting her.

Rilke stepped over the kitchen threshold into the blazing lights. He spotted Jules's shirtless man right off but it turned out the individual had his pants on and slippers, too, and was swinging a badminton racket wildly. Julia was curled up under the dining table, fully clothed. The badminton racket hammered the oak floor. Rilke absorbed a bloodied heap near the refrigerator, fastened his gaze to the racket, assessed the hairy bits of fur and leathery bits of wings woven in the netting. A final *thwack*, and then the man saw Rilke a moment before Julia did, when her hollering turned into a different class of sound altogether.

Although Rilke hadn't so much as touched his holster, the very young man chucked the racket and waved his palms in the air. An insubstantial individual, gangly and pale with floppy blond bangs on a bony brow, wiry arms, skinny bow legs. Unnaturally straight teeth, as if he'd just had braces removed.

"Calm down, son," Rilke said.

"Don't kill me, man, don't kill me."

"Shut up, Luke, shut *up*." The young man dropped his hands, limp and spent like popped balloons. "This is it, Paul, this is it, you're done, *done*." Jules was in his face, puffing that organic cinnamon toothpaste at him. She pushed him, hard, pinned him to the ovens with both fists ramming his chest; the oven handles hurt like hell.

"Okay, Jules. Let's dial it down," Rilke suggested.

"Dial it *down*?" Julia poked him in the sternum, right where she knew he had sensitivities. "Dial it *down*?"

Rilke crossed his arms to get her to back off without having to touch her and tried not to retch at the bat's carcass splayed on his polished floor, by far the worst part of this whole screwed-up deal.

"Give me a good reason not to report you." Her first words to him were out of earshot of the boy, who had the good sense not to speak or even look directly at Rilke as Julia hustled him out to the porch.

"You were screaming, Jules."

"I'm gonna get you suspended, Paul. I'm gonna tell your *mother!*"

She shivered. The cold was clearing Rilke's head. "Let's go back inside," Rilke said briefly. "Warm you up."

"You will never set foot in this house again." She met his gaze. "Did you break in just now?"

"Of course not."

"I thought you gave me your key."

"What do you think? I keep a spare. For emergencies. For maintenance." She looked genuinely surprised, as if the thought that he'd possess a duplicate had never occurred to her. She never made copies of anything.

"So here's how it's going to be." She ticked off the items on her fingers as if laying it all out for him was just by way of a helpful reminder. "First, tell your people to quit taking calls from Gary. Second, if your people are going to take his crazy calls, you can't respond, Paul. Your people must have a *policy* against you showing up here *estranged* in my house."

Rilke listened to her breathing, the shallow quick rise of it. She'd stopped shivering, as if acclimated to the cold. From the backyard came the scrape of squeaky hinges, then the hollow thud of a rubber lid being drawn and dropped back into place. The boy must be cleaning up the bat. Rilke's gut flip-flopped. "Who's the kid?"

"Your *keys*, Paul. All of them." Now that he'd controlled the gag reflex over the bat, he was feeling the temper, a quickening, the knock against his temples. Julia was flushed, her lips raised as if she'd been kissing, not yelling, her eyes glittery. "My therapist says I have to call you on your aggression issues. We're engaged, by the way."

To the best of Rilke's recollection, The Marriage had thrived on his forthright and decidedly unaggressive management of *Jules's* aggression issues. "Isn't that unethical?"

"What on earth does that mean?"

"Marrying your therapist?"

"Don't pretend you don't know I'm talking about Luke. Who you just harassed."

He almost laughed, thinking she was messing around after all. Sometimes during their worst fights she would take things so far they would end up as funny, not borderline dangerous. What else could the kid be but a joke? Half as old and twice as tall as Julia. He couldn't even look at her without stooping. If there was one muscle tucked under the flaccid overcoat of the boy's skin, Rilke couldn't detect it. Although he sure had made sad stew of the bat. "That's crazy. He's a kid."

"He's not a kid. He's *youthful.* He owns the company I work for. He's successful. He's fun. He's more available than you ever were."

Available? She used to mock touchy-feely vocab. "You can't get engaged when we're still hitched," he pointed out.

"I'm filing next week."

"You can't."

"Why's that, Paul?"

"Because," he repeated, knowing he was sounding a bit stupid, a bit confused, "we're *married*."

He could hear it coming by the curve of her mouth, the march of her chin, the unapologetic polish of her eyes. "What are you thinking, Paul? The Marriage is over."

He made a sound embarrassingly close to a whimper. He must have been projecting the stupidity and the confusion he was feeling, because all at once her brow and the pretty lines around her eyes crumpled like a wadded tissue. "Paul." She touched his wrist, and their pulses joined, the best thing and maybe the last thing he would ever feel. "It's been over for a long time. You *know* this."

Which was the source of the whole misunderstanding between them, because he hadn't known; how could he, when she'd been keeping her new man a secret?

After leaving Julia's house, *his*, house, Rilke parked at the Costco to stare at the Burger King lot. It was late, just past midnight, but a steady stream of vehicles flowed along the boulevard. Brittle light from the headlamps sparked a wretched headache, or maybe his brooding on the marital situation was making his head clang. He'd been parked only a few minutes when a bright blue SUV used the fast-food lot to avoid the Dix light, but Rilke didn't notice the illegal turn. What was most troubling, he'd decided, was that Julia thought it was all right to attach herself to a man who could pulverize a living creature the way that kid had. If a man had *that* in him, it was bound to come out again under duress. Which dynamic she'd once confessed she feared in him, Rilke. That the *hero complex* he brought to the job would sooner or later make him crazy, or resent her, or some other completely fantastical outcome he couldn't understand because she was yelling this confession at him after he'd messed up drying a special dish her mother had given her and dropped it close to her foot. Which was bare, which, by the way, going barefoot in the kitchen was a choice bound to cause lacerations..

But this exact species of altercation used to be the norm in The Marriage, nasty spats and subsequent deep ecstasies lined up like pins. Through it all, Rilke had proven himself safe, made up for every man in the world who had harmed her and might yet. He'd met every aggressive move with calm. Well, maybe a pointed comment or two had slipped out. Nothing that matched what she would say to him on the regular, downright cruel remarks delivered as if she were just offering up the daily weather report. But he'd always wait until she'd worn herself out with the scolds and recriminations and came at him with a different kind of need altogether. Always followed her lead, anticipated what she wanted from him.

Around the time Papa died, he'd even moved out without being asked. He'd finally gotten the message loud and clear that her chronic unhappiness needed air and space not occupied by Rilke. He'd pledged to do anything she wanted to make her happy. He'd tried giving up nights. He could give up being a cop. Move away altogether if that's what it took. Seeing as he'd just received a citation for reducing meth crime in the county, she'd told him he was bluffing. She'd accused him yet again of the so-called *hero complex* that violated boundaries and caused other transgressions Rilke neither understood nor accepted when she ticked them off on her fingers. No one could live up to his expectations, she'd told him, let alone live with them. When had guts and courage turned into a mental disorder anyway? was his response to that. And by the way, who really had the complex, the guy playing hero, or the folks relying on him to?

She'd drilled down then, pegging what she referred to as his increasing patterns of *stiflement* to Rilke holding Papa at a disdainful arm's length well after the man had reformed. No wonder you can't process his death, she'd concluded. Well, he'd processed that welcome event just fine, and considering that she'd cried and hugged him tight when he told her the story of the kits way back when they were first married, Rilke couldn't believe she was scolding him for an unforgiving attitude now.

He'd packed his stuff after the very next shift. The prudent course was to stay the hell away from her and the premature fiancé. But Gary might be on to something about being concerned for her safety. Just because the guy drank didn't mean he didn't have eyes in his head. Maybe Rilke was being too tough on the wrong person in this scenario.

A Mercury luxury sedan pulled into the Burger King to dodge the light. This time Rilke saw the illegal move, but as he reached to flash his lights and pull out of the Costco, a call came in for a trespass in Centennial Farms. Rilke was about to accept when a gas line rupture caused by the cold took him back to the highway ramp. A chilly hour managing the traffic around the gas guys was interrupted by an urgent summons to a barn fire on the township's southern line. Rilke met Nowak at the scene to sort the mess. The homeowners' eldest had set up making meth where the hay bales used to be stored. The barn had been awarded the state's 2008 Barn of the Year. Now the award-winning structure lay heaped in cinders, and their loser kid standing sheepishly in cuffs wasn't likely to snag Son of the Year any time this century. The Centennial Farms call suffered a steady drop in priority. Rilke wouldn't remember the call until it popped up again in the queue, but then, a trespass in an affluent community hardly constituted the crime of the century, either.

7

After Vivian left the bathroom, Lea crouched on the toilet for a long stretch of time that threatened to become outright hiding. If Bettina hadn't tapped on the door wanting to dab or poke or massage some thirsty part of her body, Lea might never have tamed her shaking legs to slip back into Karla's den. She perched on the opposite end of the sofa from Vivian. Vivian appeared not to notice her, or was ignoring her; maybe she was being discreet, maybe passive aggressive. Lea forced a smile and small talk for what she calculated was a polite interval before making a couple of purchases. While she was calculating Lea's Pleasure Points and Naughty IOUs, Sara asked whether the golden ball set had disappeared. Sheepishly, Lea backtracked to the bathroom, where she'd left it. Once she'd fetched it, she felt she had to buy the things. Sara recalculated her Pleasure Points. Lea caught Vivian staring at her when she tucked the ball set into her Party Girl bag. Fleeing Karla's insistence that she stay for the cake felt like sheer cowardice, but what was she supposed to do, confront Vivian? Pretend nothing had happened? Lea told Karla she was diabetic, a stupid lie she didn't have to tell to escape, and left.

Now she sat in her driveway, willing herself to go into the house. Jay had switched the outside lights off. She could barely see her own porch in the darkness. Was he making a point that he was still mad? Or was he trying not to scare the damn deer away? She opened the car door. The dome light shone on the Party Girl bag she'd tossed on the passenger seat, all lavender and sparkly pink hearts, as if she'd snagged a goody bag from a sleepover. She was all alone, but she flushed as if she were still hunched on the toilet, trapped by Vivian staring at her as if she'd caught Lea red-handed, fantasizing about *him.*

She tucked the bag in her purse and slammed the door.

Inside the den she flicked on the lights, a row of canister fixtures above the fireplace. The Ruger and the Mauser were back on the hearth, nestled under the crocheted throw as if Bunny had tucked them in. Lea stripped off Jay's jacket and then her sweater and threw both on the couch. Bunny's menagerie was still seated for tea. Their sightless eyes scoured the blank television screen. An empty pizza box yawned open beside the chocolate-smeared teapot. A half-eaten crust huddled in the center of the box. Lea felt exhausted. She wasn't sober at all, she realized. The vodka's blunted buzz left her desperately thirsty but perversely craving another drink. In the kitchen she filled a tumbler with soda water and drank it down. Filled it up again, this time with whiskey. As she walked out of the kitchen she saw a note on the island. Jay, telling her he'd headed outside for the night to the deer stand. Leaving the kids alone in the house, of course. She should be afraid for their safety. Or pissed off. Instead, she was relieved he was gone.

Lea took her drink into the den, fished out the Party Girl bag, and dumped her hasty purchases on the sofa. A purple vibrator with a smooth motorized bulb, downright prim by the standards of the evening. A set of leatherette ties. An amber bottle of musk oil. Those golden balls. A tube of GentleGel, the logo's dainty purple hearts shimmering under shrink-wrap.

Jay was right to call her heartless. She knew fear's cunning miscues and confusions, the insurrections it caused in the body, the mind, the heart. She should be able to block its mischief, deny its mistakes. Instead she'd annexed Jay's trauma as if his injuries were hers to claim. The attack on Jay hadn't merely reminded her of *him*. It had brought her closer to *him*, lusting, for God's sake. What made her desire unbearable was that she understood exactly what she was doing, and why. Guilt and shame over the past were easy distractions for the shameful way she'd been treating her husband. *He* was the original fear that could never be erased. Jay was her bell tone, what she most feared now. She of all people should be able to manage her response, condition herself to love the right person until she could feel again.

But when she thought of even touching Jay, the memory of him curled up on the tar, blood pooling under his head, was unbearable. The last time she'd touched him with any emotion was when she'd wept giving him CPR.

Lea stuffed the toys back into the bag. Her nose was running, irritated by the room's heat, or maybe she was trying not to cry. She wiped with her hand and caught the sharp aroma on her fingers she thought she'd washed away. Underneath that sour musk lay smoke and vanilla, the creamy scent of her children, the fear, and the trust, of animals; the fading memory of Jay's salty skin; and under it all the aroma of her own skin, still stinking of *him*.

She must have fallen asleep or passed out. Later she would remember being startled awake as if yanked from a free fall down a tunnel. Her breasts hurt. She'd been dreaming that Jay was grabbing her and shouting that she was hurting him. For a moment the house rang silent. What had awakened her? The nightmare? Kurt's sleepwalking? She rolled off the couch into a puddle of whiskey she couldn't remember spilling. She scrambled to her feet when the pounding resumed. Not Kurt's padded footsteps, but fists on her front door, the second one facing Scipio Road.

She ran to peer around the corner of the hall, half-expecting to see a living fragment of her drunken dream. Jay's rough hands flat against the panes, complaining that her skin was cutting him like shards of broken glass. But a tall, husky man dressed neatly in a blue blazer and crisp white shirt filled the grid of tiny windows lining the upper part of the door. He caught the nervous bob of her head at the end of the hallway, mimed words she couldn't make out. She was forgetting, for the moment, how bitterly cold it was outside, how strange it was that he wasn't wearing a thick coat. She was drunk, puzzled and frightened by his frantic pantomime. He might have been a kid for the round face, the wide blue eyes, except for his broad shoulders stretching the blazer's seams.

She huddled against the wall and switched on the hall light. The frosted dome fixture crackled, the burn of dead summer insects she'd never cleaned out. A broad fist again struck the glass. The door rattled in its hinges. He mouthed something. *Call*, she made out. *Cop*. Or *Dad*. He jabbed the doorknob, clearly frightened, or pretending to be.

This was the just the type of act that had lured Jay outside to be attacked. Lea stepped toward the door, just close enough to search the bushes lining the porch for any henchmen. The sudden freeze had caused the viburnum to drop their leaves all at once as if they'd been ordered to strip. Their slim trunks couldn't conceal a squirrel. But someone could be hiding behind the sucker branches clustered around the viburnum's base.

"What do you want?" she said.

The man rattled the doorknob. *Let me in*, she thought he mouthed. Later she would wonder why she couldn't hear his shouts through the glass. Had she really been so drunk? In the moment, silence suctioned the air; she could barely breathe. Her first impulse was to run past the door and up the stairs to shake Jay awake. Then she remembered he was up a tree, watching for deer. The man pounded at the door again, miming demands to open up. Shaking, Lea backed away into the kitchen. She dug her cell phone from her purse. She'd forgotten to plug it in to recharge, of course she had. She dialed Jay, but the call went to voicemail. She hung up, mangled a text that she meant to be a measured *call me back*. Later she would see her message included pleas like *he's gonna break down the door* and *help*, appeals she didn't remember typing. As she was calling 911, the phone's screen winked out. She picked up the house phone and reached a dispassionate operator, who verified her address before asking her what her emergency was. *Is he in your home? Is he attempting to break in?*

The pounding had stopped. Lea answered truthfully, *no*.

When the operator hung up, Lea slipped back to the hallway. She'd hoped the silence meant the guy had taken off but there he was, peering through the glass intently at where she'd been standing as if casting a spell for her return. Despite the cold, sweat rolled down the bridge of his nose. *Help me*, he mouthed.

She met the trespasser's eyes, tried to gauge his age. "Are you hurt?"

The man shook his head, *no*. He was behaving as if he, not she, were trapped, as if their yard were the cage, not her home. His gaze was glassy from the porch light's reflection. Or from tears. He dug his fists into his eyes. A young man, she decided. Maybe eighteen or so, no more.

"I called for help," she said. She didn't mention the cops, although she should have if she'd wanted to frighten him away. Now that her whiskey buzz was fading, the formal wear was confusing her. The kid didn't seem so threatening now, but Jay had warned her, over and over, not to fall for any innocent acts. "I'm not letting you in," she added.

The trespasser stared at her. Now she doubted he'd been wiping away tears. His eyes were dry, and their glitter seemed angry after she'd told him his ruse wasn't working. He turned up his blazer collar, shrank into it, shivering, and turned away to scan the yard. When he stepped away from the door, his whole body came into her view. From the waist down, he was nude. No pants, no socks, no shoes. Was he completely exposed? She couldn't tell; the blazer covered what she could see of his backside. She gasped and moved closer, caught a glimpse of white peeking from the blazer's hem. Not completely naked. Had he been attacked, robbed, stripped of his clothes?

Lea stepped forward to unlock the bolt just as the man, the kid, turned back to her. He couldn't have seen her hand on the bolt, the window grid was too high; but he'd spied her concern, her softening, her relaxed guard. He flung himself at the door. Lea cried out and jumped back.

"Let me in." Now she could hear him, a harsh, deep voice cutting through whatever vacuum her fear had created to suck away any sound. She'd almost fallen for it. No doubt his pants and shoes were stashed just around the side of the house. She shook her head. The kid shouted, "Why?" and started sobbing. For effect, or for real, how was she to tell? He was shivering violently now. His cheeks and nose were chapped, his knuckles bright red from the cold, from his pounding. Where the hell were the cops?

She fled to the kitchen, which started him up again, this time timid tapping. What if she were wrong and he had been robbed? If he was a lure to get her to open the door, wouldn't he take off once he realized she wasn't going to fall for it? Why would he stay on her stoop, practically naked, in this cold if he didn't have to? She tried to catch her breath, calm down. No one would blame her for just waiting for the police. But if he was a victim, terrified, frostbitten, and she'd failed to help, she wouldn't forgive herself for making his injuries worse.

Finally she worked out the humane thing to do. She would place a blanket outside the first front door, out of the young man's sight. She'd then return to the second front door and tell him to fetch it, keep warm, while he waited for the cops. In the moment, this charity, one that wouldn't endanger her family, seemed perfectly rational. She was banking on the fact that if he did have accomplices, they were sticking close to their buddy, not lying in wait at both of her doors. But just in case, she'd grab the Ruger to scare them off.

Later she'd wonder at her eagerness to carry out this ridiculous plan quickly, stealthily, *don't wake the kids*. She could also have left her phone for the kid to make a call. She could have given him a sandwich, a bag of chips, a bottle of water. Hot chocolate, like she'd offer her own children on such a terribly cold night. She could have called a cab, for God's sake. None of these responses occurred to her, although she felt stone-cold sober, alert. A freakish clarity bonded to her like a brilliant glaze, *don't be duped, don't get hurt.* Jay would think she was nuts to be concerned about this kid. He'd be furious when he found out she'd given him any sort of help.

She ran past the front door and took the stairs two at a time. The kid saw her and started beating on the door again, *come back!* Upstairs, she opened the creaky hall closet doors slowly, hoping the hinge's whine wouldn't carry to the kids. From downstairs, a loud bang made her jump. A coldness scraped her. She could still barely catch her breath. She thrust her hand into a pile of blankets they never used, pulled out the thickest, warmest one, a white throw with satin binding her mother had given her years ago.

The pounding fell silent, the quiet like a sudden drenching.

She froze, listening. She thought she heard a scrabbling, and then a hoarse yell. A dull thunk that sounded like a nail gun. He'd kicked the door in. She moved away from the stairs, blanket to her chest. Her phone was downstairs, and so were those useless guns. The one working gun they owned, the shotgun, was locked up in the garage. The front door rattled, and the pounding started up again. How could he still be beating on the door if he'd broken in? But she hadn't heard any noise in the hallway, footsteps, or his voice. She swallowed a scream, moved to the top of the stairs, chanced a peek down into the foyer.

Instead of splintered wood on the tile and the trespasser barreling at her, Lea saw a man drenched in black—cap, jacket, and straps crisscrossing his chest. He was holding a long rifle to his shoulder. The door was undamaged, still snugly bolted. The man caught sight of her and said her name like he knew her. Under the dark cap pulled low on his brow, it took her far too long to recognize Jay.

Where did he get those clothes? That rifle, a sleek, serious weapon, must be new too. She slipped downstairs and opened the door. "Jay. I didn't recognize you at all."

He pushed past her down the hall, strode into the kitchen, gun at the ready. Ammo filled the straps on his chest. Was this all for the deer? "Are you okay?"

"He didn't get in."

He lowered the rifle and turned to stare at the blanket. She hadn't realized she was still mashing it to her chest. "The kids okay?"

"They're fine. What happened to that guy?"

"I chased him off."

"Was anyone else out there?"

"Nope, just him. The jerk."

The kid had been alone, then. No henchmen. No threat. Jay looked off-kilter, eyes hard, darting around the room like an intruder might still be lurking. In the hunting gear he looked bigger, bulkier. He'd finished his military service before they dated. She'd only seen photos of his Marine days, the shaved head under the tight cover, the trousers bloused neatly in combat boots. Now he looked like the black space left behind after his image had been cut out of those photos. She wondered if he'd been shaving his hair so short to match these clothes. Did he really buy all of this stuff, and the rifle, on their nonexistent budget, or did the cull people supply the gear?

Without realizing it, she'd backed away from him until she was pressed to the kitchen island. Jay didn't notice her unease, or maybe he was ignoring it. "Why do you have a blanket?"

"He looked cold. Why were you pounding on the door?"

"You have my keys, remember?" He spoke to her slowly, as if she didn't have a grasp of the basic facts. "You took my coat when you left." Jay set the rifle down on the counter and peeled off the black fingerless gloves he was wearing. His fingers were as red as the kid's hands had been.

She did remember taking his coat; and they never kept a spare key outside, not after the attack. "So you left the kids alone in here with no way to get back in?"

"It was just for a few minutes. You said you'd be home on time. What do you mean, he was cold? I thought he was breaking in?"

"You left the kids *alone*?"

Jay shook his head. "You leave the kids on their own too, Lea."

"To work in the garden. During the day!"

Jay turned away from her. She dropped the blanket and went after him. Before she could demand to know what was wrong with him, Jay stumbled on the step down into the den, right into the puddle of the drink she'd spilled on the floor. Whiskey splashed his boots. She sprang to grab his elbow to steady him. Jay shook her off, stood gaping at the mess. The Party Girl massage oil and leatherette ties had tumbled among Bunny's menagerie and the empty pizza boxes. The golden balls had rolled to the middle of the floor. The fat purple wand was next to the hearth. Lea must have kicked the bag off the couch when the trespasser's pounding startled her awake.

Jay looked at her. "What's this?"

"Nothing." She put her hands behind her back. "Stuff from the party."

"What party?" He moved closer to her. Was he sniffing her? "Are you drunk?"

"What? No."

"You smell like a still."

"I don't smell. There's whiskey all over the floor, Jay."

"Exactly." He stooped to pick up one of the balls, wove it through his fingers like he was testing a marble.

Lea flushed. "I'm allowed to have a drink once in a while. What happened to that kid? I think I heard a scream."

"He was on our property." He glanced at the vibrator by the hearth. "Are you seeing someone?"

"Who?" Lea barely heard him. Jay would startle anyone in that gear. If the kid had yelled in fright, it was no wonder.

"Are you having an affair, Lea," Jay said as if repeating a fact she hadn't yet digested.

Lea stared at him. "What? Of course not."

"So all this stuff is for *our* love life, right?" He rolled the ball across the floor toward Bunny's possum. The ball plinked one of her china teacups. He clenched his fists. Even if she was seeing someone, would an affair spark such anger in him?

Only if he already felt that way about her.

She hoped the breath she was heaving at him stank like a still. Her fists were clenched tightly, too, she realized. Standing so close to her now, the cap so low on his brow shadowed the scars on the damaged side of his face. He looked as if he'd never been attacked.

He stepped back, uncurled his hands—maybe a de-escalation, maybe unease at her refusal to back down and apologize, as she always had before when they fought. She moved away from him. "None of what you're doing makes sense, Jay," she whispered. "Nothing has made sense for a long time."

"You can say that again." His voice cracked.

Lea walked back to the kitchen and grabbed the blanket. She walked to the front door without bothering to grab her keys. Let him lock her out.

"Where are you going?" he called after her.

She ignored him, slammed the door, hiked across the lawn to search the pines. *Could* Jay have shot at that kid? Could the sound she'd heard have been a rifle shot? The one he was using for the deer had a suppressor, so the muted noises outside made sense.

On the other side of the trees, she scouted up Scipio Road a bit in the direction she thought the kid might take, toward the city lights crowning the horizon. This would be the night when not a single car was out speeding, when the darkness snuffed out every light between her and town except for a dim sliver from the farmhouse's weak porch light across the road. Stark moonlight dusted the tar ivory. Although the kid was nowhere to be found, she called out, *are you okay?*, relieved, and then frightened, when silence answered her. Every stone under her shoes felt huge, supple, like she was stumbling over body parts. She set the blanket down near the bushes, in plain sight if the kid was hiding nearby.

When she called out to him again, *Hey, you, are you okay?*, she could only say *you* because she'd never asked his name.

Jay didn't lock her out. Of course he wouldn't. Now that she'd confirmed that the boy wasn't lying in the yard wounded, she was ashamed to have ever thought he would hurt anyone, let alone a boy. Why was it suddenly so easy to believe the worst about a man she'd loved and trusted more than anyone in her whole life? Why was she overreacting to the changes in him, when so much of what he was feeling and doing made perfect sense in the wake of his trauma? She hadn't overreacted when she found him bleeding in the driveway, except for crying a little while giving him CPR. She'd cradled his head, held his uninjured hand until the paramedics arrived. She'd been calm and collected in a resilient shock that allowed her to function but not feel.

She'd been waiting a year now for that shock to wear off, but crying in the lab earlier that day were the first tears she'd raised since the attack. For a long time now, the lab had been the only place where she could be the best version of herself: focused, doing work that mattered. Happy in her relationship with Abel, competent with the postdocs. Now she'd proven it was the only place where she could feel anything at all.

She slipped into the foyer, bolted the door quietly, intending to creep upstairs. She wanted Jay to simply fade into the night, so long as she didn't have to see him. But in the absolute stillness of the rest of the house, the only sounds came from where he still was. Muffled noises that drew her to him, a duty to her marriage vows she wished with all her heart she could disobey.

She crept to peek into the den. Jay was crouched on the hearth, palms pressed tightly together. He was weeping in that silent, severe way he denied he was doing, even with the tears running down his cheeks. He'd shed the cap, the ammo, the jacket, his boots. He was wearing his ordinary shirt, blue flannel. His shoulders should be heaving with weeping, with the grieving sounds that slipped through his pinched mouth, but he sat so perfectly still he could be a fake, a body the soul had left behind.

He wouldn't look at her. He never did, when he was sobbing. Lea went to him. She should have crouched too, taken his hands, spoken softly. But she stood above him, looking down at the crown of his head. "I'm sorry. Don't cry."

"I'm not crying." He opened his hands. He was holding the leatherette ties. He must have been hiding them from her, because they were dark with his tears, as if he'd been rubbing his eyes with them.

She drew a breath. "Okay. Cry then. Cry as hard as you can."

He wove the ties through his fingers. Cat's Cradle, Jacob's Ladder, Witches Broom, kid's games she used to play with Dinah, as if he'd long ago memorized all the same moves. "It hurts so much to think we don't love each other, Lea."

She could have said the same back. Except it didn't hurt. Like crushing those ants when she was a kid, an impulse that should feel cruel but had felt like nothing at all. She watched his hands weave old, familiar games. "Do you want to use those?" she asked quietly.

"What?"

"Tie me up."

He dropped the ties and shook his head. "So forcing you is the only way you'll make love with me?" She hadn't meant it that way, but she didn't correct him. She knelt down, unbuttoned her shirt. "Stop it," he muttered, but it sounded like a moan.

He wouldn't touch her, even after she'd removed all of her clothes, so she picked up the ties and crawled across the floor. At the narrow end of the sofa table, she lay on her back, feet facing him. Bound one wrist to a skinny table leg; he'd have to tie the other, if that's what he wanted. She stared up at the blank white ceiling and drew a breath.

Jay gave a harsh, tattered grunt she'd never heard, or maybe she just couldn't remember what his arousal sounded like. She shut her eyes.

⁞

When she opened her eyes, he was untying her gently. He helped her to sit up. Stroked her hair. Murmured loving words she couldn't hear. She rubbed her wrists.

"Did I hurt you?" he asked quietly.

She met his gaze, loving now, and hopeful. Telling him "no" would heal this marriage. But she took too long to answer. By the time she spoke, he'd turned away from her, eyes glistening.

The doorbell jangled, startling them both, and whatever he might have said to her next was lost. He jumped and yanked his pants up. "What the hell?"

Lea grabbed her sweater from the sofa and pulled it on. She couldn't be seen from the front door, but she felt eyes on her anyway, catching her nude, huddled on the floor littered with fake animals, spilled whiskey, naughty toys, tubes with fake, glittery hearts. Somewhere by the pizza box a buzzing sound nagged. "It's the cops."

"You called the cops?"

Lea remembered that Jay had tossed the vibrator across the room. That was the buzz. He hadn't turned it off. "Ages ago." He didn't move. The doorbell twanged again. Now he looked tense, worried, even. About what they'd just done, she thought. Like he was feeling eyes on him too. "On the *trespasser*, Jay. They're late."

Jay went to the door and she crawled to the pizza box, found the wand, clicked it silent.

8

It was past two when the Centennial Farms trespass resurfaced in the queue. Nowak met Rilke at the address in question. Rilke recognized the winding drive as leading to the same house that had been burgled a few months back. Lightning was striking the same fearful place twice for the meek young mother who'd hovered a half-step behind her husband while Rilke took the burglary report. At the time, Mrs. Johnson had interjected salient facts into her husband's long-winded description. She'd been the one to discover the theft. She'd come home so harried by her busy day she hadn't noticed the jamb to the second front door had been kicked to pieces, hadn't noticed the splintered wood all over her second foyer, the flat screen yanked from the wall of the den, the digital cameras and cash and microwave, all missing. She'd set to putting away the groceries in the second refrigerator in the basement, when a dread had seized her.

She swore she'd heard breathing behind the furnace.

Then Mr. Johnson had cut in to describe how his wife had climbed the basement stairs wielding a bat to discover, at last, the splinters of wood, the missing television, the ransacked den. She'd fled the house to make calls, husband first, 911 next. *I was in the house for twenty minutes before I noticed,* she'd interrupted again. She'd repeated this several times already, meeting Rilke's even gaze as if seeking his opinion. He'd assessed her then. She was poised but not bossy-confident the way suburban spoileds could be. The burglary incident had scared her, badly, which was to say the ghostly breath behind the furnace was all about a prior incident that had scared her badly *first*. He'd given her a brief it-happens nod, which raised a pleasant, pretty smile, put down at once by her husband's asking when he could get a copy of the report for their insurance claim. Rilke hadn't liked the man's attitude. He told him curtly when to expect it. Broke the news that there had been a string of incidents lately. Kids, he explained, hit the small rural communities and drive down to Ohio to sell the stuff quick. Might as well put in for replacement cost, buy new, save receipts. The man nodded, knowing it all, of course. Deep scars fantailed Johnson's cheek, trophies from a bad accident, or a bad fight. The man's nose was kinked and swollen at the bridge, wrenched by an old break. Either the guy was too tough for his own good, or too weak.

Mrs. J. had looked horrified. *But we have the serial numbers.*

I can take that information down, ma'am, he'd told her. Just in case we flag the items.

We always record serial numbers, she'd repeated as if this was highly responsible behavior bound to influence the course of justice.

"I've dealt with these folks before," Rilke told Nowak now. He rang the bell. No answer. Light seeped through a side window, the type of dim glow probably left on while the household slept. The porch light was switched off too. Some emergency. Rilke glanced at Nowak, who rolled his eyes at the possibility that this was a crap call. The development was pure crap, all right. The private roads lacked adequate lighting. The only illumination besides porch lights, useless pinpricks since the houses stood an acre apart, flooded from the up-lights pointed at the *Centennial Farms* sign at the subdivision's entrance. The streets were saddled with dumb names eulogizing the Rilke farm. *Centennial Farms Drive. Silk Lane. Cornhusk Drive* was the one Rilke couldn't believe, as if anyone would want a street address that memorialized the part of the corn folks found most annoying. Caroline had been upset when Mutti sold the land, but Rilke had approved. The sale was finalized before Papa's memorial arrangements, so Mutti must have had her move planned the entire time the old man was wasting away. Brain tumor. Might have been the PBB, or the cell phone tower down the road, or effing gamma rays, who knew, but if this was one of the delayed health effects that used to scare the crap out of Rilke as a kid, he should never have worried. The tumor made Papa a sweetheart in his final months. Who knew, maybe he'd even ok'd the sale in his final lucid moments. After one hundred years in the same family, no one was left to farm if Rilke himself wasn't going to take it over. Which he'd made clear he wasn't.

The Johnson residence here, situated directly across Scipio Road from the farmhouse, wasn't bad, a mini-manse with none of the fake bays and cobblestone detailing slathered on the other homes. Solid siding job, cape-gray paint with sharp white trim, not the barn-red and white some owners chose. Rilke tweaked the bell again.

"No sign of a trespass," Nowak said, pointing out the obvious. He was a good guy, a bit nosy sometimes, which he'd been since high school. More Julia's friend than Rilke's in those days, and he was good looking, too, tall, square-shouldered, abundant hair and generous smile, quick with a joke at appropriate moments. Rilke never understood why Julia didn't go for Nowak in the early days, and she'd never said much about that, except that she'd fallen in love with *him*, of course, forever from the first, one of those beautiful things she used to say to him, and mean, with all her heart.

Just as Rilke was suggesting they forget it, the porch light blazed on, and the door screeched open. The painful whine of unoiled hinges matched the annoyance in the man of the house's expression as he stepped outside and almost slammed the door on his wife. She grimaced and caught the door with her flat hand. She stepped out of the house, shut the door quietly, and crowded her husband's back as if she were hiding behind a rock. She was wearing a shapeless cable sweater, its color as dull as her frightened pallor.

"My wife called 911 hours ago." Johnson's impatience grated. The quasi-military garb—bloused slacks, black combat boots—was just what a guy like Johnson would hope looked bad-ass. But the civilian shirt peeping under a black coat, a silly, too-bright blue, sure undermined the tough guy image.

Mrs. J. nodded a wide-eyed confirmation at Rilke. She recognized him at once.

"Sorry for the delay," Nowak said mildly. "You reported a trespass?"

Mrs. J. said, "No, he stayed outside." Mr. J. laid a hand on his wife's arm. Rilke took out his notebook. "On the second porch," she continued. "The whole time." She indicated the walk that wrapped around the home's south corner and led to the door that had been kicked down, Rilke recalled, during the burglary. "Anyway, he *couldn't* get in. We were robbed last year." She met Rilke's eyes, a *do-you-remember?* check. He nodded a brief verification. There it was, the pretty smile, raised and dropped as quickly as a peek under a pot's lid. "We replaced the door with a real solid one after the old one was, ah, ruined. Small windows. Extra-thick glass," she added, as if that were the ticket to complete security. She'd never understand that door quality was completely irrelevant. The jamb was the way in. Shoddy modern-day quality made door-hanging like fastening iron chains to toothpicks. Nowadays jambs were manufactured in pieces small enough to ship, then glued together at the seams. Not fashioned from one solid piece the way they used to be. Easily breached by any weakling sporting a steel-toed boot or a crowbar. Which was why Rilke had replaced all the jambs in the house on Peach with his own hand-crafted ones.

"So where is the individual?" Nowak dusted his tone with just enough impatience to keep her information relevant.

Johnson said, "He took off." Rilke noted the defensive clenching of the jaw, the rigid posture. The man's scars popped from his skin, jagged in the raw porch light. More recent injuries than they'd first appeared, or the type to heal poorly.

Rilke looked at Mrs. J. "Did you see him leave?"

"I…I went to get a blanket. He was gone when I returned." Tremors in her soft voice, as if Rilke were going to scold her because the creep booked it and saved everyone some hassle.

"So no vandalism or attempt at entry." Rilke ran an assessing gaze over the home, jotted down some notes.

Mrs. J.—Lea, he remembered then from the prior incident report— scuffed her felt house shoes on the porch's blue stone pavers, real high-end stuff. She must be cold, dressed as insubstantially as she was. Johnson made no move to warm his wife.

"Can you give us a description?"

Lea raised her eyes to Rilke's. Nondescript, no color to them at all. Braced to remain calm. A bit defiant, which he liked. "A young man. Very tall. Broad build. He looked threatening, yes." She swallowed and hugged her arms. "At first."

"Adolescent? Twenties?"

"Hard to tell. He was…big." Johnson was quick with the details. "Well dressed, which was odd. Blue blazer, like schoolkids might wear. Starched shirt."

Some threat. Rilke glanced at Lea. He was startled to see her watching him as if he'd voiced his sarcasm. "Sounds like a prank," he told her.

"On us?"

He almost laughed. "Kids haze their buddies by dumping them in the middle of nowhere." Rilke recalled Homer Nixon's innocent act and regretted not ticketing the boy.

Nowak said, "We'll keep an eye out. Call in if you see him."

"After a couple of hours?" Johnson asked, and even Nowak didn't appreciate the snarky tone. "What if he *had* broken in? Would you guys prioritize us then?"

Nowak let it slide. Rilke wanted to engage the guy a bit, work out the long night's irksome residue left by other folks' bad behavior, and the unforeseen and undeserved disasters befalling innocent parties, including Julia's so-called engagement. But he followed Nowak's cool lead: "Give a call if you see the guy again."

"He was cold."

Lea was watching Rilke pocket his notes as though he shouldn't yet be preparing to leave. "Excuse me?"

"He was shivering."

"Okay."

Her soft voice pitched higher, as if he'd offered her an inadequate response. "He wasn't wearing any pants. He must have been freezing. That's why I went for the blanket."

"It's okay, ma'am." Nowak's brisk wrap-it-up tone usually cut off the wandering narrative. "These kids will ditch each other with barely a stitch on. We'll look for him."

Lea ignored him. "I had just figured out how to do it." Her husband gave the get-inside tug on her arm. "I'd lay the blanket on this porch, then lock up tight again. Then go to the second door and call to him through the glass. Tell him to go around to get it." She hesitated, waiting for Rilke's approval. He gave her impassivity. She glanced at her husband, who shook his head.

"Why are we responsible for his comfort?" he said to her quietly.

"It's just so cold out." She seemed about to cry.

Rilke gave her the nod. "You did the right thing. Never open the door." Since he didn't raise the brief, pretty smile, he knew she heard his line as bullshit. She was thinking he thought that she'd done the wrong thing entirely by not handing the poor kid a blanket, a sandwich, a phone to call home. "Where were you, Mr. Johnson?"

"Excuse me?"

"Your wife made the call. Your wife had the blanket operation all worked out there."

Johnson flushed. Not a good fit with the angry ledge of brow and tight-lipped disapproval. Made him look uneasy, in fact.

"I was outside. I'm volunteering for the cull."

"Ah." Explained the get-up; Rilke should have put two and two together. "Working with Gary?"

Lea flinched. If she'd shot the shit at all with Starkey, Rilke didn't blame her. Johnson folded his arms. "Yep."

"Bobby Gold was supposed to be out here."

Johnson looked as if he didn't appreciate Rilke having his facts straight on who was supposed to be where. "I think Gary put Bob at the back of the subdivision. By the cornfield."

Nowak said, "So you didn't see the trespasser?"

"I saw him. My wife called me. Difference was, I showed up."

"Jay." Lea touched his sleeve. A shut-up tap.

"When you showed up, what happened then?" Rilke asked mildly.

"The guy took off."

Sure he did. Now Lea looked uneasy. Biting her lip, misery etched in the soft arena around her mouth. Rilke pulled out his card and handed it to her, not to Mister Showed Up. "Call if you see him. You did the right thing, taking care of yourself."

Again she flashed him the *you're bullshitting* glance. If the glistening at the corners of her eyes were tears, he wouldn't have noticed, nor paid it any mind. He meant it; the only right and reasonable response to any uncertain situation was to protect yourself, and to hell with anyone on the other side of any door.

She took the card, of course. Tucked it right in her jeans pocket.

9

Rilke's cell rang early after his shift, when he was finishing up the night's paperwork, mouth mothballed by dehydrating sleepiness and lack of caffeine. He'd grown accustomed to days too quickly. He glanced at the ID, saw it was Caroline. Thought about ignoring it, in light of Nowak nearby; not enough coffee; the agitation from the long night he couldn't shake. His state of mind was not exactly conducive to a chat with his sister. Not that their discussions ever constituted idle chitchat. The Rilkes never placed non-productive calls. None of that just-checking-in, love-you round robin that circulated in some families. Like Nowak, routinely fielding friendly what's-up calls from his blood and intimates. Rilke's years of managing Papa's drunken, erratic moods had crafted goal-oriented communications with his mother and sister. Trim the bullshit, get to the point, avoid trouble unless trouble *was* the goal of the moment. Julia's phone habits had confirmed his view. Brisk, brief, always down to business. The management of fathers had earned him and Julia perfect compatibility as lovers, efficient and attuned to each other in public, ferociously loving in private. Ferocity that did tend to get out of control every once in a while, but always, always mended. Julia herself had explained their union to him matter-of-factly, during one of his intense moments of marvel over how much he loved her, how it couldn't be true that she could love him back. It's destiny, she'd said, how the damaged find each other. *Know* each other, by instinct.

That's why The Marriage worked, she'd said. Always had. Always would.

Rilke let the phone vibrate helplessly on his desk. He wished Caroline's habit weren't to call at this particular time of day. She'd likely just put her kids on the bus and was settled down with a fourth cup of coffee, primed to scold him by a hectic morning with those mighty fine but unruly sons, whom she allowed to walk all over her, which then gave her rights to complain about everything else under the sun but them.

Finally he answered. Caroline jumped all over his grudging greeting. "Julia called me." Scold, and that superiority, already coloring her voice.

He felt a pressure at his temples, an overwhelming urge for the coffee that would screw up his daytime sleep. He walked over to the office pot and poured a cup, understanding then that he craved movement more than caffeine. He set the cup down. "Okay."

"She's real upset this time."

"Right, Carol. Julia and I are talking. I'll give a call over, myself."

"I wouldn't do that. In fact, I'd stay away from her entirely."

"That's not the way Julia and I do things." He paused to slow his response down. "If she's bothering you, I can run interference."

"You've got things backward, Paul."

Just like Caroline to toss a sudden jab of nonsense that put him off his concentration. "I have no idea what that means."

"You shouldn't be dropping in on Julia." She slurped her coffee. "Although what you did to Julia last night hardly qualifies as dropping in."

"We got a complaint."

"Right. She told me all about the stunt you pulled, sneaking in like you did. Now look, I *know* you, Paul." Her stock preamble to a good scolding. Rilke stretched his legs, considered hanging up, *poof.*

"I know this is a difficult time and all that," she continued into his silence. The sun glinted through the front office's wide pane. The parking lot asphalt was dusted smoke-white. Same flat, colorless surface as Maple Road beyond the lot, as the low rise of a hill across the road, as the pale sky. Rilke shielded his eyes and turned away. "I also know you wouldn't hurt Julia or whoever she's sleeping with or any living soul, ever, period. And Julia knows it too. So no one's going to tiptoe around you, if that's what you're after. Okay?"

She sounded more like a got-her-shit-together sister lecturing the loser brother rather than what she really was, the immature little sister who hadn't forged a shred of adult competence despite Rilke's care of her growing up. Well, it wasn't his fault she'd wrecked everything she'd ever managed to have. Although Rilke had offered plenty of times to chip in for some classes at the community college, she insisted on raising her rambunctious tykes alone on a Target cashier's salary. In Saginaw, not exactly the lifestyle upgrade from the family farm she liked to project, and if it weren't for Rilke's check every month, her house of cards would be down around those boys of hers pretty quick.

He drew a breath. "Julia and I are working on things," he said quietly.

She paused to assess his tone. "Should I be worried about you, Paul?"

"Feel free."

"Okay. Here's what I think, although you don't care what I think. I'm heading down there later today. We need to hash out what's going on with you. Your behavior has been totally off since Papa died."

"I haven't been off since Papa died."

"Keep telling yourself that. Look, we both have feelings about Mutti staying with him until the bitter end. I get it. And you know what else I get? If you're sad he's gone, if you're grieving, that's fine. It's normal. You might be sadder than if he'd been a sweetheart, since any hope of having a loving, fully sober and present father someday is gone now."

Jesus Christ. Was everyone in therapy? "At least they stayed married. Stuck by each other."

"That's not always the goal, Paul."

"You'd know, Carol."

She drew a breath, held it fast like she'd been pulled under despite diligently treading water. "I forgive you for that remark."

His heat rose. "Papa was old school. Parents today are softies. Mostly because kids don't have to learn to labor like we did. Fine, but that wasn't how it was for us. Or Papa."

Caroline sighed. "Parents are softies today because they had parents like Papa." Which was one of her more self-aware commentaries, even if she didn't know she was talking about her own willingness to let her boys do anything they pleased. "But none of what went on in our family is Julia's fault. Let her go, okay?"

"Thanks for checking in, Caroline." He snapped the phone shut and walked back to his desk slowly to shake off the shroud of her voice, the downright offensive psychological crap. She didn't know him or anything else because his whole life he'd protected her from knowledge. Meaning the truth of some past matters, and he'd been glad to do it. Not that his conscientiousness had cultivated much influence on her adult behaviors. Plus who was she to weigh in about what was Julia's fault? Had Jules ever owned up to her hollering at him over every little thing and even pushing him around when she felt like it? Had she happened to mention her bogus engagement to a kid half her age and weight?

Calling his sister on him was a low blow, not that Jules or Caroline would see it as anything other than seeking support from the sisterhood. Carol would no doubt call Mutti next, which did constitute a dread.

Well, if Julia could marshal her forces, so could Rilke. Although he knew this move was bound to bring down more trouble, Rilke punched in Starkey's number and gave the man his cell. Told him to call any time of the day or night and he'd be happy to check on Jules. Waited patiently for the man to scribble the number on some tattered notepad. Repeated the number twice until Gary got it down right.

The office phone jangled as Rilke was snapping his cell shut, and of course it was too early for Cheryl to be on hand to answer. Nowak was returning from the men's. "You take it," Rilke told him.

"Looks like you're already in phone mode, buddy." Nowak settled back into his chair.

Rilke sighed and walked to the front desk to answer the call.

He recognized her voice at once before she supplied her name and street address, as if she were mistaking the office for 911, or maybe she assumed the law wouldn't talk to her without foreknowledge of her whereabouts and legitimacy.

"What can I do for you, ma'am?"

"I wondered. I mean, there was an intruder on our property last night and I was calling to see if he'd been, well, recovered."

"Recovered?"

"Found." She cleared her throat. "Apprehended."

"No, ma'am. No reports of that." He teased her with an unresponsive tone. But nervous Lea Johnson didn't deserve flak for his irritation with his sister's nonsense, so he recalibrated his response. "I took that call last night. I can assure you there's nothing to worry about with that situation, Mrs. Johnson. Likely the young man is already home." In truth, Rilke and Nowak had scouted around for the boy after leaving the Johnson home last night. No sign of the kid, which was no surprise at all. He'd never seen a situation where these dumb pranks led to anything worse than dehydration and one mild case of frostbite.

"It's silly, I know. Being so concerned."

"What's the nature of the concern here?" Nowak leaned over his desk with his phone pressed to his cheek. The morning check-in with his family. Anne would be herding the kids to school, asking Nowak about his night. Nowak's replies would be noncommittal, calm, projecting a night like any other, a night she shouldn't worry about. Rilke's tick of jealousy was another facet of blame he could lay at Jules's heartless outlook on The Marriage.

"That he'll…" Mrs. Johnson's breath lapsed, then quickened. Nowak snapped his phone shut. "That he'll come back."

Mired in fear, he assessed. He canvassed the details of the burglary some months back, but couldn't recall anything remarkable about the incident. "That's unlikely, Mrs. Johnson. As I explained, the whole business was a hazing prank."

"I know. I feel stupid calling like this. But it took so long for you to come. I mean, if he had been a threat—"

"We can't guarantee a response, ma'am. We used to have fifteen personnel in this office. Currently we're down to five officers." He let that radical imbalance sink in, the need to prioritize, the exhaustion of resources at the very height of the population surge caused by developments just like the one she was occupying.

Again a quickening of breath, probably to gather the resolve the timid had to muster for conversations such as this one. Out the front window a line of cars was backed up at the Maple stoplight. A film of salt on every vehicle washed the usual busy mix of color to chalk.

"Anyway." Mrs. J. cleared her throat. "I know I'm being stupid. But I can't help but think it's connected to the burglary. We were robbed. This was a few months ago. Are you that officer? The one from last night, and…from before?"

He confirmed it.

"It's probably silly to think that maybe, well, that we're being targeted." She hesitated. "I mean, is that possible?"

"Possible?" Rilke said. Nowak rose and swung through the office double doors to beat a retreat to the parking lot. The traffic had cleared on Maple. Cheryl's sedan was pulling into the space next to Nowak's Dodge Ram. Watching Nowak flash Cheryl the effortless charm and slide into his truck on his way to bed made Rilke yawn, which Mrs. J. undoubtedly heard.

"A connection." Her tone softened in deference to her perception of his fatigue and impatience, which he decided he liked. He was drawn to the rhythm of her voice, modulating to match his response, and he remembered her brief smile, which he could raise with a nod. "What if he comes back?"

"You have to understand the rationale of the intruder." He projected the professional stance automatically in response to her confusing effect on him, instead of telling her the truth, which was to quit her irrational concern over a boy who had gone home where he belonged after learning a lesson or two about the punks he chose to hang out with. "He wants to invade your home because *he* is the weak one. *He* is outside social norms." He paused. It was his set speech, one he'd worked out to pump women up in the self-defense classes he'd conducted back when he needed the income to fix up the Peach house. To compensate for their physical disadvantage, women had to learn to hold the advantage in the psychological aspect of defense. This was the particular pep talk he'd developed as the cornerstone of their protection. "And there's something else you have to understand, Mrs. Johnson. You are already proven strong *because* of your ability to operate within social norms. You have your home. You have your family. Only the strong achieve these norms and are able to maintain them, ah, long term." He paused another beat to let it all sink in. "No matter his physical attributes, the intruder is weak. You are powerful. Once you understand this basic dynamic at play between you, you can come at him."

"Come at him?"

"With all you've got."

A pause filled with her soft breathing. "You make it sound like a relationship."

"Excuse me?"

"The dynamic at play. Between *us*."

The front door squealed. Cheryl clicked in on heels and wakeful energy, flushed from the cold, ready to begin the day he was just ending. He muted his voice. "The dangerous encounter does constitute a relationship. A connection, if you will. One you didn't ask for. One you never wanted. But if you can accept that dynamic, you can prevail over it, Lea."

10

When Lea awoke that morning, she was still dressed in the clothes she'd worn all night. The morning sun was high enough to crest the shades half drawn from the windows' tops. When she showed up late for work, Abel would assume she was upset, squeamish, avoiding what had to be done. He'd never buy the excuse that she'd overslept, just as she never failed to see through the excuses he used to wall off his private life. Jay never woke her up, so she had no right to be angry that he hadn't this morning, either. But after what had happened between them last night, the mess he always made of his side of the bed felt like a trashing. The quilt draped on the carpet, the sheets twisted and rumpled, the pillows lumpy and pinched like he'd punched them.

After the cops had *taken their statement* for their *complaint* with the deadpan authority she loathed and distrusted, she and Jay cleaned up the den in silence, locked the sharpshooter rifle in the gun safe, and went to bed together as if the cops' neutral language had turned the night ordinary. They hadn't thought of not sharing a bed. She thought he'd looked relieved when she stashed the Party Girl bag in her nightstand, as if keeping the stuff meant she wasn't hurt, or angry, that they might even use these tools again, although Lea only meant to hide them from the kids. During the night, Lea had a vague sensation of huddling close, like they used to do. Backs pressed together as if, safe in sleep, their bodies interpreted what had happened between them as lovemaking. Since their troubles, he'd taken to slipping downstairs before her, leaving his side of the bed looking beaten and dazed. But if they had slept close last night, it wouldn't have killed him to linger this morning, not leave her to face him over stale coffee and soggy cereal, play the harrowing game of pretend, perfected for the sake of the kids.

Jay had left the bedroom door open when he went downstairs. From the kitchen drifted the sounds of an ordinary morning. Bunny's bright chatter, a bowl clattering on the countertop, Jay's deep murmur and steady tread. Kurt and Bunny must be late to school. Her irritation that

Jay hadn't managed the kids' schedules faded when Kurt asked if they could find the fawn today. School wasn't in session, she remembered; it was a teacher in-service day, one of the many pop-up cancellations that used to send Lea scrambling for childcare until Jay stayed home. She couldn't hear Jay's reply about the fawn, but it must have been some gentle version of *no*. Kurt's *why?* floated up the stairs, not whiny, merely curious. Bunny was complaining that something hurt. Lea couldn't make out what. She heard Jay suggest she eat applesauce instead. Bunny must have a loose tooth. No wonder she was putting her hands in her mouth so much lately.

By the time Lea padded downstairs, Jay had cleaned the kitchen. The island streaked with polish and the empty, gleaming sink disoriented her. Even the orange mac-and-cheese splotches on the floor had vanished. She couldn't remember the last time he'd washed a dish. His spotlessness felt like preparation.

Or erasure. *Leave no trace*, isn't that what they said?

Kurt and Bunny swung their legs from the barstools, dressed and ready. For what? Jay had pulled Bunny's long hair into her favorite twisty ponytail. She was worrying the loose tooth. The pearly bud poked between her lips like a puppy's fang.

Kurt's cowlick was slicked down. A perfect part sliced a fine white line through his scalp. Lea ran her finger along the little ravine, still moist from a comb dipped in water. "Where's Daddy?"

Bunny said, "Getting the pliers."

"Is the faucet broken?" The faucet looked fine. Better than it ever had, in fact. Jay had buffed the chrome to a sharp glow.

"*No*, Momma. My tooth is."

Kurt said, "Dad's going to pull it."

"You don't use pliers, sweetie."

"Dad does."

Kurt's factual tone made Lea wonder just how he'd lost the teeth she hadn't yanked herself. Lea ripped a paper towel from the roll near the fridge, now neatly replaced on the spindle instead of roaming the kitchen. She rested a hand on Bunny's shoulder. "Mommy doesn't. Open up, honey."

Bunny opened her mouth obediently. Sunlight streamed through the kitchen window, hot on her angry red gums. She'd managed to lodge her incisor sideways. Lea fought back a tide of nausea. Pulling teeth made her queasy, but mothering made mild violence a duty. She wrapped two fingers in the towel and gripped the tooth. Bunny gagged. Lea squeezed, hard, but it wouldn't budge. A strong root anchored the tooth fast. Blood soaked the towel. Tears clung to the lashes of Bunny's clamped eyes, but her brave girl never made a sound. Lea swallowed hard. "It's not ready to come out, honey."

Bunny opened her eyes. "It has to be ready. It *hurts*."

Kurt took her hand. "There, there. We *will* get it out."

Blood and spittle dappled Bunny's lips. Lea wiped her up and moved to the sink to wash her hands. The pass door to the garage slammed. Jay walked in, holding a pair of needle-nose pliers. "Good morning." His frosty tone sounded like she was being told, not greeted. He wouldn't look at her, either.

She flung his stony act back at him. "What do you think you're doing with those?"

"Performing surgery. Right, Bun?" Jay twirled Bunny's pigtail.

Bunny looked up at him. Relief and adoration lit her expression. "Mommy couldn't get it out. She said it wasn't ready."

"Mommy doesn't have the magic tool, does she." Jay did look at Lea then.

"You can't put that in her mouth," Lea said.

"My dad did it all the time." Lea tried to picture Jay's sweet, gentle dad performing this extraction with his gentle accountant's hands. "Open up," Jay told Bunny.

Bunny parted her lips. Kurt leaned over to peer in, his own mouth ajar. Lea moved to the island's edge. "Stop it, Jay. I'll take her to the dentist."

"Now, Daddy, *now*," Bunny gurgled.

"You don't go to the dentist for a loose tooth." Jay wiped the pliers on his sleeve, as if his shirt were antiseptic wash. "Here comes the alligator to pull that nasty tooth right out!" He scissored the needle nose open and shut a few times, *click clack*. Bunny giggled.

The clinking of his belt buckle right above her mouth the night before flooded back to Lea. What was wrong with him, treating their daughter this way? "I mean it," she warned. "Stop."

"Hurry *up*."

Bunny drummed the side of the island with her stocking feet. Jay stuck the pliers in her mouth and pulled on her ponytail to tip her head. Her pale, thin neck strained backward.

Lea flew around the island and grabbed his hand. The pliers knocked against Bunny's front teeth. "Ow, Momma!"

Jay let go of Bunny's hair. "Jesus, Lea. What's wrong with you?"

"What's wrong with *you?*" Lea stroked Bunny's hair and stared at him staring at her like *she* was the problem.

Bunny shook her head free. "Don't, Momma."

Kurt let go of his sister's hand. "You two shouldn't argue."

Jay placed the pliers on the counter behind him, near the sink. "Sorry, kiddo. That tooth isn't quite ready to come out."

Lea fetched a clean towel from the drawer and dumped in some ice from the maker. Bunny wailed, "But it *hurts.*"

"Bite on this, sweetheart." Lea wound the ice up tight in the towel.

Jay looked at Kurt. "Take your sister upstairs to play."

Kurt and Bunny slid off the barstools. Lea's stomach knotted at their tidy, mute obedience. She handed the towel to Bunny. "I'll be up in a minute to help."

"I don't need any help." Bunny stuck the towel in her mouth. The kids trudged down the hall and up the stairs.

Jay cleared the kids' bowls and turned his back on her. Lea said, "What's going on, Jay?"

Jay rinsed the bowls and stacked them neatly in the sink. "Are you having an affair?"

"Why are you bringing that up again?"

"We shouldn't have to make love…that way." Jay spoke so quietly she nearly missed what he was saying. "An affair, that might…make sense of it. What we did." Even the truth, *no*, struck her as caving to irrationality. She was silent. The faucet was dripping. Jay reached over to tighten the handle. "Your question wasn't really a question, was it? Are you?"

From upstairs, synthesizers squealed a kid's tune. A thump shook the ceiling. Only the kids, jumping on Bunny's bed to their music, but the familiar sounds of their favorite game startled Lea. "Am I what?"

"Having an affair."

"Is that really a question?"

"Okay. Here's a question. Ever since I got hurt, you've been treating me like I'm the one you're afraid of." He brushed past her. His passing scraped her skin, her throat, her insides, although he hadn't touched her.

"So what's the question?" she asked quietly.

He looked at her. "Truth is, Lea, I'm afraid of you."

After he'd climbed the stairs, Lea didn't know how long she stood gripping the stool Bunny had been perched on. The faucet dripped steadily, even though Jay had tightened the handle. The thumping above her, the faint sassy whine of the synthesizer, thrummed her arms and legs as though the kids were tugging on every part of her they could reach. Through the ceiling Jay's muffled voice asked Bunny and Kurt if he could play too. Lea flew to the sink, heaving. Nothing came up but bile.

The pliers lay near her hand. Shaking, she twisted the tap aerator with the plier's nose. The housing unthreaded smoothly. She thrust a finger into the washer and cleaned, rinsed, and reset it in the housing. She tightened the tap, ran the faucet, shut the water off, and waited. Above her the thumping shook the ceiling now. Jay was horsing around, jumping on the bed to make the kids fly off, hit the floor giggling, pile back on for more. Even when this game hurt, they climbed back. Jay would have to be the one to stop this game. The kids would play forever if he let them.

She stared at the faucet, the pliers forgotten in her hand. No drips. The next time she noticed water oozing from the tap, would he deny that the faucet was leaking?

11

The tiff with Jay didn't make her late to the lab after all. The postdocs were already down in husbandry, and Abel was attending a departmental meeting. She'd have some time to herself to recover, avoid questions about the puffiness around her eyes. Pulling the husbandry records and marking subjects for culling felt methodical, a soothing detachment she chalked up to exhaustion. After a half hour she pushed the records aside. She'd intended to get through the morning before calling the sheriff's office to ask after the boy. She'd convinced herself that waiting a bit would give the cops plenty of time to make sure the kid was home safe. She didn't want to admit that the delay was to avoid looking too anxious, even guilty, over his fate.

Kate entered the lab carrying a parcel as Lea was looking up the sheriff's office number. She turned away as Kate set the package on her desk. She took the hint and walked to the scope.

Lea pushed the parcel away and dialed. She didn't recognize at once the voice that answered her, the impatient beat that met her offering of personal stats, as if she were still dealing with the 911 dispatcher who'd told her flatly that their complaint had been *prioritized*. She flubbed, called the boy an *intruder*, not a trespasser. Asked if he'd been *recovered*, fumbled the correction, *found*.

I was on the scene last night.

She couldn't say why the formality felt accusatory. Must be the big cop, with his stoic judgments. She'd been surprised that the same men she'd seen at the county office had been the ones to take their complaint, the good-looking one with the military build, and the big one with the delicate features. The good-looking one hadn't changed at all, but the big cop's weight loss in the months since they'd been robbed had unnerved her. Under his coat, his gut and hips had shriveled. His cheeks had hollowed as if the flesh had been suctioned. She'd never seen him without his ridiculous teardrop shades. In the weak porch light, she'd met the flat blue surface of his gaze.

The voice asked, briskly, the nature of the concern.

That he'll come back.

The words popped out, made no sense in the context of the night's events. *Nothing to worry about. Just a prank. As I explained.*

She stared blankly at the package on her desk. Plain brown paper, twine gathered in a perfect square knot at the top. The cop's remarkable eyes hadn't been unkind, she recalled. The bellicose way he'd stood too close to Jay meant he was unaware that he'd all but shrunk since the last time she'd seen him. The oncomice she used to cultivate for Jeffers's research, too, never saw the tumors until the growth stole their fat and destroyed the involuntary functions: balance, digestion, sleep. Then the mice craned their necks to stare, incredulous that they'd missed the rude, hairless bump they'd been bearing for weeks. Some, the strongest, and the most desperate, believed the alien bulb could be gnawed through, destroyed, and then they'd get well again. They gnawed right up to the moment of their death.

The cop yawned, suddenly and loudly, into the phone, and Lea started. Why had the cop reminded her of the mice she'd engineered so long ago? Anyway, his shift must have ended with the dawn. She and the trespasser were nothing but the pesky flotsam of his long night, but at the moment her usual distrust of the police had abandoned her. She didn't want him to hang up on her.

How do I stop him from coming in?

She was crying and biting her lip so the cop wouldn't hear her weeping. Behind her, Kate moved to the refrigerator near the door, ready for her next subject. The cop's voice was warm now as if she'd reached for his hand. He spoke to her of the rationale of the intruder, the desire to invade, the violation of social norms. He explained how the cops couldn't help, how they'd never be able to help. He blamed a lack of resources for leaving her unprotected. He was prepping her for the next time. In his line of work, he'd expect there would always be a next time, one he couldn't prevent.

He told her *the intruder is weak.*

Then he told her *you are strong.*

Then he identified the dynamic at play between the attacker and victim, *us*, one that lasted forever.

She wiped her eyes. *You make it sound like a relationship*, she told him.

The cop waited for her response as if she hadn't said a thing.

She forced herself to disconnect after he kept up the silence, and then worried she'd hung up just as he was about to answer her.

Kate had returned to the scope. "Hey, are you okay?" Her voice was tentative. Lea wondered how much she'd heard.

"Fine. A bit tired. We had a guy show up on our stoop last night. I was just checking on the, *uh,* status." To collect herself, she studied the parcel. "Where did this come from?"

"It was delivered for you."

No shipping company labels, no name on the package. Flat, a box the size of an egg skillet. For security reasons the lab didn't accept un-marked packages. "You shouldn't have accepted this. Who brought it?"

"I'm sorry. It was a woman." Kate spoke as if women were a safe bet. "She was looking for a name on the building directory outside. On my way in, I asked if I could help her find someone. She said she was a friend of yours but didn't want to disturb you. I thought it was okay to bring this up."

But Lea had stopped listening after Kate's mention of a woman. She held the package by the perfect knot, snipped the tweedy threads with scissors, tried to remember the last time she'd seen a package wrapped with twine. Inside an old Bering cigar box, wrapped in white tissue, was a glass vial capped with a rubber stopper filled to the rim with cherry-bright blood. Shaking, Lea set it aside carefully to unwrap the flat object nested underneath. She tore at the tissue, not careful now. A foam tray thudded on the desk. After all these years the bones were still perfect. Bleached white, a meticulous design of scissoring limbs and curved ribcage. From the spiny feet's angle Lea saw that this frog wasn't hers. She'd dissected Dinah's too. She'd arranged the legs differently so at a glance they could tell them apart. In eighth grade Dinah was already squeamish about mutilating animals, no matter if they were long dead and reeking of formaldehyde and born anyway for the purpose of study.

But for the first time in school Lea had felt drawn to explore. Running the scalpel down the belly, peeling back and pinning the skin, seeing that the organs were arranged exactly where she'd learned they would be, sparked a rush she'd later come to realize was joy. Dissection proved that a death could be useful. Some harm in the world could make sense, or was even for the good.

Dinah, with her flair for deception, had received an A for that unit.

Mr. Bartley had given Lea a B-plus although she'd prepared both frogs exactly the same.

Lea flipped the tray over to confront Dinah's handwriting, the off-hand scrawl, the fat-bellied a's, the l's loose loops, as if the lines existed only to corral the generous empty spaces.

"What's that?" Kate was leaning over her shoulder. Lea flipped the tray right side up.

"Don't you remember middle school biology?" Remarkable how she tamed the bobble in her voice. But the tray was shaking. Lea set it on the desk, folded her hands in her lap.

"I never dissected a frog," Kate said. "That's cool."

"I had to bleach the bones." Tears scarred her vision. "The teacher was very particular. It was a big part of the grade." Of course Dinah wouldn't record Bartley's name. She never made a record of any man. She didn't understand anything about Lea's feelings for Bartley. The teacher was the first man she'd trusted after *him*. By then Dinah knew about Lea's attack, of course, although Lea had held back many details from the story she'd told after she'd shot at *him* with the Mauser. She didn't think Dinah would understand being trapped and doing what you were told without putting up a fight. Had she been afraid that Dinah would say what she always said in answer to Lea's surrenders? *You're so provincial, Lea.* Or maybe she'd been afraid Dinah would make an altogether different statement. *You were raped.* A confirmation of one thing, a denial of another, neither of which felt like the truth.

"Well, you did a good job." Something in Lea's voice must have betrayed her. Kate's tone sounded like she was bucking Lea up with cheerful approval. "I didn't dissect anything until high school. The fetal pig. So gross. But some part of me must have liked it. Because here I am."

Lea wiped her eyes with the back of her hand. "What did she look like?" She almost added, *now.*

"Who?"

"The woman who gave you this."

"About my height, long dark hair. Kind of heavy. Your age. But pretty. She had her head covered. One of those bright cashmere scarves with the paisley squiggles."

Your age. But pretty. "What did she say?"

"Not much. Just asked me to put this in your hand. She said it like that. *Put this in her hand.* She had a funny way of speaking. Kind of formal. I asked if she wanted to see you. But she said no. I'm sorry. I didn't think about security or anything."

"It's okay." But the thought of Dinah so close to the lab was terrifying. "Did you see where she went?"

"No. God, is that *blood?*" Kate snatched up the vial, popped the stopper. The blood wobbled. A fake cherry scent trickled into the air. Kate pressed a finger to the filmy surface. "Jello. Weird. Some sense of humor, right?"

Lea didn't know how to answer any question about what Dinah might find funny.

The last time Lea had seen Dinah was in Moynagh's, a bar near the Worcester campus, over whiskey shots. Several days had passed since Dinah had broken into the Jeffers lab with Lea's ID. Lea was promptly fired, a consequence Dinah may not have yet known in the tumultuous wake of her organization's so-called rescue operation. Lea was determined to be civil. The damage done, Lea simply wanted to know why Dinah had used her when she could have found another way. For resourceful Dinah, there was always another way. She must have wanted to send Lea a message, teach her a lesson, pay her back, but for what? When Lea asked point-blank and Dinah started in about animal rights and liberation, it dawned on Lea that she and her goons had not taken the animals to a safe house, as she'd assumed, but had released them in a field on the outskirts of town.

Freed them to die.

She'd said it aloud, sick on whiskey and the thought of her hobbled subjects, some with advanced-stage tumors, abandoned to the wild. When Dinah looked at her with incredulity, *you know you have killed them already*, Lea's old feelings about Bartley flooded back.

How could you fuck him?

Dinah had laughed. *What are you talking about?*

You know. When Bartley was transferred to teach advanced placement biology their senior year of high school, Lea had caught Dinah and Bartley alone together after school when she'd dropped by his classroom to ask him for help with her homework. There they were, the lights off, standing close near his desk, avoiding the windows. Bartley's back was to her but she could see enough of Dinah's hands on him and the tilted curve of her head to guess they were kissing. She ran away down the hall. After that, Bartley's attention to Lea's scientific aptitude blinked out. She saw less and less of Dinah after school. They were having an affair, she was sure of it. Dinah ruined her belief that men who could be trusted around girls did exist.

Lea had never confronted Dinah about stealing her favorite teacher from her. She couldn't bear suffering through Dinah's denials, or worse yet, a smug confirmation that would show off how worldly she was in comparison to naïve little Lea. But that day in the bar, Dinah knew what she meant, all right. Lea didn't have to say his name out loud for Dinah to shake her head and smile. *The man. Not the animals. This is what upsets you,* as if putting the man first was—finally!—a show of gumption on Lea's part.

Lea had always felt stupid for blowing up that day over Bartley, who hadn't mattered at all, or so Lea had trained herself to believe.

Kate handed Lea the vial and returned to the scope. Lea wrapped the tray up carefully and pulled the cigar box toward her. She saw the note there, not folded, the loose handwriting plainly in sight. She wondered how she'd missed it.

Release them.

"Release" was the name of Dinah's organization. But the note could be a warning, a call to arms, even. Lea stood up and hurried to the atrium walkway. Dinah couldn't access this lab, no way. In the years since the Jeffers stunt and similar high-profile rescues, security had become every lab's top priority. But Lea had to view any word from Dinah as a threat. Through the lobby's glass doors, the morning smokers, wrapped in heavy coats and scarves against the cold, huddled outside around the cobbled cement urn. Lea studied them, and then surveyed the sidewalk, nearly empty at this time of the day. She took the elevator down to the basement and scouted the corridors around husbandry. Asked the techs she met if they'd spotted anyone *unauthorized,* felt an absurd impulse to laugh at the word. Then a conviction seized her, that Dinah was embedded with the smokers, wrapped in a bright scarf, willing Lea to see her.

Lea took the elevator up to the lobby, emerged into the great glass atrium feeling foolish and angry that Dinah would, as always, drag Lea out into the open. Of course she wouldn't still be on the street. It was all a tease, the bones, the Jello, the words that were half-command, half-taunt. *Release them.* Had nothing changed in all this time?

Nothing had. There Dinah stood on the other side of the glass, breath frosting from her bright scarf, loitering patiently in the cold as if Lea were only running a few minutes late.

In the café at the north end of the atrium lobby Dinah sat silently across from Lea sipping a watery herbal tea. The young man behind the counter knew Lea, asked her if she wanted the usual, didn't identify what the usual was. Lea had refused to order. Making the statement about not breaking bread with a traitor.

"You didn't need the theatrics. Those old bones."

For all her reserve Lea never could stand silence between them. That much hadn't changed. Dinah knew the Jello and the note would make her furious. Lea needed to be picked at like a stubborn scab. You had to carve chinks in her so real feelings could seep in.

But she had thought Lea would like the bones. "The frog wasn't for show."

"You put Kate in a terrible position."

"Kate?"

"The young woman you used. Our postdoc."

"She approached me, Lea. She offered to take it." No need to point out how lax security could be, how easy it was to insinuate oneself into any place. Dinah took another inventory. Lea looked happy, she'd bloomed. Her fragility had toughened, she had meat on her bones, she smiled now. She'd grinned all right when she caught sight of Dinah through the glass, grinned with joy until she swallowed her reaction, adopted the shock and caution she assumed Dinah would expect from her. The flash of brightness made Dinah wonder if she was no longer so angry, which would defeat the purpose of this visit.

"*Release them?* Is that some kind of threat?"

"That was the theatrical part."

"Some stunt. If you know where I work, you also know where I live. I'm in the phone book."

"This is a beautiful space." Dinah set down her cup, looked over Lea's shoulder at the glass lobby. The brittle late-autumn sun reflected harshly on the directory kiosk and chrome waste cans. Tables crowded the atrium for some sort of event. The place crawled with workers and some antsy-looking suits impatient with set-up duty. Lea flinched when a metal chair leg scraped the tile. The squeal shrieked into the atrium and lingered in the vast ceiling. "So much light and air. Is your lab also so open, so *humane*?"

"Why wouldn't you just call me, Dinah?"

"Do you remember how gloomy your Worcester lab was? Those wicked basement cages. I remember thinking you could feel comfortable there, hidden away. But it was a stepping stone after all, or else things have changed a lot. Your people are letting the light in now."

"Trying to destroy useful research isn't exactly letting the light in."

"There is still something in you that doesn't want to find an alternative to killing, Lea."

"I shouldn't have let you in the building." Lea glanced at the security guard standing at the building's entrance. When she admitted Dinah into the lobby, the guard had swept them both with a practiced scrutiny as tactile as a pat-down.

Dinah set aside the tea; it was too hot, too gingered, laced with a bitter aftertaste as if the root's bark had snuck in with the tea leaves. Behind Lea, a tech wrestled a microphone with a testy stand. The tripod splayed out no matter how he positioned it. "What's the occasion?" Dinah nodded at the tables, draped in flowing white skirts. The banquet crew was setting out water glasses, rims pressed to the cloth.

"Did you appear out of thin air to ask me about the afternoon's entertainment?"

Furious—but curiosity lurked behind the exasperation. Lea would never kick her out until she found out the reason for dumping those bones on her. For Dinah, *why* was the least interesting part of any endeavor. *Why* got in the way of taking action. "I'm just asking, Lea, that's all, it looks so fancy."

"It's a hospital benefit for Alzheimer's treatments our lab developed. Care to donate?"

"You must be proud of that work."

"Cut the crap. What are you doing here?"

"You know I am up to no good, Lea. Why not alert the guard?"

There it was, a chink. Lea almost smiled. "Would Nan have any reason to kick you out?"

"Are you curious to find out?"

Lea's smile flattened. "Something wrong with your tea?"

"Not a thing." Dinah smiled. "It's delicious."

Lea sat back, waited her out. Dinah kept the silence. Lea would be expecting her to ask about her life, a husband, children, her mother and father; but then again, she would not be surprised to know that Dinah, in her sneaky and resourceful way, had learned the ages of her children, the dates her parents had passed, and exactly when she'd joined Abel after staying out of the field for years.

The tech succeeded in propping the microphone on the portable stage and murmured *check*. He motioned to an elderly woman waiting at the riser, elegantly dressed in a black pantsuit with a maroon scarf knotted at her throat. A man in a military dress uniform escorted her tenderly to the microphone. The tables gleamed with silverware and china. Dinah felt the heat rise under the coat she'd kept on to hide her weight gain from Lea. She looked old and fat, felt old and fat. Lea hadn't changed. Timid Lea, not tentative at all when it came to killing.

It was like that, Dinah had found. Those committed to cruel acts preserved their zeal and devotion, while those out to stop them burned out. But the moral was never ascendant, this was natural law. Being moral must mean going against some instinct of self-preservation, she'd decided. Dinah arranged her expression—keep it neutral, keep it friendly. The heat of the day Lea had shot at that asshole came back. Who would think she of all people would lug a gun, an ancient war trophy, clear across town to take a wild shot at *him*?

More unbelievable still, provincial little Lea had missed the guy by just a hair.

The elderly woman grasped the microphone's round head. A shrill electronic screech grated and faded. The military man—her son?—removed her hand gently. She looked at him, her lack of recognition translating as utter fear. "What am I supposed to say?" Her amplified plea echoed through the atrium.

"I'm going to speak, remember?" The soldier-son meant to soothe, but his low voice rumbled harshly through the speakers. "You don't have to say anything."

The dress rehearsal wasn't going very well, then. Lea was struggling to ignore the booming voices, her effort so familiar in her tensing shoulders, the way she had of shrinking into herself. Dinah felt the old urge to take her hand, *pull* her out into the open. "So Alzheimer's is your life's work now?"

"Was." Lea was still watching the soldier-son pat his mother on the shoulder. "I'm studying the fear response now."

"Why?"

"We're researching PTSD treatments."

"But what am I supposed to say?" the woman cried into the microphone.

"You're doing great, just great." The man nudged her away from the mic stand. The feedback whined, fell silent. Lea clenched her hands on the table.

Dinah said, "Fear is suppressed anger."

Lea unclasped her hands. "It's the other way around, actually. But there's a bit more to it than glib psychology."

Her voice was calm, Lea-prim, but she wasn't even attempting to hide her fury, never could. But Dinah hadn't sought her out to pick at the same old scabs. No more underground, no more useless symbolic rescues, no more bullshit.

"You want another shot, Lea?"

"I don't drink anymore."

Dinah laughed. "At *him*."

Lea froze, her expression blank, her old habit of slipping away.

12

Summer, 1982

"Wait until he's away from the bees."

Lea pressed the trigger. Dinah's hand flew from the barrel. The kick knocked Lea backward into the grass. The gun landed above her head. The silence baffled her, as if the gun's report had sucked in all the air. Instead of him she faced a white, empty sky.

"Jesus." Dinah was pulling on her dress strap. "That was really *close*."

Lea rolled to a crouch and peeked over the grass. He was facing the field, rooted fast, the bees swarming like sunspots on his white suit and gloves. Lea scrambled for the gun as he turned to replace the frame, carefully dusted the bees from his suit as if picking at stray threads. Lea stood up. He started toward the girls. When he reached the wildflower patch she raised the gun. But she hadn't chambered the next round. Perhaps he knew she wasn't ready to shoot because his stride was calm, measured.

Dinah tugged her. "Heaven's sake. Come *on*."

Then they were running through the field, the gun bumping behind, the grass slapping at their legs. They flew across the dirt road, hightailed it down the nowhere street, plunged into the tall cornstalks at the concrete's end. Lea didn't realize she was crying until Dinah stopped, grabbed her by the shoulders and forced her head to her knees until she caught her breath. The dizziness cleared. The sudden brightness showed Lea she'd been running in darkness, on the verge of passing out.

She looked up. Dinah's dark hair was damp with sweat. She was grinning at how easy it was to get away with anything. "You okay?"

Lea nodded.

"What did he *do*?"

There might come a time, later, not to lie. "He stole something."

"You must really want it back." Dinah helped her straighten up. "Did you see how fast he ran? That stupid hat just *flew* off him."

Lea frowned. "He wasn't running away."

"He sure was. All the way to Detroit." Dinah picked up the Mauser's barrel. "Come on."

"But he was coming *after* us."

"Are you kidding? The only way he'll come around you again is to give your shit *back*. Let's go."

The trek through the cornstalks dimmed the white glare, bringing the day back into focus: the dry crumpled stalks, Dinah's ivory skin against her dark tangled hair. The gunstock's smooth, soothing grain, the sharp bite of husks scraping her legs. She'd be cut up from this adventure like a regular girl playing in an ordinary summer. She tugged on the gun to get Dinah's attention.

"Hey. What do you care about bees?"

"What's that mean?"

"How are bees different from butterflies?"

Dinah stopped and planted her feet in the dirt. Music drifted faintly through the stalks. "Jack & Diane," the chords tinny, as if they were being squeezed out of a transistor radio. "Did you bump your head or something?" She stared at Lea a moment and then grinned. "Oh. That. You too?"

"Me too what?"

"Fooled you, that's what." She turned on her heel. "That butterfly was already dead."

"Oh." A trick. No wonder she'd been so cool about pulling off those wings. Lea felt disappointment when she should have felt relief. "Why'd you do it, then?"

"Not the first time I've been the new girl. I know how not to get hassled. Let them think you'll do anything. But don't think I'd ever hurt even a butterfly." The music stopped midway through the song. Dinah stopped at the edge of the field and grinned at Lea's expression. In the clearing beyond the stalks, boys' voices were hollering and whooping. "You're so *provincial*, Lea. You've got guts, though, I'll say that for you." She stepped into the clearing.

Lea hung back. "I don't want to."

Dinah turned, stretched out her hand. "This is your alibi. Come *on*."

Dinah pulled Lea out of the stalks. Under a maple tree on the far side of a grassy clearing, three boys stood in a loose circle around a skinny, wolfish shepherd dog. The dog's legs shook like wobbling stilts. Light-brown fur tufted the dog's bony ankles. A dented soup can glittered on the summer-singed grass. Two of the boys appeared to be arguing over a rifle. Probably about who was going to take the next shot. The boys were high school age, old enough to be plinking with .22 rifles, anyway. Lea didn't recognize any of them. She didn't think Dinah did either, which didn't stop her from dropping Lea's hand and walking right up to join their circle. Lea hung back at the cornfield's edge, clutching the Mauser's stock.

"Your dog looks sick. What's wrong with him?" The skinny dog had been staring at Lea pleadingly but snarled when Dinah approached. She reached out calmly and scratched behind his ears. Bits of fur rubbed away under her touch. The coarse hairs scattered on the thin breeze. The dog whined and snapped at Dinah's hand. She snatched her fingers away in time and stood fast, unafraid or pretending to be.

The tallest boy, a blond with a kinked scowl and bright eyes, kicked the dog's ribs. The dog howled and shrank from Dinah as if she'd been the one to cuff him. "Nothing's wrong with that dog." He pushed past Dinah to gape at the Mauser. The other boys followed him. The one with wire-rimmed spectacles had a white capture-the-flag scrap of cloth stuck in his jeans pocket. The other was bulky in the chest and arms, farmer's muscle. A farmer's sun-soaked squint crinkled his blue eyes. He wore a plaid flannel work shirt. Sweat soaked his collar, except it wasn't so hot here in the clearing. The maple leaves shielded the sun, and the breeze held a shaving of coolness. Anyway, Lea felt the cold.

"That's a German rifle." The blond boy was standing right in front of Lea but didn't look at her. Her sundress had slipped low, barely covering her chest. Dinah had broken the strap she'd tugged on to get Lea to run from *him*. Lea hadn't noticed her bared skin until the boy failed to.

"It's not real." Spectacles reached out to touch the stock. Lea stepped back.

"It's real, you dodo," the blond said.

The farmer said, "Bet it doesn't shoot." But he wasn't looking at the gun, like the others. His gaze halted on Lea's broken strap, then her bare shoulder. When he saw that she'd noticed, his jaw tightened, and he looked away.

Dinah stroked the dog's trembling back. It tolerated her touch, too afraid now, or tired, to snap at her. "I'll take that bet."

The boys all looked back at her as if seeing her for the first time. The blond looked twice. Ran his gaze down her dark, wind-tangled hair, tight black tank top, long, pale legs. Dinah tossed a careless sexy look back at him like a casual volley.

"If you're so eager to bet, you know it shoots." The blond turned back to Lea. Absorbed the gun with the same hunger he'd absorbed Dinah.

"Bet you my friend can blow away your crummy tin can with one shot."

Lea flushed, shook her head at Dinah. Dinah gave her the same look she'd lobbed at the blond. A natural flirt, but Dinah knew how to pick the right targets, not become the target.

"No way." The blond studied Lea, dismissed her pinched, plain face. Too timid to say a word to a pack of boys, let alone shoot a big gun. "She doesn't even know how to *hold* it."

"*She* knows exactly how to hold it. Wanna bet?"

"What do you wanna bet?"

The farmer noticed Lea's flush, her nervous, shifting feet. "Leave her alone, Rick."

"This old dog." Dinah's grin was sheer brightness, but Lea, watching her play with the dog's ears and thinking of the butterfly trick, saw the hard, muscular curl along her clenched jaw.

Spectacles curled a fist around the white kerchief in his pocket. "That's a stupid bet."

"Whoever owns this dog is too stupid to take care of it right."

Rick walked over to Dinah, shadowed her with his chest. Dinah's glassy, teasing smile never wavered.

After a moment, he relaxed. "You got a dog of your own to bet?"

For a moment Lea expected Dinah to offer up the Mauser, but she must have sensed that her command over Lea's alibi did not include the gun. "I've got a pack of my stepdad's Hav-A-Tampa Jewels and some SweeTARTS."

"I don't smoke and I'm pronated to cavities." Rick laid a hand on the dog's head. The shepherd's knees locked like tree knots. The farmer and Spectacles joined him to ring Dinah.

Being penned didn't seem to bother her in the least. "Prone."

"What?"

"*Prone* to cavities." Dinah slipped her hand into her shorts pocket.

Popped a SweetTART in her mouth and rolled it on her tongue. "Plenty left for you boys." Flecks of spittle gleamed on her lips.

Rick stretched a finger to her bare wrist and tickled his way up her arm. *Itsy bitsy spider*, Lea thought he whispered. She lodged two fingers in her mouth, whistled sharply. From an oak on the other edge of the clearing, a bird trilled back. A sparrow, probably.

Startled, the boys turned to Lea. Dinah and the dog didn't flinch.

Lea took the wicked dirty cards from her sundress pocket and held the packet out.

Rick mumbled something rude and crossed the clearing to take the packet. The boys crowded around as Rick unwrapped the tissue and flipped through the cards. Lea expected them to laugh at Hitler squished between the naked woman's breasts, or grabbing the woman's tit by accident, but the boys didn't so much as crack a smile. Although he drank up the images greedily, a flush crept up Spectacles's neck. The farmer glanced at Lea uneasily, stepped away, and refused to look more at the cards. Rick looked back at Dinah, who teetered on tiptoe behind him to see what Lea had dragged out *now*. She answered his questioning look with an arched brow, *see what I mean about her?*

Behind glinting lenses, Spectacles took in Lea's flat chest, her broken dress strap. He was thinking she wasn't at all like any of the grown women being defiled in the pictures, but what would he say if he found out that she was exactly like them?

Rick wrapped up the cards and stuck them in his back pocket. "You're on," he said.

Lea stepped to the middle of the clearing.

Dinah swiped up the soup can from the grass, looked around for a stump or a rock to place it. "Where do you set this thing up?"

Rick grinned. "Right on this old dog's back."

The farmer crossed his arms. "Come on, Rick. Leave them alone."

Rick cuffed the dog and held out his hand. Dinah handed over the can without a word. A low whine rumbled from the dog's throat when the soup can touched its back. Bleak black eyes fastened on Dinah.

"No way did you shoot that can off this dog's back."

Dinah glanced at Lea uneasily. So Dinah had nerves after all, she wasn't always the cool girl. Well, good. Lea chambered the round calmly. The bullet's click rang out like she'd already plinked the tin.

"Guess you'll have to take my word for it," Rick said.

Lea guessed by the dog's terrified lockjaw that the boys had shot at it, all right. Controlling that much fear took training. "Take it off," she said. Too loudly. Her voice echoed off the trees.

Rick grinned. "The mute speaks. Bet's off, then."

"I'd watch that mouth, sport." Dinah stepped away from the dog, her bright eyes on Lea.

Lea hefted the Mauser. Still a struggle, but it pillowed in her shoulder's hollow naturally. "Take it the fuck off or I'll shoot *you.*"

Spectacles made for the oak tree. The farmer laughed at him. "What the hell, man. She can't even hold it up all the way." He looked at Lea, his blue eyes glittery and distant, like the bauble of sky she'd seen after her first shot missed the man she wanted to kill with all her heart. "You don't have to do it. It's okay."

Lea aimed at the empty space beyond Rick's elbow. The recoil knocked her flat again. This time the rifle's boom filled her ears. How had silence swallowed this roar when she'd shot at *him?* The boys yelped and scattered. *Crap.* If her father was home by now, the noise would bring him on the run. Not for a moment did she think that she'd actually hit anything. In her fantastical view of guns, a wild aim was destined to miss.

Dinah's loose, tangled hair blotted out the sun. She was grinning. Even with the sun behind her, Lea could see every detail of her wide smile and shining eyes. Dinah admiring, the one joy of that summer. But her hands were shaking as she grabbed the gun and helped Lea to her feet.

The dog was still frozen in place. The light brown rings around its ankles quivered. The can was nowhere in sight, and the boys had fled to the clearing's edge. Spectacles looked ready to dive headfirst into the withered cornstalks.

"Jesus Christ." Rick's voice cracked.

"You're an asshole," the farmer said. He was staring at the poor shivering dog, so Lea couldn't tell if he meant Rick or her. She deserved it. Her own knees were shaking as badly as the dog's. What if she had hit this dog, or Rick? Or Dinah? What was wrong with her that her impulse to shoot had obliterated any thought of harm?

Dinah turned to Rick. "Pay up, twinkle toes."

"Shit." Rick left the oak tree's cover and came out into the clearing. "My dad's gonna go ballistic."

"What does your dad care?" The farmer's watchful, wondering gaze shifted to Lea.

"Socks is his fucking dog."

"Socks is a fucking cat's name, man."

"Fuck you. I didn't name it." Rick snapped his fingers. The dog limped over to him. Rick pinched the scruff and hauled Socks over to Dinah. "All yours, beautiful, but don't your crazy-ass friend here deserve the prize?"

Dinah clapped the Mauser barrel back and forth between her hands. The dog leaned into her leg. "Seeing you shit-scared was her prize, sport."

Rick shook his head and dug out the wicked dirty postcards to give back to Lea.

"Keep them," she said and turned on her heel.

"That's one sick girl." As Lea slipped into the cornfield, one of them, probably Spectacles, spoke just loudly enough for her to hear. Maybe by accident, maybe on purpose.

Dinah caught up with her a few rows from where Lea would take the path through the trees back home. Lea heard the Mauser bumping along before she saw Dinah burst through the stalks. Socks trotted at her bare feet.

"Well, Lea, there's more to you than meets the eye." Dinah gave her back the gun. "Guess you have your alibi. They'll never forget that as long as they live. Where'd you get those crazy pictures, anyway?"

Now that she had the Mauser back, Lea's one thought was to get it up on the pegs before her father came home. The stalk's shadows splashed the dirt furrows in front of her and the air was dense with pent-up heat, but it could be any time of day. Lea had no sense at all of how long it had been since she stumbled upon Dinah on her way to *him*.

Socks came up to her and sniffed her hand. Lea touched his bony head. Tears rose to her eyes, the sting so unfamiliar she couldn't for a moment understand why the dog's ruff was blurry. Nothing had made her cry since before *him*. "You shouldn't have made me do that."

Dinah grinned. "Now that's an interesting perspective on the day's events."

But you did, she wanted to say. Lea was nothing but a joke to those boys, right up until the moment she fired. They didn't believe the old war gun would actually fire, or that a girl like Lea could shoot it. But

Dinah had known and let her go through with it. She'd even risked her own hide. Lea might just as easily have shot her by accident as Rick or that poor dog.

Dinah was studying Lea with her already familiar appraisal, half teasing, half sizing up, *you're so provincial, Lea.* "That asshole's right. You won this dog fair and square. But you don't look like you have it in you to take care of him." Her voice dropped, softened. "Do you, Lea? Maybe you need to be taken care of too."

Socks shook his head and loped back to Dinah. Lea wiped her eyes. Suddenly she wanted to be rid of this girl. She wished she'd told her to fuck off in the first place. Sharing *him* with Dinah was dangerous. So was Dinah's fake sympathy, stupid and mean after egging her on to shoot. "I don't want that scrawny old dog," she said coldly. "I already have a pet."

Dinah shrugged. "Good thing I want him, then. See you around. Be careful."

Dinah slipped through the stalks, Socks at her heel, feathery tail swaying in an almost-wag. She was heading east, back toward *him.* For the first time Lea wondered where Dinah lived. Perhaps he was her neighbor and Dinah hadn't said a word about it, which would be her typical sleight of hand, wouldn't it?

After she'd hefted the Mauser back on the pegs and returned the chair to the dining set, Lea grabbed a fistful of the rabbit food her father had bought. She ran to the pen behind the garage. The bunny was lying on its side. A slow shudder rippled through its slack belly as if it had been popped. Lea had mistaken for fat these empty rolls of fur. How could she have missed this wasting, the dull varnish on the eyes? She bit off a piece from a pellet, held the chip close to the mouth. The rabbit nudged her hand gratefully before nibbling the food.

Maybe it was fattening that bunny right back up or maybe it was her clumsy potshot after all, but when her father called later that summer as promised, *he* refused to come to dinner, continued to refuse any invitation.

Even after she'd grown to hate her with all her heart, a part of Lea would always love Dinah for giving her that alibi.

13

2008

From that summer on, Dinah stuck to Lea, admiring her and teasing her, pulling her into the open. Their friendship had even survived Lea's suspicions about Bartley. But the Jeffers raid had proved she'd been out to use her, from the very day she'd baited Lea to be the one to shoot so Dinah could rescue that pathetic dog. She wasn't about to be used again. Lea had left Dinah sitting alone in the atrium and was now alone in the lab with the bones and the vial of fake blood. Anger at Dinah's manipulative choreography flooded her again, the rage only Dinah could prod from her. *You want another shot, Lea?* When she'd shot at *him*, she couldn't recall feeling much of anything. Nothing like the impulse she'd had to throttle Dinah as she sipped her tea calmly, like they were two old biddies catching up on a few inconsequential years.

He was the first thing Lea had checked before moving back to Michigan from Worcester. He moved away years ago, her still-clueless father had told her. His house had been razed for a new subdivision.

What happened to the bees? Her question popped out, as if the insects were what still mattered after all this time.

Her father hadn't remembered that his friend had kept bees.

At the time she'd convinced herself that his complete erasure was some justice, some safety. His return now was some kind of heartless, karmic taunt, another reminder of how incapable she was of healing herself, let alone helping her husband to heal. Had she sensed he'd come back, and that's why she'd thought of *him*, in Karla's bathroom? Or on the phone with that cop, when he'd made her see what happened with *him* as a relationship?

If he *had* returned, if this wasn't another of Dinah's games.

As she stared at the bones, something catastrophic was turning inside of her, a compulsion to call Dinah's bluff, their friendship's sadistic undertow Lea had both hated and craved and would never admit now that she'd missed. Firing that Mauser with Dinah staring at her in disbelief had been the best feeling, hell, the only feeling, she'd had after *him*. She'd fallen in love with that gun's kick. After her first shot, she was sure the recoil had dislocated her shoulder. She'd wondered if the German soldiers had all returned home with bad shoulders, if that was the reason American soldiers like her grandpa didn't use such guns. She didn't remember whether the kick had hurt on the second shot in the clearing. What she did recall was Dinah's surprise as she helped Lea to her feet, and then, the admiration she'd been quick to disguise. Lea had spent years trying to get her to look at her like that again.

Until the Jeffers raid.

Lea would always be an operation to Dinah, had been since the days Dinah had used her to earn her grades, steal her favorite teacher, destroy her career. *Fool me once* was the only rational response to Dinah's latest attempt to sandbag her.

Dinah had planned for them to meet at the commuter lot that afternoon on the edge of campus to take Lea to *him*, or so she claimed. Lea planned to let her stew right there in her car. She'd prove once and for all that Dinah couldn't just show up and drag Lea out into the open, not anymore.

Lea stuffed the bones and the vial into the Bering box and grabbed her purse. With the postdocs and Abel away at the benefit, Lea should slip down to husbandry alone, perform the cull in solitude, work quickly, efficiently, quietly, the way she'd been trained. Dinah would nurse such greedy satisfaction, that her offer had made Lea too sick to do what she had to do; but then Dinah would never know, would she, that Lea had left the lab in tears instead, clutching the cigar box as if she'd rescued these long-lost bones herself?

At home, she locked herself in the first-floor bathroom before Jay had a chance to ask what she was doing home in the middle of the day. His heavy knocking brought the kids on the run. A debate sprang up about what could be wrong with Mommy that had sent Lea to her knees, face in the bowl, wishing she could throw up her guts, her spine, her capillaries and cartilage, flush everything she was made of down to the sewers, hope that the offal that made up her heart flowed through pipes and drains and came out cleansed in faraway waters.

She heard Jay send the kids upstairs. She jiggled the toilet handle, splashed water on her face, and stepped out. Jay was in the den, pulling on his new black jacket. He didn't ask if she was all right. He barely looked at her at all.

She longed to tell him that Dinah had come back. Jay had considered Dinah's betrayal appalling when she'd told him the whole story. But Jay headed to the front door without speaking to her.

"Hey." She followed him into the foyer. "So we aren't going to talk to each other at all now?"

"I think we've said everything."

"I don't," she said quietly.

Jay almost smiled at her tone. "Guess that's your cross to bear. I'm going to the range."

"Guess shooting innocent things is your cross to bear."

Jay actually seemed to think about her retort, as if she were being sympathetic to this duty. "That's an interesting way to look at it. I used to think euthanizing animals for research was morally squishy, even though my wife made a living doing just that. But you always rationalized that your research does good in the world, and over time I came to agree. I guess I should thank you for showing me how humane cruelty can be. Under the right circumstances."

He slammed the front door. She walked back into the den. The room's cleanliness felt like a cover-up. Why hadn't she gone after him? She'd let things between them deteriorate to the point where he was using a word like *humane* as an accusation.

The Mauser's barrel poked out from one end of the throw, pointed at her ankles. She crossed to the hearth and scooped up the guns. She meant to check on the kids, but she could hear their voices float down the stairwell, happily occupied. It would take only a moment to store the guns where they belonged. She left the pass door ajar and crossed the garage to the window facing the driveway. Jay had bolted rows of metal shelves floor to ceiling along this wall to store tents and coolers and fishing rods they hoped to use again one day. The Mauser she would lock away with the shotgun in the safe, but Jay kept the Ruger out of reach on the top shelf, in its original case. Boxes of shot lined the wall on the next shelf over, left over from the grouse hunting and skeet shooting he used to enjoy up north, until having the kids kept them homebound. She searched for the Ruger's case but couldn't see it right away.

Outside the window a deer nibbled at the hedge near Centennial Farms Drive. Two fat crows, glossy feathers tinted bruise-blue, settled on the grass as if awaiting their turn. Lea set the Mauser and the Ruger on the worktable Jay had rigged from an old door and two sawhorses and looked around for a stepping stool. He'd recently tidied up out here, too, she saw. They parked the cars in the driveway to leave space for projects, so Lea only ventured out here to stuff a trash bag in the bin near the pass door. He'd always kept their previous home's garage spotless, but after the move here, he seemed to prefer disarray. Dust and fat, linty cobwebs had filled the corners and the garage door tracks. Toolboxes and wood scraps littered the walkways Jay had formed from subdividing the space with shelves and pegboard. The cedar planks of the chest he'd begun crafting before the attack had been scattered around the bandsaw as if he'd kicked the wood in frustration when he'd tried to finish.

Now the concrete floor and open rafters were swept clean. Even the grooves of the door track gleamed. A cedar plank rested on the bandsaw. The sugary odor of freshly cut cedar sweetened the air. Cans of stain stood stacked on the work table. The sample dot on the label was the color of an autumn maple leaf's earnest fire. She had no idea he'd resumed woodworking. That he'd chosen a stain meant he expected to finish the chest. She couldn't recall hearing the saw's grating chords. The only hobby she knew of were the visits to the shooting range or association meetings about the cull.

A roar from an unmuffled exhaust rumbled down Centennial Farms Drive. Lea glanced out the window. The pane was still streaked with cleaner, smelled faintly of lemons. The crows flew away, wings snapping like Jolly Rogers in a sharp breeze. She would remember thinking the birds' sudden flight, not the vehicle's racket, startled the deer, and that was why the animal bolted into the road right in front of the car. A burgundy sedan, speeding well above the drive's low limit, struck the deer with a wrenching thud Lea could hear through the window pane. The deer was knocked back to the spot it had just fled. The car sped toward Scipio, hung a left at the development's entrance without yielding at the stop sign.

Lea ran to hit the garage door opener.

The engine's roar faded down Scipio. Near the hedge the deer lay on its side, chest heaving. One leg lay twisted, mangled by the car's fender. When Lea's shadow blanketed its face, the eye staring up at her widened, bloated with panic and pain. The deer kicked its front legs out, struggled to stand up. The mangled leg flopped. Blood poured onto the grass. Lea watched the deer watch her. Wariness had scrubbed the panic from its eye, but not the searing pain.

Lea's hope waned, that she wouldn't be forced to do the humane thing. She hiked back to the garage. Just inside the open bay door, Kurt was tiptoe on the wobbly stepstool she'd been looking for, reaching for a bin up high on a shelf. "Honey, what are you doing?" Lea grabbed him by the waist and lifted him down.

"Getting the string."

Lea reached up for the bin he'd been seeking, full of twine and cord, bright blues and greens jumbled up with the usual plain brown. She handed the roll to him. "Where's your sister?"

"Upstairs. Thank you, Momma."

"Stay inside, 'kay?" She waited until he disappeared into the foyer before fetching the gun safe key from its hiding place in a toolbox and retrieving the 12 gauge. She stood on tiptoe to grab the box of ammo she thought was right and hurried down the drive before she lost her nerve. In her absence the deer had scrabbled to try to hide underneath the hedge. She'd torn up the grass but failed to move at all. The head was half-raised from the shredded grass. The black eye darted, bleak and wild.

She hadn't worked a gun's action since that summer's day with Dinah beside her, goading with her amused silence, but the jolt of the shotgun's break felt like muscle memory. She loaded with trembling hands, shouldered the gun, stepped back for better aim. Which shot would be most merciful? To the head? The chest? The heaving, swollen belly? The only euthanasia she'd ever practiced used a quick motion of her wrist, or a syringe, in a sterile environment.

The deer pawed the grass. The rear end quivered. The muscles under the skin twitched to get up, run away. The eye teared. Lea closed her eyes and pulled the trigger.

Because she'd never heard a deer make a sound, and this deer hadn't so much as whimpered in its wretched pain, she assumed the kill would be silent. The scream that rang out so closely mimicked a human cry of suffering that Lea retched. The legs flailed helplessly. The deer raised its head, screamed again. Shot peppered the fur's delicate velvet between the eyes. She'd thought she was loading a slug. But she'd grabbed bird-ing buckshot instead. How could she make such a mistake? It wasn't like she knew nothing about guns.

The deer fell silent. Lea moved out of its sight to relieve the deer from the terrifying sight of her. Perhaps it would die after all. But then it struggled, rasped that high-pitched scream. Lea stepped back. She'd have to run to the garage to fetch the proper slugs.

A man rounded the corner of the hedge. Lea started and clasped the gun to her chest. He was wearing a canvas jacket, jeans, boots. His brown hair ruffled in the cold breeze. She didn't know him, he wasn't a neighbor. But he knew her, it seemed. He reached for her gun. She drew away. He hesitated, and then rummaged in his pocket. But then she recognized the big cop's blue, distant gaze and didn't need to see his badge.

She surrendered the shotgun, thinking, in her panic, that he would arrest her.

<h1 style="text-align:center">14</h1>

After Rilke hung up with the timid and elusive Mrs. J., the usual pleasantries with Cheryl on how tired he looked after the busy night distracted him from puzzling over what he viewed as her extreme concern for the kid, which he'd already guessed was cover for some other fear which might or might not have had basis in the reality of living all snug and well off in a ritzy subdivision. Hard to tell with the sheltered types what exactly they were afraid of, although Rilke might suggest, if Mrs. J. ever gave him the chance, that his money was on her own husband as a safe bet for unpredictable behavior. Something about the guy struck Rilke as off, in the two seconds he'd spent thinking about the man at all.

The chitchat with Cheryl also prevented any serious examination of the confounding hold Mrs. J.'s—Lea's—questions had kindled in him. If he'd thought it through, he would have dismissed any notion of attraction. The woman merely had a nice, soft, very sweet phone voice, which any man would appreciate hearing after a long and exhausting night; but then again here he was, denying to Cheryl that he was tired at all lest the banter start about how nights suck and days are great and how could Rilke actually want the graveyard shift when, with his seniority, all he had to do was ask for a more humane schedule?

But Cheryl gave such tiresome comments a swerve and released him into the brittle sunshine with a wave and a smile. Rilke drove to the cottage brooding over how Julia could act as if Rilke had no idea The Marriage was over, when they'd never even discussed divorce. Maybe her rash engagement was another of her ruthless gambits to humble him.

When Rilke reached the cottage, he undressed and slipped under Omi's fluffy quilt without drawing the blackout shades. Not that he dreaded falling asleep in a manufactured night, but sometimes worrying about the trouble with Jules caused him to be sick. Nothing felt more lonely than throwing up in the pitch dark.

A shotgun shot rattled Rilke awake before he even knew he'd been asleep.

A peaceful silence followed. He might have questioned hearing anything at all were it not for the quiet's pressurized feel. Likely some over-eager resident of Centennial Farms was indulging some illegal target practice for the open hunt after the sharpshooter phase. Offering cash for kills was bound to prompt rash behaviors, he'd pointed out to the county plenty of times. He dressed quickly, pulled on a Carhartt jacket and boots, and slipped his badge and weapon into a pocket.

He moved briskly around the cottage to the narrow dirt path he'd beaten through the abandoned corn rows. The path wound through the brush-filled ravine he used to traverse to fetch Papa home from working the southwest field. That gully now bordered the Johnson yard. After scanning the front lawn for trouble, Rilke hiked along Scipio's shoulder to Centennial Farms Drive. His breath pooled in the air. These endless cold days had whitewashed the resolute green from the pines fronting the Johnson property. It was late morning, so traffic was diminished until the midday school buses and part-timers rushing home to their kids streamed into the sub. All quiet on the road. He hiked up Farms Drive a bit and scanned the clipped yards, pocked with dejected patches of frost-bitten brown. Such was the impeccable maintenance of these homes that the blighted grass looked freshly and evenly mowed.

Rilke rounded the curve that wound to the Johnson drive, flanked by shrubs and a decorative rock garden meant to conceal the drainage pipe under the drive. The smothering silence was downright unnatural. Old Peach Tree Court had a contingent of stay-at-homes, so there were always little tykes roaming bravely on tricycles or miniature motorized cars, listening for the sound of their mothers hollering commands at them to *watch out, stay close, come in.* This emptiness felt like folks couldn't wait to get out of the sub for the day.

He was about to turn back, doubting that he'd heard anything at all, when the unmistakable clench of a shotgun barrel being broken and loaded rang clear. He scanned again and determined that the sound came from behind a neat hedge of evergreens along the street-side boundary of the Johnsons' backyard. A shot rang out. The sharp report raised a shrill animal squall. Rilke took off at a run but slowed on the approach. The profound silence had descended again.

He slipped around the hedge to confront the confounding visual of slight Lea Johnson bundled in the bulky cable-knit sweater, clutching a 12-gauge to her chest and looking up at him, eyes wide with pure fear.

Before her lay a fat-bellied doe, stuffed with her last feeding, struggling on the brown grass. The animal's hooves dug into the dirt with agonized spasms as she eyed Rilke with the frantic absorption of the final terror she would ever see. One of her legs was shattered. Rilke ran a gaze over the tawny fur stippled with buckshot like pellets of black acne. Buckshot peppered the taut white fur between her eyes.

Lea spoke up, voice wobbly, but with that bit of defiance. "I didn't know what to do."

She hadn't engaged the shotgun's safety. He reached over to take it from her because if she didn't know enough to load the gun with a slug instead of bird shot to perform a mercy killing, Lord knew what else she didn't understand about firearms. He was put off guard when she clutched the gun to her chest, and then he understood. It happened a lot that folks didn't recognize him out of uniform. He gave her a nod and showed her the badge. Her expression cleared. Recognition, relief, then wariness mixed up in there.

She surrendered the shotgun. He pulled the safety and put the gun out of her reach. The doe scrabbled at the frosted grass, raised a shoulder as if to leap up and flee, screamed its thin, helpless shriek. Lea shrank into her lumpy sweater like she was hoping to fold herself out of sight. Her quick breath sent wisps of vapor his way. Rilke looked down at the panicked glaze filming the deer's eyes. He wanted to bundle the animal in his jacket.

He withdrew his service revolver and fired.

The doe's dying shudder raised a gut wrench. Rilke brought a hand to his mouth, suppressed a gag, and wiped a frosty slough of spittle from his lips. Lea watched his hand tremble.

"Mom!"

A stout brown-haired boy ran up, clutching the hand of a towheaded, pretty little girl. Dangling loosely in the boy's other hand was a coal-colored pistol with a nicely buffed walnut stock. A vintage Ruger MKI target, the sport cousin to the old Ruger handgun Papa had given Rilke to clear the coyotes from the traps. Nicely preserved and maintained, the steel scrubbed to a cobalt sheen, maybe a rust patch on the barrel. Not loaded. The boy noted Rilke's attention to his weapon and stared at him flatly. His soft fist tightened defensively around the stock. Rilke was still clutching his own weapon. He returned it to his pocket.

The girl stared at the carcass with solemn fascination. She was gripping a pair of needle-nose pliers in her chubby fist. "Is the deer asleep?" Her voice was her mother's, wobbly but clear, a bit defiant.

"I told you to stay in the house." Lea's steely, brusque tone was not one Rilke would imagine she'd use on children. She took the boy's gun. "I'm disappointed in you. I told you never to touch this gun again."

"I heard shooting," the boy said defensively.

"When will she wake up, Momma?" The girl stuck her thumb in her mouth. Rilke's nausea bubbled at her steadfast gaze on the doe.

"We're not supposed to be alone in the house," the boy reminded Lea.

"We're supposed to wear our coats outside," the little girl reminded him.

"There wasn't *time*. Anyway Momma forgot hers too."

Lea swore under her breath, another personality facet Rilke wouldn't have expected of her. She took the pliers from the little girl. "These are sharp. I don't want you touching them again, young lady."

"Oops, Momma." The little girl popped the thumb from her mouth like a cork. "We don't say bad words in this house."

"We're *outside* this house." The boy planted his feet in the defensive posture.

Lea rested a hand on his shoulder. "All right, that's enough. I'm very disappointed in the *both* of you. Take your sister inside." The boy turned and marched his sister dutifully up the driveway. Lea watched them go. When she was sure they were out of earshot, she swore again. Profanity didn't suit her at all. The lightweight, ineffectual curses, and the steely stance she'd taken with her kids, were making him sick all over again.

"They won't leave this thing alone." Lea raised the pistol as if surrendering it to Rilke. She offered no explanation for the pliers, which she stuck in her back pocket hastily as if hiding them.

Rilke swallowed against a bitter taste on the rise. "It's a natural fascination for a boy his age."

"I wish I could get him to understand how dangerous it is." She looked at him uneasily. Did she think he was going to cite her? "I meant, the attraction to guns. But this one isn't dangerous. It's just a target pistol."

"Yes," he managed. "I had one like it. As a boy."

Lea looked at him as if he'd just issued a warning, not a reassurance. She tucked the Ruger under her sweater and the gray tee beneath into the waistband of her jeans. Rilke absorbed the view of her navel's puckered basin. "I didn't mean for them to see," she said. "They love deer." She stared at him. He expected her to register unease at the killing, and her children's witnessing of it, or at him at this moment, neither cop nor civilian.

"Thank you," she said.

A weakness, pure folly, washed over him. His knees gave out. He crouched, or maybe it was a stumble to the damp grass. Cold flooded the seams of his jeans and jacket. He was aware of indistinct orientations, a tipping, the unyielding chalk on the land. He assumed for a moment that he was unconscious until he felt her near. A warmth hovered at his cheek, and then a comforting pressure.

"Do you need help?" Lea asked.

Her hand cradled his jowl as if cupping jelly. He fumbled for her other hand and closed his fist on a bedrock of bones clustered under a slippery down blanket. He'd thought her skin might have this feel. Then he thought the bones of her wrist bundled in her wool sweater might have this feel. He glanced down to confront the confused visual of his hand clamped around the doe's leg. The hoof's black knot poked out from his fist like a top hat.

Lea followed his gaze. Slid her hand from his cheek to lay over his.

He assessed that she was about to laugh.

"Don't," he urged, meaning the laugh, meaning that she might spark a fit in him.

She snatched her hand away. Crimson blotches stained her cheeks. She stood up without meeting his eyes.

Throttling their connection was most definitely what he didn't mean. He stood, clumsy and outsized, hovering over her confusion. "Okay," he said.

"What do I do now?" she asked.

He searched for the right answer. Wondered why she hadn't said *we*.

Into his silence she said, "With the body."

He cleared his throat. "Oh. It'll need removal."

"The county should take it."

"The road commission doesn't provide that service." He fumbled for the professional cadence. "The homeowner assumes the cost of removal."

She didn't like his answer. Rilke detected a delicate paling under her flush, like the flash he'd caught of her belly. The defiance returned to her voice, stripped of the uncertain wobble. "Well, with the cull. I mean, the county's removing deer anyway. Why can't I leave it on the extension for tomorrow's…pickup?"

"It'd put the deer down tonight," he explained. "Having the carcass laid out so close to the bait site."

"It's not fair." She looked about her, at every blade and bush and hoof and not at him. "I didn't hit it."

"The wildlife service can come on out for you on a special run." He paused a beat. "I have the number. If you don't want to have to look it up. Much cheaper than Critter Control."

She crossed her arms. "I don't want to use that service."

"I know the owner. I can call for you. If that would help."

Lea's shudder was a visible ripple of her thin shoulders. "I don't want to deal with him at all."

He had every sympathy for her queasy outlook on Gary. He indicated the hedge, tried for a more palatable tack. "Look. Isn't this your neighbor's property?"

She did look at him then. "No, it isn't. And passing the buck doesn't make it any fairer."

"Okay."

"Bad pun," she said.

"Excuse me?"

"*Passing the buck.*"

Rilke nodded. "Except she's a doe."

Just like that he raised her brief pretty smile, and when it quickly extinguished, a light lingered in her gaze. *All right.* He took his hands from his jacket pockets and assessed an efficient route to his field across her front lawn. A pickup trundling down Scipio wove into the oncoming lane to avoid a cluster of potholes. The tires crunched on the frozen pavement. "Tell you what. Do you have a tarp? I can remove her for you."

"No," she said quickly. "I shouldn't have given you a hard time. It's not your job."

"It's no problem at all. Just take me a jiff."

She relaxed, then. "I appreciate it. I do. But no. I'll take care of it."

"Did you see what happened?" He was moved to extend the familiarity between them. He sensed her shivering at the cold, her restlessness over her kids, alone in the home, her residue of irritation over their behavior.

"A car hit it. *Her*," she corrected. She wrapped her arms tightly around her waist. Her pallor had turned carnation red again. He should have offered his jacket to her. "I'm not good with cars. Makes or models or anything."

He reached for the 12 gauge and handed it to her cautiously. "Keep the safety latched. Do you know how to engage it?"

"Yes. I just forgot to do it before."

"Okay, then."

"Aren't you going to ask to see my permit?" Her timidity returned with her uncertainty.

"You don't need a permit for a rifle until you transport it for the purpose of hunting." He turned to leave her, to prove she wasn't in trouble.

Her voice stopped him. "Officer?"

He faced her, gratefully. "Rilke," he said, and then "Paul."

She was hugging the gun to her chest like before, when he'd moved to take it away. "The young man from last night."

He waited. Wondered what aspect of the incident they hadn't covered over the phone. Relieved that her recovered shyness had to do with her nagging concern over the kid, not with him.

"I want to tell you. I was getting a blanket for him, like I said. When I came downstairs, my husband had chased the boy away. He was carrying a rifle. Because of the cull."

Rilke closed his expression. "Your husband said the kid took off. Did you see him chase the boy?" He put the question neutrally, doubting that this was a confession instead of yet more irrelevant information, but with a flaky, aggressive homeowner like Mr. Johnson, who knew what foolishness the man might bring down upon himself and his wife.

A shift in her posture. Nerves. But it could have been the cold breeze sweeping lightly over them that raised a flinch. "Well. I didn't actually see him chase the boy, no."

"Did your husband discharge the weapon?"

"No. Of course not." Her heat was up. "He wouldn't do that. There wasn't anything dangerous about what I actually saw Jay do. But given what you told us about pranks"—she caught her breath, hung on to it for a moment—"we overreacted. I just feel terrible about the whole thing."

He gave her a nod, waited it out.

"Anyway. I put the blanket out for him. In case he hadn't gone far, or in case he was, you know, hurt or something. Out at the road." She indicated the line of pines along Scipio's shoulder. Pointed to a spot Rilke had passed on his way to her. He didn't recall seeing a blanket. "I wanted to report what I'd seen. When I called this morning. Which wasn't much, but anyway."

"You didn't break the law."

"I didn't mean that. I mean, that's not what I'm worried about."

"What I mean is you're allowed to defend your home if you feel threatened. If your husband did chase the kid, that's fine."

That made her uneasy. "But you said the young man wasn't a threat."

"I said he likely didn't constitute a threat." He kept his tone neutral. "We're discussing your—*your husband's*—perception."

"My husband has a permit for that gun. I'm sure he does." She was avoiding the eye contact again.

As if he was bound to check her husband's papers right there and then. He fought against the impatience she raised in him with her timid outlook and her tiresome references to the ineffectual and foolhardy Mr. J. "Look, if the kid ran away, that's an end to it." Not that the assurance was going to ease her mind. "There's really no need for concern. Likely he's home safe by now."

"Have you heard for certain?" Her expression cleared. The sun gleamed on her chafed skin, a hard, frosty shellac. He had a vision of her thawing, her crimson blotches drained, her limbs freed from their stiff, worried stance. He imagined her peeling, exposed. She wasn't a beauty. Brown hair cut blunt to a narrow chin, a fragile slimness to her hips and shoulders. She dressed as women dress who don't care how others, how *men*, view them. Under ordinary circumstances Rilke wouldn't give her a second look. But now that he was close to her, he saw that she was pretty, in a way. Not a knockout like Julia. Not the type of good looks women lob at men to see who can catch.

She was gazing at him, awaiting an answer. She wasn't shivering anymore. "No," he told her. "But I've never seen an adverse outcome from these pranks."

"I don't know what I was afraid of, exactly." She tried for a light tone, now that he'd relieved her worry. "I should never have called the police."

"Sounds like your husband was the one who was afraid."

"We both were afraid. My husband was attacked last year. It happened at home." At Rilke's sharp glance up the drive, wondering why, last night, he'd recalled the burglary but not the more serious trouble that had visited the address, she added, "Not this house. We lived in town then. Kildare Drive." She paused to allow this information to settle in. "So you see. Why we were nervous last night."

Yes, he remembered the Kildare assault, a brutal, senseless crime. Neither the home nor the victim's car had been burgled. He recalled, too, that there had been some question as to whether the victim would live. That Mr. Johnson was the man whose survival had once been on the wrong side of the odds irked Rilke all the more. "I remember that incident."

"I wanted to mention that over the phone too," Lea said. A plea crouched in her voice. "When I asked whether he would come back. I was thinking of the break-in. When we were robbed here, I thought, I don't know, that they'd found us somehow. Because they were never caught after they attacked my husband." She fell silent as if to cuff the plea in her voice. "I don't know why I didn't explain it all to you. So you'd understand us. That we're not just some privileged types calling the cops for minor stuff. Like the police are our personal protection or something."

Rilke directed a glance to the deer. He didn't like her reference to *us*, when what he recalled of Johnson's hostility, in Rilke's view, had included nervous Lea. Rilke had been in the middle of too many domestics not to recognize a man's fury toward his wife. "I'm glad you're telling me now. Sure I can't come back and take care of this for you?"

Lea shook her head. Had he said something wrong? But her voice was clear, a bit defiant, familiar again when she said, "No need to come back. Not for that."

15

Out of curiosity and because he was wrought up over the deer incident and the weakness he'd given in to, and the laying of Lea's hands on his, Rilke skirted the path leading to the guest cottage and jogged up to Scipio Road. His thinking was that she'd fibbed about laying out the blanket, given that she'd likely have been too fearful to hike up here in the dark. Not that an act of guilt wasn't possible. Although the Johnsons' driveway connected to Centennial Farms Drive, the front door was oriented toward Scipio. She'd only have to cut across her lawn instead of taking this long way around. Manageable, even for the timid.

He reached the shoulder, then scouted down a half mile past the Johnson home. He felt stupid, because what did it matter that he wouldn't find the blanket, that she was white-lying to compensate for a reactionary husband? The vulnerable routinely fibbed as a defensive maneuver, which was why he'd always had such solid trust in Julia. She never fibbed. She'd never projected weakness, not even when her papa was battering her. What put her in the hospital those times was her smart mouth baiting the bastard. Of course, once she'd married Rilke he'd seen to it that she never had cause to feel vulnerable. But even if she did go all in with loose-cannon Luke, for a time she'd stay tough inside and out. Men's behaviors, the best and the worst, had little effect on who Julia really was.

But Lea was quiet, diminished. She abdicated quickly to the man on the scene. Kept to a pretty smile that might once have been laughter. That tendon of defiance might be the leftovers of strength. Her fearful outlook might once have been earned through endurance, or bravery, but was now just terror.

Rilke backtracked down Scipio, scudding the gravel shoulder with his boot. He kept an eye on the tangle of winter-dried milkweed and yellowed heaps of blackberry vines curled in the drainage ditch, hoping to spot a neatly folded white scrap.

The shooting of the doe was bound to make him ill, but it was Lea's hand on the loose tuck of jowl that had confounded him more. He was ashamed of the droops at the deltas of his cheeks and chin. Julia always said he carried his weight everywhere, indiscriminately, even in the folds of his face, and that was one reason she'd stopped touching him there, and then at all. The urge to respond by gently taking Lea's lips to his had been so different from his passionate impulses with Julia as to be a different class of desire altogether.

It stood perfectly to reason that the blanket was nowhere in sight.

The wind kicked up as it often did on this stretch of Scipio, bounded as it was by disused fields. The breeze tunneled him in an unexpected flurry of snowflakes and papery flakes of corn husks. Cold leaked through his seams. His hair grew damp with sweat and snow. He wanted a hot shower, a bit more sleep.

He wanted to see Lea again.

He wanted to make love to Julia.

And when he squinted into the wind at the cobblestone farmhouse across the road, the brass centennial plaque reflecting a sunny gleam, he longed to spot, on the worn planks of the sagging porch, his mother beckoning him inside.

What he saw, instead of Mutti, was a Buick LeSabre parked on the shoulder, kitty-corner to the house.

The vehicle was oriented east, so the license plate was facing Rilke. He moved in, confirmed the numbers on the plate, assessed conditions. The rear window was absent the silhouettes of passengers. As he approached he made out the indistinct slope of shoulders draped over the wheel. For an uncertain pulse the outlook was alarming. The slack form didn't stir as Rilke stepped to the driver's window. Just as he was about to tap the glass, the body twitched. The head straightened, slow to acclimate to Rilke's appearance. Rilke's scrutiny moved from the unfolding of Homer Nixon to a spackle of bloodstains carpeting the passenger seat.

His hand jerked the door handle, *locked*, rapped the glass.

Nixon raised tearful eyes.

"Step out of the vehicle," Rilke told him. As Nixon sat upright, Rilke took it in—his soaked jeans, his hand wrapped around his arm, blood bubbling between the fingers like droplets of oil. Nixon moved his hand away long enough to roll down his window and went back to clenching his wound. A cut, Rilke saw, a surface injury that bled all out of proportion to its harm. Nixon's gaze was fixed on Rilke's as though his eyes were stuck.

"He never came home."

Rilke assessed the interior of the car. Besides the blood, all was ordered, clean, well maintained. A heavy down coat was folded neatly on the rear driver's-side seat. "Who's that, son?"

"My brother."

Rilke ran a gaze over the exterior, noting the dent creasing the front panel, the headlight smashed, the dimples in the bumper. "You hit something, Mr. Nixon?"

"A deer. *It* hit *me*. Ran right into my car."

"All right, then."

"It was just a *prank*." Nixon broke down again.

Rilke peeled off his jacket, unbuttoned his shirt. The funneling wind sluiced his arms when he removed his flannel, wound it tight, and handed it through the window. Nixon gaped at Rilke's bare chest chafed red by the wind. Rilke slipped on his jacket. "Put pressure on that cut."

Nixon's ineffectual first aid resulted in the shirt dangling useless from his shoulder. Not exactly the type to self-administer care. The clumsiness could be a symptom of withdrawal, so maybe Nixon was giving the sober life a real go. Rilke helped him into the passenger seat, showed him a thing or two about wound pressure, and backed the vehicle into Mutti's drive.

The front door was unlocked, as Rilke expected and was always working to correct. Mutti still operated as if she were back in the days of farmhands populating the place, the habits of old rural ways when a locked door was uncivil. After he deposited Mr. Nixon in a chair and went rummaging in the cabinet under the sink for antiseptic and bandages, Mutti glided in mid-fold of a bathroom towel.

"What's the trouble, then, Paul," she said briskly, as if Nixon's weeping arm was just the latest minor farm emergency to patch.

"Where's the first aid?" Rilke answered her with matching matter-of-factness. A relief swept over him at the sight of her bluebonnet print housedress, her navy felt slippers, her silver hair knotted tidily at her neck. Every socket of his physical aspect felt calmer with her near. He was never clear on whether he was just the type of guy who'd never outgrown his mother, or the relief was a stubborn holdover dread that Papa had done something to her.

"What happened, dear?" Rilke turned to tell her and saw that she was addressing Mr. Nixon.

"I cut my arm." Nixon sniffled.

"Good heavens. Let me peek." She peeled away Rilke's shirt, soaked through, clicked her tongue the way she used to over Rilke's boo-boos, which caused Nixon to tear up again. Rilke dived back under the sink. "Son, what are you doing tearing up my cabinets?"

"Where's the first aid?"

"Above the microwave."

"Well, if you weren't always moving things around the place." Rilke uncurled from the plumbing and moved to the skinny cabinet above the microwave.

"Haven't kept the Band-Aids below the sink since you moved out. Being that you were the one who always needed them in reach. Be careful with that," she admonished when Rilke rattled the spice jars.

"I *am* careful." He fetched the silver box he'd always kept stocked with supplies, an old Scout tin with a stippled insignia punched in the lid and a square handle. Mutti mopped Nixon's arm while the kid swiveled scrutiny from Rilke to Mutti to the overall visual of the farmhouse kitchen. To Rilke the room was his second skin, but judging by his raw expression of dismay, to Nixon the kitchen was the latest consternating and unplanned facet of his ill-fated prank.

Besides the dark cabinets being sorely out of date, the color contrasted rudely with the vintage porcelain sink and swan's-neck faucet fixtures. And the clutter didn't help, with plates and coffee cups stacked on the counters, not tucked away in cupboards, as if Mutti had just cleaned up after a full farmhand lunch. The trash lid bumped open from an overflow of bags and peelings. That evening's dinner, a block of livid pink beef, lay thawing at the sink, bleeding juice down the drainboard's grooves. Seemed like a big roast for just the two of them, but Mutti knew he liked his beef. In a colander a heap of mushrooms, glistening from a recent rinse, tangled their beige limbs and caps. The coffee pot still blinked on, baking the morning's last cup to sludge. The room carried the smoky odor of burned grounds and raw meat and root-cellar apples, and mixed up in these aromas was Mutti's scent, cornhusker lotion and dryer sheets and dishwashing detergent.

Maybe Nixon's mama kept a more orderly domestic situation. Mutti staunched the flow on his arm with practiced efficiency. Nixon flinched.

Rilke placed the kit on the table. "It's okay, son."

"Moisten a towel, Paul," Mutti ordered.

Rilke brought a clean dishrag and a mixing bowl of warm water. After Mutti sponged and dried the cut, she held Nixon's arm steady.

"Use the peroxide."

Rilke poured straight from the bottle. Bubbles foamed the length of the cut like condensation along a crack in a pipe. Nixon winced again but didn't cry. Mutti dabbed the foam and watched Rilke press gauze to the cut before starting the wrap. Nixon's fine curly hairs grazed Rilke's fingers as he wound the bandage tight. The kid's skin, rough with goose pimples, radiated heat. When Mutti accidentally jiggled the arm, Rilke moved to cup Nixon's elbow, felt the nudge of a skinny bone when the boy relaxed into the palm of Rilke's hand.

"What's your name, dear?" Mutti asked gently.

"Homer," Nixon said.

"Nixon," Rilke said.

Mutti laughed. "Which way round?"

"Homer's first," the kid mumbled.

"By the look of that cut I'd guess you got into some barbed wire. You'll want to see a doctor, make sure you don't need a tetanus shot. What were you doing way out back?" Mutti was referring to the development's northern boundary, where a row of home sites lay abandoned by the housing bust. The farm's rusted barbed wire still stretched the length of the adjacent field, hidden by straggly brush.

Homer gave Rilke a nervous glance as Rilke taped the bandage firm. "Looking for my brother."

"What's his name?" Rilke asked quietly.

Homer pressed a fist to the bridge of his nose. "Russell."

Mutti poured a glass of water and handed it to Homer. He gulped it down, trembling. "You want something to eat, dear?" she asked.

"No, thank you, ma'am." Homer eyed the oozing roast.

"I'm taking you in to report Russell missing. Then we'll have the arm looked at," Rilke said.

"You're going to have to change out of those pants, dear." Mutti's glance at Homer's bloodied lap raised a look of stark terror on the boy. "I'll fetch a pair."

"You got a shirt for me, Mutti?" Rilke asked.

Mutti headed for the hallway. "I'll see what I can do."

"Not Papa's," Rilke called after her.

"For heaven's sake, Paul, you'll wear what I bring you."

Rilke set to cleaning up the surgery, as Mutti used to call the aftermath of scrapes. Homer hugged his bandaged arm to his narrow chest. "You in pain, son? You want an ibuprofen?"

Homer shook his head.

"Pretty cold to be out traipsing around in shirt sleeves. If you'd been wearing your jacket, you wouldn't have gotten cut."

Homer shifted in the chair. "My dad would get on me if I tore my coat."

"Seems like messing up your coat is the least of your worries. That where you dropped Russell? Back by the fence?"

Homer shook his head. "On the road. But he coulda gone back there to find the girls, hitch a ride home."

"Got friends in the neighborhood?"

Homer looked at Rilke warily. "My sister and my cousin were here working." As if he anticipated what meaning Rilke might assign to that statement, Homer added quickly, "They're in sales," which didn't exactly clarify his relatives' activities. Rilke's prompt as to what exactly was being sold raised a flush and a stammered *merchandise*. Rilke maintained the impassive act for a few beats before Homer broke down. "Naughty shit for rich chicks, okay?"

Rilke recalled the tasteless object that had rolled from Nixon's glove box along with the vehicle registration. "Okay."

"They give these parties. They make a lot of money." Rilke believed it. Despite the economy, lady parties were still a big business.

At Rilke's clouded frown, Homer's tone reoriented to the defensive. "We hauled the merchandise to the party, then dropped Russell where he'd know to find his way back to Jacky and Sara if he wanted. But he didn't need the girls anyway. Should have been nothin' for him to just walk down the road to the Burger King or something."

"It's a pretty good hike up that road," Rilke pointed out. Not to mention navigating the confounding twists and turns of the development's narrow roadways in the dark. No wonder Russell had landed on the Johnson stoop.

Homer's eyes filled. "When I did it, they ditched me in the middle of nowhere. Had to flag someone down to call the cops to pick me up.

Russell's a dope, though. He's younger than us. Kind of immature too. We made it easy on him. Only he messed it up."

"He was seen last night and he was fine." This piece of information didn't appear to soothe. Nixon rubbed his arm and looked at Rilke doubtfully. "We'll find him," Rilke reassured him. "He wouldn't have any reason for not seeking help? For hiding out? Trouble at home? A prior record?"

Homer shook his head.

"Not a very nice thing to do to your brother, leaving him out here alone, then."

"It was a *prank*. Plus he wanted to do it. He's been nagging for months. He always wants to prove he's man enough to take anything we dish out."

The tears looked ready to spill. Guilt had overtaken the fear in Homer's expression. "Kids like to fit in," Rilke agreed. "Especially younger brothers."

Homer lost the battle with the waterworks. Rilke rose to tear a paper towel from the roll next to the microwave and handed it to Homer. He jammed the paper to his eyes. The distressed lump in his throat bulged like a stone.

Rilke said, "We'll bring him home. Don't worry."

Homer sniffled and finished mopping up the tears. "You live here?"

Rilke snapped the kit lid shut, engaged the latch, pushed it to the middle of the table. "Not anymore."

"You always talk to your mama that way?"

"What way is that, son?"

"Like, I don't know. I never heard a name like *Mutti*."

"It's not her name."

"Why do you call her that?"

"It's German," Rilke said, as if that explained things.

"What's it mean?"

Rilke tossed him a look. "*Mama*. And maybe you should think about spending a little more time with yours once we get your brother home, Mr. Nixon."

Homer's look was pure bleakness. "I just live with my dad."

"Okay. Does he know where you are?"

"He don't know none of it." Homer swiped at a runaway tear. "He thinks Russell stayed the night with a friend. I'm supposed to look out for him, but he kept saying this is what he wanted to do. We're always being pushed around, especially Russ. He's big, so he looks older, but he's not strong. We aren't rich like the kids at school. Dad pays our tuition out of insurance Mom had. On top of what I did to you, my dad is gonna kill me. For real." Nixon stared at Rilke's arm.

Rilke had every sympathy for what a dad might do when faced with challenging family matters. "I'll give him a call, then." When Homer shot him a nervous glance, Rilke gave a nod. "I'll handle your papa. It'll be okay."

"But how do you *know?*"

"I know how to deal with fathers."

"I mean, about Russell."

"You got home," Rilke pointed out. "So will he."

Homer looked down at the seeping bandage on his arm. "Actually, when my friends ditched me in the middle of nowhere. That was the night I got in trouble with you."

"That right?"

"Yeah. I got high, then they left me, I don't know, somewhere. By the time I got to the Costco I was pretty out of it. Obviously. I don't even remember how I ended up there. I don't remember a lot of what happened that night."

"Did Russell get high before you dropped him off?"

"No, sir. Russell would never do drugs."

Nixon had been fully clothed the night of their tussle, Rilke remembered. "Why'd you take his pants?"

"The girls were working so close by. We thought it would be funny if he showed up at one of those parties with no pants. Serve those rich chicks right."

Rilke absorbed this tasteless and reckless visual. "Wouldn't serve your brother right, I don't think." Homer bowed his head. The new remorseful aspects didn't impress Rilke, but maybe his vulnerable state of mind would jog his memory. He cleared his throat. "That night at the Costco. Did you have a, *uh*, pet with you? A kitten?"

Made him lightheaded just to mention it. Which Homer noticed. "A kitten?" The kid's tone was more curiosity than confusion. Rilke nodded. He was almost too queasy to notice Homer suppressing an uptick at the corner of his mouth, which unchecked might have unfurled a satisfied smile. "Wait, was that what I was holding? I just remember something, ah, *soft*."

Before Rilke could respond to this fresh line of smartassdom, Mutti arrived with an armful of denim and plaid. She showed Homer the bathroom off the den. Rilke removed his jacket. Mutti returned in time to see Rilke's bare chest. He pulled on the shirt and buttoned it up. Farm plaid, reeking of molded hay, fertilizer. And stale, sour whiskey. His gut clenched. "You look thin."

"That's one thing I'm not." He took up his jacket, avoiding her gaze. He was still feeling squeamish. His mother's gaze raking his flesh wasn't calming the stomach acid, that was for sure.

"Caroline phoned me this morning. About the trouble with Julia."

This made him look up. "Caroline doesn't know anything about it," he stated carefully. Without static, but Mutti saw right through the so-what act.

"I don't like to butt in, but your behavior is crying out for interference."

Paul could do without being lectured to while swaddled in Papa's fabrics and odors. "We're working things through. Me and Jules. Together."

"I'm thinking of what's best for you, son."

"That's fine."

A strand of silver hair had loosened from the knot and floated along her neck. He traced the flow of her curl instead of her stern gaze. She sighed. "You understand that what you *mean* to do isn't the same as doing what you mean?"

"Do *you* know the difference?" Rilke couldn't tame the snotty tone.

Mutti didn't cave to the childish attitude. "You can't force Julia. Your love is your own business, if she doesn't feel the same."

Did Papa force you *to love him*, he wanted to snap back, but wouldn't that comment land him square in Caroline and Julia's nosy therapy outlook. Anyway, the whole credo Rilke lived by, both personally and professionally, was to figure out quickly whose business was whose and act accordingly. Rilke pulled on his jacket and messed around with the zipper all to avoid her gaze, which he couldn't read and didn't want to.

Nixon appeared in the doorway bundled in dungarees and plaid a size or two generous. "Whose clothes are these?" Rilke asked.

Mutti crossed to the sink to fuss with the dishes. "Yours. From high school." Nixon gave Rilke a strangled look. "I'm expecting you for dinner," Mutti reminded him.

"Ready to go, Homer?" Rilke tried ignoring her, his old teen trick, which she didn't truck then and wasn't going to truck now.

"Paul?"

He tried his other trick, which she did truck, then and now. He kissed her cheek. "Love you, Mama."

16

At the station, while Cheryl soothed Homer Nixon with hot chocolate and cookies left over from the Toys for Tots drive, Rilke contacted the father and doled out the facts while dialing down the agitation the man naturally presented over Russell's absence. Rilke impressed upon Nixon Sr. the expected outcome of this admittedly worrisome development, which was that most missing kids under *this type of circumstance*, meaning the prank and not some sudden and unexplainable disappearance, almost always turned up safe and sound. Rilke kept the notification brisk and reassuring, but kept Homer's role in the deal minimal. Homer gave him a sober look that might have been relief, even gratitude. He hung up, then checked in with the day staff to make certain the facets of locating Russell and caring for Homer were in play before signing out a vehicle to drive back home.

Only instead of returning to the guest cottage, he turned into Centennial Farms' west entrance, the one that looped to the back of the development, to poke around for Russell. The cops on duty would be looking for the kid, and anyway, chances were good that what he'd told Nixon Sr. was accurate—no cause to worry too much, too soon—but neither did it hurt to check whether Russell had run, not toward Scipio Road as Lea had reported, but away, as Homer believed.

Which led Rilke to the abandoned home sites and the stretch of rusted barbed wire hidden in brush. Beyond stretched the field, trampled matchsticks of dried cornstalks frozen to the frosted earth. Papa had spent the last of his years here growing decent corn, getting decent prices. His end had been gentle. The weird benevolence that had transformed the old hateful Papa was characteristic of brain tumors, the family was told. Although Rilke noted that the kindness coincided with being too sick to get drunk.

Before hospice, Papa had taken to wandering. An aspect of the illness, the specialist told the family. It fell to Rilke to fetch the old man back. Rilke often found him here, at the barbed wire. Papa would be shivering in his pj's, or, nearer the end, in his birthday suit. It had crossed Rilke's mind once, he had to admit, to let the old man freeze to death. But he'd always ended up helping Papa home. They would ride back to the farmhouse in silence. Papa would insist on holding Rilke's hand no matter how firmly Rilke pulled away. He couldn't stand touching the hands that had given Rilke the strap plenty of times, shot those cows, bludgeoned those kits, made love to—or hurt—his mother. But once Rilke gave up and endured the contact, Papa would rub Rilke's fingers gently. The ritual made it difficult to steer straight. Likely the old man had no idea who or what he was caressing like a damn pet, was what Rilke reminded himself whenever he got suckered in to feeling glad for the connection.

Rilke ruffled the bushes near the fence. Blood spotted the juniper branches where Homer must have cut himself. He stepped over the fence carefully and scouted the idled home sites. Under his jacket, Papa's shirt scratched his skin. With no sign of the missing Nixon, the priority now was to change out of Papa's clothes and knock on some doors prior to his shift. Prior to dinner with Mutti, he corrected. A metallic taste tickled his throat.

He drove slowly through the neighborhood. Hillocks and berms fabricated to camouflage above-ground utility boxes obstructed his sight line. Wasteful expanses of manicured grass sloped to the cheap manses. The place was as deserted as ever, except for the occasional SUV almost running him off the narrow road. He swung around the corner to curve past the Johnson home. For a moment, at the head of the loop, he had a perfectly unobstructed view of Lea's side lawn just past the hedge.

A bold crimson smear bisected the flat, brown grass.

Jesus Christ.

He mashed the brakes, gasping at the sharp pressure of his safety belt. It took a moment to calm his jangled nerves. The line of blood originated near the hedge. And the fallen doe was missing. *All right.*

He exited the car. Skirted the hedge. Saw that the ribbon of blood was still wet. He spied Lea on her front lawn midway to Scipio Road, slight hands wrapped in the folds of a sky-blue tarp. She'd managed to slide the doe partway onto the plastic but tugging the load had obviously proven too much. Her solemn little boy traipsed behind the doe, struggling to hold up the hind legs. Floppy lemon-colored latex gloves stretched to the kid's elbows like a lady's fancy gloves. A dust mask was strapped to his face like a cotton snout.

Rilke jogged over. Despite his approach, right there in plain sight, she didn't look up until he was upon her. "I said I'd take care of this." His tone was irritated, demanding explanation, not at all what he meant to project.

The little boy dropped the hooves and stared at Rilke over the mask with round blue eyes. Lea straightened stiffly, put a hand to the small of her back. Sweat beaded on her brow, glistening in the golden sunlight. She was wearing the oversized cable sweater with the sleeves rolled up. Rilke dropped his gaze to study the setup she had going with the deer. She'd wrestled the animal admirably onto the tarp, all except the rear end, which was leaking blood freely like the flow from a loose gasket.

"I'm taking care of it," she said defensively, which was some of the truth.

"Who are you?" The boy's voice, dampened by the mask, came out gummy as he stared Rilke down. The boy didn't recognize him from that morning.

Lea answered before Rilke could. "Remember, Kurt? This man was just here to…help Mom. It's okay." She flashed Rilke a neutral look. "He's not a stranger. He's the police." When the boy relaxed, Lea smiled briefly. "They just had the stranger danger talk in school."

"Why didn't you call Critter Control?" Rilke bent down to scoot the doe's hindquarters square to the tarp's center. He noted how the boy tamed a shudder, a grown-up valiance.

Lea cleared her throat. "They wanted three hundred dollars to remove it."

"Sounds about right."

"I don't have it."

Rilke swept a gaze over her two acres, her vast house.

"I don't have it," she repeated, drawing her arms to her chest.

"Okay." Rilke took note of the boy's shift in concern from the doe's lurid presentation to his mother's posture. "Tell you what, son. I'll take it from here. Why don't you take your mother in for a hot chocolate."

Kurt looked to Lea as if this were by far the best idea of a very long morning. But Lea shook her head. "I can't ask that."

"You aren't asking." At her doubtful glance, he gave her a nod, and was pleased to see it raise her smile, as before. "It's my pleasure," he deadpanned.

She laughed outright. "I'll bet." She turned to Kurt. "Go in and fix some hot chocolate for you and Bunny. Lock the door. Dad should be home in a minute, and I'll be in soon."

"You did a good job here," Rilke said as the boy gave the doe a final wary assessment. Kurt trundled to the house, avoiding the crimson stripe on the lawn like a crack in the sidewalk. Rilke would stake cash that the boy wouldn't remove the protective gear until the door was tightly shut behind him. He glanced at Lea. Her brow had wicked dry in the cold breeze, and she'd rolled her sweater down to her thin wrists. She'd been standing long enough that the cooldown of her exertions was raising shivers. "I don't need help," he told her. "Why don't you go home."

"The feet. I mean, the hooves…they drag and get caught. I tried to do it alone and ended up having to get Kurt." Her steady gaze dared him to judge her for exposing her son to this upsetting visual. "I'll hold them off the ground. It'll go faster."

Rilke unzipped his jacket and removed it. "Bundle up, then."

Her gaze attached then to Papa's shirt, frayed at the collar and cuffs. The odor of his sweat mixed up with fertilizer and whiskey rained over Rilke. A fine shirt to ruin, he thought as he handed the jacket to Lea and bent over the tarp.

Lea's plan had been to take the short route across the lawn to dump the carcass on the north side of Scipio Road just down from the farm-house. When Rilke told her they'd dump the doe in his field instead, she'd frowned until he explained that his family owned the farmhouse. Either way the doe would end on his land. She nodded then and grasped the back edges of the tarp in a stalwart non-finicky way he liked.

With her autumn fat and bloated belly, the doe was a strenuous haul. As they dragged the carcass along the road toward the narrow path to the guest cottage, Rilke was surprised, and then impressed, by Lea's strength. He was dragging most of the doe's weight, of course, but in defiance of her slight build and nervous aspect, Lea lifted her end of the plastic with apparent ease. The doe's blood flowed into the deep cup they were forming with the tarp. Golden beads of sweat popped from her brow again, and her cheeks blushed roses from the effort, but she maneuvered the deer coolly. When they reached the path, brush and prickers entangled the doe's hooves. Lea dropped her end to free the legs. The collected blood streamed from the tarp, almost splashing her boots. Rilke cautioned her, and she stepped aside in time to let the blood cut a dark vein into the hard earth. Rilke detected a paling underneath her flush.

"It's not far now," he told her. "I can manage from here."

"I'm fine," she replied, answering a question he hadn't asked.

"Okay."

She hefted the hooves. "Where are we taking it…her?" She'd remembered the joke, was attempting a tense smile.

Rilke nodded to a stretch of the field downwind from the cottage. From here it was a matter of rhythms and modulations as they moved the doe through the brush onto the brittle half-masts of old cornstalks. When Rilke shifted the doe's weight to avoid a stone or bush, Lea compensated to keep the burden distributed evenly, to prevent more spilling of blood. If a hoof caught, she disentangled it deftly with one hand. His slightest movement was balanced by her intuitive match. They performed the final yards of the haul smoothly.

Rilke led her up a slight hill and paused at the mouth of a deep pit, a scrap graveyard where Papa used to pitch rusted parts and empty cans. He wiped the sweat running down his cheeks. Lea waited, hooves in hand. She mistook his rest for hesitation.

"What's wrong?"

He looked at her high bright color, the quicksilver paleness gleaming underneath like a foundation of nickel plate, and he had a sudden, grieving sense of missing her, even with her still so near. Flustered, he looked down. The doe's nose rested close to his boot. The sightless black eye stared back at him. The buckshot freckles nested on the bridge of her snout raised a brief nausea. He said, "You can let go." When she did, he gathered the sides of the tarp and heaved the doe. The tarp flapped sharply. Blood dribbled down his shirt sleeve. At the pit's bottom, the body crumpled, the belly thrust upward. The stiff legs shuddered as if they'd scampered down the slope. The head bumped up against a rusted spiked plow Papa had used to dig the first weeds of spring.

"Sorry about the tarp." Rilke brushed the blood on his sleeve.

"It's fine. I wouldn't want to have to clean it," Lea said. "Will it—she—be okay here?"

He took in her shallow breathing. "Come again?"

"I mean, she won't stink too badly or…be inconvenient to you?"

He smiled at the naïve outlook. Buzzards would strip the doe to her bones as soon as any odor pledged them a meal. "Nope on both counts."

Her labored breath frosted the air between them. Her gaze latched onto the blood on his sleeve, and he realized then that she was holding her hands out awkwardly as if uncertain where to put them. Blood smeared her palms and laced her wrists like ruby cuffs. She was trying not to mind. Her eyes were glazed. Shock was worming into her.

"Lea," he said, but already she couldn't answer.

She broke out trembling. He gathered dried leaves and twigs, pressed them to her hands. Her fingers were stiff as stone under the blood. He cleaned her as best he could, pitched the leaves into the pit, cradled her hands in his palms, carried them to his lips to warm her, comfort her, bring her *back*.

In the guest cottage, Rilke took the jacket from her gently and showed her the bathroom. Turned on the water until it ran warm, since Lea was moving slowly. In case she outright fainted, which was presenting as a real possibility, he left the door ajar while she washed up. He listened to the sounds of her scrubbing and assessed an increasing vigor, so she must be coming out of it all right. He peeled off Papa's shirt, balled it up, and tossed it outside to burn later. When he turned from closing the door, Lea was standing outside the bathroom. She'd removed her bulky sweater and whatever blouse she was wearing underneath to reveal a plain cotton T-shirt, charcoal gray, tucked into the skinny-waisted jeans. Water glistened on her thin arms.

She kept her eyes gamely on his face to avoid looking at his exposed chest. "I'm sorry," she said. "But there's no towel. I looked."

Rilke flushed and moved quickly to fetch a cotton dish towel from a drawer in the kitchenette. "Sorry. I'm due for the laundry."

She took the towel and disappeared into the bathroom, shutting the door firmly. Rilke dressed quickly in a clean canvas shirt before scrubbing up at the kitchen sink. By the time she emerged again—a loose-fitting print blouse pulled over her tee, the bulky cable sweater draped over an arm—Rilke had dried up, buttoned his sleeves, and filled the coffee maker. He was relieved to see her eyes had cleared. As she surveyed the cottage's single room, her movements were no longer slow. Rilke relaxed a bit. She seemed past the point of trouble and at ease with him, a counterweight to his own unease.

"Thank you." She gave him an open, pretty smile. "Again."

"My pleasure."

"Wasn't it just." Her smile veiled. A hint of paleness crept under the flush the cottage's humid heat had raised. No matter the season, the place was always steamy. The coffee maker brewed a bitter caramel odor that gummed up the air. Good insulation job, bad venting, which he'd fix if he planned to stay, which he didn't. "Sorry I got woozy."

"It's natural."

"I'm not usually squeamish about blood." She was standing in the middle of the room, hugging her sweater. "Why would she bleed so much...from there?"

Rilke cleared his throat. "Come again?"

"I—*we*—didn't shoot her there. From behind."

"She'd have been injured internally from hitting the car," he explained.

The rational explanation calmed her. She asked after the missing boy, if he'd heard anything. Rilke pulled out a chair from the laminate table he'd placed at the sill of the picture window overlooking the east field. "Nothing yet. But nothing yet to worry about." He felt it prudent not to mention that the missing kid's brother had hit her doe.

"I feel ashamed that we scared that boy. You don't think what we did caused him to get lost?" She hesitated. "Or hurt?"

He shook his head. "Coffee?"

"Think I'll need something stronger after that experience." She slouched into the chair.

Rilke didn't stock alcohol in the cottage. "Can't help you there."

She shrank, timid again, as if he'd judge her character by the need for whiskey after an upsetting incident. Rilke poured a cup of coffee to occupy himself with something other than brooding over half-formed notions concerning how confounding feelings for Lea kept creeping up on him.

When he turned to lean against the counter, she was studying the room. Papa's bed, pushed to the far corner under a trio of square, pine-trimmed windows. When Rilke moved in, he'd burned Papa's frayed chenille bedspread and replaced it with a quilt he remembered Omi sewing on long winter evenings, a pattern of interlocking rings banded in daffodil yellows and tangerine and scrub-brush green. A squat, heavy oak bureau stood opposite the bed, the polished top gleaming where he usually tossed his handgun and wallet. Both were now stowed in his jacket pocket hanging on a hook by the front door. The kitchenette was as sparsely populated as the rest of the room, with uncluttered laminate countertops, a half stove and half-sized fridge. A tidy, empty place, bright with the whitewash of brittle autumn sunlight gleaming from the eggshell walls, the polished silver appliances and waste can. The cold, reflective light did nothing to cool the infernal humidity that trapped every odor and discomfort. She took it all in and then glanced at him curiously. "You live here?"

"It's temporary," Rilke told her.

She shrugged. "It's nice. I've always thought it would be easier to live like this. One room. Simple to keep up. Everything in sight and reach. You can *hear* everything too."

Before the gentle ring of her voice now filling the space, the only sound he'd ever heard since he moved in was silence. "It's simpler," he agreed.

Her gaze rested on the cat's old spot just past the kitchenette, the only facet of the cottage Rilke had changed. He'd built shelves into the wall, floor to ceiling, and tried to fill them up with pots and the mismatched dishes Mutti had lent him. But he didn't have enough kitchen run-off to clutter them properly, and the shelves near the floor lay empty. "That's a beautiful cabinet. Cherry wood?"

"Stained pine." He swallowed a hot stream of coffee, winced at the burn. "Covers up some dings to the floor there," he added, although it made no sense to say it.

But she didn't react, except to say he'd certainly found an elegant solution to the problem of the damage.

"Your boy have a pet?" he continued as if the question were a natural aspect of the conversation at hand. This, however, did raise her confusion. "A rabbit?" he clarified.

She looked at him searchingly and then smiled. "Oh. You mean Bunny. It's a pet *name*. For my daughter. Her real name's Barbara. After my husband's grandmother. She was a sweetie but I don't like that name, so I took to calling her something similar."

Rilke nodded. Drank more coffee. Assessed the monumental effort it would take to sit at the table with her.

She smiled. "I guess not liking a name isn't a very good excuse for nicknaming my daughter after a helpless thing."

"Rabbits have good survival instincts," Rilke responded.

She'd been gazing out the window at the tan, broken stalks of dried corn and the eyelash fringe of the willows waving at the far boundary of the field. At his observation she tilted a startled look at him. "What did you say?"

"Rabbits." He cleared his throat. "They're skilled at precise movement and timing. Knowing the exact moment to run. Or when to freeze while looking for the way out. If there is one, they typically find it."

Lea's pretty mouth twisted in dismay. Her eyes widened, filled with tears. Until now, their color had been obscure, unremarkable, a dimpled pond of hazels and browns. Coated with tears, the mixed-up hues smoothed out to a heron blue. Rilke was caught off guard. The only tears he'd ever raised in a woman, besides during the routine sibling horseplay he'd shared with Caroline when they were kids, occurred as a response to speeding or light-dodge tickets in women who thought the charge was unfair, or who hoped to weasel out of the fine with a display of drama, which never worked. Julia never cried, which he was never sure whether to appreciate or fear.

"Constant vigilance makes them sharp little critters. Most folks think they're dumb. Like, dumb as a bunny." This explanation seemed to upset her more. He added hastily, by way of reassurance, "The point being, it's a fine pet name for your little girl. Bunnies aren't helpless."

She pressed her fists to her eyes and bowed her head. *Jesus Christ.* What was he doing, running off at the mouth about rabbits?

He didn't stock Kleenex in the cottage either. A clean kitchen rag would have to do. He set down his cup. The clap of Mutti's china against the laminate startled Lea into collecting herself. She dropped her hands. Her bulky sweater lay crumpled in her lap. Her thin shoulders shook, and then stilled as she looked about her, at every surface and cabinet and cup and not at him.

"What you said about relationships." Her gaze landed on the china at Rilke's elbow. "I've been thinking about that all day."

"I'm married."

As soon as he'd blurted it, he tensed. But she lifted that small brief smile, lidded it, and her eyes were dry now. "I mean the one you have with the person who hurt you."

"Okay." He struggled to remember what, precisely, she was recalling.

"You said the relationship with that person lasts *for the time of duration.*" She hesitated. "Of the dangerous encounter."

"Yes." He did remember now. Over the phone.

"I haven't found that to be true."

She met his eyes then. Rilke gave her the nod that had always raised her fleeting smile, which failed this time to raise any expression at all.

"I've found that the relationship continues. I've found that I think about him every day." She appeared more relaxed now. Her shoulders had fallen to the chair's vinyl back. "Every single day, at least once. Sometimes more. Sometimes every moment. In the empty spaces." She looked down at her hands. "Since I was thirteen." She rearranged the sweater in her lap to blanket her legs. "My parents weren't home, so I wasn't supposed to open the door to anyone. But he was a family friend." She glanced at him then, maybe to assess a response to the error in her judgment. He nodded, *all right*.

"He said Dad had sent him to repair the furnace. He was carrying a toolbox. He'd visited us, my parents, I mean, plenty of times. So I opened the door. He knew where the furnace was in the basement so I went back to watching TV. *Sir Graves Ghastly*. Remember him?" Rilke told her he did. A show he'd watched with Caroline, plenty of times. "And then he called me down. I thought he needed help cleaning up. *Come here*. He sounded scared."

"What did you do?"

Lea stared at him. "What he told me to. No one's ever asked me that before."

"I didn't mean—"

"No. I know you didn't. I haven't told anyone about this to speak of, except my best friend, a long time ago, and only because…well…"

Rilke told her that he shouldn't have asked it that way.

"I can answer, though." She held his gaze steadily, an act of will he recognized. "I could tell you everything I did. Every detail." She paused to assess his reaction. She must have found his neutral posture encouraging. "They always say, I mean other girls do, that while it's happening they, you know, go somewhere else. Like it's happening to someone else. But it wasn't that way for me. It felt, well. It felt like it was happening to me, all right. It still does, to this day, this moment. Sometimes I think *the relationship* would, I don't know, *wither*, if I could just detach. Pretend I was someone else and it happened to them. Once upon a time."

"I understand that," he said.

"During…things, I hit some switch on the furnace and a buzzer went off. He told me I'd broken the furnace." She paused. "His voice was awful. Matter of fact, like we were just working on the furnace instead of, *um*, having sex. After that he stopped telling me what to do. He was rougher than he might have been if I hadn't hit the buzzer. If I'd kept pretending to go along with it." She bit her lip. "Afterward, I stood up. I…I think that freaked him out, that I could stand and, *um*, face him. He left, all of a sudden."

Rilke tensed against the shudder in his gut. For the moment he kept it impersonal. "Did you report this?"

"I never told, no. Well. I did end up telling the police. Sort of."

"Did they follow up?"

Her defiance flashed. "No. I told the cop at school. You remember how Officer Friendly used to visit every year?" She drew a sharp breath. "We were supposed to go to Officer Friendly when we needed help. So I did. But he didn't do a thing except tell me never to open the door to strangers. I know I wasn't making myself clear. It was confusing to talk about. I couldn't get the details straight. And I hadn't told my parents. Because I *knew* I wasn't supposed to open the door. And once or maybe twice, I'd flirted with him. When my dad was out of the room. So maybe, I was thinking, this is what flirting meant. Plus I did whatever he said, so, I mean, I told myself I'd as much as said *yes*. It made a certain sense out of what happened, I guess. I was…young. So I was scared to tell. To *report*. But I couldn't get it out of my head, that Officer Friendly should have *known*. Because he was the police." She shook her head. "The dumb things we're taught to believe about the authorities when we're kids." She smiled. "You must get that a lot. In your line of work."

In your line of work.

And Rilke understood then what she wanted from him. It was what Julia had wanted. His measured response. His knowing what to do, and when and how to do it. She wanted half of the relationship. Her share, not his. Lea would never want to know that Rilke, too, had opened a door and been summoned into a room where something happened that wasn't supposed to happen. That he, too, had been alone with the worst of men and it was all his fault for walking right in.

"I do," he agreed. "I get that a lot."

"I felt that. Whenever I saw you. After the robbery. After the young man…after he left. And over the phone. When you said that about the relationship." She gave him a timid look. "And then you didn't like shooting the doe. It upset you."

"Yes."

"So I know something about you."

This, too, Rilke agreed with.

"Sometimes…about *him*," she ventured. "I've been married for ten years. I have two kids. But. Sometimes I think that's the only real relationship I've ever had."

At this Rilke had to turn away to keep it together. "That's not the case, Lea."

She crossed her arms and looked out the window. "I often think if I'd managed to hurt him back, I wouldn't think about him so much. That the relationship would never have…persisted."

Rilke allowed as to how she might feel this way.

"Then I think… Sometimes I think if I hurt something…someone *else*, that would help end things between us."

Rilke said gently, "It wouldn't end old things. Only begin new things."

She glanced at him and flushed. "I shouldn't have said that."

"All I meant was, if you train yourself to prevail over anything that makes you feel like that individual made you feel, you'd be surprised at what you can do."

A part of his stock speech in his self-defense classes, which typically relaxed his female students, but Lea's faint, pinched smile had nothing in common with reassurance.

"I only prevail, as you put it, over the most helpless things."

He thought of her brusque manner toward her little tykes. "That can be a start," he assured her. "I've seen women get strong by practicing discipline in their work. Or at home." She flinched at this. He said lightly, "Or maybe you just go for broke. Once I saw a girl shoot a can clean off a dog's back."

Another anecdote he trotted out for his classes, that mousy girl and her war gun he and the guys had egged on when they were all stupid kids with too much time and smart-ass swagger on their hands. He always left out the part about the German pornography those girls had with them. The story usually raised disbelief and amusement among the women. But Lea's odd smile vanished. "What?"

"Yeah. It was one gutsy move." Lea looked bewildered. She glanced out the window again, a hand clutching her other arm as if he'd nicked her. Must be sensitive to animal welfare. "It turned out okay," he told her. "The dog wasn't hurt at all. She saved its life, in fact. But you'd never have thought, looking at her, that she was a crack shot. My point being, I don't think she knew it, either."

Before he could explain the whole story, about the bet, about the girls taking that dog with them when they left, how Rilke had thought from the get-go that the mousy girl could sense that dog was being abused, Lea stood up abruptly and walked to the door. *Jesus Christ.* Rilke cleared his throat, was about to plead with her to hold on a sec, when she stopped at his jacket, drifting slackly from its hook, and plunged a hand into one of the pockets.

The exact correct pocket, as it turned out. When she turned to face him, she wasn't exactly pointing his weapon directly at him, but close enough that his prior experience with her skill set in that arena provoked a sweat. "Why are you people always so *condescending*? How about you find my husband's attackers? I mean, you can't even get my TV back." That odd, tight smile was back. "Although you were a real help with the deer."

The ongoing work of locating Johnson's attackers was no doubt in the hands of one of his underappreciated colleagues in that jurisdiction, but facts were clearly now beside the point in the heat of emotion. Although Lea was projecting the opposite of emotion with her flat eyes and off-kilter grin. "You gonna use that?" He adopted the aggressive tone, to put her off her footing.

She wasn't buying it. "Do you deserve it?"

"Does it matter?"

That got through to her. She lowered the gun a bit, looked out the window again as if assessing how far the cottage was from the empty road. "It does. It should, anyway." She was speaking to him differently now. Patiently, as though he needed things explained to him. Which didn't change the angle of the barrel, sort of pointing at him again and disconcertedly steady. "Sometimes I don't know who I hate more. Him, or you."

That hard look was back, as though he'd failed to do something. The same look he'd seen her flash her husband behind the man's egotistical back. "Okay. What's the plan here? How are you going to hurt me?"

Throwing her words back at her made her pause. Her eyes glazed over again. "Nothing I could do would hurt you." She set the gun on the table, orienting the barrel toward him, not that she realized it.

"That's not true."

She stared at him then. Assessing him. Maybe wondering why he hadn't moved to secure the gun, which was a question he'd ask himself when he looked back on his half-assed response to this situation. Instead he unbuttoned his shirt, starting at the waist. What the hell was he thinking, with the gun unsecured and the distance in her expression, like that startling coldness she'd shown toward her tykes? She watched the unclasping of the shirt buttons, the removal of the shirt, the folding and the placement on the polished oak floor. He stood, arms draped at his hips. She was looking at his chest the way she would stare at an empty wall. Not demanding to know what on earth he was doing. Not into it, either; that he could tell for sure.

He'd never stripped like this in front of Jules, who preferred to be in charge of who was stripping what from where during their intimate encounters. But in the absence of any reaction from Lea, how could he avoid looking like a chump, except take off the boots? The socks came off of their own volition. A damn shameful sight, those thick yellow nails he hadn't trimmed for a while, and the oak flooring was frigid. He detected a slight nod, or thought he did, so he undid his belt buckle. Waited for her to say something. He slid the denim down to his ankles. Folded up the socks in the pants and placed them neatly on top of the shirt.

She drew a breath. He stood very still. "Go lie down," she said in a voice he'd never heard from her. Clinical was the word that came to mind. She picked up the gun and pointed it straight at him this time. Two-handed grip, steady and ready. As though she knew exactly what to do with him now. *Jesus Christ.*

A scream sounded outside the cottage window. Just a fox, but Lea must have mistaken it for a human cry and started. The gun clattered to the floor.

Rilke retrieved the weapon and set it on the kitchenette counter. "It's just an animal."

Lea had gone pale again, timid and scared. Back to the helpless act, which he now recognized as just that. "You're not even going to look?"

A plea to *see*, when she wouldn't so much as give a glance at him standing right there in front of her in his briefs.. "I don't need to." He gave her the brusque tone. Which she could take as condescending all that she pleased. He pulled his pants back on.

Lea crossed to the window. Likely saw the critter hauling ass across the field. "There's a woman out there," she said.

Jules. Shit. He grabbed his shirt and went to look. Lea stood there with him, head to shoulder as if nothing that wasn't completely natural had just happened between them. But it was Mutti, threading her way through the brittle cornstalks close to the cottage's walkway. She was holding Papa's shirt, which had landed right in her path when he chucked it outdoors.

"It's my mother," he said.

"Why did she scream?"

"That was an animal. Like I said." He didn't mean to sound impatient, but she could see for herself his mother was fine. But maybe the screech reminded her of the doe. She was so pale, with that flat, leaden look in her eyes. Lea picked up her sweater from the chair, pulled it on, and rubbed the static from her mussed hair. He stifled the impulse to touch her shoulder, her hand, any part of her he could reach, and why was he about to let her just walk out after she'd pointed his own gun at him?

Lea saved his mother the trouble of knocking by leaving the door wide open when she left. If she exchanged any pleasantries with Mutti, Lea harassed and hurried, his mother suppressing her surprise to see a female who wasn't Julia bolting from her son's place, Rilke couldn't hear a word.

Rilke's mother had nothing to say about the woman who'd hurried past her in the middle of the day, in the middle of the family field, nor did she so much as glance at Rilke's socks and boots and belt in the middle of the floor. When she pointed out that his shirt was buttoned askew, she might have smiled a bit as he sorted himself out. Mutti had always been loving to Julia in the practical sense. She ran meals over when Jules was working long hours. She knit beautiful scarves and shawls in doubtful shades of gray and green, colors Rilke would never think suited Jules but ended up bringing out colors in her eyes and skin he'd never noticed before. She'd never once butted in with a tiresome question about whether they planned to have kids. But his mother always went silent when Julia was around, a pained concentration as if she were treading water until help arrived. She set Papa's shirt down on the table and refused Rilke's offer of coffee.

"What on earth was this doing outdoors? Looks like there's a tear on the cuff too."

She looked genuinely upset. Rilke apologized, which Mutti didn't seem to hear, gazing at the shirt as if it were Papa's very corpse, not a rag she couldn't scrub the reek of whiskey from. He expected another tart word or two, but she asked after the Nixon boy instead.

"He's fine. Worried about his brother. Another prank night."

Mutti nodded. She was familiar with kids being dropped in the sticks. She'd helped a few find their way home on nights when the farmhouse was the first civilization they reached. She took her eyes from the shirt to look around the place. "Very nice, son. It's good to see it looking like a home." The compliment turned his stomach. He thanked her. Of course she could tell he was being insincere. "What are your plans, Paul?"

"You're looking at them." He meant it as a joke, but she looked at him sharply.

"You know you're welcome to stay here for a bit longer."

He waited for her to define *a bit longer*, or what exactly she meant by even questioning whether he felt welcome. But she let the words hang, or speak for themselves, or whatever intent she was projecting. Except he couldn't figure out why she'd trekked over only to inform him there was a fuzzy timeline to occupying the cottage he'd renovated and now maintained.

"Got another tenant lined up?"

"I'm putting the house and the land up for sale."

His surprise shook him. He'd never once thought she wouldn't stay in the house until she couldn't anymore. In the way of adult children who only ever knew one home growing up, Rilke's mother and her house were one and the same bedrock. "In this economy?" He decided to focus on the practical instead of questioning why she'd *want* to move, given that the prior land sale had made upkeep on the house plenty affordable for the foreseeable future. And thanks to Rilke and Mutti both, the farmhouse was in impeccable shape, even if the kitchen needed an upgrade, which he'd offered to do for her plenty of times.

"I've had some interest. I'll do fine." Interest she hadn't shared with him.

"Where are you going to live?"

"Saginaw. Carol can use the help. And I could use more time with the boys while I'm still healthy enough to enjoy them."

So this was Caroline's plan, then. Rilke should have seen it coming in the chronic mismanagement of her life that seemed, at times, deliberate.

"Anyway, I wanted to let you know in plenty of time to make other arrangements."

He fought the impulse to offer to buy her out, annoyed that the thought would even pop into his mind. He should be grateful to Carol for offering up a clean break with all that was left of the life and living Rilke had refused to carry on. But he couldn't help the feeling of confusion, maybe even grief, at the thought of her moving away from him. Or maybe he was feeling some deep fear that he'd let his mother down, although she'd never said a bad word about his decision to choose law enforcement over farming. "Okay, I appreciate knowing." He wasn't used to seeing such marked relief in her expression. She'd been dreading the telling, which made him feel more confused, or sad. Or like a fuck-up. "I'll be happy to clean out junk, of course. Repairs, and if you want the kitchen redone?"

She shook her head. "I don't want to put a penny in I don't have to, if someone will take it as is."

To tear it down, was Rilke's gut-flipping reaction. Build more manses on the other side of the recession, houses with no character or quality and occupants too busy with their careers to use them as much more than hotels. "You can afford to hold out for the recovery, you know."

"That's good advice, son." Mutti moved to him, gave him a tight, fleeting hug that warmed him, and let him go in the same quick movement. "Make sure you follow it yourself."

After his mother left, cradling Papa's shirt with a fondness he never would understand, Rilke downed a glass of warm, cloudy water, too thirsty to let the tap run cold. On the dresser, his cell screen lit up. An unfamiliar number, which he would have ignored if he hadn't thought Lea might be calling, forgetting for the moment she didn't know his phone number.

His mouth went dry at the anticipation of her voice. But Starkey's briny wheeze was the disappointment that crawled through the receiver.

"There's a disturbance, Paul."

"Gary. It's the middle of the day."

"Just notifying you regarding the goings on." Starkey slurred his words. Drunk already. "Per your request."

"I'm off duty." After Lea, he couldn't face Jules, not right now. He didn't want to see her again, ever, period. Miraculously, this conviction didn't feel lonely at all. "How about you just go inside and shut your door."

"I am inside, Paul. I hear through the walls. There's no avoiding it."

"Try shutting that door real tight." Rilke stepped to the window. Moisture dimpled the frame's whitewashed seams. Outside the sun was low behind the corn's bent stalks. Later than he'd realized. Had he been with Lea for that long? Their boots had beaten down the grass around the guest cottage. He couldn't see any new prints leading away from him. When she left, maybe she'd retraced their impressions.

Starkey said, "You *said* to call you."

Not a reminder Rilke needed at the moment. "I'm hanging up, Gary."

"I'm afraid for her damn safety here, Paul." Starkey must be holding the phone catawampus because a thudding sound, and then an outright thump, filtered through the wheezy breathing. The man must be stumbling around the place like a pinball piloted by a loser. "She's my girl too."

"Okay." And welcome to her too. Rilke quashed the sarcasm, which anyway would be lost on the inebriated, doomed as they were to the literal interpretation. A breeze ruffled the trampled grass. The impressions, his and Lea's, softened on their way to vanishing. The last paver on the cottage's approach was crumbled. Weathered, or he'd dropped something heavy there without seeing the damage. And the window would need caulking. Since he'd moved in he'd neglected basic maintenance. Well, he was pledging right this moment to mend that too.

Starkey amped up the threats. "I'm going over myself."

Another thump, like a door being thrown wide. The knob had punched through the drywall if Rilke was any judge of sound effects. "Okay, Gary. Just stay inside. I'll check it out." He disconnected the call. He'd drive by, all right, and ticket the old man if he didn't find at least a misdemeanor disturbance in progress.

PART 3

FEAR EXTINCTION

17

After she left—fled—that cop, hightailing it past his mother, of all people, Lea cowered in the half-bath off her kitchen, retching into the toilet. Above her, the kids played in Kurt's room. The ceiling shifted under mysterious movements that left no clues to their quiet game. Kurt had locked the doors just like she'd told him to. Jay hadn't yet returned from the range. When the sickness passed, Lea pressed her brow to the rim, but the pine odor of toilet bowl cleaner made her sick again. Her fingers stung as though the nerves had been cauterized. She stood up and ran hot water on her hands. Her fingers stung worse. Had she cut herself in places she couldn't see? The ceiling rippled like a rolling body bearing down.

How long had she left the kids alone? *Why* had she? She recalled the doe crumpled in the pit, her back against the rusty plow's teeth, and the cop's—Paul's—concern over the blood on her hands. She'd been woozy, she couldn't have made it home. She'd had no choice but to go with him. Then he'd stripped, right in front of her, and she'd gone for his gun. Or was it the other way around? She'd told him to go lie down, before the scream. That she remembered. What would have happened if they hadn't been interrupted and he'd done what he was told?

Could it be true that he had no idea who she was when he told her he'd seen her shoot at that dog? But then, she hadn't recognized him. She still couldn't place him. Why would she? Those boys that day had been the first details she'd forgotten whenever she recalled shooting at *him.*

She splashed hot water on her face. From upstairs a door slammed. Bunny screamed. Dripping water, Lea called her name and raced up the stairs. Blue twine trailed from the banister knob. A green string hung limply from her bedroom doorknob. Down the hall, Kurt threw open his bedroom door, the yellow Latex gloves still swallowing his thin arms. Bunny stood solemnly on the other side, cradling her cheeks with her hands. Blood streamed down her chin and blotched her shirt like polka dots. Plain brown twine waved from the doorknob, a bumpy pearl lassoed at the end.

"Got her." Kurt peeled off the gloves and plucked the tooth from the twine's loop.

"Thank you." Bunny pressed a fist to her mouth.

Lea grabbed a cloth from the hall closet and knelt to dab her chin. "Oh, honey. Does it hurt?"

"Your breath is stinky, Momma." Bunny turned her face away and curled her arms around her neck.

The hug felt like welts on her skin. Lea drew back. Bunny's sparkling gaze unnerved her. Her poor mouth looked so raw. "Kurt, that is not the way we pull teeth in this house! We wait for them to fall out on their own. When they're ready."

Kurt said, "Daddy does it this way."

"I asked him to, Momma." Bunny pulled away. "It took *so many* tries to get it out! Will the tooth fairy give me extra?"

"Me too." Kurt handed his sister her tooth. "I'm the one who pulled it."

"The fairy doesn't visit helpers," Bunny told him.

"Only when she doesn't know who the helpers *are*. I'm gonna leave a note for her."

"Not under *my* pillow," Bunny said.

Jay's voice drifted down the hall. Kurt ran to his dad. From the landing, Jay absorbed the bright twine hanging from the knobs, his son's eager tale, his daughter's triumphant gap already crusted over with a dark clot. "What happened to the lawn?"

"Did you put the kids up to this?" Lea demanded.

"Lea. There's blood on the lawn." Jay spoke slowly. He was acting like he was working to get through to her, when she could hear every word.

"The deer died there," Kurt explained to his dad.

"The deer *died*?" Bunny's eyes widened.

"The deer is resting, sweetie. Someplace safe." Lea looked at Jay. "Hit by a car."

"It might be the fawn's mom." Kurt frowned.

"Not likely, buddy." Although it was *very* likely, Lea thought, resenting the reassuring lie she herself would have offered if Jay hadn't.

"Good work on the tooth. Let's see your jack o' lantern, sweetheart." Jay grinned at Bunny. She ran up to him and grinned back.

"I did it by myself," Kurt boasted. "While Momma was out."

Jay stopped smiling. "You left the kids alone?"

Lea rubbed her hands together. "I was only gone a moment."

Kurt said solemnly, "It was a long time. The man said he would help Momma so I got sent inside. I locked the door."

"It's okay, Daddy," Bunny said. "We got a lot done here."

Jay ruffled her hair. "Hey, kids. Go downstairs and play, 'kay?"

"What about my tooth?" Bunny held up her little pearl. "It might get lost down there."

Jay took it and slipped it into his pocket. "I'll hold on to it. Such a pretty tooth." He watched the kids race down the stairs before looking at Lea. "So is that the guy you're sleeping with?"

Lea laced her hands behind her back. "What?"

"The man coming over in the middle of the day? That you leave the kids to see? Is that why you came home early today?"

"He did *not* come over! He helped me with the deer. He's a cop," she added.

Jay took in her nervous slouch, the sweat blistering her brow. "You're lying to me. You never used to lie. Not ever."

From the den, the television blared the theme song from a cartoon Lea used to watch with the kids during lunch when she was a stay-at-home, before Abel hired her. Why was she sweating when the hallway was so cold? The cop's house had been hot. Now that heat was *attached* to her.

"Are you in love with him?" Jay asked quietly.

The harder she clenched them behind her back, the worse her hands tingled. Kurt's twine stirred on the doorknobs, bits of color set in motion by a breeze she couldn't feel. Did Jay know he was blocking the stairs so she couldn't get past? She relaxed her hands, and the pain stopped. She wasn't cut, or bruised, she hadn't been harmed at all, and had Jay just had the *nerve* to ask her about love?

She headed toward him, hoping he'd get out of her way so she didn't have to push him. "Let me by."

He stepped to the side with an irritating flourish of his hands, like a game show host. "Did you think I wouldn't?"

He was just taunting her, but Lea slipped past him, gripped the banister, and looked up at him. The stubbled silvery hair, the scars that from this angle looked fresh, angry, newly slashed into his skin. Was he perfecting his aim with all that practicing he was doing? It would never occur to him to wonder what she was capable of doing with a gun. What she'd almost just done to Paul. What she'd decided she was about to do to *him*.

She turned away to head downstairs. "Does that mean you're going to see your cop?" Jay called out, louder than he had to. Did he want the kids to hear?

She ignored him on her way out the front door. What would he make of the truth, that to escape him, and him, and *him*, she was going to run to Dinah after all?

<h1 style="text-align:center">18</h1>

Damn Starkey for not erring on the literal side when it came to behavioral suggestions, or even direct orders. When Rilke arrived at Peachtree Court, he nearly knocked the old man down when he exited his vehicle. "Gary. I told you to stay inside."

"I went in after her, Paul," Starkey wheezed. Rilke assessed the house: drapes drawn, unusual for the daytime since Jules loved sunlight. Door shut tight, all orderly that he could see. He suppressed a gag at the man's unwashed breath, which purred with milk, not sour grain. Maybe the slurring words and erratic behaviors of late weren't entirely about the booze. The loony outfits, wholly inappropriate for the cold weather, sure didn't project a guy still in possession of all his mental facets. A hole-riddled robe was knotted over canvas pants. The collar of a proper weight work shirt cinched the sagging neck under the robe's moth-eaten placket. The man must have grabbed that rag instead of his coat. Ditto the slippers, white fuzzies rammed onto his skinny bare feet. He'd accepted long ago that in the absence of relatives, Rilke himself would have to step up on the care front if it came to that. From the looks of things, that front was moving in fast. "I knocked, anyway. She's not answering her door."

"Her prerogative whether to come to her own door." Across the court, Grace what's-her-name was staring out her living room window. Nothing for the woman to see besides Gary, which was entertainment enough. Except for a rust-splashed Honda parked carefully at the legal distance from the hydrant, the court was empty of cars.

"This used to be a peaceful street when you lived here." The man stumbled again, right into Rilke's chest. Almost knocked them both down.

Rilke righted Gary with a firm hand that skirted the territory of a shove. "Seems pretty peaceful at the moment. How about we get you inside?"

"I miss you, Paul."

"Not a lot of opportunity to miss me, Gary, since you call me over here so much."

"You treat me with respect. You both do. Your Julia looks me in the eye, when most folks don't see me at all."

Starkey was damn near hugging Rilke now, and there was real potential for weeping in the near term. "She's not my Julia. Let's try to ease up on the self-pity," Rilke suggested.

"Will *you* look at me, Paul?"

It hadn't occurred to Rilke until that moment that he'd taken in the old man's clothing, the legally parked Honda, both men's firm footing in Julia's drive as a result of his salting, and the flutter of Grace's drapes as she withdrew into her house, all as a way of not raking a glance over the bloodshot eyes or the liver-spotted nose or the face's rubbery skin. He'd avoided looking directly at Papa too. Hated seeing the delayed effects—of alcohol, of aging, of cruelties both practical and unjustified—that scarred their bodies, or maybe Rilke hated that the best he could do against these men was to avoid looking.

"*Will* you?" Starkey swayed backward to give Rilke plenty of room to focus.

Although Rilke was put off by the sentiment, he couldn't refuse a direct request from a long-term acquaintance. But the degree to which he had to prepare to apply genuine scrutiny to the pellets squinting from under the puffy bags and narrow lids surprised him. Beneath these obstacles, Starkey's eyes shone in the slanting sun, making their benign gravelly color almost attractive.

"That's good, Paul." Starkey held his gaze for an interval far past comfort. "Feels good to be *seen*."

Rilke crossed his arms and decided he would not be the man who looked away first. "Agreed there, Gary."

Maybe something in Rilke's tone communicated that he was managing the old man. Starkey scuffed his fluffy slippers on the blacktop like a kid. Best to salvage both their dignity and move him inside. Rilke propelled Starkey to his porch. Starkey managed to insert one more upsetting sentiment before Rilke could open the door and stow him inside. "Can't you make it up with Julia and come home?"

During the escort to the porch, Starkey's robe had fallen open. Rilke saw now that blood dotted the canvas work shirt underneath. "You hurt there?" Rilke nodded to the stains.

Starkey plucked at his shirt and scratched at the blood like pesky evidence. Black flakes lodged under his nail. "Sometimes I'm careless handling the deer."

Rilke looked at Starkey's slippers to avoid the nauseating spatter. "Tell you what, Gary. I'm coming for you tomorrow off my shift to get you checked out, all right? Call your doctor first thing. Book a long appointment."

Starkey tried to say something, *thank you, fuck you,* who knew? Rilke slammed the man's door, as if enough force would seal the jamb forever. Through the man's front window, Rilke watched Starkey shuffle to the home's shadowed interiors, he hoped to collapse on his bed and stay there.

Across the court Grace what's-her-name peeked out again. In all the years they'd been neighbors that couple never once had made a public display of any nuisance, including excessive affection. He, Rilke, was a quiet man. One of his primary faults, according to his own wife, mother, and sister. Yet he'd managed to manufacture noise out of every aspect of his life. Until Lea, his reticence had naturally drawn him to involvement with the raucous. Or maybe women were just predisposed to view a man going about his business as withdrawn.

He glanced at the house, feeling a certain pride that he could look at the place without a shred of care. The drapes were new, and a heavier style than he would have chosen. Mutti preferred the lacy sheer look for the farmhouse, so he'd grown up with light filtering through any weather. They were tightly enough drawn to look sewn together. Free of Starkey's loud voice he became aware of a pulse through her walls, maybe the bass line to one of those party songs she liked to crank up. As he walked to his car, the faint throb crystallized to music. Jazz stuff, like they played on the local public radio station. Which Julia never in her life had tuned into. A busy piano trill fluffed up the melody like a swatch of Mutti's chintz. Rilke studied the house, wondering how he could hear the music if the door was shut. He saw that it was in fact, slightly ajar. And the door looked odd.

He took a moment to absorb why. The lock's shiny, bland aluminum face was wiped clean of a keyhole. Only Jules would change her locks and then leave her door open, and did she really think installing a fancy smart lock without telling him was the way to operate with basic trust and respect moving forward?

Rilke took the porch steps and pushed the entry door open. The hallway was dim, no wonder with the late afternoon sunshine choked off, and she had the heat cranked up too. It felt like a sauna. A screwdriver and an installation manual for the lock lay on the foyer table. Voices spilled from the kitchen and the living room both. Way too many to fit in a Honda. The vapor of weed floated down the hallway like the stoner welcome wagon. Rilke unzipped his coat. The jazzy piano plinked on, brittle as a migraine.

In the living room several individuals huddled on his plush carpet nursing red Solo cups. Through the gloom Rilke recognized Jim Wagner from high school, lolling on a pot belly attached to where football muscle and his rosy future used to be. Melissa Green, who, in another life where she still had looks and a sweet voice, sang the lead in the high school production of *Lil Abner,* was sitting cross-legged next to him, alternating between sucking on a pencil and a joint. Rilke had already ticketed Melissa a couple of times for possession, so this one would land her in felony trouble. The green equalizer lights on Rilke's stereo flashed furiously to the jazz piano as if chasing down the erratic beat.

"Do it again," a young woman Rilke didn't recognize begged Jim. She looked to be little more than a teen, way too young to be hanging with a high school has-been in Rilke's living room. If she pulled on the joint, he'd be busting Melissa for providing drugs to a minor too.

Jim leaned over the coffee table. "Open sesame," he intoned into a remote.

The drapes swept open on the silky hum of a motor. Startled, Rilke ducked out of sight behind the doorway jamb. In the sudden splay of light, he saw that calculators and heavy books took up the real estate on the coffee table not covered in rolling paper, clumps of weed, and ash. A burgundy blot near the sofa dampened the tasteful gray wool carpet he and Jules had sweated to pay for and was barely a year old.

The underage girl giggled. "Neat."

Melissa switched from chewing on the pencil eraser to smoking the joint. "Luke's a maniac. He's got everything connected. I mean, who needs smart drapes?"

"You can program them any way you want. Even fake being home when you travel," Jim pointed out.

Melissa exhaled. "Wonder what Jules thinks of him being able to control the whole house remotely?"

Jim took over the joint. "It's not controlling. It's *convenient.*"

Leave while you can, Rilke's wiser self suggested, but Julia's high, busy voice grating from the kitchen, not to mention the irritation he could no longer pretend wasn't messing with his new, healthy resolutions for the future, blotted out the counsel. He pushed down the hall and stood assessing at the kitchen doorway. The music, now a cloying trumpet ditty, leaked from a source Rilke couldn't identify. Bright new LED bulbs he certainly didn't install above the island sprayed rainbow hues on the scene. Partying all around, the guests thick around a blender filled with ruby sludge, as if it took a village to whip up a beverage. An unsteady young woman with pink eyeshadow was peeling a banana. Someone ran the blender without tightening the lid, and the ruby drink splashed over onto the counter. Some joker licked up the puddle, tonguing the granite Rilke had, himself, installed.

Julia, golden hair mussed at her shoulders as if she'd just come from bed, was bent over the table littered with junk-food packaging, backside to Rilke in those tight jeans he'd sworn never to study with interest again. Rilke looked away to see deep gashes cut into the floor polish. Damage from skinny Luke's fancy work on the bat. The blender motor whirred. Laughter hummed along with the motor's whine. Now the young woman hadn't put the stopper in the lid. The joker lapped the blender lid and then the girl's hand.

Through the distractions, Rilke became aware that Julia was leaning over to talk to someone hunched in a chair, clutching a throw around his shoulders as if he were freezing, despite the furnace chugging along full blast.

Rilke had to look twice to assess fully whom he was seeing. "Mr. Nixon," he said, loudly. Somehow through the trumpet and debauchery, the young man made eye contact. Julia jumped too, a jerky straightening like a salute, which was a satisfaction. Why was she wearing glasses? Her eyes were enormous behind big round tortoise-shell frames straight out of the '50s. At least she looked utterly surprised before the pissed-off attitude descended.

"What are you doing here?" she demanded.

"Cool off, Jules." He kept it brisk. Nixon stared at him. He appeared not to recognize Rilke at all even though he'd seen him out of uniform. How Homer had ended up in Rilke's kitchen clutching a red plastic cup, with Julia's busy mouth at his lobe, was an irreconcilable visual. But something about Homer's face was off. The eyes were oriented closer to the nose's bridge than Rilke remembered. The face was rounder, the neck longer. Slowly, Rilke took in other facets. The flash of a navy blazer under the throw. Bare knees peeking out from the folds. And the throw. Thick white cotton, hemmed with satin ribbon.

Lea's blanket. *Jesus Christ.* That she hadn't been lying after all was more of a relief than a surprise.

"You can't just walk in here, Paul," Julia scolded as if she hadn't left her door open for anyone to do just that.

From the living room the drapery motor whined. Peals of laughter rolled into the kitchen. Rilke crossed to the kid, which meant nudging Julia a bit because she refused to move out of the way. She shoved him back, her version of pouting. Rilke floated a name, *Russell?*

The boy nodded, impassive, a wary blank slate. A deep cut on his brow had barely scabbed over, probably sustained from a tree branch. He appeared to be favoring his left arm too. Rilke scanned the blanket for any sign of blood and was relieved to find it clean. He looked in okay shape. Despite his size, the boy looked much younger than fourteen. The red plastic cup held something green, flecked with ice, probably a margarita. The kid reeked of corn nuts.

Rilke took the cup away and plunked it down among the Fritos and cheese curls. A textbook and notes on lined paper detailing some species of learning Rilke didn't recognize occupied the other end of the table. He pressed a hand to the blanketed shoulder. The kid flinched. Rilke asked him if he was all right. Russell nodded. *No way am I talking,* the kid's silence seemed to say, not while the blender churned on.

Julia was crowding Rilke, waging shrill words into his ear that overlaid the whiny trumpet like just another track. He gave her another shove. She grabbed the tabletop as if he'd pushed her hard enough to lose her balance. Her glasses tilted as though he'd knocked them, but he'd seen her hand make that sneaky adjustment. "Cut it out, Paul," she cried, a few decibels louder than her usual complaints. Russell stared at them like he'd been scalded and scooted the chair back, rocking dangerously on the two back legs.

A man came over, hair greased back like an achievement. "Hey, watch the lady. You okay, Jules?"

Julia mouthed at the guy, *don't.*

"Back off," Rilke said.

"Back off where?"

Julia tossed her glasses on the table. "Leave, Paul. Right now. Unless you're gonna be petty and bust us for the weed?"

"You a cop?" Back-off paled and backed off to the counter.

Rilke looked down at Russell shivering in the blanket and asked if he'd called his dad yet. Russell shook his head. Rilke took his phone from his coat pocket. The movement disturbed his jacket so that the kid saw his holstered firearm. He erupted in screams and bolted, blanket streaming, to the other side of the kitchen island. The blender crowd whooped *what happened* and folded young Nixon into a scaffold of protective arms and Julia cried out, "Nice work, Paul."

Skinny whiz kid Luke rounded the corner from the direction of the bathroom bearing a sopping towel, a Costco-size box of Band-Aids, and a spray bottle of Bactine. Water streamed onto the wood flooring. The boy genius couldn't even wring out a towel to avoid stains and the slipping hazard that now had Mr. Fiancé skidding in his own puddle. Maybe he couldn't do anything practical unless it involved wireless control. The insubstantial tailbone whammed on the floorboards. The Bactine skidded toward Jules. Band-Aids leaped from the box and rained down on Luke's lap. *Whoa man* was the feeble reaction from the floor.

"What the fuck, Paul," Julia yelled as if he'd tripped her man.

Russell buried his face in the blanket. Back-off was rubbing the kid's shoulders like a prize fighter, as if deep massage was the key to controlling the situation. Julia pulled Luke to his feet. The fiancé was such a lightweight she could haul him up with one delicate hand. At least they'd hushed their mouths. Any minor griping as they rounded up the Band-Aids was swallowed by the mellow saxophone that had replaced the long-winded trumpet.

Rilke approached the island, provoking general consternation. "It's okay, Russell." He drew out the badge and slid the wallet across the sticky counter.

Russell peeked over the blanket's hem. "Shit," someone said. The pink eye shadow swallowed wrong and sprayed her drink back into the blender canister. "Are we busted?"

Rilke said, "Anything illegal in that blender there?"

The young woman's gaze slid to the hallway, in the direction of the living room stoners. "It's a smoothie, sir."

"Sure it is. Clear out. Take your buddies in the other room with you."

The migration was noisy but efficient. Julia pitched in with the herding, ushering folks out the back door, keeping her cool out of spite, Rilke imagined. Jim and Melissa slunk past, clutching book bags crammed full, pretending not to recognize him. Did Melissa realize Rilke was letting her off? Jim had once been Rilke's worse tormentor, the expert in wise-guy farmer cracks. Better to keep up the pretense of strangers than be beholden to Rilke for setting them free but stoned into the late afternoon sun. The party crowd fanned out through the backyard and headed for the footpath bounding the neighbor's lot to Apple Blossom Lane. Explained the empty court. He glanced at Julia. She shut the door and shrugged.

"You always ticket them when they park on our street."

Luke had shepherded Russell Nixon back to the chair to administer the Bactine. The radio programming was now in pledge-drive mode. The announcer's droning repetition of the drive's phone number was driving a headache straight between Rilke's eyes.

"Turn that off," Rilke told Julia.

Luke fished a phone from his pocket. "Kitchen off," he murmured into the device.

The rainbow bulbs above the island glowed, then dimmed. The announcer fell silent in the kitchen. From the living room the pledge-drive break yielded to a clarinet boogie.

"Living room off," Luke mumbled.

The clarinet cut out on a woodsy shriek. Luke stowed the phone back in his pants and moved to the counter to mop up the mess.

Julia called out, "Thanks, sweetie," in a sugary tone designed to get Rilke's goat even more than mating speakers with light bulbs and connecting the entire house to the guy whose name wasn't on the mortgage. "By the way, Paul, pretty soon you'll be working with Luke. Our company just landed a contract with the county sheriff's office. GPS, CCTV, gunshot detectors. No more waiting for service calls. The system scans for disturbances and dispatches you right away. Then you won't be able to even take Gary's bullshit calls."

Rilke decided to ignore everything about what Jules had just laid out for the future of policing, including the *our company* crap. Plus, with her lifestyle choices, what made her think this house wouldn't be tagged right away as a disturbance? He turned back to Russell and set his cell phone on the table. "Call your daddy. Then we're going to get you checked out."

"I don't want to go nowhere but home."

"We'll get you there." Rilke turned to Julia, amped up for real now and trying not to give her the satisfaction of knowing it. "I need to speak to you."

"I don't have anything to say." She flashed a look at Luke, not so manly now with a sopping dishrag rather than the badminton racket in hand.

"She doesn't have anything to say," Luke echoed feebly, although he did manage to puff up the flat poster board that passed for a chest. "I think you need to leave." Luke stepped toward him, a tiptoe maneuver that looked anything but territorial. Rilke almost felt sorry for him.

"Come any closer and you'll need that badminton racket again, son," he advised.

Jules said calmly, "With threats like that, maybe you'll be interested in our BWV project."

"Let's not escalate…" Luke started in, but Julia grinned.

"That's Body Worn Video, for your information. Cops in the UK are reporting that harassment claims from the public are down forty percent or something when they have the body cams on. We're betting on it being the next big thing in police reform over here, right, Luke?"

Luke's mouth stayed firmly shut.

"Sounds like a solid move in the direction of public confidence," Rilke pointed out, instead of what he wanted to say, which was to strap a camera on him any time he was around his wife and let the public sort out who was harassing whom. "Alone. Now, Jules."

She folded her arms. "Or what?"

That did it. He grabbed her by the elbow and steered her to their bedroom. On his maintenance visits, he'd never ventured into this room. No appetite for the reminder that he still thought of it as their room, for one thing. It was a surprise, he had to admit, to see it clean and orderly. Just as he'd always kept it, since Jules never had the patience for housework. Oak flooring clean and buffed. Bureau top neatly lined with her childhood knickknacks, unicorns of porcelain and pewter and some hand-knitted ones with sagging horns and fraying eyes. Sweet mementos her mother had given her over the years. Divorcing Jules's dad would have been the most productive gift by far, but Jules loved these tokens and insisted on marshaling them there on the bureau so she would see them first thing every morning. Only the bed was mussed, with the corners all untucked and the quilt shaped into a bolster near the headboard. He couldn't squash the visual of his Omi's quilt being used for some sexual exercise, because why else would an heirloom assume that unnatural position? The shades were up. Just across the grassy strip between the houses, the blinds were up on Starkey's bathroom window too.

Rilke struggled to keep his voice level. "This kid has been missing, Julia. Why didn't you report it?"

Julia crossed to the bureau and dug a breath mint from a tin. "He just walked in, Paul. I thought he'd been *invited.* I was just asking him who he was when you descended on us."

Now that he was turned to face her, he saw a puddle on the other side of the bureau, from some drink she'd spilled and hadn't bothered to wipe up before it warped the boards. Typical thoughtlessness leading to easily avoided damage that he'd have to repair. He'd picked up after her almost every day of their lives. Likely the floor was crap-free now because Luke had been promoted to cleanup duty. "Invited? He's wearing a blanket. He doesn't have any pants on."

"I thought it was one of our blankets. You heard him. He said he was *cold.* Plus how was I supposed to know he was missing his pants when he wouldn't take the blanket off?"

"He's fourteen years old and you're giving him margaritas because he's cold?"

"How am I supposed to know what he doesn't tell me? You always expect me to be a mind reader. Well, guess what, he's drinking a smoothie, not a margarita, and by the way I don't live inside the head of every guy who shows up at my door. I legitimately thought he was from class."

"Class?"

"Calculus." She gave him a look, pissed but wary. "We were having study group. I'm taking classes at the CC."

The textbooks in the kitchen and the living room made sense, and then didn't. "You failed Calc in high school, Jules."

"That's why I'm in the *intro* class. Which sometimes has teenagers in it because some of them are *accelerated.*"

"Are the potheads accelerated too?"

"Jim Wagner's in my class, okay? He's turning his life around, fyi on an example you could stand to follow. Some of the old crowd tagged along, so what. Doesn't give you the right to just walk in here."

She didn't even have the sense to be grateful that he'd let the so-called old crowd off the hook and since when had she re-buddied up with the very bastards who'd harassed Rilke the worst back in the day whenever Rilke's quiet act failed to keep him under the radar? Jules got up close, like she always did when she was messing with him. Under the breath mint seeped the odor of cheese curls and coffee. He felt a coil, then, of missing her. Why did he always want her most when she was being mean? He met her eyes, bleary, still enormous even without the scholar glasses magnifying the hell out of them. Although she was facing the window, her pupils hadn't shrunk, he realized then, and felt the fool.

"Are you on something, Jules?"

She gave him a hard push. "What I'm on is *you*. On your *ass*."

Her lips were plumped up. From sex; what else? He glanced pointedly at the quilt roll. "That how he makes love to you?"

She drew back a step. "Wait. I don't make the bed and your dirty mind takes a detour? I mean, when are you going to grow up, Paul?"

He stared at her lips. "Maybe your new man should program the shades to shut when you two go at it."

A response he would change if he could.

"Oh my God." Her mouth went slack. Sunlight burrowed in the troughs fanning from her pout. The fine wrinkles crinkling her eyes looked chiseled. It occurred to him that the flat sheen on her gaze could reasonably be exhaustion. Or nearsightedness. She marched over to the bed and pulled something out of the ripples of slouched pillows and rumpled sheets. Something fluffy and soft. Long, tender hairs, pink and black button nose. His stomach lurched. A kit, snuggling close to Jules without waking up, except who could tell on the slumber front since the long messy hair erased the face.

Jules nuzzled the head. No purr. Either the cat was hostile, or the cat was really a dog. One of those toy breeds, more fur than flesh, that served no deterrent purpose at all.

"You hate dogs, Jules."

"You're the one who hates them, Paul." She kissed the nose. A tiny pink tongue snaked out lazily. Too lazily. There was something wrong with the animal. "Or wait. Maybe it's cats you don't like."

He classified that last remark as another dig rather than a cruel loss of memory about his history with cats. "What's wrong with it?"

"*He* just had surgery. Sleepy guy. So you can stop fantasizing about why my bed's sloppy."

Not too sleepy to piss on the floor. Rilke went to the bureau, slid open the second drawer where his T-shirts and briefs used to be kept. Still there. Skinny Luke's insubstantial garments hadn't pushed his out yet. He grabbed a Hanes stained yellow beyond salvage and dropped it on the puddle.

"I'm sorry," Jules said.

He'd never heard her apologize for anything, period, which put his guard up, all right. He mopped up the piddle and tossed the tee in the laundry basket on the other side of the dresser. "Can't blame the little guy."

"I don't mean the pee, Paul. Look at me." A command he was happy to obey, although her soft tone and overall gentle vibe was giving him the creeps, if he was honest. Under Rilke's stare, the little dog flopped his legs around Jules's neck and nestled under her chin. "I'm sorry for all the times I got in your face. I'm sorry for all the anger I have, and all the unhealthful ways I expressed it. I take full responsibility, and I regret my behavior."

She wouldn't meet the attentive gaze she'd asked him to shell out, so who knew where she was going with the contrition. "Working this out in therapy, then?"

"Yes, in fact, I am. And besides sorry, I want to thank you. For taking care of me. Dad never hit me again after you dealt with him. No one's ever hassled me since. You were…effective."

Effective. Was that what loving him was to her? She was saying more about where things now stood, how she was trying to make her life better, the words distant as if they were flowing from the window, not her. "We grew up together, Paul. But we didn't grow. You know? So, can we get a divorce without any more drama?"

From the hall, the baseboards clacked from the heat ramping up. He shouldn't care about the d-word anymore. He should recognize his nauseated reaction as the stupid reflex he always suffered during an out-of-control situation, but he was hardwired to take everything about Julia to heart, and maybe what gets started as kids can't ever be outgrown, and what did she mean, *make my life better* when the life he'd made for her had been pretty good, fucking great, actually, and why couldn't he just walk out of this room right now and leave her the hell alone?

"I wish I'd never saved you from your dad," Rilke said quietly.

She did meet his eyes then. "So that's your answer? You wish that old man had ruined my life forever?"

"I only meant, I wish we had dated under different circumstances."

She moved toward him. He braced for one of her typical outbursts, some re-engineering of who wished for what and when. But she didn't say anything, or else she had nothing to say, for once. She shrugged the lapdog's paws from around her neck and handed the pup to Rilke. The dog didn't exactly assume the lovey pose it had bestowed upon Jules, but it didn't tense up either. Must be the sedative. Animals did tend to sense Rilke's general uptight attitude and act out accordingly.

Even with the soft little obstacle between them, they were leaning into each other; and the kiss, if it had begun, might never have ended if Rilke had any say about their lips and their love and their wishes, past, present, and future.

Luke appeared in the doorway, cell in hand as though he was prepping to install voice command over whatever might be happening in the bedroom. He skidded to a halt when confronted with the visual of his supposed fiancée in a near cuddle with her husband. "Hey! Don't touch my dog!"

Who would have guessed that skinny kid could project like that? That booming voice cut right through the sedative. The animal's deep growl and the sharp teeth that sank into Rilke's lower lip were the last insults he would have expected from a puppy, not to mention the impressive blood flow that stained the little thing's nose. Luke hollered something panicked and rude as if man had bitten dog and Julia, probably more embarrassed than regretful at being caught so close to her husband, snatched the pup away. She adopted a defensive stance, light and steady on the balls of the feet. Ready to flee or to come at him with everything she had, just as he'd taught her when they were still only kids.

19

Dinah had thought Lea would stand her up, but there she was, parked two rows away, although she could have pulled into the empty space next to the Jetta. She'd seen Dinah right away and driven by as if having second thoughts. Now she approached Dinah's car with shoulders hunched like she was riding out blows. Lea always did crave a dare. One only had to nudge her to get her to do anything. Her valiant attempt to act unfazed, that Dinah had—of course!—waited for her, was failing in the old endearing ways. Her relief showed in her quick walk and half-life smile. Her coat flapped open to reveal a stained sweater. Shaggy, uncombed hair blew in the wind sweeping the commuter lot. Lea had been hiding her body in such disarray since they were kids. How unchanged she was by the bulwarks she'd built, her home, and her family. Or maybe she *was* changed, for the worse, which itself would be an improvement. Through the window, Dinah waved like she was the out-of-town sister dropping by for her regular visit and tossed the brittle grin she knew Lea would find mocking. Raise the hackles, yes, get her on the defensive where she so loved to be.

Lea slid into the passenger seat. She wasn't about to say anything about being late. Let Dinah eat silence. But Dinah merely grinned at her as if she'd been considerately punctual and turned onto State Street toward town. The rusted silver Jetta would have suited her ten years and twenty-five pounds ago. At every light, the engine growled on the idle like a complaint.

When Dinah hung a right onto Hill, named for a local founder, Lea knew she was heading for the lab. So *he* was a ruse after all. She tried to remember if she'd read anything recently about Release and their bullshit tactics. Dinah wouldn't try to steal her ID again. She must have another way Lea wasn't picking up on. "You're not getting into the lab," she warned. "I told security to deny you entry to the building from now on."

Dinah glanced at her. Lea always looked so distressed when she was lying. She'd pressed herself to the door as if to leap out of the car, so afraid that Dinah would reply, *no, my dear, you didn't report me to your security.* Near Washtenaw, she turned right onto a residential street. Away from the lab. That should make Lea wonder. "What happened, Lea?" she asked mildly.

Lea looked down at her hands. At one time in her life, Dinah would have guessed Lea's secrets before she realized she was holding any, so at first she assumed Dinah was referring to the cop, Paul. "Nothing."

"To Jay."

Lea was startled. Jay hadn't mentioned Dinah, which didn't make sense. He'd be as shocked to see her as Lea had been. "You saw Jay?"

"In passing. Not to speak to. I drove by your house yesterday." Jay had been in the front yard playing catch with a little boy and a little girl, so Dinah had parked on the road to watch. Dinah had expected Lea to choose a house like this, no character, far too large, the type of big bland fort Lea would seek for shelter. Pretty children, though. Throwbacks to a more beautiful family line. The girl didn't resemble her mother at all. Neither did the boy. Poor Lea, so unlike them she might not be related at all. The wide eyes, the cheeks rosy with the cold, the light hair tumbling from their hats, were all Jay. At least, the Jay Dinah had last known. Even from a distance, she could see terrible scars on his face.

Lea hadn't asked yesterday whether Dinah had a family. Probably she knew how impossible children are for some women.

When Dinah had turned the engine over to drive away, Jay had glanced up. His expression hadn't changed. He must not have seen her behind the windshield's glare or recognized her if he had.

"Did he have an accident?" she pressed.

"Yes. I mean. Not exactly. He was attacked." For once Dinah didn't have a remark at the ready. Lea refused to fill the silence with details.

"I'm sorry," she said at last. "Was this long ago?"

"Last year."

Dinah glanced at her. "It is difficult to speak of?"

"Not particularly."

Dinah hesitated at an empty four-way stop, rolled through the intersection. "Then you can tell me."

Lea ignored the demand. Once she shared Jay's injuries with Dinah, other intimacies would be demanded. "How did you know where I live?"

"It is easy to find you, I have found you many times. I have kept tabs."

"Why, to use me again?"

"For my own selfish purposes, yes. I miss you."

As if Lea could ever be fooled again by her bullshit sincerity. If Dinah had been *keeping tabs*, why hadn't she known about Jay's attack? It was in all the papers. Lying as usual, humming into the silence, spinning the wheel with a practiced hand as if these streets were *her* home.

Dinah turned down Cambridge and pulled up to the Asian grocery store at the end of the street, a cramped market where Lea used to shop when she and Jay lived closer to town.

Lea stared at her. "Why did we come here?"

"He lives here." Dinah pointed to the second floor. Burred cedar shingles dangled from the battered siding. The landing of an old iron fire escape clung precariously to a cracked window. Traces of that morning's frost still dusted the sill.

"There's no apartment there." Ang's shop was a cherished, tucked-away local secret. The block building formed a rude outcropping on a three-sided curb, as if tossed by accident onto a street of rented bungalows and subdivided Queen Annes. When Lea had first moved to town, the shop was a tea house for the Russian and Eastern European immigrants seeking work with the university and a peaceful life on a quiet tree-lined street. Now the neighborhood housed Asian university students who would take their education back home. Ang's was the transient community's bedrock. Lea used to buy star anise and the rice threads the kids loved here. After the move to Centennial Farms, she stopped shopping here, not because the shop belonged to their old life, but because it was no longer convenient. She'd never even noticed the upper floor. If she had, she'd have assumed the space was used for storage.

"Apartment is a loose term, but yes."

Lea studied the second floor window. No shades, no sign of life. The glass pane reflected the fierce sun back to her. "How long?"

Dinah maneuvered to the curb between a rusty pickup and a Buick missing a wheel. Ang's triangular lot didn't have room for parking. Dinah pulled in too tight, rolled up on the curb. Lea felt the lurch as a wave of illness. "I didn't ask."

"You've been…in there?"

Dinah cut the engine. Across from the Jetta, a power line sagged from the listing poles like a playground jump rope. That she could have run into him anytime on this street made Lea shudder. More troubling was the thought that she had seen him and hadn't recognized him. That he would no longer be familiar was unthinkable.

"I befriended his sister; she leaves him in my care sometimes."

"He has a sister? How can he have a sister and—" *And do what he did to me?* But she couldn't say it aloud. Was this woman a monster? Had she belittled him, abused him, made him hate young girls? Or was it Lea who'd been different, nothing at all like the sister he loved?

"He's got a sister. He had a mom and dad. He got married and divorced. He moved to Indianapolis, became a teacher of industrial arts. He has lived an ordinary life." Lea leaned against the passenger door. Dinah added gently, "Nothing about him has ever been extraordinary, Lea."

"Except what he did to me."

Dinah reached for Lea's hand. They held on for a moment in the old way. Palms pressed tightly, fingers curled to form one fist. How many times had they clasped hands while running through fields or horsing around on the playground? Such easy contact then. This habit lasted into adulthood. As late as Worcester, just before the Jeffers raid when Dinah had appeared on her doorstep, she'd taken Dinah to the seaside, thinking the ocean would help soothe her latest heartbreak. They held hands on the beach, shared whiskey straight from the bottle. Lea had wondered then why they weren't lovers, and then chalked up her wonder to her usual confusion of affection with sex. *He*'d conditioned her to experience any touch as sexual. On the beach, with the waves caressing their ankles, their toes girlishly painted pink and tucked into the soft sand, Lea knew that if Dinah meant them to be lovers, they would be. Drunk on whiskey and the thin salty air, with Jay waiting for her at home, Lea didn't trust herself to question what she wanted.

But that day on the beach had proven to be the usual bullshit, Dinah's broken heart the ruse to steal her lab ID. This sudden appearance out of thin air, too, must be a lie, *he* the ruse. Lea yanked her hand away. "Why are you really here?"

"The single time I hold pure motives, you think to ask this question?"

"You're a liar. He doesn't even live here, he can't."

A woman holding a plastic bag pushed open Ang's door. Chopped spiky hair, a nose ring studded with steel beads the size of ball bearings, flowing leather coat. Green shoots poked from the top of the bag, scallions and chives. Dinah caught Lea's brief stare at the nose ring. "You're still so provincial, Lea."

"Take me home."

Dinah gave her that appraising look. Under the bright scarf her gray hair tumbled to her shoulders. A yellow undercoat shadowed her skin. Dark pouches rimmed her eyes. Age and fatigue only highlighted her loveliness but the old ferocity still made her beauty a deterrent.

"I don't mean that as an insult. You're reliable. Consistent. I must turn to you when I need someone. After all this time, I still have only you."

"When you need someone to use. What is it this time?"

"I told you. I owe you another shot."

"Got a gun?"

Dinah sighed at Lea's snide smugness. Lea would think she was calling her bluff. Dinah stared out the window at the shopper. Just the type of woman Lea would stare at, someone with the guts to be herself. But poke Lea and she'd shake off her conventions, this Dinah could count on. After the Jeffers operation, she'd gone bonkers in that bar. Yelled at Dinah for fucking Bartley, as if the lab raid didn't matter at all. Before Dinah could ask her what on earth she was talking about, nothing ever happened with Mr. B, Lea had cried out *I told him all about the frog, I told him you were a cheat.* This ridiculous outburst had summoned the bartender to demand they leave. Dinah hushed him with a stiff tip. *There's no one even in here,* she'd told the man. The professor in the tweed and elbow patches scanning student papers over spectacles and a Bloody Mary looked up then. The two utility guys in blue canvas jumpsuits drained their ale, studied Lea curiously as they passed the women, break over, back on the job. Typical Yanks surrounded by Yank bar kitsch. The bar made from Babe Ruth's bowling lane, polished, glowing in the gloom. Colonial blacksmith tools sharing the walls with cheap mirrored Samuel Adams ads. What did Lea see in these dark places, her labs and bars with their patriarchal bullshit? For a girl who mistrusted men, Lea sure barricaded herself with them.

Lea could have turned Dinah in to the police after she stormed out of Moynagh's, but she hadn't. By keeping quiet, Lea ensured that the raid was Dinah's first and best success, the one that had made Release a going concern. Lea would think Dinah owed her for the break-in, but the real debt lay in her silence. In the bar that afternoon, Dinah could have revealed that the film was staged. The mice only appeared to vanish into the tall grass and wildflowers. In truth they streamed into a portable corral just off camera to be delivered to animal care experts. When Lea had cried out, *released them to die,* Dinah could have told her the truth, but fuck it, Lea was the one who'd mutilated them. She didn't deserve, did she, to know what was only for show?

Seeing Lea now, shrinking against the passenger door, clenching her hands together, Dinah still didn't regret the omission. Lea's fear had always struck Dinah as artificial, a demand for attention, a deflection from the ruthlessness the assault and her troubled parents had instilled in her. Dinah had always marveled at the sheer loneliness of Lea's home life. That mother, draped in nylon scarves and boozy vapors, who locked her bedroom door whenever Dinah came over as if the girls would burst in on her vodka tonic binges. That father, who after work grabbed the leftover boxed mac and cheese the girls had made for their dinner and parked himself in front of TV shows like *Wonder Woman* and *Charlie's Angels.* Still, by the time Lea hit college, her parents had cleaned up their act. The mom swapped vodka for boutique coffee, the dad took up imitating Julia Child recipes and watching history docs on cable. They attended parents' weekends and honors convocations. They paid Lea's bills all the way through her PhD.

Dinah couldn't count the times she'd turned to Lea for grocery money when her own parents, both finance types who could well afford to help, refused after Dinah dropped out of Mount Holyoke to work for the rescue foundation full time. Unlike Lea, Dinah had had an easy childhood with cool, involved parents who took her skiing and paid for acting lessons and hugged her every damn time she passed through a room. Up until she went off script. It wasn't that her folks never spoke to her again after the first rescue made the news. Being cut off for good was a slower burn. Anyway, the estrangement was as much Dinah's fault as theirs, for moving around the country without always telling her folks where she was.

Lea was so different from her, always had been, but they shared the same origins. Privileged girls, plenty of middle-class family money at their backs so long as they did what they were told. Dinah wondered then, as she sometimes did, what she and Lea could have accomplished as partners. After the Jeffers raid, losing Lea had tangled Dinah up in grief. She'd realized, too late, the love that lay in her impulses to goad Lea, the pleasure she took from Lea's tantrums and vengeances. At times she'd allowed herself to believe that Lea's faithful taking of the bait had been love too. Like a fool, she'd assumed that the raid would be the final push Lea needed to stop seeing living beings of any kind as subjects and join Dinah's team. Love had caused her to mistake Lea's intensity toward her work for unhappiness, hell, a *conscience.*

The shopper walked to the rusted pickup parked in front of Dinah's sedan. She glanced at Lea through the glass before stepping quickly up into the cab. In this temporary neighborhood of strangers, everyone earned a quick glance, a hurried avoidance. Unpunished crimes could languish here. Secrets could wither away into forgotten lives. But forgetting was not forgiveness. "What if I did have a gun?" Dinah asked.

"I said, take me home."

"Get out, then. Call a fucking cab."

The pickup pulled away from the curb. When the motor faded, Lea said, "I hate you." Childish, to believe those words would hurt.

"I hate you too. I really always have." Dinah opened the car door, slipped outside into the cold. She wrapped her scarf more firmly around her hair before heading around the back of Ang's store.

Lea caught up to her at the cheap plywood door behind a row of dented aluminum trash cans. She meant to have it out with Dinah, say everything she should have said in the car just now, in Moynagh's years ago. But Dinah slipped through the door into a cramped, run-down foyer. What choice was there but to follow her?

The foyer was freezing. Wind whistled through cracks in the door-jamb and siding. Black scuff marks slashed the cheap white tile. His name was written on a smudged paper scrap stuffed crookedly in a mailbox name slot. Nick White. Ordinary, a name of no significance. A flyer from the local Kroger flapped in the mailbox's lip. Someone had bothered to find this door, stick an ad in this solitary box. A phone book, still shrink-wrapped, lay on the floor below the box. He had no use for a community of names.

The women climbed a listing flight of pine stairs flanked with an ornate carved banister. Light from the upper landing's cracked window shone on the polished wood. The staircase was missing treads. The rotted boards shuddered and creaked, but the elegant banister glided up to the second-floor landing like a velvet rope. Lea couldn't imagine who had thought to decorate this shabby entryway with something so lovely. Also how the staircase bore the weight. With every step's shrill whine, she expected to tumble down to the foyer, shatter a bone, welcome the pain that would pierce her numbness. She told herself that Dinah was playing with her. Lea would follow her through the door at the top of the landing, find Ang's overstock neatly stacked on shelves, and Dinah would grin, *I really had you going.*

At the landing, Dinah rapped on the only door. Behind them, cold air hummed through the windowpane's jagged crack. The sharp aroma of star anise and wild mushrooms filled the landing. Ang heaped the mushrooms high in raised rectangular bins, the moist, sticky stems laced together like raw tentacles. When she untangled the long stems from the caps, Lea would plug her nose against the raw dank odor that reminded her of a cellar. Although she hated the smell, she loved their earthy taste. Jay and the kids wouldn't touch mushrooms; she used to eat them alone.

Dinah opened the door without waiting for an answer. By this Lea knew how often she must have visited. Lea slipped in behind her. The apartment was as cramped as the foyer. An efficiency, with a kitchenette on the far wall, a neatly made hospital bed lodged in the nook where a dining table should be. Sealed mover's boxes made a corridor to *him*, reclining in an easy chair by the room's only window. The reek of iodine and, faintly, urine reached her before she saw the stand looped with dangling tubes and an IV bag next to his chair. He lay deeply unconscious. Another of Dinah's tricks, not warning her of his illness. Next to him, on a water-stained love seat, a bright granny-square throw lay neatly folded. Syringes, tubes, a urinal and wipes on a cart next to the sofa. A cloth stained orange draped on a plastic basin. Medical supplies offering comfort and dignity to a man who deserved neither.

Lea's numbed wade closer to him felt like curiosity, not shock. Under a thin, faded nightshirt dotted orange—the iodine—a Hickman port wormed from the sallow chest. A growth below the waist poked at the nightshirt's loose fabric. Angry purple veins popped from the drooping hands like rain-swollen crawlers. Thickly ridged nails curled toward the palm like branches sloping toward sunlight. One of her terrors, the memory of how he'd scratched her with them.

How could she have ever thought she wouldn't know him? But he wasn't anything like he'd been. Swollen purple pouches under his shuttered eyes and plump bleached lips bloated his most familiar features. The mustache had been weeded, the round naked head a faint mustard color. She should have recognized jaundice right away, but she was disoriented by a swooping feeling of flight. She blinked, stepped back, brushed against Dinah. Dinah must have thought Lea meant to touch her. She slid an arm around her shoulder.

"Where's the sister?" Lea whispered. She was terrified of waking him, witnessing his slow dawning recognition. A lack of recognition would terrify her more.

"She often takes a break at this time. Grabs a smoke and coffee. He is usually out cold so she feels she can leave him safely. Lately I've been coming to sit with him. It won't surprise her to see me here."

He didn't react to their hushed voices. Lea watched for a flutter beneath the eyelids. He might have been dead except for the pulse at the throat's hollow and the chest's uneven rise.

"His liver?" Lea's voice registered high, unfamiliar. The room must be cold. The iron radiator behind the sofa was steadfastly quiet, but a prickly warmth seared her back and neck.

"A sarcoma. Rare, I'm told."

He stirred. A hand curled into a fist. The nails dug into the yellowed palm. Had he meant to scrape her back then, or were his nails so long he couldn't help it? He'd been on top of her. The furnace fan was whirring in her ear. Hot air fanned them both. If the furnace was broken, why was the fan working? It would take her days to understand he'd lied about the repair. Stupid, she was so *stupid* to have let him in when her parents weren't home. But he wouldn't have had to lie. He was her father's friend, a man she'd flirted with, even held hands with once when her father couldn't see. He used to call her sweetheart. She loved hearing him say it. Shit, she'd loved him. She would have let him in no matter what he said, with her thirteen-year-old rash craving to find out if he loved her back.

The yellowed hand relaxed. Blood rose to a crescent notched in the palm. A sour taste tickled Lea's throat.

Dinah pushed her scarf back. Her hair spilled out over her coat. Dinah's weight struck Lea then as it hadn't before. Her lips were pinched red slashes, her eyes slits snipped from the flesh plumping her cheeks. A musky odor clogged the air. His wasting, or Dinah's sweat, or the worn floorboards steeped with mushrooms and spice.

"Sally will be back soon. You have to decide what to do. Lea?"

Lea stumbled to the kitchenette and vomited into the sink.

The radiator clanged. A hiss spiraled from the valve. Lea wiped her mouth with her hand. She refused to touch the stained towel draped over the faucet. Dinah was moving around the room. "What do you mean, decide what to do?"

She turned to see Dinah holding a gun, a chunky revolver straight out of some cheap western. A kid's toy, just another jab. Dinah was the last person to carry a weapon. Self-defense wasn't nearly as colorful as martyrdom, and besides, Dinah wasn't afraid of anything.

"What are you doing to me?" Not what she intended to say, and why was she pleading? Words slipped out of her sloppy, out of whack.

"I promised you a second shot." Impatient, as if explaining it all to Lea for the millionth time. "Or if you prefer, euthanize him like one of your animals. Look in the cupboard there, you'll find his medications. You must know which drugs you can use. Look at him, you can see death will be a mercy. The gun is licensed to me, I will be blamed, and I will say I did it. But if you use medical means, no one will know his death is not natural. No one will question, he is so close to the end. Your choice. Revenge on us both, or just on him."

"That's ludicrous."

"Or you can forgive us both. Decide quickly." Dinah watched Lea's gaze flicker to him. Incredulity and anger softened to thoughtfulness. Or curiosity. Reliable, ruthless Lea. Dinah relaxed. How little Lea had changed, how easily she slipped back into the fearless child who had swiped her grandfather's war prize, determined to kill her rapist. Lea would never for a moment believe how close Dinah held the memory of her courage. But Lea needed to quit picking the wrong weapon for her targets. "We can leave. If you don't think you can."

Lea would never simply leave. Dinah watched her approach, her gaze on the gun. For a moment it appeared she would snatch it from her. But then, she froze.

"Show him to me," she said.

"What?"

"Show me." When Dinah didn't move, Lea pointed to his waist. "The tumor."

Of course Lea would want to observe him, that was her way. Dinah set the gun down on the sofa and knelt heavily at his slippered feet. She rolled up the nightshirt's frayed hem. Under the wafer-thin eyelids, his eyes fluttered.

When she had arranged the fabric above the belly, Dinah sat back. The adult brief was bloated with urine, Lea saw. Above the mesh band, the tumor was a tight balloon of flesh protruding just under the rib cage. Patchwork veins laced the skin like leather stitching. His original body was feeding this complex structure, this new body forcing its way into existence to destroy what was nurturing it to life.

Dinah said, "Just think. If you'd stayed in cancer research you might have been his cure."

Lea cried out and lunged for the gun. Heavier than she expected, not a fake at all. She pointed and squeezed the trigger, realizing too late she was aiming at Dinah. He tipped forward, struggled against the jutting leg rest. The IV tubes rattled on the stand. A gurgle rose in his throat.

Had she shot him?

Dinah was on her, fist closing around the barrel. "Thank God I keep it chambered on an empty cartridge." The gun clicked and was in Lea's hand again. "Just don't aim at me this time, you numbskull."

The room oozed heat. Her arm steadied. Lea felt a revulsion too close to grief and raised the gun. He moaned and opened his mouth as if swallowing her aim.

"I'm wet," he said.

Age, and cancer, hadn't taken away his familiar voice, a soft tread on the deep rumbling understory she'd crushed on when she was a stupid kid.

Lea lowered the gun. Dinah groaned. "Jesus, just *shoot*."

"Please." He stared at Lea. Did he recognize her? Did he even see her? The bleary eyes gave her no clue. "Help me to the bathroom."

Lea set the gun down on the box and went to him. Even with Dinah's help, lifting him from the chair and trekking to the bathroom would take too long. That diaper was saturated. She took the urinal from the cart and knelt down at his feet. He watched her. A rich blue under the irises' calm surface. She'd never been close enough to his eyes to see they weren't really black. He didn't recognize her, she was sure of it now. But she was just as sure that his gaze held relief. And gratitude.

"Lea, don't. Please don't."

Dinah's pleading was the voice Lea didn't recognize. She ignored it. More bullshit. It was always bullshit with Dinah. She'd lured her here so Lea would tend to him—kill him or put her hands on him. Either way could be called a duty to care. Dinah was just forcing her to choose which mercy she could live with.

Lea tugged at the diaper's waistband. She'd have to lift him high enough off the chair to pull it down. She stood up and worked the diaper down to his hips. The jostling brought tears to his eyes. "I can't hold it much longer," he pleaded.

"It's okay," she said. "You don't have to."

Dinah was on her, then, pushing her away. "For heaven's sake. I'll do it."

Dinah worked fast. Stripped off the diaper and positioned the urinal like she was used to caring for him this way. Lea threw the wet diaper in the kitchen trash. By the time she'd washed her hands, Dinah had set the urinal on the floor and was slipping a fresh diaper past his knees. "Are you going to flush that or what?" she said to Lea.

He reached out to clasp Dinah's hand. "Thank you."

Was Dinah squeezing his hand back? She must have been too distracted to hear footsteps on the landing outside. When Dinah yanked her hand away and stood up, Lea started.

"She's here." Dinah grabbed the gun, broke the cylinder open, tapped the bullets from their chambers. Slipped the revolver into her coat pocket casually as if stashing a joint.

The apartment door swung open. A woman impeccably dressed in wool slacks and a camel coat slipped into the room. As Dinah had promised, she didn't seem surprised to see them. She threw the coat on the sofa back. The lining was moth eaten. Some relic from a shabby closet. "Oh, thank you so much for changing him. Dinah, cover him up, would you?"

"Sure, Sally." Dinah took up the granny-square throw and bent to wrap his legs. His eyes fluttered closed. He became as lifeless again as Lea's first glimpse of him, the throat's pulse a faint restless skitter under the brittle skin. Dinah took the urinal and crossed to the bathroom. Lea couldn't breathe. When she returned, Dinah saw her distress, shook her head, *keep it together.* But Dinah was pale, for once as rattled as Lea.

"It does reach the point when you just wish him gone," Sally said. "It's not Nick anymore, is it?"

Lea's eyes filled with tears.

"Oh, I am sorry." Sally clasped Lea's hand. "Of course, seeing him this way is a shock. Are you all right?"

Lea pulled away from Sally's clammy palm against hers. The radiator's hiss crawled along her skin. There wasn't so much as a hint of him in Sally's steely gaze, no family resemblance in the features. Shouldn't his healthy ghost lurk in his sister?

"You should call hospice. They can help manage this." She didn't say *better*, but from Sally's sharp look Lea guessed her meaning was plain. Over Sally's shoulder, Dinah touched him. Showing Lea how he didn't move, how he couldn't feel.

"Better to have a quiet passing, and I am perfectly capable of seeing to that," Sally said. "But how nice that you came in time. How do you know Nick? Were you a student, like Dinah? Nick insisted on moving back home here to pass. A few of his former students have managed to find us and send condolences." She smiled brightly. "Dinah said Nick was her favorite teacher."

Of all the ruses Dinah could have used, she chose Bartley as their cover. Dinah removed her hand from his shoulder. Smiling a little, but exhaustion lined the crescent wrinkles at her mouth. She waited for what Lea might do next.

"Yes." Lea's voice was distant, but calm. "He was our favorite teacher."

Dinah smiled at Lea. She was such a cool liar, ruthless to the core once she was poked. Interesting that Lea had aimed at Dinah first. Likely a heat-of-the-moment slip, but they never would be certain, would they?

20

Back at the cottage, Rilke checked the lip in the bathroom mirror. The swelling was impressive and he was spotting a bit. Dried blood marched along his shirt's collar. The pup's bite had been *effective*, all right, although he didn't think the wound would need stitches. In Jules's kitchen, while whiz-kid Luke pretended he was kicking Rilke out of his well-programmed environment, Rilke had dealt with the Russell situation. He asked if he'd called his dad, and Russell nodded. When Rilke removed the blanket, Russell shivered like he was still cold, although perspiration had stained his collar. Maybe a fever, and he had cuts here and there, a bruise on the arm he was favoring, but nothing more serious that Rilke could see. Luke had covered up the big scrape on his brow with a tidy bandage job. Well, Julia could go ahead and add *effective* nurse to Luke's plus column, then.

On the way to the station, Russell had worried the bandage, sucked in his breath when he touched it too hard. When Rilke questioned him about whether he was hurt badly and where he had spent the night, Russell's detached *no, sir,* and *outside, sir* didn't strike Rilke as evasive. He'd handed Russell off to Karr, the deputy on duty. Shrugged off the lip as no big deal and not Russell's fault.

Now he glanced in the bathroom mirror once more. Well, it was down to this. If Rilke didn't stay away from Jules, she'd spend their lives coming at him and blaming him for everything that spiraled out of their control. When the d-word was accomplished, and now he was happy to proceed with the legal rigmarole on that score, wait till the relationship with the fiancé blew up in her face. Watch how she'd manage to find a way to blame that on Rilke too. Everything Rilke had given Julia he'd built with his hands, including laying those hands on her bastard of a father. Luke was counting on his wireless gadgets to make her happy. Well, good luck with that plan. How long would it take for her to accuse Luke of being too controlling with all those damn controls? Anyway, if there was anything Jules demanded from men, it was the hands-on approach.

He splashed water on his face and dried off with the kitchen towel he'd given Lea that morning. What on earth would he tell his mother about his mouth at dinner that evening? He'd have to go straight on shift from the farmhouse, so he folded up his uniform and placed it in a duffle, heated up the coffee left over from what he'd brewed with Lea there. Through the window near where she'd sat, the silver sun hovered low over the back fields. He couldn't, now, bear to think of her as just another of the guest cottage's departed. Well, finding the Nixon kid gave him just the excuse he needed to see Lea again. He had just enough time before dinner to swing by the Johnsons', tell Lea the good news, prove to her he'd been right all along about the usual outcome of these mean pranks. Gauge her attitude, learn if it constituted the beginning of something or the end of nothing special.

Even with the sun sinking fast, the Johnsons weren't in a hurry to turn on the porch lights. Rilke stood shivering in the gloom between the oversized pillars, the blanket neatly folded and tucked under his arm, waiting for an answer to his knock. One car was in the drive. He hoped it wasn't Mr. Johnson's, although maybe he was up a tree by now. There was talk of lengthening the cull to a whole season rather than rely on good weather and clear sights over four nights to manage a major over-population problem. Close the county parks, stage snipers on the trails all winter long. The move had the advantage of bypassing homeowner permission and complaints. If the enterprise went that route, Rilke hoped the DNR would manage the operation A to Z and the sheriff's office could give the whole deal a swerve. Maybe there was something to the argument that exposure to a fear would lead to a cure, but Rilke wasn't buying it, never had, never would. He was the last guy in the world who should deal with animals, period.

He knocked again, and then tweaked the bell. The silence that followed the chimes' echo wasn't a positive sign. Maybe she'd seen it was him through a window and wasn't going to come to the door.

A light flashed on in the foyer. Lea opened the door. From her expression of surprise, he gathered she hadn't peeked out first. She had to strain her neck to look up into his face. Earlier, when he was stripped down before her, he'd felt small and insubstantial. Now her spare, hunched posture, like a trampled blade of grass, reminded him of his true size relative to hers. How had he ever dismissed her as pampered and unattractive?

Her surprise settled on his lower lip and lingered there. Back at the cottage, he'd managed to convince himself the cut didn't look so very morbid. Lea's stark expression challenged that assessment.

But if she had anything to say about the wound or felt any concern for his basic well-being, she apparently wasn't about to let it show. "Oh. I didn't think they'd send *you*."

That unexpected greeting confounded him, all right. Rilke held out the blanket and forgot to say what he'd rehearsed, which was, *Lea, I've brought you your blanket.*

She stared at the thing, utterly unimpressed. He cleared his throat. "We found the boy, Mrs. Johnson. He'll be safe at home by now. I thought you'd want to know."

He'd sworn not to call her Mrs. Anything. Her prolonged confusion, fast threatening to become irritating, could be chalked up to a vast weariness or a very slow road to grasping basic facts. The muted light from the foyer's brass surface mount shone on her neatly clipped hair, no longer the dull brown it had seemed in the cottage's natural light, but streaked through with rich auburn. He couldn't see her eyes properly, which were her prettiest and most reassuring aspects. He was glad when she hugged herself in the familiar way, in that ridiculous tent of a sweater she was always wearing that hid so many wonderful facets. The impulse to hold her swept him. Knowing how easily Jules picked up on his signals made him fidget from nerves, and Lea was making no move to take the blanket, or invite him in. They stood, stupid and silent. He hoped she was growing as embarrassed as he was by their mutual confusion since sharing discomfort was sharing something, at least, and anyway warded off any chance she was merely hoping to get rid of him.

A padding of feet sounded. The boy Kurt peeked up at Rilke from under Lea's elbow. "Hi, Officer."

Rilke smiled at him. "Hi, sport. You take good care of your mother this afternoon?" Which he meant as a softball flirtation. Lea reacted by turning pale.

"I didn't let my sister touch any guns today," Kurt informed him.

"That's fine, son," Rilke approved dutifully.

"My sister lost a tooth." Kurt stared up at the lip. "Did you lose one too?"

"Adults don't lose teeth." Lea laid a hand on the boy's shoulder. "Not like kids do."

Now she and the boy both were staring at the lip. Rilke touched the bite. A dot of blood smeared his finger. He ran his tongue over the wound, wished he'd thought to bring a handkerchief. "Just a little mishap there." He smiled to show the boy the intact interior. "Nothing serious," he added, in case one question led to another with the young man's curiosity being what it was.

"We were gone when the tooth fairy barged in," Kurt said.

Well, that made no sense. Rilke shot Lea a glance.

"She never barged in before in the daytime," Kurt continued.

"Go finish your dinner." Lea's mean tone he recognized as the one she always took with her children. In some mothers' commands the *honey* or *sweetheart* coda would be implied if it wasn't stated. Lea's voice was missing those gentle implications. Mutti had always taken the harsh approach with the Rilke kids, but he and Caroline deserved the tight ship attitude due to their natural rambunctiousness. Lea's kids seemed dutiful and compliant, no trouble whatsoever.

"Mama always said she's not the Fairy but I never believed her. Then the Fairy broke in today when no one was home. So Mama was telling the truth."

"Best to believe in what your mama tells you, son." Rilke thought he saw Lea shudder. Under the sweater the bodily cues were hard to assess.

Lea gave the boy a pat. "Run along now."

Kurt padded back into the home's recesses. Lea stepped away from the threshold. "Look, I guess. If it's to be you, you better come in and take a look." She swung the door wide. Now she was avoiding looking at him at all. As he entered, she slid the blanket from him. She seemed to take care not to touch any part of him. His desire to touch her was bordering on debilitating, which was why he hung on to the blanket long enough for the carefully folded corners to unravel into an untidy heap.

Lea caught at the folds as they tumbled out of her grasp. "Although you'll just tell me what you told me last time. What you people always tell me. That there's no way to catch who's responsible, right?"

You people. What category was he being thrust into now? Her voice held that abrasion she used on her children. He helped her gather up the blanket and arrange it in her arms. She treated the billowing mess gingerly, as though he'd handed her a snowbank.

"Mrs. Johnson." *Shit.* "Lea. I'm not following…"

But she was walking away from him, the blanket drawn to her chest. Also, she hadn't said anything about the Nixon boy being safe, when earlier she'd been so concerned for the health and welfare. He followed her through the generic den common to these Centennial Farms homes. The polished Pergo was littered with stuffed animals and bits of glitzy wrap. The place smelled of alcohol, with a sharp undertow of peppermint and musk, like a bunch of fancy women's scent bottles had been dumped out all at once. Up a step from the den, the boy Kurt was seated in the open-plan kitchen alongside the pretty little towheaded girl. The kids perched on long-stemmed stools at a curved granite counter. The girl tooled around a batch of bright orange macaroni and cheese with her spoon. Bunny, she was called, he remembered. Watching the child play with her food was to witness what Lea would look like happy. Loose fine hair, eyes like shiny pendants, her mother's bright smile that wasn't smothered the moment it was released. The little girl waved at him. Orange powdery smears streaked her lips. Her front tooth was missing. Even from his distance Rilke could see the bloody gap, as exaggerated as a clown's goofball smile.

"We aren't allowed upstairs right now," she informed him.

"Okay, sweetheart," he said. Best not even to try to puzzle out anything these children said.

Lea had disappeared through a doorway. He heard her quick patter up a set of stairs. He entered a hallway after her and took the stairs two at a time. On the second level, Lea was standing in front of a hall closet, refolding the blanket into a lumpy rectangle. Beyond her the bedroom doors lay open, the kids' rooms, cheerfully decorated with painted rainbows and shelves lined with plastic dinosaurs. The beige wool carpet was littered with the same disarray as the downstairs. Up here the mess didn't hold the air of family unraveling but the carefree play of imaginative children. The den's bordello odors yielded to the tidy, commonsense aroma of clean linens and freshly vacuumed fibers. Mutti had always demanded cleanliness in the bedroom, which Rilke was better at maintaining than Caroline. Caroline had received plenty of mouth from Mutti about the state of affairs in her room. Rilke towed the line, as he always did, but secretly thought kids deserved a little slack in their private arenas.

Rilke unzipped his coat. Lea turned at the metal teeth's crisp separation. "May I help with that?" he asked.

She gathered the last corner, tucked it into the center of the mess. "I'm surprised you came so soon. I thought there was usually a long wait for a response."

The sarcastic tone again. Her voice was funny here too. Muffled and distant, dampened by the plush carpet. She stuffed the blanket into a stack of whites and slid the closet door to.

"I just came to let you know about the boy being safe." He tried not to broadcast that he had no idea what she was talking about and that he was, by this point in the game, downright hurt by her distance.

Lea stared at his shirt, the dressy white button-down he'd put on for Mutti's sake, under his open coat. "Oh. You're not on duty?"

"Not yet. What's this about, Lea?"

"I called the office to report it. I thought, actually, of not calling this time. Given the lack of resources in the sheriff's office. I remember that's what you called it. Lack of resources." She was worked up now. She leaned into the closet door as if needing to be propped up. The hallway light fixture was one of the cheap frosted plastic jobs. The unfriendly yellow light on her pale skin excavated dark, hollow pools under her eyes. "We can't guarantee a response, is what you said. Do you remember?"

"I do." He struggled to keep up the neutral tone. Sweat pearled on his back. He hated the distant sound of their voices in the carpeted hall. "I remember everything we talked about today, Lea."

The straightforward approach did the trick. She straightened up and looked at him. "I'm sorry for what happened. It was all very, um, *slow.* I'm not like that. Usually."

"It would be okay with me if you were."

He might have gone too far with that remark. She shouldered the closet door again. Her straight hair hid her expression. In the inadequate lighting the auburn highlights muted to the lifeless brown. The leached color now struck him as forlorn, not plain, and the stark part down the middle revealed a chalky scalp. The right move might be to go to her now, but in her own home with her children below and that inflammatory husband likely to walk in at any moment, it was probably best to keep his distance.

After a moment she looked up. "I'd better show you, then. It's in my—our—bedroom. Which is why. Anyway."

She moved past him abruptly, once more taking that cautious, irritating care not to brush up against him. She swung open a door on the other side of the landing. He followed her down an unhandy step that served no purpose at all. The room was one of those attic afterthoughts, carved from eaves and gables and the roof's hard, unforgiving slant. An asymmetrical eyesore, too cramped in some places, like where the bed was situated, and too open in others. Like the downstairs and the kids' spaces, the room was a mess. Heaps of clothing were stacked up on the bed, a week's worth of neglected washing at least. The night-table drawers yawned open. Objects stuck out catawampus like a disorganized yard sale.

The room's saving grace was the window wall facing west, a line of clean glass framed with pretty white sashes and trim. Even in the twilight the sashes lit the room more than the weak stand lamps mashed into the tight corners and the row of canisters above the closet doors. The daylight effect must be spectacular. He couldn't help the vision of lying here tangled in Lea, the morning sun warming them.

Lea was staring at him, waiting. He cleared his throat. "Is there a problem here?"

"The whole room is a problem. Someone broke in and did this." She moved toward the bed. "Look." She fished a pair of delicates from the laundry pile. He flushed when she brought the delicates over and placed them in his hand. Silky nylon, bikini-style things. Except they weren't bikini-style, he realized when he ran his fingers through and the fabric frayed. They'd been cut to a tiny size.

She was staring at him steadily. "All of my underwear and my bras. Cut down small to look like, I don't know. Thongs or bikini tops, or whatever. And look." She pointed to the other side of the bed, near the pillow. A pair of khaki pants lay neatly pressed and folded. "They look like part of a uniform. You know. Like, that kid was wearing a school blazer, so. I mean, it's weird he would leave his pants like this."

Rilke roved an eye over the room again. The stuff in the drawers had the look of being tossed. Of course he should have noticed at once. "Anything missing?"

"I don't think so. But I haven't checked carefully. Some of the underwear has writing on it. *Slut*. Juvenile stuff like that. With a Sharpie, it looks like."

"When did you discover this?"

"When I came home. Just a little while ago."

"How long were you out of the house after we were…together?" He put her dainty things down on the bureau behind him.

She hesitated. "I don't remember. I mean, a couple of hours."

"With your little ones?"

"No. They were with their dad."

"Any sign of forced entry?"

"This doesn't look forced to you?"

"You said someone broke in," he reminded her patiently.

The practical, investigatory side of the matter seemed to confuse or frighten her, as he'd grown to expect from their previous encounters. She folded her arms. "I guess I didn't notice if the door was unlocked. But no. No sign of damage."

She was standing near him now. He hadn't noticed her retreat from the bed. Her head came up to his shoulder, no higher. Thanks to the dim, ill-positioned lights he couldn't see her expression at all as she stared at the bed. "Where's your husband, Lea?"

"Jay? Why?" The wariness he hadn't expected. She moved away from him a bit.

"It's a natural question under the circumstances."

"What does that mean?"

"It means, that if you're asking me to do my job here." His lip throbbed. He touched it to make certain it wasn't weeping. His finger came back clean. "Part of that job is to ask where your husband is."

Lea turned to him, thrust the steely lockjaw at him she'd used on the kids. "Why else would I have you in my bedroom, except to do your job?"

The wall-to-wall plush did nothing to mute the blistering tone, which could be hurtful if he let it under his skin. Also he didn't care for the language. Her attitude demanded the type of tough dispassionate response he never ever wanted to take with her again. Sweat soaked his good shirt. He removed his coat and stepped to drape it on the bedstead's foot rail. "So answer my question and we'll move past that line of thinking. Why did you find this and he didn't, for example. Was he out of the house, too, this afternoon?"

She was staring at his holster. "You're implying that he did this."

"I'm not implying."

"Well. Those sure as hell aren't my husband's pants."

He unfastened the holster and slid the gun under his coat, out of sight. Time to let the impasse between them play out, move her from the pissed-off stance to consideration of the possibility that he'd called it. The damage to her personal effects, the fact of the entire rest of the house being unscathed. The apparent lack of burglary. The room reeked of an angry man. Of course he'd been involved in domestics where the woman herself destroyed her things, a desperate move to clear the man out before the dynamic escalated.

Lea simmered down and took time to consider. She sat on the edge of the bed, nearer his coat than the heap of ruined clothing. A noise leaked into the room. The door lay open, the landing ablaze with the cheap yellow light. He might be hearing the heat kick in again, or the kids downstairs, scraping their chairs.

"Shit." Her voice shook. It took him a moment to understand that it was smothered laughter rocking her voice, rippling her thin shoulders. If she found the state of this room amusing, she and Mr. J. must share some sort of alternative outlook on marital relations. In her position he'd be packing a bag.

"I don't see what's funny here," he pointed out.

"No, it's just." She wiped at her eyes. "I'm sorry. It's just, when I first came in and saw this, before I got frightened, I was thinking how much *better* the room felt this way. Isn't that stupid?"

He deemed it prudent not to answer.

"I hate this room. It's so closed in. Seeing it trashed made me feel, I don't know. *Released.*" She burst out laughing, although Rilke couldn't see anything funny about the comment. "And then my kids ran in and they thought… They thought the tooth fairy did this. Oh shit." She looked up at Rilke, divined some demand in his expression for more information about her children's ghoulish interpretation of fairy tales. "I keep the tooth fairy treats in this drawer." She pointed to the nightstand closest to her. "And Bunny lost a tooth today. So, you see, when they saw the drawer, it made sense to them, that the tooth fairy was here. That she would do this."

Rilke let her laugh it out while he approached the drawer in question. Packs of gilt-edged, busy-looking cards and dyed rabbit's feet were jumbled up with various unmentionables. Fancy lubricants in lurid containers, stout rods sporting stouter heads, more dainty things with very little real estate to them. Slim leather restraints, suburban S & M lite. A candle with a vague scent he couldn't place, the wick still clean.

Lea stood up. "Don't look in there."

"You might have closed it up, then," he said mildly.

"Aren't we supposed to leave things as we find them? For the report?" Her voice wavered between embarrassment and defensiveness. "Anyway, I didn't think it would be you who responded."

"I came to see you," he reminded her. "I'm off duty."

That simmered her down. She dropped the hard act. "Well. I don't want you to see any of that."

Rilke slid the drawer shut. The items looked brand new, never used, so maybe the state of affairs in the bedroom here were similarly underutilized.

Lea sat back down on the edge of the bed. "We fought earlier today. I haven't spoken much to him since."

"Since when?"

"Before."

"Before we were together?"

"No, after that." She drew a breath, looked nervous. "Like I said, I was out this afternoon. An, *um*, appointment."

"Okay, so you saw him before your appointment." He took a chance, sat beside her. She didn't move away or toward, either one, which could mean anything. Her hands were tucked up high under the sweater sleeves.

"No, after, too. But just for a moment." He waited out the muddled timeline. "He took the kids to Chuck E. Cheese. They'd only just got home when I did, and then Jay, uh, left right away. Again. Look, I mean, I'm sure Jay wouldn't do this. Wouldn't that young man do it, to get back at us?"

"The boy was at the station, and then went home," he told her. He chalked up the paranoia about the wrong guy, the kid, instead of her volatile husband, as a typical denial of a domestic situation gone permanently south. He dared to reach for Lea's hand. He took a knitted cuff, slightly damp, as if she, too, were perspiring, and pushed it gently up her wrist. Her fingers fit to his naturally. "And there would be signs of a break-in." She let him tighten his hold on her hand, even squeezed back gently. *All right.* "Which, you said, there weren't."

"No," she agreed. Then she said, "Was the kid okay?"

"Perfectly fine," he confirmed.

"That's good, then." She worked his fingers like she was rubbing pennies.

"Are you going to arrest the Tooth Fairy?"

Lea slid her hand away. Bunny was standing in the doorway. Kurt was lurking behind her shadow on the landing, shifty, as if he'd egged her on to enter the room.

Rilke stood up clumsily. Kurt moved to take his sister's hand. "No, sweetheart," Rilke assured her.

"The tooth fairy didn't mean to do it." Lea's sharp interruption startled him.

"She didn't?" The girl sounded genuinely curious. Or maybe disappointed.

"See?" Kurt told his sister. "If it was on accident, you don't get arrested."

"It doesn't look accidental in here." Bunny stared at the bed.

"Go downstairs, kids. I'll be down in a sec." Lea had stood up. Kurt yanked on his sister's hand dutifully. They filed away in silence. Their retreat cast a single shrinking shadow on the landing. When the kids' footsteps on the stairs faded, Lea stepped closer to Rilke. "I don't want to make a complaint about this."

"That's not the real issue here, is it?"

"Why? I mean, if you're off duty. Are you obligated to report this?" She looked at him as if all he could save her from was further hassle instead of an unpredictable husband.

"Look. You and the kids need to come away."

"Meaning, come with you."

He saw at once by the way she drew into herself that she was envisioning the guest cottage. The lonely bed and the tiny kitchenette, the hidden dings in the floorboards. "My mother lives across the street. You can stay there until things sort out."

"Your mother?"

He crossed his arms, matching her posture, and nodded toward the far wall as if the farmhouse beyond were visible through the drywall. "No worries about being a bother. My mother loves children."

"Extraordinary." She gazed at him with the inscrutable intensity he recognized from the cottage. "You're bleeding."

Damn Jules and that pup to hell. He brushed his lip, brought away a finger brimmed with blood. Lea plucked a shirt from the bed and handed it to him. "Here. It's ruined anyway." He pressed the jersey to his mouth. Infuriating crimson dots peppered the fabric. Wasn't a mouth supposed to heal quickly? "You know what I said before? How I'm not like what I did? Or might have done?"

"I do remember." The shirt muffled his response. Her jersey was fast becoming a gruesome spectacle. He wondered if she could properly understand him. She was getting away from the point of the moment, which was some type of agreement about the future they could have together, but if he'd learned anything about Lea, it was that the best strategy was to play her out with a little extra line.

"The thing is, I am like that."

"I don't see it that way," he reassured her.

"Do you know what I'm going to do tomorrow?" She settled her gaze on the crook in the elbow he'd propped up to apply pressure to the bite. "As part of *my* job? I work in a research lab. I'm going to dispose of mice. A lot of them."

Rilke took the shirt away and licked his lip. His blood tasted like iron and sweat. "I didn't know you worked with animals."

She nodded. "Do you know what I mean by *dispose*?"

Rilke indicated that, yes, he had a good idea of what she meant.

"I'm going to snap their necks."

Being sick all over her beige plush was becoming a distinct possibility. "Probably that's the humane way to do it," he observed.

She nodded. "I'm very good with humane measures."

Her work on the doe sure didn't speak to that particular skill set. "That must be an asset in your line of work," he told her.

The echo of what she'd said to him struck her as funny. She covered her mouth to smother a laugh. "I'm actually very good at killing things. As long as I don't have to aim at them." She giggled at this too. Rilke couldn't follow a word of what she was saying. "What I'm trying to tell you," she said, "is that I can handle my husband." She looked now like she might cry.

He took away the shirt so she could hear him clearly, and anyway the flow had mercifully ceased. "That's what I love about you. You're strong, Lea. If it were right to make love with you now, that's what I would want. It's all I want."

He should have anticipated that she'd react badly, there in her intimate room, among her ruined things, with her odd little tykes awaiting her downstairs. She backed away from him. Meaning to gesture, *it's okay,* he instead held out the bloody shirt. She moved closer to the bed, then seemed to realize he might take the move as an invitation and ducked quickly into a spot between the nightstand and the cramped dim corner, trapping herself under a low-slung eave.

He wished he could snatch the words back. "I mean, *right* now isn't right."

A sound crawled along the back of her throat. "I think you should leave."

Just to show her he was the type of man to honor, with promptness and respect, a woman's command to get lost, he took up his holster and fastened it, and slipped on his coat. With her fancy shirt stained, it didn't seem right to pile it on the bureau or on the bed's pretty quilt. He balled up the shirt in a sodden ball and tucked it under his arm. "Just so you know, I'm obligated to report this incident." Not, strictly speaking, true. He didn't know why he said it, or why he steeped the words in the professional cadence.

But she seemed to find this funny too. Back over the shy mouth her hand went to shield the brief pretty smile from him. "Which incident will you report, Officer?"

If she were a snarky woman, like Jules, she'd have finished him off by tacking on "Friendly." Make of him the hated cop from her girlhood days, who hadn't understood what she was so desperately trying to tell him.

21

Downstairs Rilke hurried past her little ones' wide-eyed stares at the bloody shirt, through the messed-up den that looked as much like a crime scene as her bedroom. He was halfway down the long, dark driveway to his car when her voice came after him, his name coming breathless as if she was in pursuit. When he turned, she halted by the spindly lilac bushes near the garage. *Jesus Christ.* Would it always take him leaving to get her to move? An icy breeze rustled the pines along Scipio and blew strands of her delicate hair about her tensed shoulders. She hadn't switched on the porch light. With the moon clouded over, he couldn't see whether her arms were crossed or down at her sides, whether her silence and that uptight, defensive posture were her way of inviting him back.

He stood right where he was.

The wind whistled through the lilacs. The bare branches scraped against the garage as if stripping paint. Her startle at the sound, more than any desire to approach him, must have caused her strange, birdlike skip to him. Her head barely crested his chest. He resisted the urge to engulf her in his arms. She stood with her feet planted, mimicking her son's stubborn stance. Clouds of her breath touched his coat when she spoke. "What I really want to say is, thank you."

He struggled with the context. Typical of Lea to put things off kilter just when he thought they were squared away. "Thank *you*," he responded. When she didn't reply, he told her, "I wish bad things had never happened to you."

"Yeah, well." She crossed her arms. His heart sank. "Again. I'm sorry."

"I don't want an apology from you."

She stepped up to him then, ran her fingers under his coat collar, placed her palms flat to the shirt underneath, *all right*. He dipped down, careful not to connect with any bit of her that wasn't, now, stretching up to meet him. He barely felt her arms slide lightly around his neck, and anyway he couldn't embrace her back without dropping her blood-stained shirt on her house shoes. His size and awkward hunch were bound anyway to doom close contact. But she reached up to him easily. Her mouth pressed his open with a fierceness that surprised him but was as natural as breathing, or sleep.

He leaned into her, drawing her waist to his with the free arm. But the moment he wrapped her up, she stepped back and drew a hand across her lips. The childish gesture of wiping away his kiss almost broke him down. Then again, she might just be cleaning off his blood. Her silence could mean regret, or a desire for him to step up, now that she had. Always confounding, to read her body language. Julia's acting out of exactly how she felt at any given moment had dulled his instincts, or maybe being married for so long had made him clueless to nuance.

He cleared his throat. "I'd like to come back." Which didn't come out right. He'd meant to say, come back *in*, stay together. Why couldn't he just say what he meant to this woman without sounding like a chump?

Lea looked away. "How I feel about you doesn't make any sense at all."

She shuffled to her porch. When she went inside the house, the oily click of the deadbolt felt louder and lonelier than if she'd slammed the door.

"That your girlfriend?" An unanticipated voice seeped from the ill-lit environs down the driveway. The owner of the vocals, taking skinny shape as Rilke approached, was leaning against Rilke's car. Rilke might have called the stance nonchalant if the body type could support a ballsy attitude.

"And what can I do for you?" Rilke moved only as close to whiz-kid Luke as necessary to demolish the kid's bravado.

Luke straightened up in a hurry and shriveled under the cool-guy leather bomber he was sporting. Like stretching a wet noodle, although the height factor was impressive. If the sun were up, the kid's shadow would swallow Rilke and march straight to Lea's front door. "You've got it backward."

Well, maybe the kid was learning his lessons from Jules after all on the confounding wordplay front. Rilke said, "We can hammer out the details of what's backward, or you can scram. I like option B."

Luke crossed his arms. "Option A works for me. What I can do for you, for example, is advise you to bow out of dinner at your mother's tonight." Before he could question how Luke came into possession of this inside track on Rilke's evening, Luke continued, "And what you can do for me is apologize to Julia and never go near her again."

"Which is it?"

That seemed to force the smart mouth off the road. "What?"

"Apologize? Or stay away?" Rilke messed with the kid mostly to modulate his growing and hard-to-ignore desire to deck him. Luke had rearranged his body again to lean against the vehicle, which now looked less like casualness and more like a gambit to remain upright on his knock-knees.

"Okay, I get it. Ha-ha and all that. Here's the deal, and I mean that literally. Apologize to Julia, 'cause you should, man. That scene in our bedroom was not cool."

Rilke let the *our bedroom* part of the deal pass, not without some real effort, considering he'd painted the walls and stripped and refinished the oak boards of that room himself. Not to mention stained the bedstead by hand—which, by the way, had belonged to his omi just like the quilt Luke was using as a dog bed. "Okay. And then the staying away part comes after that. Got it." Rilke dabbed his lip with Lea's bloody jersey and winced on purpose. Luke performed the avert-the-eyes routine on that fact that Rilke could call animal control on his aggressive mutt.

"I get it, the sarcasm. I understand the place that's coming from. I'm just trying to work things out like men. Reasonable men," Luke added.

"Uh-huh. Speaking of places, how did you find me?"

That put the kid on the defensive, but now that he'd waded into man-to-man territory, Rilke had to hand it to him, he wasn't going to cave to intimidation just yet. "Do we have a deal?"

"What's the deal again?"

"Information, man. Julia and I were invited to join your mom and your sister for dinner tonight. Tell me you'll apologize to Julia and I'll tell you what's going down right now at your mom's place." Rilke glanced at the pines lining Scipio. Through the branches, he could just make out the farmhouse porch light. Luke said, "Shake on it?" and stuck out his hand.

Rilke stared at the long knobby fingers that looked screwed to the palm. "Tell you what, Luke. You get yourself up to the house, and I'll be along, too, and we can find out what *the deal* is together."

"It's an intervention."

The words clacked and tumbled like dice out of the shaker. "Excuse me?"

"Everyone thinks you need help."

"Help with what?" Rilke wasn't being obtuse. He didn't drink. He didn't do drugs. He didn't gamble. He used to border on obsessive eating back before Jules ripped out his appetite along with his heart, but nothing he would classify as addictive. Anyway his mother would never spring such a trap on him. She'd told him straight plenty of times when he needed to clean up his act. Caroline, too, hadn't exactly kept her views to herself.

"Toxic control issues would be the milder diagnosis I've heard. Grief over your dad's death is the benefit-of-the-doubt version." Rilke balled his fists at that one. Luke noticed and met Rilke's impassive gaze full bore. "For the record, I don't think you need help. I think you need to stop being a dick."

"Are you aware I could arrest you for that remark?"

"Are you aware of the definition of protected speech?" So Cool Hand had a spine keeping the whole spongy apparatus afloat after all. "For example, it's within my rights to tell you to stop being an asshole. Or a prick. 'Cause I'm not threatening you or interfering with your duty as an officer. The way you threatened me in my kitchen, for example. Which would be harassment. If I reported it. Which, at Julia's request, I am choosing not to do."

Rilke ignored the jabs about whose kitchen was whose and the exact definition of harassment. "Been to law school, then?"

"Did you know that the lady I saw you kissing is married?"

Rilke glared at him, a bit diluted on the stern front by having to lob it over Lea's soaked shirt parked on his lip. "Yeah, I do know. You friends with the Johnsons?"

"The husband called my company for a quote on a smart alarm system. Does he know you're sleeping with his wife? 'Cause that could be our deal. If you'd prefer. You stay away from Julia. And I'll keep my knowledge of the Johnsons' security needs private."

"Tell me if this speech falls in the protected realm, expert. Fuck off."

Rilke may or may not have squeezed this crack off before a sound behind him, a brittle scrape like feet being dragged, made him turn. Luke may or may not have cried out *oh shit*. A trio of piercing lights blinded him at the same moment Luke shouted *hey!* and darted—who knew the kid could be so lithe when he wanted to be—in front of Rilke. He wasn't fast enough. A lumpy shape flew from the light show straight at Rilke's chest and thumped his neck and shoulders. He staggered and fell to the asphalt. The lump landed in his lap. Something furry. Rilke had the vague impression of brambles and loam. Was a hoof nudging his crotch? A stubby white tail brushed his knee, and the white spots sprinkled along the creature's fuzzy back could be his vision's backlash against the bright lights. And who was swearing a blue streak, him or Luke?

It turned out that Luke had his knobby and surprisingly effective grip on the man of the house, swearing that streak, decked out in the black shooter's costume, a headlamp strapped to his brow. Not the small one-lamp deal a regular guy would wear for taking out the garbage or making a repair in a close dark space, but an expensive three-lamp sportsman's model. Rilke struggled to regain composure and his footing, but as he pushed the furry, sad little bundle from his lap, which was, in tragic fact, a dead fawn, the headlamps splashed light on an alarming spread of blood, which Rilke took to be a torrent flowing from his lip. The cusswords-on-parade pouring from Johnson had reached upsetting decibel levels, not to mention content. Luke's valiant and, considering that he might enjoy seeing Rilke get whipped, wholly generous effort to keep hold of Johnson failed. Johnson launched on top of the fawn as if to protect the poor thing.

But the planting of fists in certain tender areas and the bashing of the headlamp gear against Rilke's cheek matched the frenzy of Johnson's reckless accusations involving Lea and other not-quite-yet-accurate interpretations of the relationship. The fawn's pathetic tangle of lifeless legs and sharp hooves was messing with Rilke's defensive maneuvers and the asphalt scraped his other cheek and hurt like hell and how had Johnson flipped him facedown with the fawn mashed underneath? Luke was yelling *they were just kissing, man!* Rilke thrashed and kicked ineffectually and Johnson had Rilke pinned now in a fairly expert wrestler's clinch. Hooves and holster dug into Rilke's ribs.

The headlamps winked out like stars fleeing the scene. A splash of light from the porch illuminated frayed house shoes with a hole above one big toe, revealing a toenail painted a girly shade of pink Rilke hadn't noticed before and would never have expected to see anywhere on Lea, planted right at Rilke's nose.

The rest of Lea was bowed over her crazy husband, plucking at the back of his coat. Obvious questions such as *what the hell are you doing* did the trick of reorienting Mr. J. to the reality that he'd pummeled a man and done it well but now might be the time to heed his wife's suggestions to *stop it! get off him!*

Luke's gentle assistance in hauling Rilke to his feet, the reassuring clap on the shoulder and the *are you all right, man?* competed with Lea's round-eyed intake of Rilke, and then the poor fawn all crumpled up on the drive, for the most-humiliating-scenario-of-the-year prize. Lea's hand entwined in her husband's plunged the whole deal into the territory of downright disheartenment. Johnson was gasping as if Rilke had clocked him, not vice versa.

Of course blood was pouring from his lip, and he'd lost the jersey. He fumbled around in his jacket pocket for anything to staunch the flow and managed to knock his cuffs to the asphalt. At the clatter of metal, Lea started. Luke handed him a handkerchief, a fussy little square. The enormous LK, monogrammed in a prissy gold script, would be a pleasure to stain.

Johnson said to Lea, "Is this the guy you're sleeping with?"

Lea said to Rilke, "Are you going to arrest him?"

Luke said to Lea, "He's off duty. Technically he can't. Not for assaulting a cop." Luke glanced at Rilke. "Unless you were here to perform official duties?"

"Are you *sleeping* with him, Lea?" Johnson tugged on her hand.

Lea ignored her husband. "Are you a lawyer?" Lea asked Luke.

"Nope. Just like to know my civil rights." Luke bent to scoop up the cuffs and handed them to Rilke.

Rilke could do without Luke's daddy's-helper routine. He stashed the cuffs out of sight, out of mind, and told Johnson, "In fact, I was here to look into a break-in. Your wife reported it."

"Well, then, technically he *could* arrest you," Luke offered up.

That got the man's attention. In the light streaming from the porch, Johnson's glossy scar, irritated by the cold, ran raw all the way to the eyelid's rim. The injury crammed his features like the moon trapped in a fractured phase. The lamps strapped to his brow dominated the head like an undignified close-up of a fly's eyeballs. He turned to his wife. "What happened?"

Rilke said, "You did quite a number on your wife's things in there."

Johnson rammed a gaze at Rilke and then looked back to Lea. The bellicose posture shifted, some sort of tell Rilke couldn't read. At least he finally let go of his wife's hand. "What things?"

Lea laughed, a quick, harsh sound. "My things." Her hand fluttered to her mouth.

"We were robbed? Again?"

Johnson was managing the fake disbelief efficiently, but Lea wasn't buying it. "Nothing was taken." When she dropped the hand, she wasn't laughing anymore. "None of your things was touched at all. Not one thing."

Johnson's gaze dropped to her chest. "His blood is on you," he said quietly.

Lea looked down. Rilke's crimson dotted the cables of her sweater. She plucked at the wool. "Don't, Jay," she murmured.

The front door yawned open. The little tykes crammed solemnly onto the porch, bare feet mingled together. Lea swiveled to face them. Johnson groaned. Luke stepped next to Johnson, shoulder to shoulder, to block the kids' view of the fawn.

"Go inside." Lea's harshness toward her kids didn't surprise Rilke anymore.

"You've been gone a long time, Momma." The little girl corked a thumb into her mouth as if she hadn't meant to speak.

Kurt said, "The tooth fairy made a big mistake in your room, Daddy."

Johnson kept an easy stride with his little tykes' oddities. "It's okay, honey. We'll fix whatever mistakes we find. Go inside."

When the kids stayed right where they were, Lea shot Rilke a look that he would prefer were oriented a bit more toward a united front. "My husband may not be in full, um, control. Of himself."

"I know exactly what I'm doing," Johnson said, which was a distinct and unfortunate possibility.

Rilke nodded at Lea. "It's okay. Really."

Lea gave him the brief pretty smile that was fast becoming the best part of Rilke's life and walked away from the possibility that her husband's behavior was his version of a rational response to the news flash that his wife might be in love with another man. Luke waited until the door was firmly shut before stepping away from Johnson and glancing down at the fawn. "What happened to the little guy?"

Johnson's shoulders slumped. "I shot it. Stupid mistake."

Explained all the blood Rilke had thought was his own. Luke took in Johnson's black camo get-up for the first time. "Why are you out hunting at this time of night?"

"I'm not hunting. I'm culling. Who are you, again? Are you friends with this guy?"

"Look, gentlemen." Rilke interrupted the fact-finding mission on who was friends with whom. He dabbed at the lip, which finally seemed to have scabbed over. "Let's get her out to the shoulder and move on with the evening."

"Meaning move on with discussing what you're doing with my wife?"

Rilke gave Luke the let's-wrap-this-up glance. "Give me a hand here?"

Luke nodded, all grim and busy. He bent to reach for the body, but Johnson laid a hand on his arm. "I don't want my son to see her tomorrow. She's kind of…a pet."

"Doesn't make sense to bring her to your driveway in the first place," Rilke observed.

Johnson turned to Rilke, almost contrite. "I was thinking I'd bundle her up in the garage and… Anyway. Can we put her to rest somewhere out of sight?"

Rilke had to admit it wouldn't do for the little tykes to see Starkey cart the tragedy away and nodded. Johnson clicked on his headlamps and kneeled before the fawn. Lights roamed over her body like a second veil of spots. He lifted her gently, looking as if he might cry over the little thing. Well, Rilke could relate to how hurting animals brought a man down, all right. But Lea might be right too. Johnson may be suffering from permanent damage in the self-control department. Maybe he didn't even remember messing up his wife's things.

He sure remembered killing this little fawn, as the tears now tumbling breakneck onto the fur testified.

Although Luke could have taken the opportunity to book it, as Rilke had suggested, the kid followed along to form a pathetic funeral procession to Scipio and down the road a ways to the cornfield's icy furrows glimmering under the moon.

When the men reached the guest cottage, Rilke skirted the walkway that led to the front door and took them around back. Johnson's headlamp lit a winding path through a clump of brambles, up the low, gravelly rise. With the light, Rilke could just make out the rocky lip and the pit below, gently rounded like a basin of dark water. Johnson drew near to peer down. In the headlamp's bob glinted a pile of paint cans, the old irrigation pipe, the glinting teeth of Rilke's granddad's horse-drawn plow. Luke stood near Rilke, breathing hard. Maybe the kid was getting emotional. Johnson's sniffles weren't exactly keeping Rilke's stomach acid on the even end of keel.

Johnson laid the fawn down at the pit's edge. His lights swept past the plow to illuminate a hoof attached to a long, tapered leg. He roved the light over the body of Lea's doe, lingering on the bullet wound piercing the animal's brow. Likely this fawn belonged to her, out looking for mama right in Johnson's trigger-happy line of sight.

Johnson said, "They won't be alone, then."

Rilke made a grim, faraway sound. Johnson nudged the fawn with his boot. The body's splayed, stiff legs ground into the dirt like a kid's stubborn scuffing.

"Hold on." Rilke swallowed the sour taste bubbling up in his throat and knelt down. He scooped up the fawn easily, as if she'd become weightless, and rested her back on the pit's incline. The body scudded down, swaddled in a cloud of frost. Rilke's nausea vanished. He felt no urge to rage, his usual response to sad and utterly pointless outcomes. It felt good, in a way that shouldn't feel good, just to kneel there, hands pressed to the cold dirt. Lea had said that about her room, after her things were damaged. That it felt better, all messed up.

Johnson said, "We keep hurting all the wrong things."

Luke wiped his eyes and rubbed Johnson's shoulder. "It was an accident."

Rilke rose. "Who do you mean by *we?*"

The snotty tone sure reoriented Johnson's attitude. The headlamp beams bobbed up, gleamed straight into Rilke's eyes. "You and my wife, for one. I suppose, if you're sleeping together, Lea told you what she was doing with that kid. Must be why he broke in later and messed up her stuff."

Rilke sidestepped the light show and blinked away the black after-spots. "Your wife and I discussed how I didn't see any evidence that someone broke in, Mr. Johnson."

Johnson skated right past the accusation. "He was inside our house the night you people didn't show up. She tell you that?"

Rilke gave him the impassive stance. "Okay. You were doing the kid a favor. Cold night. Cops running late."

"I wasn't doing that kid a favor." Johnson switched off his headlamp. The cottage roof blocked the moon. Luke and Johnson dimmed to gray outlines against the darkness. "My wife was the one who let him in. I found them in the den together."

"The kid who showed up at our house?" Luke piped up.

Rilke gave him the shut-up nod, which he doubted Luke could see in the gloom. "Okay, then. What about it, Johnson? What did your wife, *ah*, do?"

"Lea had gotten drunk earlier that night and bought a bunch of sex toys. Guess she wanted to have some fun." The nightstand overflowing with barely used lurid objects made some sense, then.

"That kid was really scared. He'd been looking for help all night long." Luke plucked this unhelpful comment straight from the no-kidding bin.

Rilke ignored him. "You want to go someplace warm, Johnson? Talk things through?"

"No, I don't want to *talk things through* with you. Maybe she bought the sex stuff for you, right?"

"She didn't buy anything for me," Rilke said.

"I think you're full of shit." Johnson crossed his arms.

"What did you guys do to that poor kid?" Luke insisted.

Rilke stood worrying a rock with his boot toe like he was nudging a golf ball out of the rough. "You know what's full of shit, Johnson? My wife's been sleeping with some young guy. A real punk."

"Whoa, now, wait a minute." Luke stepped toward Rilke. "Punk? Really?"

"In protected speech terms, yeah. Punk. Or maybe dork." Rilke worked the rock out of the dirt and rolled it around. "Anyway, Johnson, I'm working to straighten things out there. Maybe I've even sorta threatened the guy once. Maybe I will again. As long as he gets the message in the end. Right, Luke?"

Johnson dropped his arms. "You're sleeping with *his* wife?"

"She's my fiancée." Luke looked at Rilke. The exact expression of distaste was lost to the darkness. Too bad. "And you *are* a dick."

"Stay tuned for how much of a dick I can be, son." That stopped the kid's slow and ill-advised advance. At least he was consistent on the ineffectual front. "Look, Johnson, I'm telling you about my situation by way of saying I sympathize with *your* situation. I do. I mean, you got beat up by some punks who were never brought to justice. Can't risk that happening to you and your family again, right? What's the harm in sending that kid on his way with a little warning about your property rights?"

"I know how much you sympathize with my wife."

"I'm not sleeping with your wife. God's truth. I'm being honest with you. Why not be honest with me?"

The moon crested whatever final barrier, the cottage, or the trees along the ridge, was blocking its shine. Johnson was surveying Rilke with a lifeless gaze, as though a part of him had burned out. "Okay. I walked in on Lea with that kid in our den. Sex toys on the floor, him with no pants on. I don't think he was trespassing at all."

"That's vile." Luke slid his hands into the bomber's pockets and shuddered.

Might be a lie. Or maybe she *had* let Russell in and was hiding that fact. Either would explain a great deal about Lea's behavior. "That kid is fourteen years old. Are you saying your wife was seducing a child?" Rilke pressed.

Johnson's jaw knotted. "God. He looked way…older. More mature. Anyway, she sure acted like she knew him. Pretty well too."

"That must have got to you, Johnson. I know what I would do to that kid. Not to mention my wife," Rilke said. "What *did* you do about it?"

"I chased him out of my house."

"Did you fire your weapon?"

"I defended my property."

Before Rilke had a chance to think through Johnson's bullshit response and if Lea knew her husband had gone after the kid, why would she then go outside to offer up a blanket? Luke ground out some repetitive insult, *God you're both such dicks*, and took his hand out of his pocket and barked an order at his palm: *Ariel Zap!* A buzzing drifted from the vicinity of Johnson that sounded like bat wings and then like pissed off bees, and Johnson yelped and slapped at his neck and danced at the edge of the pit as if his pants were on fire. And, although it meant that Rilke would have to scrabble down the pit, pluck Johnson from the mother-child heartbreak on the pit's floor, wrestle with the man's outraged thrashing, and then tend to the gash on Johnson's neck from scraping the plow's teeth, when Johnson tumbled backward over the edge, hollering the whole way down, Rilke made no move to save him from the fall.

Or maybe Rilke was distracted by a mild vibration on his own shoulder, little shocks that tickled through his jacket. Maybe the clever little remote control self-defense prototype Luke would later admit to planting on him was named Ariel, too, and Rilke was meant to join Johnson down there in the pit. But he plucked the device off his coat and gave it back to Luke without a word. He was willing to give the kid the benefit of that doubt, and anyway who could blame a punk for wanting to shock the crap out of every dick who had it coming?

22

Later, at the station, Johnson whined on the phone with Lea to come get him, which was not going to happen, as the man was on his way to jail for the night for going after Rilke and possibly the Nixon boy. Which Rilke had explained, along with the advice that Johnson spend his dime contacting a lawyer. Once Russell Nixon was questioned, odds were that lawyer would be collecting plenty of Johnson's dimes. But despite throwing around some despicable accusations about her there at the pit, it was Lea's voice Johnson wanted to hear. How a man like Johnson could so passionately love and ferociously hate a woman at the same time, and yet keep her so securely in the dark about both depths of feeling, was a feat Rilke recognized. Feat, hell. A *necessity*, depending on the woman. Anyway, he had to admit that hearing Johnson's self-pitying vocals fill the station's night-shift silence made Rilke jealous as all get-out. No doubt Lea felt beholden to her husband's remorse, not to mention his dependency on her. Interesting how Johnson made no mention of what he'd said she'd done to Russell Nixon. Rilke's decision to leave her out of his report felt more like a reflex than a choice. Either he was ignoring a lie or covering up the truth. Neither reality was one he was inclined to spend any time pondering.

Whiz-kid Luke, he'd learned, had planted a GPS tracker on Rilke's vehicle to pull his surprise appearance act there in Lea's driveway. Illegal, by the way, as Luke would know. But Rilke let that slide too. Risking it all for Jules was a ballsy move that deserved respect. Luke was tougher than he looked, and not just against helpless creatures, either. Maybe he'd end up giving Jules a badly needed run for her money, which Rilke could see himself cheering on from the sidelines of his own happier future. Plus, when he called Mutti to tell her he had to miss dinner, he could have sworn he heard Jules's voice mixed in with Caroline's in the background there. Luke's intelligence had made it possible for Rilke to intervene later against their ill-advised intervention, so some gratitude was called for on that score.

Once Johnson was finally stashed away in county, a call came in.

A broken water main down Oak Street was gushing havoc near the township line. Since everyone else was by now out on calls, Rilke had to skip thumbing through the day-shift reports and the usual pre-shift updates. He headed out to the lot, skipped the patrol car check too. Buckled himself in and just sat for one brief moment that felt utterly stolen. His clouded breath curled back on itself to mist his nose. The silence felt like a second body, cozy and comfortable. The township hadn't replaced the burned-out lamps over the station lot. The quiet darkness lulled Rilke into missing sleep, real, proper slumber wrapped in true night, not the artificial sabotage of light he'd manufactured over the years. He remembered what it was like to fall asleep as a kid, with babyish thrills like monsters in the closet pulling him into the depths he used to slip into so easily. But, too, the night could be depended upon to shroud the grim. After he'd filed the reports, his memories of the broken and the deceased would turn to gauze. Inaccurate recall was the real reason he preferred this shift, he realized now. With time, most haunting visuals were locked in a chamber of passing dreams.

Mutti always said nights were the problem with him and Julia. No man could be a proper husband dead on his feet during the daylight hours, the normal times when everyone else lived. *What do you know about proper husbands*, Rilke would say.

Don't brood, Paul, Mutti always replied.

I won't brood, he always said back. In the patrol car now, he punctured his brief rest by pledging it aloud, that *from now on* he'd quit thinking, quit feeling, quite so much. He pressed on his lip, just checking. The wound opened up again, which is what he deserved for messing with it. Rilke pressed his arm to staunch the flow, not caring about his jacket.

He turned the engine over and cranked up the defroster when the windshield fogged. The fan crystalized the vapor on the glass to a pattern of spindly crystals like the doilies his omi used to tat. Rilke scraped a neat porthole through the latticework and swung onto Maple, headed toward the county line to reroute traffic around the submerged country lanes.

On the other side of rounding up SUVs and tiny electric cars floating down the road like canoes lashed together, a call came in for an attempted break-in that proved to be a homeowner prying open his own window because he'd forgotten his key. The teen occupant had taken the spare hidden under the fake rock in the landscaping, the guy explained, a divorced dad with no one at home to let him in. After a couple of speeding tickets issued to some lead foots, one of whom turned out to be the insensitive teen rushing home with the spare key, Rilke was famished. All the day's drama made him crave the calories he'd missed out on at Mutti's.

Rilke's socks hadn't yet dried from wading in the water when he cruised past Costco, pulled into the Burger King lot, and cut the engine. He fished a napkin out of the glove box to press to his flowing lip, not realizing that he'd made a habit of chewing the scab open. When he opened the car door, his mirror almost scraped a silver Lexus the color of frost. A black Expedition with tinted glass was parked near the entrance. Behind Rilke, pulled in tight next to the rusted dumpster, a Pontiac crouched next to a forest-green Windstar.

A crunching under his boots drew Rilke's gaze to bits of thick glass sparkling on the blacktop. He checked the Lexus and the Expedition and saw that the Ford's rear window was smashed. Looked like Bobby Gold's vehicle, the other sharpshooter in Lea's neighborhood. Except with the air temperature cranked back up tonight to a reasonable late-autumn chill he'd be up in the stand by now, and Rilke couldn't see a locker box in the back for weapons. The owner of this vehicle might be cheek deep in a Whopper and not yet realize he'd been broken into. Through the store's glass panels, the dining room's fluorescents splashed puddles of light on the walkway all the way to Rilke's boots. The place was quiet, the tables near the entrance empty because the best places to sit were in the back, out of sight, near Rilke and Julia's old favorite booth, where Julia would tease him about the ketchup on his chin, and the way she wiped him up suggested what they would get down to doing in the car as soon as they polished off the burgers. No line, either. The roped-off area in front of the service counter's silver rim, all Rilke could see of the kitchen, was empty. He swung through the door. Above him a bell tinkled a thin, high note.

"Stop!"

A tall punk with heft in the shoulders, hoodie pulled low over his face, stepped out from behind a column near the condiment counter. By the time the door chimed shut, the punk was standing between the ropes as if waiting his turn in line. The .243 sharpshooter rifle Rilke was staring down had a suppressor attached to the barrel's mouth. What an *unbelievable* fuckup, to assume Bobby was up a tree.

"Okay, son." Rilke raised the hand not clenching the napkin to his lip. Over by the booth where he and Jules used to hang out, a chair rested on its back, legs poking up. A bucket-sized cup of pop had been thrown over. Ice and Coke puddled on the tabletop and sluiced over the edge to the tile. Cartons and cups overflowed from the trash receptacles under the condiments bar. On the bar, napkins fanned from a dispenser. Ketchup oozed down the trash receptacle, glazing the floor almost to the rope line. Despite being apparently abandoned, the teenage girl behind the counter was keeping it together pretty well. Ash-gray uniform, the red-lined neck yawning open at the fluttering throat swallowing panic, an oversized name tag Rilke could almost read from where he stood. A black ribbon clutched a pretty sweep of hair in a girlish ponytail. One hand was thrust deep in the register drawer; the other clutched the countertop's sterling rim, knuckles shining. Rilke gave her a slight nod as she locked eyes with him and then stared at the blood-spotted napkin. Her relief melted into fright as if a split lip diminished his competence, or maybe she was afraid the punk had beat him up before entering the store.

Rilke looked past the girl to the kitchen's gleaming metal surfaces to confirm all was clear. The fry cooks had slipped away, and Bobby and the other customers too. Better for getting this situation under control, but Rilke felt a surge at the craven fact of the girl left alone.

The kid waved the weapon at Rilke like a handshake. The boy was completely out of his league. A more seasoned hood would have gauged Rilke's uniform before making so much as a twitch with the gun in his direction, would have kept the gun trained on the girl until Rilke moved his ass out the door. This hapless wonder was aiming right at the bloody napkin stuck to his lip as if the pup's bite constituted the whole threat.

The napkin muffled his voice at a critical juncture. "Let's calm things down here, son, and lower that weapon." The napkin's tail flapped with his breath.

"What?"

"Lower your weapon," Rilke said again. He bit at his scab, raged at Julia's distant bewitchment that was keeping his blood flowing.

"How do I do that?"

If he'd been less agitated by his half-assed tumble into this situation, Rilke might have recognized a kid's plea to get the hell out of this mess. At the counter, the girl was working her jaw as though she was chewing on some rash action. Rilke said, "Cut the mouth, son, and drop the rifle."

Bad move on the cop tone. The barrel jerked like a bumper car. "I can't *cut* my mouth." The voice, a bit too high and precious for the boy's size, seemed familiar. Now Rilke absorbed a garment detail he'd missed on first inspection. Neat white cuffs peeped from the sweatshirt. The Nixon kid.

"Your dad know you're here, Russell?"

The unexpected identification had the desired kick. For a moment the gun rocked to one side. "You know my dad?"

"I know he wouldn't like what you're doing here."

That comment sent the barrel back up. The girl behind the counter sneezed, a windy release on its way to a scream. Russell flinched but kept the gun straight, which either showed admirable focus or the preamble to a comprehensive freak-out. Rilke wished he could see more of the boy's face than the back end of a nose behind the rifle's scope. At this close range the napkin must be magnified to a flag of surrender. He pressed on the wound. His finger came away wet. "Let's give your dad a call to take you home. Again," he suggested.

Russell lowered the gun a touch, which might have diffused the situation except for another sneeze. The girl had removed her hand from the drawer and inched backward toward the kitchen's shiny interior. Russell gave a garbled shout *go back* or *stand back* so the girl didn't know what to do and froze with her mouth open. A movement at the girl's waist startled Rilke. A head of hair. Two heads, then three. Blond, brown, brunette bobbing all in a row. Fucking Snap, Crackle, and Pop. A Burger King visor tenting a panicked eye peeked over the counter's rim. *Jesus Christ.* The customers and cooks hadn't abandoned this girl. They were corralled under the soft-serve machine behind the register, the machine's nozzle oozing a beige cream. A crown of thick black hair and black eyes bobbed up next to the visor. A mustard smear slashed the customer's chin. The guy must have hustled behind the counter mid-bite. To the left near the drive-thru window, a fryer bubbled around an abandoned batch of fries.

The girl wiped her nose with her wrist. Russell cinched up his aim again on Rilke's lip. "Homer!" he hollered.

The visor ducked back down out of sight. Where was Homer lurking? Out of range of Rilke's sloppy intake, that's where. Down the narrow hallway to Rilke's right the men's restroom door yawned open. Homer walked out in shirtsleeves, wiping his hands on his jeans like the head had run out of paper towels after a routine pee. He was still wearing the bandage Rilke had dressed at the farmhouse, now stained with dried blood. At the sight of Rilke, one hand aloft, the other pressed to the crimson-soaked napkin, he stopped cold by the ladies' room. "Shit." He moved out of the hallway, eyes on Rilke. "I swear to God I did not know he was going to freak out. All he said he wanted was a burger on our way home."

"Did you clean up the mess in there?" Russell demanded.

Now the girl's sneeze sounded more like a moan. Homer said, "We're in good shape, Russ. How about you put the gun down now?"

Rilke thought he heard a click from the rifle. Could be the safety engaging or disengaging. Could be the minutes ticking down on any reasonable salvation of this situation. "What's the mess in the bathroom, Mr. Nixon?" he asked quietly.

"Russ pissed on the floor, man, okay?"

Homer's wise-ass tone might have put a check mark right in the accomplice column, but his gaze, fluttering between Rilke and the rifle, was pure panic. Homer moved to the counter. He picked at the bandage's edge fussily like digging at a hangnail. "Russ, you do not want to mess with these people no more so why don't we just leave, okay?"

Out the long window the dining area's harsh fluorescent lights made a dense black wall of the darkness. A sedan cruised away from the unmanned drive-thru. The occupants gaped at Russell. Russell aimed the rifle at Rilke's waist. The hood slipped from his head. "I'm already in trouble, Homer. Big trouble."

From the fry station a bell pinged. The girl implored, "The fries are done," as if burning the potatoes was next up in the evening's queue of misfortune. Fat sizzled and crashed against the metal baskets. A crisp, golden odor wafted from the kitchen. Behind the counter the visor was on the move, propelling a pimply individual in an ochre Burger King tee to the fry station. The kid popped up just long enough to lift the baskets from the oil. The quiet rescue escaped Russell's notice.

"We can stop the trouble right here, Russell, if you put the gun down on the floor," Rilke said.

Russell's aim lingered at Rilke's knees. "Liar!"

"Christ, Russ. Put that motherfucker *down*," Homer demanded.

"He's gonna shoot me!" Russell cried.

Homer stepped over to Rilke, pulled the service revolver from his holster.

"I wouldn't do that," Rilke warned him.

"Yeah, except my brother's right about you. I was too high at the time, but I remember now how you damn *tackled* me at the Costco. Before I even knew you were there, wham, my knee's totally fucked up. I was acting in self-defense when I attacked you. Which you lied about." Homer slid Rilke's revolver across the tile to Russell. "Why do you people stash such a big-ass weapon outside the Burger King anyway that any fool can steal?"

The mustard beard behind the counter offered, "It's for the cull."

Homer looked over at the girl. "What's a cull?"

"It's where they kill deer. Overpopulation. My mama's getting a petition against it," the girl said.

Homer winced. "Russell, we're going home, like, *now*. Put that *down*."

"I'm not leaving without her," Russell said to him mournfully, as if betraying a secret regret. The counter girl gasped and plunged her hand back into the register as if to remind the Nixon boys this incident could still amount to just a simple robbery. At her waist heads bobbed in consternation. At any moment the strain would spur some tapped-out individual to execute a dash to the door.

Homer pleaded, "Let's just go, Russ, okay?"

Rilke nodded. The napkin peeled from the scab and fluttered to the tile. "Good plan, Russ. Just set the weapon down and walk right out that door."

Russell, nobody's fool, lowered the weapon just enough to stare at Rilke without the napkin. "Wait a sec. I know you. You're that man from the lady's house. You're *that* cop."

Rilke affirmed, calmly, that he was that guy and also that cop. Russell looked at Homer. "He messed with the lady that rescued me."

"No surprise there." Homer looked at Rilke like that was all the confirmation he needed about the accuracy of his miraculous recall concerning the Costco incident.

"Her dog messed with *me*," Rilke reminded Russell. Then he added, "She's my wife."

The hood wrinkled like a wink. Up went the barrel again. "Being married is no excuse."

Tears breached the girl's valiant squint. "I'm not married!"

Before Rilke could figure out a reasonable response, which judging by a new unstable commotion under the oozing soft serve nozzle was way past due on the swift and unerring front, a buzzer cried out from the kitchen's gleaming depths. The girl and the fry cook looked behind them, called by instinct to attend such keening and the customers had gone restive, all grab and groans, and Homer warned them to *cut it out* and *stay down* and judging by the rummaging some serious disregard for Homer's instructions was brewing. But as he processed the range of possible complications to this miserable situation, Rilke was not at all prepared for a slender woman, whose straight brown hair he'd utterly failed to recognize, to stand up.

"He means me."

Maybe Lea meant to meet Rilke's consternated gaze calmly and bravely, but all she could manage was to stare at the empty space over his shoulder. Then her odd little tykes bounded up, too, clinging to her waist. Their tousled heads had been so completely hidden from view, Lea must have been right on top of them down there in the huddle. Bunny's velvety pink princess coat looked doused in soft serve. Kurt was wearing those big latex gloves, the fingers splayed like floppy daffodils against his mother's baggy sweater. They stared at Russell with big eyes and pursed mouths that wisely sensed it was a good time to keep quiet. Lea pried them away from her and pushed them toward the register.

"Go stand over there, kids. The lady will take care of you."

"Yes, Momma." Bunny slipped to the girl's side. Too scared to make a peep. Kurt wouldn't budge from Lea until she gave him another little push and a whisper Rilke couldn't hear.

When Kurt had joined his sister, Lea stepped forward. "You did mean me, right?" Russell nodded. The rifle bobbed.

Homer backed away from the counter as if Lea were after him. "Russell. Cut this shit out now."

"It's okay," Lea said. "I was…it's okay to hurt me." She glanced at Rilke. "Not him. He's here to help."

Russell lowered the weapon a bit. "I don't know what to do."

Lea slid over the countertop toward Rilke's lonely spot in the rifle's sight. Rilke shook his head at her. She gave him the brief pretty smile.

"Momma. Come back," Bunny cried.

A clack like a stubborn ignition sounded from the kitchen's depths. Russell lowered the gun's snout all the way to the tile. Had Rilke leapt for the gun the incident might have ended there. But as he made a move to recover his weapon the noise from the kitchen ratcheted up and startled him so badly he chomped his lip hard and the wound cracked open. The pain messed with his reflexes and Lea's approach went blurry. From the kitchen an alarming char reeked from a gleaming grill box straddling the flame broiler's conveyor belt; and the girl started screaming and Homer hollered *shut up* and some individual behind the counter wailed unhelpfully, *oh Jesus* like the stench of burning burgers was simply intolerable.

Russell made up his mind to aim at Lea.

Lea said, "That's good, that's right," and what a stupid time for a timid woman to muster her courage, stupid and cruel considering her children were watching her with wide and desperate gazes, too confused to cry. Kurt's latex flapped on his cheeks. The register girl made a sound that might have been *oh crap* or maybe the cry was Homer's because Kurt wasn't hiding his face behind the gloves but had tucked his daddy's Ruger into the floppy fingers and was taking aim at Russell.

"Leave my momma alone."

A shrieking alarm chased a black smoky plume from the kitchen depths. Someone yelled *fire!* and Russell jerked the barrel toward Rilke and fired. The glass entrance door shattered. The voice clarified *no! fire!* An oval flame landed at Rilke's boots and as he lunged for Russell Lea flung her arms around him with her back plastered to his chest, entirely the wrong orientation for a protective embrace, and Homer cried *aw fuck* and the customers bolted over the counter and fled out the shattered door. The fry cook was manning the grill box, flinging ignited patties at Homer and Russell with a pair of tongs. A fireball kited over Russell's head. The napkins poking from the dispenser behind him popped into flames and *shit* the ketchup streaming down the trash receptacle might actually be very thick blood and Lea was standing between Rilke and effective action with her hair stuffed in his mouth.

Through the shattered door a siren whined. The register girl had the Ruger now and she shoved Kurt and Bunny down and waved the pistol wildly, totally unaware that the weapon she was bearing was an ineffectual target pistol, and stared at Rilke as though pleading with him to keep it together, be her *hero*, and Rilke told her *get down* and grabbed Lea hard by the shoulders, shoved her toward the broken glass and the comforting melody of multiple sirens screeching from all four corners of that crappy Dix intersection, *go,* and she obeyed in the wrong direction over the counter and on top of her children. Homer shouted at the fry cook *stop that, motherfucker,* and yanked the rifle from Russell. The fry cook dropped the tongs and fled out the back and the men's room door tilted open and a body in black camo crawled down the hallway, bleeding from the mouth. The body arose and unfurled, hands aloft in surrender and supplication and Homer yelled *run, Russ! Run, Russ!* and Russ clamped his hands around his ears as if Bobby the sharpshooter's suffering was a terrifying noise instead of a terrifying vision.

No doubt about it, the girl was aiming the Ruger at Rilke. Russell grabbed Rilke's revolver, Homer swept the rifle from the sharpshooter to the girl and Rilke stepped in front of the barrel. Later, ballistics would have to figure out who fired when and upon whom, but the bullet that pierced clean through Rilke's thigh and into Homer's gut swept Rilke into a dream. Just before he passed out, Lea flew over the counter and draped her body over his.

23

After enduring a grueling hospital stay for the rest of the week, the best part of Rilke's convalescence was being confined to his boyhood bed's twin mattress, an extra-long that made the bed hard to dress because Mutti had to special-order the sheets. He'd only ever had one set of sheets at a time which, whenever he wore a hole or worried a fray in the satin binding with his night thrashings, he got the strap. After a time, Mutti'd given up supplying the proper fit. Dressing the bed became a weekly wrestling match with corners and angles impossible to cover no matter how hard he stretched the cotton. He usually resorted to keeping one corner exposed like a joint stripped of flesh, and when the fitted sheet balled up with his sleep quivers, he'd safety-pin it down. Maybe being shot constituted a special occasion because his sheets fit perfectly now and carried pleasant aromas of lilacs and sugar, and there wouldn't be any thrashing about with his leg propped high on the plaid throw pillows Mutti had fetched up from the living room sofa.

Not that he was any fan of pain, but the wound, a clean passageway straight through his leg, felt good. If he'd been able to sit up far enough to peel away the dressing and squint straight into the chute, he imagined he'd see neat layers of muscle and vein stacked and orderly, healing dutifully. He refused the Oxy and stuck to guzzling Tylenol with pop and coffee and Mutti's fatty roasts.

One thing Mutti had always been good at was nursing him back to usefulness without a ton of fuss. She'd herded Caroline and the boys back to Saginaw after a hospital visit resulted in some well-meaning but painful overtures from the energetic tykes that involved snuggling with Uncle Paul in ways wholly counterproductive to keeping a wound closed up and sanitary. Caroline's late contribution to the thwarted intervention was not to chide her fine boys to be a bit more gentle, but to kiss Rilke's cheek while whispering *heal up, now, and I don't just mean the leg, you jerk.* By the time he'd come home, he and Mutti had the house to themselves. She cooked up a storm, kept him clean, changed the dressings with a brisk, efficient handiwork. In the closet, she'd hung the clothes he would need when he was well, all laundered and reeking of fabric softener, even the jeans, bless her. If it weren't for the nightshirt bunching up in his crotch every time he repositioned the pillow tower, he'd be perfectly content to lie here for time infinite, swaddled in the luxury of losing track of night and day, barely aware of whether it was the sun's beams or the moon's trying to pierce through the broad slats of the shade he insisted Mutti keep drawn.

Mutti's ministering to his wound meant they spent moments together that could be conducive to the type of conversation he'd always thought they should have. Get some questions out there, hope for some answers. As a kid he'd always chalked up the silence between them on certain topics, and her physical reserve, to her temperament and his own fears of finding out why exactly she could love a man who didn't love his children. But her lack of affection could have been a response to his serious, aloof nature that, to be fair to his mother, most folks found off-putting. Now, as he shifted his body in response to her touch, he understood their silence as a merciful collusion to just *be*. Mother and son, nothing more nor less, a bond much better left unquestioned.

Maybe buried under daily life was where family troubles belonged. Wasn't forgetting the better part of forgiveness? What was the point of asking what your papa had been up to back then, with his hand at your mother's throat? Why spend a life wondering what segment of that activity spurred your papa's erection, or whether your mother meant that *yes*, or whether you'd even heard her right, or saw them right? Could he swear that what he'd seen was violent, or was that a false memory suggested by other awful recollections of his father's brutal stances? Maybe, too, he'd always been wrong about the cat and her poor kits. He'd always assumed that Papa made him slaughter those kittens as a revenge of sorts, for catching him with Mutti, for thinking the worst. But what if his papa had been telling the truth, that he was out to toughen up his sensitive son just the way his own papa had, so Rilke would grow into a strong man who could, if he had to, shoot his own herd without flinching? Which was the greater shame, that Rilke was capable of such violence toward a helpless little thing, or that he'd gone on to be so afraid of his papa, and of his own self?

Still, Rilke wondered what kind of man he'd be now if he'd had a sober and gentle father. Sure as hell wouldn't be the man he was now, grateful for the hole in his leg, wondering if he'd ever care to leave this room again.

Most gratifying of all was Julia's prompt appearance at his side, the pretty sincerity of a crying jag still reddening her eyes. He'd barely come home from the hospital when she was, simply, there. When he'd first opened his eyes after a prolonged nap that could have lasted an hour or a whole blissful year, she was hovering over him, so close that her hair was brushing his cheek. He wondered for a groggy moment whether she'd kissed him awake. When he stared at her, her loveliness skittered out of his vision. The chair he kept by his dresser scraped across the oak boards. She'd never developed the courtesy and basic good sense to avoid damage to the floor by hefting anything. Then she was sitting near, clawing at his hand, serving up satisfying sentiments like *I can't stand losing you* and *I can't stand to see you in pain.* He didn't mention that the pain, while bad, felt pretty damn great, and his silence was rewarded with the real kicker, *I can't* stand *what Pup did to your face.* The bite still did feel nasty and had blistered into a hard black knot that constituted a real disfigurement, so there was plenty to show off about the damage the little guy had caused. Rilke rode out the comprehensive list of all the other behaviors she'd perpetrated that she now couldn't stand. All in all it was a lot to take in after Jules had made it clear for so long that what she really couldn't stand was Rilke.

He chose not to point this out, either. He'd been hell to live with, was what she was really communicating. Rilke's discipline, his moral outlook, his loyalty, could trim certain boundaries of autonomy and sensitivity. But just try taking away the right to take him for granted. Look at the grievous outpouring *that* raised. Who else but Rilke even possessed a moral outlook anymore? Certainly not Jules, or Johnson, or PC guys like Luke. To bring sense to the world, as opposed to pumping feel-good nonsense through a bleeding heart, morality had to be *applied.* Who wanted to live with that, was what Jules was really saying.

Well, it felt good to have her near, anyway. They'd fooled around in this very bed as teens, although they'd never gone all the way out of honor to the boyhood nature of the bed, and the fact of his mother always just downstairs. He was pleased that these memories raised only a genial fatigue. He didn't ask whether her solicitous attitude meant a status change for whiz-kid Luke. On her other hand, the one she kept at a respectful distance east of her lap, sparkled a pretty nice diamond, set in a sleek and curvy gold band that suited her slender finger. Well, Luke sure had good taste and the income to match, which at the moment Rilke was experiencing as an unexpected source of comfort.

After Julia left, Mutti told him that Jules had wanted Paul to convalesce at Peach Tree Court. Thank God his mother had the sense to take over his care. Rilke couldn't imagine conditions more challenging to efficient healing than Jules wrinkling her lovely nose at his wound when she changed the dressing.

❧

Still he brooded on Jules. How beholden would Rilke feel to his vows if, on the next visit, Julia had abandoned the fancy diamond? They'd been together since they were kids. If she wished to stay together until death did them part, what part of him could refuse? He worried that the confounding state of not brooding anymore about genius Luke's various activities with his wife wasn't a symptom of being out of love, but ever more deeply in it.

Just after breakfast the next morning, Mutti's sharp knock and her stock joke, *are you decent, Paul,* rattled his door. Real funny because pop and gravy stains from last night's meal dotted the short nightshirt he still wore for ease of changing the dressing. The radiators were knocking like hell, steaming the room against the cold seeping through the sash. Sometime in the night he must have suffered from the heat because his blanket was crumpled sheer across the room, and the top sheet was tangled around his good leg. More than two feet were shuffling around out there in the hallway. He thought he heard Jules whisper something brisk and apologetic. He tried to shade the jewels as best he could, literally girding the loins for whatever she had for him next.

He'd admit to being startled all right when the hushed pretty voice Mutti ushered over his threshold turned out to be Lea's. Well, he should have known that voice was too hushed to be Jules's. Why was she showing up at all, seeing as she hadn't returned his anxious calls to find out how she and the little tykes were doing? He'd had to ask Nowak for the update that Lea and the kids had come out of the incident okay. Now her faded jeans and loose, untidy shirt shrank her frailer than ever. The blouse's bland color was so like her flesh he couldn't decipher the hue right away as a worn-out shade of yellow. Mutti said *here he is* as if the fact of him laid out before the women didn't speak for itself. Even more confounding than Lea's arrival was the vision she cut in close proximity to his mother's robust facets. Mutti had several inches over Lea. Her silver hair streamed from the ineffectual tether of a hurried bun. Her sharp features that a neighbor had once called *patrician*, which Rilke as a young stupid boy thought the woman must have confused for *pretty* until he looked up the word, walked their usual line between impatience and solace. Compared to his mother, Lea's hunch and shuffle, her wary roving gaze, appeared, as ever, scared. But if she was still truly frightened of him after defending his life in the damn Burger King, why had she bothered to come?

When Mutti shut the door firmly, he smothered the impulse to call his mother back. Lea hung around the threshold as if she, too, would rather dart after Mutti.

"Hi," she said.

A single syllable was all she had to offer, then, after all that had happened, and all she must know he knew. The radiator hissed. A plume of steam raised a rashy sweat on his chest and neck. "Hi," he responded.

She looked over every boyhood memento on the dresser: the Cub Scout crap, the miniature mineral collection pasted to cardboard which his omi had bought him at the county fair once, a girl's hairbrush that might have been left behind by Caroline or a teenage Jules. Her flitting gaze, avoiding the sight of him on the bed at all costs, could be interpreted as aversion, or pity, or shyness, and why couldn't he ever read her right?

"How are you feeling?" Her brisk tone flattened any concern to a required pleasantry.

"Real good. Well," he corrected.

"Really?" She ran her hand over his dresser, drummed her fingers nervously.

"Really," he confirmed. "It's not as bad as it looks."

His satisfaction with his wound seemed to unnerve her more. She clasped her hands behind her back, and her limbs vanished in the straits between her shoulders and hips. He wished she'd have the good sense to sit down without being told. Hadn't they moved beyond invitations? When he finally asked her to pull up the hardback chair by the dresser, she declined by staying right where she was. New, fine lines formed shallow waves around her mouth, like a stone that had skipped across her skin. He wondered how long it would take her to tell him about what she and her husband had done to Russell Nixon, to make him freak out the way he had. Why else would she refuse to lay eyes on him except to confess?

Lea moved to the window, tripping on the braided rug's upturned edge. She smoothed the curl with her heel but the border sprang back like a duty to imperfection. That edge had curled no matter how many times Mutti had wetted it and stacked up the encyclopedias to flatten it down.

Lea gave up mashing the edge and jostled the shade to peer out at the backyard. Sunlight striped Rilke's general untidiness. While she was distracted, he might as well cinch himself up, if he could free his ankle from the sheet. At his lame attempt to sit up, Lea pulled the shade up and crossed the room to help him. When she drew the covers over his exposed lap all the way to his chest, the instinct was to lock his fingers with hers. Her hand was cold. The sticky heat seeping from Mutti's effusive kitchen and the enthusiastic radiator hadn't warmed her at all. He hadn't meant to pull her to the bed, but she sat readily, her leg pressed to his hip. *All right*. He realized then that he'd been lying about his overall state of health. He hadn't felt good, not at all, until she was touching him.

"Are *you* okay?" he asked.

She reached with her free hand to brush his hair from his brow. He wished the gesture didn't feel so motherly. "Yes, thank you."

"You're welcome," was all he could think to say.

"I meant, thank you for saving us the other night." She untangled her hand from his hair. Her fingers brushed his sore lip on their skip back to her lap.

"More like you saved me. How are the little tykes doing?"

"All right, I guess. When Jay called to say he'd been arrested, I didn't even try to find a babysitter. I didn't think it through. Lots of things, I didn't think through…anyway. It's all my fault."

Now she was staring at the headboard's spiral oak spindles. Her hand was still cold as if his grasp was a biting wind. "Nothing's your fault," he said, more to gauge her reaction than to offer any reassurance.

Her eyes met his briefly and skated away again. "How is the young man who was shot?"

"Homer's hanging in. No damage to any internal organs. From what I hear." Rilke had also heard that Homer claimed he'd hit Bobby with his rifle butt, no doubt to atone for the prank that had caused this whole mess. The damage to Bobby's mouth hadn't been a gunshot wound after all. Nowak and Rilke had pieced together that Russell had mistaken Bobby for Johnson in the Burger King and assaulted him, maybe out of revenge, or just plain fear. Well, who attacked whom would be proven soon enough. Anyway, Russell's lawyer would no doubt mount a diminished capacity defense, exacerbated by physical and mental cruelty, cruelty that originated with the Johnsons.

"What about that sharpshooter?"

"He's fine. Turns out he wasn't shot. Looked a lot worse than it was."

Lea looked down at their hands as if their clasp had wandered in from another room. "What do we do now?"

He squeezed her fingers. "What do you want for us?"

She took her hand back and tucked it in her lap. "What will happen with Jay?"

His surge of anger was all his own fault. He should have guessed that her concern for her husband's fate would turn out to be the real reason for the visit. Had it occurred to her to wonder why she wasn't also under investigation? He must have choked off any comfort in his expression, because her eyes startled wide. "I mean. It makes a difference to us, doesn't it. What happens to him."

"Does it?"

"He's...yes, it does." She fled to the window again, as if the view of the claustrophobic backyard, with the rusty old swing set listing by the shed, could be any haven.

"I won't have anything to do with what happens now," he said.

"I didn't mean—" she said. "I just wanted to know. What happens next. What to expect."

"What *I* mean," he clarified, "is that it's not my responsibility anymore. You should talk to your lawyer."

"Okay. You're right. I'm sorry. I should have understood how things work."

Rilke didn't dignify that with a response.

Lea spoke into the silence. "The doctors told me over and over that his behavior was in the normal range for a traumatic head injury. I was always thinking, if he was normal, then it's me who's *not* normal. You'd think I'd have known better how to manage. It's my field." She pressed her brow to the windowpane like a kid breathing patterns in the frost.

"I guess you don't care to hear this, but he did change a lot after he was attacked. Except he's always been such a good father. That didn't change. Mostly."

The good-father check in the plus column seemed unlikely, but then Lea wasn't exactly one to judge warm and loving parenting, from what he'd seen. "Again, sounds like good information for your lawyer."

"We weren't so unhappy before," she said as if overall marital satisfaction were the real issue.

"You probably shared a lot of things before." Rilke paused to let that sink in. "And probably quite a few things afterwards too."

He let her mull that over, there at the window, bathed in the late morning sun. The shine plucked at her new worry lines, setting alight the tiny pieces of her accustomed to being concealed. "Yes," she said at last, as amiably as if she were agreeing with him about the narrow view his window offered her. The air's shimmer, the sky's unblemished blue, the fields unrolling beyond the cramped backyard, the orderly rows of slumped, dried husks from which Rilke used to pluck his insensible father so he could have one more opportunity to die. "Jay said he told you everything."

"Did he tell me everything?"

"Jay's usually truthful."

"Aren't you?"

She wrapped her hands around her waist. "No. Not really."

The accuracy of that nullification irritated the hell out of Rilke. "Why did Russell Nixon cut up your things, and not your husband's, Lea?"

He'd say this much: she knew how to project a convincing show of surprise. "I thought…did that kid do it after all?"

Neither Russell nor Homer had confessed to the act, but it made sense they'd done it. The boys' father had said they never did come home. Between the time Homer had picked up his brother and the stop at the Burger King, they'd had unaccounted for hours of opportunity. "Sounds like he had good reason to."

"You convinced me it was my husband."

She had the accusatory tone down too. Which Rilke decided was high time to put a stop to. "What did you do to Russell, Lea?"

She flushed. The radiator had fallen silent. The unseasonable cold was again seeping through the seams, but the fresh air wasn't cooling his prickly sweat. While sleeping days, he'd sought quiet the way the victims

of the past night's crimes must one day again seek hope. He'd manufactured oblivion with blackout shades and white noise. The oppressive
vigil in Papa's cottage had taught him not to confuse the absence of
noise for peace, but Lea's quiet spells were damn skirmishes.

"Lea?"

She turned from the window. "What did my husband tell you?"

"Your husband said you were propositioning the boy when he walked
in." He said it roughly, and there it was, the anger, like he'd nicked her.

"What? That's…that's disgusting. Jay's lying."

As if that information was hot off the press. But Rilke said, "He
sounded sincere to me."

"That boy never even came into the house."

It confirmed something or other that she wasn't avoiding his eyes
now. "Your husband claimed you let the boy in," Rilke informed her.
A rumbling vibrated the floorboards, waves of sound from the kitchen
below. The radio, blaring the golden oldies Mutti liked to blast while she
cleaned.

"Well, I don't know why Jay said those things. Because they aren't
true. I read that the kid is just fourteen years old. Why would Jay…" Lea
tightened her grip on her waist as if hoping to squeeze herself out of
existence. "Wait. Did you *believe* him?"

"I thought Russell's revenge there in the Burger King was pretty
convincing."

"Then why wasn't I arrested too?"

"What makes you think you won't be?"

She chewed on that one for a while. Her jawline's tumble routine
signaled that some decisions were about to reached and others discard-
ed. Mutti turned the radio down a bit. Lea said quietly, "While I was
upstairs getting the blanket, I heard noises. Yelling. Another sound, I
couldn't really tell what it was. When I went back downstairs, the kid
was gone. Jay may have… Anyway, I went looking for the kid. To give
him the blanket. But you already know all of this."

He remembered Russell wrapped up in the dirty blanket in Jules's
kitchen, how surprised he'd been to see that Lea had been telling the
truth. He nodded.

"I don't think Jay knew the kid was so young. But I think I can guess
why he lied. His dirty prank on me. All of this, it's been just one big
prank, right? Not that it matters."

Rilke straightened up against the headboard. He wished he could make her leave. Then he wished he could lock his door, seal his window, keep her in this room forever.

"*Does* it matter?" she asked.

She dropped her arms. The shirt's cuffs still hugged her elbows. With her wrinkled shirt-sleeves bunched up around her thin shoulders, she projected naïve and helpless mitigations for her and her husband's behavior.

"If you say your husband's lying, then I believe you."

"I didn't come here to talk about my husband."

"Right." He turned away to stare at the peeling wallpaper. Hurt feelings were an insult to self-respect but she might as well have poked his wound for the pain her wavering voice raised; and *Jesus Christ* his scooching up straight had messed up the sheet so she could now plainly see facets he'd rather she not see at that particular moment.

"Thank you," she said.

The phony gratitude forced him to look at her, to take in her flush, her slack bob and skinny shoulders. Through the bland yellow collar, her neck's hollow rippled like a strained muscle. "Don't mention it."

She stared at his leg, aloft and helpless. "It's like I told you at the cottage. I can't love. Not properly. Not like other people. I think that's my whole problem."

"It's not a problem," he told her.

Her hand floated to her waist. Her fingers worked the buttons through the pinched, fraying buttonholes as if she'd never removed this shirt. The blouse's peel revealed the sturdy plain harness Rilke used to examine in his mother's Sears Roebuck catalog when he was a kid, as if his whole future with women depended upon deciphering the workings of this garment. Lea stepped out of her sneakers and stuffed her socks into their caverns, the toe ends cascading from the heels like shadows tossed away. The jeans' shedding uncovered practical, high-waisted undies. "Put your hands away."

Which made no sense at all. He took her in, the fluttering hollows, the gentle curves. In the sunlight the muscles on her arms and legs stood out. Strength she took pains to hide in her bulky clothes and shrinking posture.

She nodded at the headboard. "Don't touch me. Please."

He obeyed. When he'd gripped the spindles, she crossed to him and slicked her cool skin against his sweaty rough patches. When he dared to move his hands along her waist, her hips, her long slender back, she didn't pull away, she didn't leave him.

Then she whispered in his ear, *I'm that girl from long ago, why don't you know me?*

<h1 style="text-align:center">24</h1>

After leaving the farmhouse, Lea stopped at the hedge near the driveway to watch Jay, Kurt, and Bunny clustered together in their front yard. The kids were bundled like roly-polies in parkas and scarves and bulky wool hats. Jay had dressed them properly, only his notion of *proper* was a day too late, now that the air had warmed. Whatever Jay was showing them was lighting them up with wonder. Above the family's huddle, a black crow bent the topmost branch of a tall pine on Scipio Road, the burly silhouette charcoaled against the blue sky.

Well, maybe this was an innocent moment she shouldn't judge. Since Lea had brought him home, the kids had seemed to banish the Burger King to a remote harbor of remembrance they would dredge up one day while trying to recall exactly when their parents' marriage had ended. But Jay would never be who they recalled when they remembered that boy bursting through the restaurant door. They'd remember, before they'd been forced behind the counter, how the boy with the rifle had gaped at Lea, and how she had cried out when she saw him. Someday Kurt and Bunny would understand that Russell and Lea had recognized each other. Paul had believed Jay's story about her. Weren't children also susceptible to believing their mother capable of anything, just as Lea had believed her mother knew *he* had defiled her? She must have already sensed this when, on the way to pick up Jay from the county office, Bunny had seen the Burger King sign flash by and piped up from the back seat, *I'm hungry, Momma,* and Kurt chimed in, *I want some fries,* their recital whenever they spied signs with golden crowns or arches, or little freckled girls with orange pigtails, desires that, when she fulfilled them, always felt as dirty as bribes.

Kurt took his hands from his pockets. He was wearing those Playtex gloves again. Since helping her with the deer, he called them his work gloves and refused to give them up. She and Jay would end up arguing about whose carelessness had led to Kurt having the Ruger that night, whether he would need therapy to work through what she viewed as trauma and Jay saw as courage. Jay handed Kurt something that Lea could now see was the shotgun she'd used on the deer, then showed him how to break the barrel. After what the kids had been through, was he actually going to allow Kurt to load it while Bunny watched?

Lea swore under her breath and moved past the hedge.

On the other side of the bushes, slow-moving Vivian from "book club" was approaching the drive, bearing a shotgun. "Pardon me," Lea said before reminding herself that the woman had stopped short on her driveway, in *her* way.

"That's all right." Vivian spoke as if she expected Lea's apology. An orange hunter's vest clashed with her burgundy parka. She was made up tastefully like she'd just come from the salon. A subdued rouge dusted her cheeks. Dusky blue eyeliner traced her gray, steady eyes. Her silver hair bobbed in a tight, girlish ponytail, the neat *v* of her widow's peak bulging like a stuck-out tongue. On the lawn Jay pulled on a ski mask and fished a piece of orange netting from his coat pocket. "Jay looks all set to go," Vivian remarked.

"Go?"

Vivian smiled. "It's volunteer day."

Just beyond the pines bordering the Johnson yard, Gary Starkey's trailer trundled down Scipio and pulled over on the gravel shoulder. The winch rattled with each bump. The crow took flight, wheeling over the forested ridge to the field beyond. Vivian was watching Lea with that arch expression she'd weaponized in Karla's bathroom. Lea flushed and was about to give her a dressing down, when, behind Vivian's shoulder, she saw a neighbor in blaze orange walking up the road toward the back of the development, a rifle slung on his back. Three doors down, a man, also armed, in canvas Carhartt leggings and jacket, strolled down his drive.

"Are you participating?" Vivian asked.

Lea shook her head.

"That's right." Vivian pulled a pair of fingerless gloves from her pockets and slipped them on. "You never qualified to be a volunteer, did you?"

Vivian's manicured nails shone like new fillings. That night in Karla's bathroom, the nails had been chipped and uneven, a match for her knotted knuckles and ridgeback tendons. Even now the woman's arched brows and unabashed gaze felt like a salacious drop cloth. Had Vivian hovered outside the bathroom door that night, listening in on her?

"I didn't see you at any of the training sessions," Vivian continued. "Do guns make you nervous?"

"Not really." Lea tucked her bare hands into her sweater sleeves. "I have terrible aim."

Vivian appraised her as if, based on what she knew of Lea, this wasn't a joke. But maybe she was thinking of the long day ahead culling does on what remained of the Rilke farm. A humane solution, begun with good intentions.

Jay slipped on the hunting mesh and took the rifle from Kurt. *Go on in, kids.* His eyes shone bright through the ski mask's kohl. His relaxed voice carried to Lea on the breeze the way his strong, steady cheer used to close any gap between them. Before the attack he'd based his life on a misreading of the Golden Rule. Not the "do unto others" part, but the "as you would have them do unto you." He'd never understood that *would have* was a wish, not a promise or a quid pro quo. She'd witnessed it herself so many times in the lab, once she understood that the freezing pose was not a defensive posture, but a last-ditch possibility. In her subject's intelligent eyes shone the fear she recognized, one that knew their single, lonely death heralded the greater tragedy of extinction. But behind that fear lay the fierce belief that if stillness was absolute, predators wouldn't see them at all. Danger would pass. Mercy would be irrelevant. A silly faith, but it meant that the final instinct she was recording from the animal's postmortem neurological patterns wasn't fear after all, but hope.

Perhaps she and Abel would one day discover the neurological switch to throw and thus repair Jay. Or maybe they'd prove once and for all that Jay's world, in which it was just common sense to teach even the youngest children how to load a gun, was the true reality, and instead work to fix Lea. Dinah would tell her to stick around for the fix, save Jay, save herself; why shouldn't both be possible? She'd say Lea had a duty to keep her finger on that switch like a village girl forever sealing a dike.

Kurt and Bunny raced each other to the front door facing Scipio Road, the one Russell Nixon had pounded, cold and frightened, seeking help to find his way home. The door was locked. Laughing, the kids ran around to the porch facing the drive and disappeared inside. Jay shouldered his rifle, glanced down the drive, and saw Lea watching him with the harshness he'd come to accept as her new natural expression. He was exhausted, banged up from the tumble into the pit, the long march back across the fields, the hours in county jail waiting for Lea. The cut on his throat from the plow's teeth stung like hell, one of those annoying superficial wounds that hurt worse than a serious one.

Sometimes the serious ones didn't hurt like they should. After the attack last year, when he'd been forced awake from a medically induced coma, he'd been cocooned in an absence of pain. The gauze on his vision could mean he was alive or dead. He couldn't pick Lea out from the blank silhouettes of hovering bodies surrounding him. He'd awoken to these shapes buzzing around wounds he couldn't feel one other time in his life, when he was still in the service. During training, he'd been in a road accident while riding in the back of a carrier that overturned on a California highway. He'd knocked his head hard enough to concuss. The guy next him had been killed. All that practice for combat, only to be casualties to a teenage driver who'd swerved to avoid an animal on the road and hit the carrier head on.

After he'd recovered, the medics warned him that a future serious blow to the head could cause permanent damage. *How far in the future?* he should have asked, to hold out hope that a time would come when another injury wouldn't matter.

Eventually, the bliss those tubes were pouring into his arm after the attack was dialed back and pain ruled. Only it wasn't pain, it couldn't be. The searing along his skull and jaw radiated down the side of his body, screwed into his gut at some befuddled axis below the waist. This pain wasn't doing its job. It was cold, like the first numb moments of a burn before the nerves catch up to what the mind is already braced to feel. He'd been driven from his body, as if this pain didn't know all the rules yet on how to make him suffer. Confused in the space outside of himself, he'd seen Lea for the first time, sitting stiffly in a vinyl chair just out of reach. She wasn't even looking at him. She wasn't looking out the window at the parking lot, or the oak and maple rustling in the local park beyond the lot. What the hell was she seeing in the bare beige wall she was staring down? Her expression was empty, like she'd vacated, too, like she didn't wish for him to awaken, like he wasn't even in the room at all.

Eventually, *eventually*, Lea had realized his eyes had opened. Then she'd arisen from the vinyl chair to fall upon his body, mad with weeping. The spectacle had struck him as professional, a mourner hired for her practiced lamentations. Her weight hurt like hell. He threw up. Pandemonium descended on the distraught wife of the beating victim. Lea had been pulled from him by the staff appointed to save his life.

That was the last time she'd really touched him. Since the attack, she couldn't hide her repulsion, her blame, her anger. She believed his desire to protect their family, to help the neighborhood, even to love her, meant he was broken, dangerous even. He shouldn't blame her. He'd never told her about the first accident, the original blow to his head. The intense anger he felt toward his wife should be proof enough that the doctors had been right about the delayed effects of another head injury. He should have wondered, too, why he felt nothing toward his attackers. But he barely thought of those kids at all, even when Lea would question him, and the police: *What happened? Can you describe them?*

Lea and his doctors thought trauma had damaged his memory, but he remembered their faces perfectly. Kids with round, pale faces, straight teeth shining through tight, gleeful smiles, T-shirts with popular grunge-band names, sneakers. *Ordinary kids* is how he would have described them; ordinary, except for what they'd done to him. At the time, identifying them simply seemed beside the point.

Now, even looking at Lea jarred his memory of a pain that didn't know the rules, the rude lurch out of his own body, the fear he might never be allowed back in. And, God help him—the outrageous story about Lea and Russell Nixon he'd told that cop she was sleeping with. That, too, erased the pain. How was he to know that kid was only fourteen? He'd looked much older, like a young man perfectly responsible for his actions.

Trashing her side of the bedroom had felt great too. He'd lost his temper after she left the house. Parked the kids in front of the TV in the den. Tossed those sex gadgets out of her drawer like a toddler. He didn't have a clear memory of destroying anything. Ripping up her underwear. Writing insults on them. Wouldn't he have savaged his own stuff too, if he'd gone that far? Useless dress shirts and the ties he used to wear to work? Those khaki pants he'd bought right before the attack that he'd laid out on the bed to see if they still fit? If he'd lost control like that, could he have taken the kids out to Chuck E. Cheese afterwards as if nothing was wrong?

He'd continue to insist it wasn't him. Let Lea find out, in time, when that boy's brother had recovered, that her cop was lying to her.

When Lea returned to the lab the next morning, Kate asked if she was all right. They'd all seen the news. They were all worried sick, Kate assured her of this. Abel overheard Lea's quiet *yes*, took in her pallor and evasive brush past him to her station. He'd tried calling all last week to check on her. Lea hadn't answered her phone.

"Oh, hey. Did you ever catch your friend?" Kate must be watching her too. She must have decided this was the only safe question she could ask Lea.

Lea glanced outside. A film of frost dusted the window's glass. The iron chimney billowed white steam against the gray sky. "Yes. I did catch her."

Kate turned her attention back to the scope. Abel approached with a sheaf of bills he'd corralled in her absence. "Should you be here?" he asked.

Lea nodded.

Abel took her silence as a rebuff. "We okay?"

"Perfectly."

"I can have Tom cull if you'd rather not do it."

He thought she wasn't up to it; he thought he was being kind. But he hadn't ordered the euthanizing done in her absence, either. Nor had he performed the work himself. Abel wasn't squeamish or sentimental. He was ruthless about the priorities of discovery and the imperative to cure. Some particular reason must lie at the core of his waiting for her to come back.

Abel hadn't pulled up his stool, as was his habit when they spoke. He was avoiding her eyes as she was avoiding his, worrying his hand with the familiar anxiety. Lea shuffled the bills and laid them aside. Michelle's drawing from the day she and Abel had first discussed culling the mice poked from the stack. The amber circle was a ring of fire after all, not the sun. The empty space within the flames was colored a bright, cheerful blue. Beyond the ring, a roller coaster's skeletal frame loop-delooped around a single empty car on the track. On the other side of fire, Michelle had drawn the thrill she hoped to ride one day.

Better than married.

Well, she knew what Dinah would say, that the wedding's proof lay precisely in Abel's waiting for Lea to perform the cull.

"I'm perfectly fine, Mike. I'll take care of it. After hours today, okay?" Lea handed him the drawing. "I never heard about Michelle's appointment?"

If he felt relief that the same old Lea was back on the job, he didn't show it. "What controls her symptoms best is what zonks her out the most. Nothing's going to change that. Except us, right?"

Even if Abel's research led to new drug development, Michelle would be living with her soul's flight for years, fragments of her life forever missing. When she still thought of memory as a wound, Lea used to envy Michelle's brief escapes, those few moments of simply being, stripped of meaning. Now the thought of existing, even for a fleeting time, without the meaning of love, or anger; forgiveness, or even fear, terrified her.

"Right," Lea agreed.

Late in the day, when the others were wrapping up work, Lea placed a call to social services to request a welfare check on *him*. After double checking the operator had the correct address, she called Paul. Their brief check-in, the reassurances that they would see each other later, already felt both routine and as surprising as discovering that they had met way back when Lea had proven herself a crack shot and Rilke was the only boy there to guess what had steadied her aim.

After Paul hung up, Lea went down to animal husbandry. She suited up and stepped into the cage room on her way to Lab Will Care. No stickers had been mounted on the cage's identifying cards indicating which mice would be euthanized. Every detail of the cull had been left to her.

And every opportunity.

She clicked off the cage room lights and entered Lab Will Care. After days away from her, the mouse, skittish, clawed at her hand. In the acclimation room, the needling claws clicked on the metal table, fought for a grip on the cool steel. Lea scooped him up gently, over and over, imprinting the arc that would soon carry him to fear. Before long he would re-acclimate to her scent and then to her touch, believe that every journey down would be safe in her hands.

When she was certain the lab was closed, the building empty except for security and a few graduate students on deadlines, Lea left Lab Will Care. Down the hallway, on the far east end of the lower level past the loading dock, the access door was alarmed but unguarded. Lea disabled the alarm, propped the door open, and stepped out into the chilly night. The loading bay was empty. So was the sidewalk. They'd agreed to meet here after dark. Dinah had promised, first, to come alone. Her people could join later, after Lea had left. Dinah had made a play for Lea to meet the others, record a statement, be part of the footage they would upload of this rescue. Lea had refused. She still didn't agree with Dinah's tactics, but she didn't tell Dinah that. Instead she'd said, "I'm nobody. Not a leading researcher, not even a scientist anymore. What use would my conversion be?"

Dinah had laughed. Behind her beat-up Jetta, the campus commuter bus had swung wide, nearly grazing the car's fender. Neither woman had noticed. After leaving *him,* they'd spent hours talking in Dinah's car, holding hands in their old way. "Your conversion is the only one that matters, Lea."

Should she feel relieved or disappointed that she didn't see Dinah here now, that her conversion didn't matter after all?

Well, at the moment, all she felt was cold. Shivering, she stepped back inside, kicked the doorstop aside. But as soon as she'd stopped searching for Dinah, of course, here she was, slipping through before Lea could shut her out.

"You came," Lea said.

No use whispering, they were completely alone. But Dinah's reply, *what made you think I wouldn't,* was so muted Lea thought she might be speaking to herself. In the hallway's harsh fluorescence, she looked pale, almost nervous. Lea wasn't used to seeing Dinah worried. They'd worked it all out. Which subjects to rescue, where they would find sanctuary. Old hat to Dinah, Lea had assumed, but watching her now, breath catching in erratic gasps, gaze flitting down the bright hallway, she realized Dinah was terrified. Of being caught. Or of Lea betraying her.

Dinah relaxed, her breathing calmed. Lea wasn't coming with her to rescue the animals. She would slip out now, and Dinah would let the others in. Lea's refusal to join might be fear, or principle. Or it might be that trap. Would any outcome matter to how Dinah felt about Lea? Dinah doubted it. She'd meant what she said. Changing Lea was all that mattered. Women like her were harm's managers. Risk-averse wives and mothers who worked stable jobs with good intentions. Lea had enough imagination to battle human ills, but not enough to see how inhumane that battle had made her.

Dinah took Lea's hand. Lea held on for a moment, palm to palm. Letting go felt lonely, and lovely too. Better than friendship, better than passion. Lea held out her access card, the one she would tell Abel had been stolen. Or maybe she'd tell the truth, that she'd given it up freely. She'd be fired anyway. She'd never find work in a lab again, not this time, with her record, in this economy. There was no reason not to help Dinah now. But she didn't want to see her subjects cower as they were removed from the lab, tremble as they were freed for the cameras, petrified when they were rounded up again and swept to a strange place they wouldn't understand was safe shelter.

Dinah took her card. "They won't be hurt, not at all, you know I can promise this."

Lea knew all about Dinah's promises. "Release them," she said, and left Dinah to find her own way to the cages.

Dinah watched Lea walk past the loading dock and disappear around the building. She still wouldn't put it past Lea, that this easy access was a ruse, a trap. One never could quite trust Lea, but the damage wasn't her fault, was it, and her untrustworthiness was what Dinah had always loved best about her. You could lead her anywhere, put anything in her hands, and you never knew what she would do. Whom she might hurt, and whom she might forgive.

Book Club Discussion Questions

1. Despite her expertise in studying the fear response, Lea finds herself unable to cope with the lingering aftereffects of her husband's recent trauma. Why do you think Lea fails to understand and sympathize with Jay's complicated recovery?

2. How does the fact that the subdivision where Lea lives was built on land that used to be a part of the Rilke family's farm influence Paul Rilke's behavior towards the Johnson family and the search for the missing teen?

3. Lea's unexpected re-connection with her childhood "frenemy," Dinah, surfaces old anger at Dinah's act of betrayal. Why do you think Lea is as drawn to this complicated friendship in adulthood as she was as a teen, especially when Dinah is still maddeningly condescending towards Lea?

4. The novel explores characters who were drawn to jobs where a certain amount of moral ambiguity is a part of doing business, but who now find that they are losing their ability to justify the means to an end. How do Lea and Paul's changing attitudes toward their professions play a role in confronting their fears and past traumas?

5. A local deer cull plays a central role in the novel, as does Dinah's work as an animal rights activist. How are Dinah's activism and the cull linked in the novel? What is the novel saying about the impact of human activity on the animal and natural world?

Acknowledgments

My heartfelt thanks to Jaynie Royal, Pam Van Dyke, Elizabeth Lowenstein, and everyone at Regal House Publishing. Bringing fiction into the world is a leap of faith for both the author and the publisher. Jaynie and her fantastic, dedicated team keep the faith with their unfailing expertise, wisdom, and kindness. I'm very grateful *The Meaning of Fear* found its way to the Regal House family.

I'm grateful to the journal *Arts Saves Lives International* and to Wayne State University Press for publishing the short stories that later became the foundation for *The Meaning of Fear*. My deepest gratitude to Susan Neville, Megan Staffel, and CJ Hribal for their indispensable critiques of my early drafts. I owe a special debt of gratitude to Kevin McIlvoy, who first encouraged and guided this work from story to novel. Mc, the writing world misses you dearly.

I'm lucky to have had so many friends who championed this novel. Dorene O'Brien, Lolita Hernandez, and Kelly Fordon, brilliant writers all, gave me invaluable critiques, steadfast support, and eternal optimism. Many thanks to Jennifer Allison, Laura Kasischke, Annie Martin, Ian Ross Singleton, Daniel Madaj, and all the writers and editors who have supported my work over the years. My deep gratitude to Emily Schultz, whose expert editorial insights and feedback helped *The Meaning of Fear* find its final shape. Many thanks to Dr. Geoff Murphy for providing crucial background for Lea's story. Any errors in science and the details of a laboratory scientist's work are my own.

Love and gratitude to my husband, Ron, who makes everything possible, even, and especially, the impossible.

To my mother, Carol Church, the strongest person I know—thank you, Mom, for being there, always.

9 781646 036783